"THE AUTHOR OF *THE CONVERSION OF CHAPLAIN COHEN* GIVES US A HILARIOUS, WITHERING, YET NOT AT ALL CONTEMPTUOUS ACCOUNT OF WHAT MIGHT BE ANYBODY'S SUBURBAN JEWISH CENTER. HIS YOUNG RABBI . . . IS CONFRONTED WITH THE JEWISH LUAU THAT IS THE BAR MITZVAH PARTY, THE FASHION SHOW THAT PUSHES SERVICES OUT OF THE SANCTUARY, A PILLAR OF THE BOARD WHO IS A SLUMLORD. MR. TARR WRITES ALL THIS WITH A CONVICTION AND FERVOR, MASKED IN HUMOR, THAT IS IN THE BEST PROPHETIC TRADITION. HE LOVES THE PEOPLE AND HATES WHAT THEY ARE DOING . . . ONE HOPES THAT THE IDEAS WILL GO OVER AS WELL AS THE STORY."

—The New York Times

RAVE REVIEWS FROM

"TARR IS A HILARIOUS WRITER . . . an author whose comedy is also based in the incongruities of contemporary religion."

—San Francisco Examiner

"I was as DELIGHTED AND CHARMED with it as I was with his first book . . . RUEFUL WIT, LIGHTENED WITH GOOD HUMOR and a dash of charity, is very rare in this world, and it is a treasure to be nurtured and encouraged."

—Taylor Caldwell

COAST TO COAST!

"SO WHAT ELSE IS NU? AND FRESH AND FUNNY AND SOMETIMES SERIOUS? HERBERT TARR'S NEW NOVEL. UNRESERVEDLY."

—The Kirkus Service

"A JOYOUS BOOK."

—Hartford Times

"FUNNY, WRY, OCCASIONALLY TOUCHING—BUT MAINLY FUNNY."

—Book-of-the-Month Club News

"TARR'S STORY . . . TOLD WITH WARMTH AND WIT . . . SURE TO ENTERTAIN MEMBERS OF ALL FAITHS."

—Buffalo Courier-Express

HEAVEN HELP US!

A Novel by

HERBERT TARR

This low-priced Bantam Book
has been completely reset in a type face
designed for easy reading, and was printed
from new plates. It contains the complete
text of the original hard-cover edition.
NOT ONE WORD HAS BEEN OMITTED.

HEAVEN HELP US!

*A Bantam Book / published by arrangement with
Random House, Inc.*

PRINTING HISTORY

Random House edition published February 1968
2nd printing .... July 1968
3rd printing .... September 1968

Bantam edition published March 1969
2nd printing
3rd printing
4th printing
5th printing
6th printing
7th printing

*Copyright © 1968 by Herbert Tarr.
All rights reserved under International and
Pan-American Copyright Conventions.
This book may not be reproduced in whole or in part, by
mimeograph or any other means, without permission.
For information address: Random House, Inc.,
457 Madison Avenue, New York, N.Y. 10022.*

Published simultaneously in the United States and Canada

---

*Bantam Books are published by Bantam Books, Inc., a subsidiary
of Grosset & Dunlap, Inc. Its trade-mark, consisting of the words
"Bantam Books" and the portrayal of a bantam, is registered in the
United States Patent Office and in other countries. Marca Registrada.
Bantam Books, Inc., 271 Madison Avenue, New York, N.Y. 10016.*

PRINTED IN THE UNITED STATES OF AMERICA

FOR FLORRIE AND ERNIE

who wanted me to be an uncle

AUTHOR'S NOTE

Since this novel's leading character and I are both rabbis, some readers may be tempted to conclude that *Heaven Help Us!* is autobiographical. Resist this temptation, please, because all the characters depicted herein are strictly fictitious. Happily, moreover, I have never served a congregation that did not enlighten me; I can only hope that the reverse is also true.

H.T.

JULY

CLERGYMAN RUNS AMUCK,
FUSTIGATES 18 TEMPLE TRUSTEES!
"I'M SORRY," RABBI ABEL SAYS,
"BUT YOU CAN'T LOVE THEM ALL."

YES, I know it wrinkles the man-of-the-cloth image to fantasy neglecting the Golden Rule eighteen times in one swoop, but what the hell? Allowances must be made for ministers, especially those whom a board of trustees has just treated to a way-off-Broadway revival of the Spanish Inquisition. Like me, for example, brooding back here to the Rabbinical Seminary dorm from the Hillendale Temple, which will be notifying me later tonight whether I've been chosen its "spiritual leader." Now, after five years of divinity school, I'm wondering whether the rabbinate is, after all, a likely profession for a nice young Jew in possession of all his marbles.

I became a rabbi, as near as one can figure without that Rorschach test administered nowadays to candi-

1

dates for theological seminaries (heaven forbid an
Ezekiel or Paul should slip in!), out of passion to
devote myself to learning and to teaching others, as
the man said, without fear of being called square, to
do justly, to love mercy and walk humbly with God.
The synagogue seemed the logical base for this kind
of life—the synagogue, where for thousands of years
Jews have come to open their souls to the Divine,
their minds to the Torah and their hearts to their
fellowmen. But after flunking so many congregational
interviews—two in New York hostelries were so shat-
tering that it's with fear and trembling I register at
any hotel now, even when I'm alone and carrying
luggage—and after tonight's fiasco, I suspect that
Somebody up there may be trying to tell me something.

Happily, this last grilling enabled me to see a whole
board instead of representatives thereof. The only
trouble is the trustees got to see me too. One person I
can outstare (just fix your eyes on his hairline; it'll
drive him crazy), but how do you look eighteen people in the eye at once, while they're raking you up
and down like it's a police line-up?

They let me stand in the doorway so long I expected someone to whoop, "That's the man, Officer;
he's the one who done it!" And I was readying a
statement when a man said, "Won't you have a seat,
Rabbi Abel?"

There was only one eyeless chair present—at the
far end of the table long enough to be the last mile
in fruitwood. Around it in gauntlet fashion sat the
trustees, who scrutinized my every detail as I bravely
worked my way up the room, churning ripples of
whispers in my wake.

"He doesn't look Jewish."

"So *blond*."

"Hmmm, nice and tall, and with shoulders."

"He's sat in something. There's a big stain on his—"

"I like the way he walks."

"God! He looks just like Harry Belafonte bleached."

After what felt like a four-day journey through the Jewish bush, I reached table's end. There a mouth stood up to bark, "I'm Barney Singer, president of the temple." A massive man of about forty who looked like a pillar of the congregation, literally, he held out a loglike arm. "Welcome, Rabbi."

"Thank you." We shook hands.

I sat down, facing the board. Yes, they were still there, all those matched sets of irises; only one person interviews candidates for Secretary of State or Supreme Court Justice, but here for a rabbi eighteen people had to be in on the kill. Swiftly I turned back to Mr. Singer's horn-rimmed two eyes, which—not to press the analogy, but one brown one was slightly larger than the other—resembled knots in pinewood.

"How was your trip here?" he asked.

"Oh, fine. Just fine."

"How long did it take you to drive out from Manhattan?"

"About an hour and a half."

"An hour and a half?"

"Yes, I think it was an hour and a half."

"Strange. It takes no more than sixty minutes after the rush hour. Seventy minutes tops."

"Well, I guess it must have taken longer this time."

"Yes."

"There was a strong headwind." (A charming try, you understand, at breaking the ice.)

The room remained so quiet you could have heard a smile.

Mr. Singer said, "Really?"

Our conversation dropped dead right there. Gevalt! Had the interview been terminated because my car took too long to drive out to Hillendale? You think that's silly. Well, did I ever tell you about the other interviews?

On my first one the rabbinical placement commission sends me to a Waldorf-Astoria suite to see the vice-president of a Southern congregation. After I say how pleased I am to meet him, which retroactively turns out to be my biggest lie of the day, the man confides he's come to New York to help secure the Presidential nomination of that great statesman so needed in this perilous hour of creeping communism, graduated income taxes, mounting sex fiends, crime in the streets and/or the Negro Insubordination—the only one who can maintain freedom for America and stability for the dollar while paring welfare rolls and scaring the pants off the commies and the University of Berkeley, because he's fearless, high-minded and not one of those Eastern smart-asses. And the V.P. was speaking of none other than, as if I had not already guessed, Ronald Reagan.

Is it my fault an inadvertent guffaw transferred a sip of Scotch from my mouth to my host's face? Ronald Reagan was never even nominated for an Oscar, for crying out loud! Well, next thing I know, the veep is wiping himself off and concluding the interview (he was his state's chairman of the GOP, it turns out; yes, there are Jewish Republicans—why didn't anyone ever tell me?).

On my second interview I get a break: the pulpit committee is anxious to settle on a rabbi because they're all leaving for Honolulu that week. About to give me the call, the chairman remarks, "I don't imagine you'd object to our having a detective bureau run a routine check on you before signing contracts, Rabbi, would you?"

Benignly I reply, "Not if I can run a routine check on *you*, Mr. Ribalov." Fair is fair, right?

Mr. Ribalov, alas, didn't think so.

No grass grows in *my* head, so I go to my next interview resolved to volunteer naught but my name, profession and, if pressed real hard, religious persuasion. What happens? I hardly make it through the door. A second vice-president takes one look at my hair and asks, "Say, aren't you Whitey Abel? Weren't you a camper at Camp Cheyenne Judea?" That ends that, for as the man explains, "How could I accept as my rabbi somebody I remember as a bed-wetter?" My convincing him that Bud Schinler was the one, not I, cuts no ice; neither can my former counselor see himself following spiritually after somebody he used to wrest *Playboy* from after lights out.

Where was I?

Oh, yes—Mr. Singer and I had just finished comparing travel time from New York; now we were mulling over the results, I looking at him, and he, not to be outdone, looking at me. Perhaps I should have said, "I can even things up by driving back to the city in forty minutes flat"—but this time I was taking no chances.

Finally the president spoke up, hesitantly. "Rabbi, how about starting things off with an invocation?"

Who can deny the reality of today's religious revival? This year alone I've been invited to deliver invocations at a Little League game, the openings of two new delicatessens and the cornerstone-laying of a Turkish bath. It's a good thing God doesn't have to acknowledge each fall-up from the invocation explosion, else He'd never have time to mind the world. Yet if I declined to invoke here, the trustees were liable to think me a goy or something, maybe even the anti-Christ. "Well," I said, impulsively risking the truth, "I like to save invocations for more appropriate occasions."

Surprise, surprise! That wasn't a goof at all. Everyone looked relieved, as a matter of fact. Apparently nothing pleases people so much as not doing what they never wanted to do in the first place.

"Now that that's over with," Mr. Singer said, "let me tell you about our temple, Rabbi. We're only four years old, though this beautiful estate must have made you think we're established a good ten years, didn't it? Like most congregations, we organized primarily for the sake of our children. It was a terrible thing; come Sunday morning all the gentile neighbors' children would be asking ours, 'Where do you go? Don't you have any Sunday School? Didn't anybody ever die for you?' It was really anxiety-provoking. Or take what happened to friends of mine: their son came home one day, crying because somebody called him a dirty Jew, which his parents had never told him he was. So some of us families got together and started a Sunday School—that was four years ago. Two years later we raised enough money to hire a rabbi, and last month we bought this elegant property. It's the old Beardsley estate; he was the famous banker, you know. Well, that's how it all started. You might say our little children have led us. Don't you think that's a wonderful thing?"

"No," I said. (Using the same rationale, Mr. Singer and company could have founded a poolroom. It would have given their kids somewhere to go Sunday mornings where they would have enjoyed themselves, and you can imagine how anxiety-provoking it would have been for gentiles to hear *their* children gripe that every Sunday Sammy from next door goes to this joint down the street, shoots pool, drinks beer, smokes cigarettes, curses, so why the hell make them attend some crummy school?)

Happily, the president never heard me, he being the type who assumes everyone agrees with him, even when you say you don't, unless, to get your disagreement across, you knee him in the groin. While I marveled at my narrow escape, he went on: "In four years our membership has zoomed to a hundred and forty families. We have over two hundred children in our religious school; also a sisterhood, men's club, youth group, some twenty committees and an expansion fund. We are, you see, a very active temple."

"Your sisterhood, men's club, youth group—what have they been doing?"

"Oh, a lot. Once a month sisterhood has a luncheon, and men's club a stag dinner, catered; and every Sunday night the youth group throws a rock-'n'-roll pizza party. They sure can pack away that pizza, our young people."

"Yes . . . ?"

Mr. Singer matched me. "Yes?"

"Don't the sisterhood, men's club and youth group do anything? I mean, anything more. I mean, do they have programs? projects?"

"Certainly," the president said, and listed in bookkeeper fashion sisterhood's bowling league and play reviews, men's club's World Series baseball pool and Turkish Bath Night, youth group's weenie roasts and socials, the shul's gala affairs and original shows, like this year's *My Fair Sadie*. "And then on the first Sunday of every other month—we can do this because we're still a modest-sized temple—the whole congregation gets together for a nice intimate lox-and-bagel brunch."

Could anything be more *gemütlich?* It was like Lindy's had opened a suburban branch.

Mr. Singer continued: "As for what we want in a spiritual leader, we have very high standards. You see, our former rabbi, Dr. Terman, was wonderful, very popular with the Christian community too, not only with us. Irv was a fine speaker, a thirty-second-degree Mason, a member of Rotary, and he never missed a single temple function. It was a perfect match between spiritual leader and congregation, also between his wife and sisterhood, and their four small children and—but then—" He paused, took off his glasses and wiped his eyes.

What a tragedy such a fine rabbi had died, orphaning four children. I felt bad.

Mr. Singer put his glasses back on. "Dr. Terman got a wonderful offer from this big temple in California. We were all so proud," he said.

"Wha—?"

"The second or third largest temple in Los Angeles. Naturally we hated to see him leave, but nobody expected Irv to stay here for long; he was too good. Rabbi Jacobson of Hillendale's other temple, of course, has remained ten years; he'll *never* leave. Well, to sum up—what we want in a rabbi is an all-around man who has vigor, vitality, personality, a go-getter who can sell our temple to unaffiliated Jews and earn the respect of the gentile community too."

Could the Fuller Brush Company have put it any better to their salesmen?

"Now, Rabbi Abel, suppose you tell us about yourself—your age, secular education, previous experience and such."

Welcoming the chance to speak, I listed a few statistics: twenty-eight years of age, a B.A., M.A. and Ph.D. in English, a bachelor's and master's degree in Hebrew Letters, no congregational experience, since I had been ordained the month before, a hitch in the Marines—

"Marines!"

"I told you I liked the way he walked."

One man addressed me. "Rabbi, I didn't know the Marines drafted anybody."

"I enlisted."

"He enlisted! In the Marines!" two women exclaimed, as if in comparison with that feat, walking on water were a snap.

(Was it unethical of me not to explain that I had enlisted in the Marines five years before because at that time they alone still offered the six-month escape hatch from the two-year draft? Probably. But had David conceded his knocking off Goliath with a rock had been a lucky shot? He had not, and I did not.)

Everyone wasn't won over, however. "Rabbi," one woman asked, "you're only twenty-eight?"

"Yes." That was my opportunity to say I was going on twenty-nine, and I would have seized it if I weren't twenty-six—almost.

"Only twenty-eight," she repeated, then muttered in a whisper that could have been heard by Helen Keller, "My *problems* are older than him."

Another trustee sympathized. "So's my Scotch."

A long pause. The people just sat there, becalmed, their eyes rolling ever so slightly from side to side of me.

I broke silence. "What else would you like to know?"

My query seemed to capsize them. They listed, turning to neighbors and pointing with chins. When nobody spoke up, they began to nudge one another. "Ask him something."

Finally it came. "Tell us, Rabbi, what do you think of Russia?"

My inclination was to endorse the John Birchers' contention that the Russian government was infested from top to bottom with Communists, but I forced a pleasantry instead. "Well, I prefer the United States myself."

The trustee announced to the board, "I'm satisfied." To me he explained, "You see, there was a Protestant minister here in town who was a terrible agitator." He looked me straight in the eye, man to rabbi. "You haven't, have you? Signed the wrong petitions, I mean."

"Frankly," I said, risking being taken for a wall-flower, "nobody's ever asked me to sign any petition."

"Would you have, Rabbi? Signed, say, the Stockholm peace petition?"

"That's an iffy—which is what Franklin Delano Roosevelt used to call questions that can't be answered except through the benefit of hindsight (and hindsight, of course, is always twenty-twenty)." Hastily I added, "I think Roosevelt was quoting Herbert Hoover."

"Mmmm." The man nudged a neighbor. "You ask something."

Came the next question. "Since you have a Ph.D., shouldn't we be addressing you as Doctor?"

"Rabbi means more to me."

"Dr. Terman preferred to be called Doctor."

"Well, my Ph.D is in the drama. No doubt Dr. Terman took his doctorate in a Jewish field of study, which I hope to do too—"

"His Ph.D. was in Spanish."

"Spanish? Oh. Well, Maimonides spoke Spanish. And he was a great rabbi. Also."

A longer silence this time, only now I welcomed it as a respite from questions. These were my people here, so tell me, why were they persecuting me?

"Rabbi? How do you feel about the State of Israel?"

This was like my first date all over again, with the girl asking anything that came to mind and my chattering away because we both fearfully regarded silence as something that existed only to be clogged, like a sewer. "Well, even before reading *Exodus*—"

I hadn't said anything, had I? Yet all of a sudden the trustees began to chant, *"Exodus! Exodus! Exodus!"* It was so soul-warming, eliciting a response at last, that when the roar abated, I couldn't resist starting it up again. "Yes, even before *Exodus*—"

They were off. *"Exodus! Exodus! Exodus!"* they exclaimed, as in "Two-four-six-eight, who do we appreciate?" Above the clamor rose the voice of the "only twenty-eight" woman: ". . . so I really didn't want to go to Miami all by myself, but that first morning at the Fontainebleau, walking out to the pool, with *Exodus* my sole companion, what do I see but everyone swimming was also reading *Exodus!* I'm telling you, it felt like I was home . . ." And then she asked me to bear witness. "Rabbi Abel, tell us what you think of *Exodus.*"

Caught off-guard, the truth slipped out. "I never could finish the book. Since I majored in English—"

"You didn't finish *Exodus!*"

"Oh, I'm pleased it's so popular—because I share Uris's passion for the land where our forefathers lived, and my own grandfather—"

"*You didn't like* Exodus?"

"I love *Israel*." I'm not proud of what I added, but what would you have said with people regarding you like an unsmitten Egyptian first-born? "You see, I think the characters in the Biblical Exodus are better developed, more appealing, and it's better written too, the Bible is—in *some* parts—"

Mr. Singer turned from me, announcing to the board, "He didn't like *Exodus*."

Nu, nu, don't ask what happened then. Nothing. Whereas before, the trustee had struggled to fill the silence, now silence filled them: silence so deep and dead it felt like a group entombment. Believe me, at this point I'd have welcomed questions on flying saucers, the frug, the possibility of Jewish life on the moon—anything.

But nobody questioned, nobody spoke, nobody so much as spit on me. Damn! Why wasn't anybody asking about what I'd been studying for five years?

"Mr. Singer, would you like me to give the board my views on God?"

"God?" he repeated, as if waiting for me to add His surname.

"How about the function of the synagogue?"

The president stared at me blankly; he couldn't seem to place my face.

"Jewish education? social action? civil rights? how to *live* our Judaism?"

Mr. Singer shook his head. "Thank you, Rabbi. I think you've told us enough." He stood up. "If you'll please excuse us. We'll phone you later tonight with our decision."

Rising to my feet, I sank down the deep room for what felt like the third time. Now no whispers accompanied me, and all eyes were averted, like from a traffic accident that hadn't produced enough gore to make gawking worthwhile.

"Oh, Rabbi—"

Had I heard aright? Was someone addressing the pariah? "Yes?" I paused at the door and turned around. "Yes? Yes?"

A sweet motherly man inquired, "You didn't need this position, did you? I mean, do you have a large family, like Dr. Terman?"

(Some days you're ahead if you died the night before.) "I'm single."

"Single?"

"Not married?"

"A *boy!*"

(My grandfather used to dismiss his neighbors, two satyrs who lived with a succession of assorted women, as "the boys," simply because they were bachelors— and each of their beards was two inches longer than his. To devout Jews, you see, James Bond is a boy.)

I fled. I'm willing to die for my religion, of course, but who wants to be oppressed? The door behind me was thin, however, the voices inside loud, and as I tarried—not eavesdropping, just tarrying—I let myself be inundated by sound waves. Barney Singer spoke first. "Nu?" he said.

"A bachelor rabbi?" was the first response, a male one. "What could he know about our troubles?"

"Oh, poo. Rabbi Abel is right for us"—this from the "only twenty-eight" woman. "Yes, I think he's just right."

The Russia man: "But you said before, he was too young."

"Only twenty-eight" woman: "So I can't change my mind? You didn't fight on the same side as Russia during the Second World War?"

"What's the Second World War got to do with Rabbi Abel, for crissakes!"

Another lady: "I agree with Maurine Levenson. Rabbi Abel is perfect for us."

A male trustee: "By 'us', you don't mean your unmarried sister, do you?"

Some other woman: "What a nasty thing to say even if it *is* true."

Hubbub!

Mr. Singer: "Ladies, ladies, gentlemen, please . . ."

Eventually things quieted down. Things did, not I. Well, how would you like being just right for exactly the wrong reasons?

Mr. Singer: "May I make a suggestion? May I? As an accountant I always try to be scientific. Let's try that here. Suppose we make two columns on the blackboard, call one Rabbi Abel's debits and the other Rabbi Abel's credits, and then simply compare . . ."

If you think I've been exaggerating tonight's pogrom up till now—certainly I have, but within proportion— here is a list of my credits and debits, which I memorized verbatim, because how many people have been personally audited, like General Motors?

DEBITS	CREDITS
"Too young."	"He doesn't look Jewish."
"He doesn't *look* like a rabbi."	"I'm *sure* Rabbi Jacobson from the other temple is a four-F."
"Five degrees—he must be a bookworm."	
"So intense, no sense of humor."	"He looks like an albino Belafonte, doesn't he?"
"A *boy*."	"He's single!"
"Maybe we can do better?"	

"For God sake, how could
  any Jew not like *Exodus!*"
"What was he doing in the
  Marines?"
"I loved Dr. Terman."
"Where did he get that tie?"
"He doesn't seem to have
  inner strength, you know
  what I mean?"

And that's when this fantasy came to me of smiting
eighteen trustees, male and female alike. Yet con-
ditioning is an insidious thing; one can't suddenly
transform twenty-five years' indoctrination of Love
Your Neighbor as Yourself into Chop the Board Up
with Karate. (Besides, what would the gentiles have
said? Or those fretting about the Vanishing American
Jew?)

So it was back to the Rabbinical Seminary dorm
for me with clean hands, though I may yet run
amuck tonight after two shots of Jewish booze—a
double feature at the movies. Come to brood on it,
maybe that's what's missing now in organized religion:
amuck-runners—to explode this chummy coziness of
churches and synagogues, with their food-fetishistic,
social-swirling, edifice-complexed kaffee-klatschness.
This is a religious revival?

It's occupational therapy.

The phone rang as I opened my door, but I was in
no hurry to hear "We wish to inform you, Rabbi Abel,
you're lucky indeed to have escaped Hillendale with
neither tar nor feather." Nothing if not courageous,
however, I picked up the phone three hundred seconds later, when it rang again.

It was Mr. Singer. "You made excellent time getting
back, exactly sixty-five minutes. Well, congratulations,
Rabbi Abel—"

"Oh, it was nothing."

"Nothing? Oh, you mean your return trip. Rabbi, my congratulations were in reference to"—he cleared his throat—"to the board's choosing, by majority vote, to award you a year's contract as our spiritual leader ..."

I zoomed into shock.

Mr. Singer continued, but I heard nothing until ". . . and to celebrate your election, I'd like you to join my family for dinner tomorrow night. If you would pick up my sister, Millicent, in front of the Americana at five-thirty, she can direct you to our home with a minimum of ..."

Out of shock I catapulted. So this engagement was the prerequisite of another kind of engagement. Oh, you think I'm jumping to conclusions? You think this humble rabbi is a conceited ass? Well, let me tell you something, friend: you don't know my people. What Mount Everest is to mountain climbers, bachelors are to Jews. Because we're there: affronts. And unless I miss my guess by a light-year, the trustees elected this boy their rabbi only because a majority have girls for him.

". . . a superb gourmet cook. Millicent works as food editor at ..."

Naturally I had to decline the position. For this I attended five years of rabbinical school? For this I studied Bible, Talmud, Midrash, theology, philosophy, education, homiletics, history, archeology, comparative religion, Hebrew literature, the Code of Laws, pastoral psychiatry? Just to get in shape for a honeymoon? "Thank you," I said, "but perhaps you should get somebody else."

"For dinner tomorrow night?"

"For your temple. You see, I've been thinking of going into chaplaincy work. In prisons or—"

There was a commotion at the other end of the phone—evidently several trustees were auditing the conversation—and I heard:

"He wants more money."

"They're very independent nowadays."

"So offer him seventy-five more dollars a year—and settle for three hundred."

"Maybe we can do better elsewhere."

"But did you ever see a *blonder* rabbi?"

"Sign him for a year. If he doesn't work out, next June we simply drop him."

Know what? Barney Singer did offer me more money, rather "a more substantial honorarium." (Divinity students of the world: forget your Hebrew, Greek, Aramaic, Cuneiform, and learn Euphemism; it's the only language. Without Euphemism in the ministry—where clergymen are "spiritual leaders," hired is "called," and "called" means either your predecessor got himself a better deal or was fired—you're dead. Or, as we say in Euphemism, you've "passed on," as if life were something you were merely touring.)

"Who's asking for an increase?" I said. "You see, Mr. Singer"—and that's when I told this great big fat lie—"I'm engaged to this girl from Westchester." Not a hundred percent great big fat lie; I was simply loose with my tenses. I *had* been engaged to a girl from Westchester, until we broke off.

The trustees reacted in echo-chamber fashion:

"He's engaged!"

"Engaged?"

"*Engaged!*"

"Sonofabitch."

Mr. Singer's response shall long live in glory, for it demonstrates how high the human spirit can soar when it doesn't want to look like an Indian giver. "Rabbi Abel," the president said, "we want you, starting August twenty-eighth, anyway." (Covering the mouthpiece inadequately, he muttered something to the board about a letter from the placement commission.)

"Well, in that case, I accept."

You're shocked? Let me explain. I am answering the call of the Hillendale Temple for one reason alone: revenge.

Perhaps also because sweet too is the injunction of *Ethics of the Fathers:* "The day is short, the work much, the laborers laggard, the reward high, and the Master urgent. You are not obliged to complete the work, but neither are you free to abstain from it." So consider this my bit to help convert the religious revival into something more than a Pax Grossinger's.

Charge!

א

——*Hello, Rabbi? This is Barney Singer.*

——Hello! How are——?

——*Rabbi, there's been some mistake. I just got your letter about coming to Hillendale next week. Don't you remember? You're due on August twenty-eighth, not August first.*

——I know. But I'm anxious to get started.

——*Started? On what?*

——Why, my work . . . the congregation . . .

——*We agreed you'd start four weeks later. It's in our contract: August twenty-eighth.*

——Yes, but—

——*Rabbi, the temple doesn't have the money to pay you for all of August. It's not in our budget, and we're so strapped for funds we may have to run* two *bazaars this year.*

——Oh, I don't care about the money. Let's say August is on the house, not on the temple.

——*That's really decent of you, Rabbi.*

——Not at all, Mr. Singer.

——*Very decent. I mean it. Only—*

——*Yes?*

——*What would you do here August? I mean, during August everybody is busy. Rabbi, you can't expect people to attend meetings in this heat.*

——Well, I can get to know the congregation, conduct Sabbath services—

——*In August?*

——August isn't a good month for Sabbath services?

——*Well, you see, Rabbi, well—*

——Who's conducting them now?

——*Who's conducting what?*

——Sabbath services.

——*Oh.*

——Who's conducting them?

——*Well, the truth is—well, nobody. I mean, there are no Sabbath services to conduct. We canceled them last June fifteenth.*

——You *canceled* them?

——*Well, look, the temple isn't air-conditioned. Besides, the children are away at camp, the women hang out at the club, the men golf. You know how it is during the summer, Rabbi.*

——I see.

——*Of course, I appreciate your offer. I'm glad to*

see you're not money-mad; too many people are these days. But I really think you should report on August twenty-eighth, as scheduled. You want to start off in the temple with a real bang. Isn't that so, Rabbi?

א

AUGUST

A T precisely the twenty-eighth of August, I arrived in Hillendale, a grassy, well-fertilized sub-
urb which looked like any other community that had
won its war on poverty by pricing it's homes upwards
of forty thousand dollars. This, local real estate agents
informed me, prohibited my living in town; on my
salary I couldn't afford it. Yet when Barney Singer
learned of my plan to live in the city and commute
to the temple, he reacted as if I were turning to
Christianity instead of to Manhattan.

"You *can't* do that!" he exclaimed. "We need you in
Hillendale for people to see." Immediately he formed
an apartment committee that combed the area block
by block—methodically efficient, Barney Singer could
systematize chaos; all he needs is to be programmed

—until they found me a local pad, former servants' quarters on a small estate, which enabled me to become a sleep-in rabbi.

It was only after moving into my cramped quarters that I learned my predecessor's contract had stipulated that the temple had to provide him with a Hillendale home rent-free. Why hadn't the same been done for me?

Barney Singer explained. "Dr. Terman was a family man, you see, and a better bargainer."

Now that there were no more interviews to render me paranoid, I found the congregation consisted of genial people—friendly, attractive, very maid-oriented, liberal, keen on golf and children's summer camps, good-humored—except for dapper Rick Adler, who dresses as if the prom were still in progress. After remarking that my sixteen-year-old green Ford looked like something extruded by a sick Mack truck, he volunteered to introduce me to the Buick dealer in town because—the well-vehicled trustee told me, very much disturbed—his own maid drove a brand-new Chevrolet.

"Ah," I shot right back, "but is she fluent in Hebrew?" That stopped him; he could figure out my *non sequitur* no better than I.

Other trustees took an even greater interest in me. Pete Schuster, for one, a muscular gipsy type, who has the self-satisfied, cruel good looks of somebody who loves 'em in *order* to leave 'em; with a sunnier disposition he'd be perfect casting for Heathcliff. I had hardly unpacked when Pete Schuster came to visit. "You have no idea how anxiously I've been awaiting your arrival," he said, and then lavished me with advice on what to say at my installation and how long to say it in; which congregants were worth cultivating for their donations; how to make ours the biggest temple in the county. "If you listen to me, Rabbi," he guaranteed, "there's no telling how far you can go."

(Did that mean that if I did not harken unto Pete Schuster, I would also go far—away?) "I'd appreciate your help."

"Good boy." He whipped out a piece of paper. "Now, Rabbi, here's a list of things you have to do— to *begin* with . . ."

At the first opportunity—it arose during a meeting, when Barney Singer asked about my wedding plans; he didn't want me inadvertently to choose the evening of an important temple function, he said, like the President's Ball—I announced that my engagement had been broken. So what if it happened fourteen months before? To these people it was fresh news.

"Why did you two break up?" somebody wanted to know.

"I'm sure they had good reason," said Maurine Levenson, the temple's executive vice-president. "Didn't you, Rabbi?"

Could I explain that my fiancée and I had discovered in time that what we had most in common was a difference in sex? "No," I said, and everyone chuckled.

Laughing loudest was Dore Redmont, an easy name to remember because I'm sure it used to be Isadore Rosenberg. "I like a rabbi with a sense of humor."

"I don't," Pete Schuster said. "Watch it."

Curt Langer scowled. "Dr. Terman didn't have a sense of humor."

Early the following morning Maurine Levenson and ten other women, all most sympathetic, called to express their sincere regret over my broken engagement, before giving me the phone numbers of sisters, cousins, nieces and kind aunts. (Dating them, I suspected, would be akin to trying to make out in Macy's window.)

For the next few days, till the Sunday of my formal installation, I was kept busy answering the question "Why did you become a rabbi?"

I'm always asked that. (A thousand to one it's never asked of doctors, lawyers, accountants or millionaires—and only by Jews, come to think of it, never by nons-.) Clearly people worry about a rabbi: Does he believe in God *that* much? Didn't he know it takes longer to study for the rabbinate than for medicine or law? Couldn't he stand the sight of blood? Doesn't he want to make something of himself?

Each time automatically I thought of Zayda, Dad's Orthodox father and the saintliest man I've ever known; he knew every grandchild's teacher by name and his report card by heart, he treated his employees like family and paid them the highest wages in the industry, he could quote from the Bible and Midrash at the drop of a yarmulka. I was a child when he, a man in his seventies, left the United States to settle in Israel, and during his farewell party he came over to where I was sulking in a corner. "Please don't be mad at me for leaving," he said. "I have to go live in the Land; I'm a Jew. Soon they'll be declaring Israel the first independent Jewish State in two thousand years." I said everybody was a Jew, but they weren't going anywhere, and he told me, "In America? Who's a Jew here? Here Jews are inside-out Marranos." When I denied being a moron, Zayda explained: "Not morons, Marranos. They were Jews during the Spanish Inquisition who made believe on the outside they were Catholics; but all the time on the inside they remained Jews. In America now it's the exact opposite; on the outside Jews here are making believe they're Jews, but inside they're all of them Rotarians."

Yet I never mentioned Zayda, because even to me there seemed no direct connection between his leaving a million-dollar business to live in Israel and my becoming a rabbi. (Or was the rabbinate my way of memorializing Zayda's murder, while at prayer in a Jerusalem shul, by an Arab soldier at the outbreak of the Israeli War of Independence?) Instead I kept previewing my installation sermon, quoting from Abraham Heschel ("Where could one learn the eternal wisdom of compassion? The fear of being cruel? The danger of being callous? . . . We are in danger of sinking into the darkness of vanity; we are all involved in worshiping our own egos. . . . We are constantly in need of self-purification. . . . It is in the Synagogue where we must try to acquire such inwardness, such sensitivity") and Jacques Maritain ("Judaism gives the world no peace, it bars slumber, it teaches the world to be discontented and restless so long as the world has not God; it stimulates the movement of history").

Yes, you are absolutely right: I do lean on quotations. But they're my way of saying, "You wouldn't have the nerve, would you, to disagree with Moses! with Isaiah! with Maimonides! with Freud! For shame."

My parents drove out to Hillendale the morning of my installation. Undemonstrative family that we are, we didn't kiss or even raise eyebrows at each other; we never do. Nobody has ever so much as

seen my parents shake hands or heard them go so
far as to say they like each other—to this day I
suspect I must have been voted into existence—except at their silver wedding anniversary party, when
Dad toasted Mom with words so beautiful they sent
a neighbor into the kitchen, bawling, "Why doesn't
my husband say things like that about me, the sonofabitch!" and the next day another guest at the party
brought divorce proceedings against his wife.) Mom,
the only plump middle-aged woman in her circle who
also doesn't sport premature blue hair, had come to
kvell from her son the rabbi, while Dad, whom Belafonte resembles, was there to kvetch. "I promised
your mother I wouldn't say a word," Dad said, "about
what you're doing to yourself and to me."

Mom poked him in the tie pin. "Sol, you're starting?"

"Lena, all I said was—"

"Too much. You can nod every once in a while;
that'll be plenty. Look, if *I'm* not saying anything—
and I'm a *mother* yet—"

It was an old story, Dad's antipathy toward my
vocation. He'd had other plans for me—namely, Treasure Chest, which Zayda had founded. Dad's also
Jewish, you see, and it's an unnatural Jewish father
who doesn't yearn to give his only son the business.
In the beginning Dad created scenes that played like
The Jazz Singer perverted. "A rabbi you want to be?
What kind of *Jew* are you!" he exploded. "A Jew is
somebody who's in business for himself. Which rabbi
is? And why have I worked so hard all my life, building up Treasure Chest into the fourth largest independent business of its kind in the whole world?
Why do you think? It was for you, Gideon, and all
my grand-children you're going to give me." And

more: "Did I ever say a word to you about your goings and doings? Did I? Did I ever try to stop you from majoring in English instead of business administration? Or from running around on freedom rides and sit-ins and God knows how many orgies at Fort Lauderdale in between? I did not. Because I had confidence your hormones would finally balance themselves out. But now—*now!* Throwing away the fourth largest independent business of its kind to work for five hundred bosses. With the richest ignoramus in the congregation the chief boss. The rabbinate! I can't think of an occupation better designed for making a man an anti-Semite."

I had quoted William James ("The great use of a life is to spend it for something that outlasts it"), Karl Jaspers ("What a man is, he becomes through the cause he has made his own") and Freud ("Only religion is able to answer the question of the purpose of life"), but Dad had rebutted them all with "Strangers you listen to instead of your own father? What kind of *son* are you! You know in 1942 the United States government no less gave Treasure Chest top priorities, they thought it that important to our country's defense? Top priorities, mind you, in the middle of the Second World War! It's so hard to take, Treasure Chest is? A useful business, a respected business, a growing business, a business a person can take *pride* in."

When I tried to explain that while I appreciated his generosity, what excited me were people and values, not brassieres (which is what Treasure Chest is, and not, as you might have jumped to conclude from Dad's description, the Holy Grail), he had snorted, "Appreciate? Is that a word to use to a father? Who wants appreciation? Who needs appreciation? Just accept, take over the business, prosper. Later, when you're older and smarter and a father yourself, you'll understand things; *then* you can appreciate what I'm doing for an ingrate like you."

Where was my mother during my five-year argument with Dad (on the night before ordination, he had taken me aside to ask, "Gideon, you're actually going through with this?")? Also hoping for a change of heart. Mom, you see, always wanted me to become a doctor. When I announced my plans to enter the rabbinate, she said nothing at first, and then, "If I seem shocked, Gideon, it isn't because I'm not happy with your choice; I am if you are. It's just that people we know—well, they don't *do* that sort of thing." Which, of course, is the curtain line in *Hedda Gabler*, after the woman has committed suicide.

But don't get us wrong. The truth is, and I blush to admit it because nowadays it's so way out, I love my mother and father very much despite all my faults. Oh, the bull sessions I've sat through where parents were blamed for everything from halitosis to tight ids to loose stools to orgasms of non-earthquaking proportions. Me, I shep nachas from my parents (in addition to everything else, Dad is not only his industry's biggest contributor to charity but also its only anonymous one, and Mom does volunteer work twice a week at the Chronic Diseases Hospital, a place I can't visit without having nightmares), and if this be treason against billions of motherfaulters and fatherdamners, screw 'em.

Showing my parents around my apartment—that was easy: they could see its two tiny rooms from the front doorway—I related its history as servants' quarters, and Dad remarked, "Who was the butler, Tom Thumb?"

"I like it," Mom said. "The grounds outside are lovely, the refrigerator looks roomy. Come, Gideon, help me unload."

Over my protestations—it was easier for me to eat out all the time; besides, there was no room in my apartment for food—Mom shlepped out five cartons from her car trunk; one packed in dry ice was marked Meat, and the others were full of enough S. S. Pierce canned goods to see me into the twenty-first century. I don't know why Jews have this hang-up about food, but we do; food is meat and drink to us, and sex too. Even in the Marines the Jewish personnel would sit around, munching salami and canned gefilte fish provided by the Jewish Welfare Board; then everyone would lick his lips, give such a sigh, sometimes moan, as if he were undergoing a religious experience. As for Jewish mothers, I don't have to tell you; they have this tremendous feeling of guilt because their breasts provide their babies with only milk and no variety.

(You want examples? I got examples. My first overnight hike in the cub scouts: we gather around the bonfire, and the thirteen gentile boys pull frankfurters out of their knapsacks. I, the only Jew in the group, open *my* pack, and right then there was nothing that would have given me greater pleasure than immolating myself, together with the marshmallows; Mom had packed two lamb chops and three chicken livers.)

My mother opened the refrigerator. "Books?"

There was no place else to keep them—the kitchen cabinets and stove were also filled with books, because my office had no room even for a window—but did that deter her from emptying the refrigerator, loading it with meat and shifting the books to my car trunk? Of course not. Then she served us a seven-course brunch, before asking to see the temple.

"Yes, we're dying to see it," Dad said, his face looking like a black armband.

On the way over, Mom gave me a run-down on who recently became engaged, who got married and who looked like she was late that month. Dad, a less oblique type, said only, "Even Frankenstein found a bride, Gideon. So what's with you?" (Parents, according to my own unpublished survey, are people who nag you to get married when you're single, when you get married they nag you to have a baby, when you have a baby they nag you to have a second, and when you have your second child they nag you to stop.)

Dad's expression gradually brightened as we toured the converted mansion. The seven upstairs bedrooms were classrooms and a storeroom, the linen closet was the library, and several walls of the first floor had been torn down to form a sanctuary that seated almost 193 people. "Nice!" he said. "Why didn't you tell us the place was so nice?"

"Who cares about a building? It's what goes on outside the temple on account of it that makes a temple a temple." (Now there was a homily worthy of Bing Crosby at his priestiest. If I wasn't careful I'd soon start calling congregants "My son" and begin Sabbath services with "Good Shabbas, dear friends, and welcome to another service of the Hillendale Temple;" which Rick Adler wanted me to say in order to advertise that ours was the *friendlier* synagogue.)

"Gideon, Gideon!"

"Sol, you promised."

I took them through the kitchen and into my office, formerly the pantry. "The temple is overextended financially," I explained, "but they did assure me a window if the bazaar goes well."

"Not a word!" Dad swore.

It was time now for Mom to take my emotional temperature. "All I want to know, Gideon, is if you're happy." She's the kind who when anything happens to anyone, it happens to her too. When somebody marries, or gives birth, or makes Dean's List, or gains weight, my mother shares in the joy; and if misfortune strikes anyone, God forbid, she feels that also. Don't think it isn't wearing, growing up with a woman who's elated one day because Elliott Roosevelt just took his fifth wife and this time it looks like the real thing, thank God, and his mother is such a fine person she deserves some nachas already from her son; or who's depressed another day because Adlai Stevenson can't seem to find himself a mate, what a pity such a fine man should be lonely in addition to having been gypped out of the Presidency by some ten million votes. "*Are* you happy, Gideon?"

Dad beat me to an answer. "Why shouldn't he be happy? He has five hundred bosses to *make* him happy. That, and the knowledge that he'll always be in the wrong. It stands to reason: how can a rabbi ever be right when whatever he does, he can't avoid antagonizing somebody? Ask him enough questions during the year, let him take enough stands, and a rabbi's lucky if by June, seventy-five percent of the congregation don't vote to throw him a lynching party."

"Thanks a lot, Dad! Tonight's my installation, and already you're having me canned."

"Gideon, when you were a little boy, I was on the shul's board, and in all my life the one time I saw trustees happier than when they were interviewing and hiring rabbis was when they *fired* them. But I promised your mother not to say a word, and I intend to keep that promise." (Mom sighed.) "Gideon, you know what I wish you now, don't you? All the mazel in the world. The brassiere industry's loss is certainly Judaism's gain. I mean that sincerely. May God have mercy on you."

Mom intervened. "Suppose we change the subject now altogether. Gideon, there's an article in the Hadassah Magazine I want to show you—about Maimonides, the rabbi. Did you know that in addition Maimonides was a doctor?"

After having stayed up till four o'clock that morning, revising my installation sermon, I spent all afternoon revising my revisions, wishing all the while I could have tried my sermon out in New Haven to see whether the reviews warranted my bringing it into Hillendale or closing myself out of town.

(Do I sound overanxious? Well, I sure as hell am. It all goes back to my youth, Doctor, to the first time the seminary sent me out to preach—someplace in Long Island, where a group of Jewish families were meeting in a school auditorium until they had acquired enough members and their money to plunge into the great American religious sport of building. The service is about to start when I discover something missing. "Where," I ask, standing on the stage, clutching my twenty-one-page manuscript in two sweating palms, "where is the lectern?" Well, nobody knows. Nor could anyone find me a music stand or so much as a high chair, because the storeroom had been locked up for the weekend. But I *had* to have a stand; how could I preach, shuffling twenty-one pages of manuscript with the insertion on the back of page seven, and the asterisk at the bottom of page ten telling me to proceed to the first two paragraphs at the top of page thirteen, then return to page eleven?

"Service time!" somebody shouted, and there was only one thing to do: panic. Pulling out a grand piano from the wings, I set up shop on it, and that's how I conducted the service: snuggling into the curve of the piano with my prayerbook on top—I was lucky at that; the piano could have been an upright—feeling throughout like Helen Morgan reincarnated, so that when the time came to preach, it seemed inappropriate for me not to start with "He's just my God, an ordinary God . . .")

In the evening I drove my parents to the railroad station to pick up my installer, Dr. Isaac Tchernichovsky, dean of the Rabbinical Seminary. A broad-shouldered, erect seventy-six-year-old six-footer, with whirling white hair and brows that topped his olive skin and bright black eyes like whipped cream, his entrance into Hillendale was that of a Moses; indeed, he made all the passengers there look like a sea waiting to part before his mahogany walking stick.

"Installation," he snorted, when I thanked him for coming. "Wouldn't you think another term could have been found to distinguish between a rabbi and a washing machine?"

We all got into the car, I with a dozen prepared questions about Spinoza, Buber, Niebuhr and God. (Making small talk with the dean would be as sacrilegious as playing Ghost with Einstein; besides, I feared what Dad might say.) On the subject of God alone, there was much to ask. For the dean regarded man not only as the partner of God but His challenger, whose function was constantly to remind God of *His* function—to ensure the triumph of goodness in the world; and whenever He falters, man should take over for the Lord, who draws strength from the struggles of His champions. Perhaps—this was the dean's fascinating idea—the Lord was not perfect or omni-anything in the beginning, but is now *growing* toward perfection, which He cannot achieve without man's help; for his faith will compel the Lord's total emergence in the end. "'On that day,'" Dr. Tchernichovsky was fond of quoting from Zechariah, "'the Lord shall be One and His name one.'"

Alas, while I was starting the car, Dad jumped in with the first question. "Dean? You think my son has a future here?" he asked, as if the temple were a get-rich-quick scheme, in which case he'd no doubt offer to set me up with a chain of synagogues, and I felt like drowning myself in the gas tank.

"Mr. Abel, do you think Judaism has a future?"

"Here in Hillendale, you mean, or in general?"

Mom interceded to keep Dad from giving the dean the benefit of his doubts. "The reason my husband asks is, on the drive out I mentioned maybe we should move our cemetery plots nearer Hillendale so Gideon shouldn't have to travel so far to visit. But that's only if he'll be remaining here, you understand."

The Dean sighed. "There are storm clouds in the Jewish future, that's true. Judaism no longer dominates the life of our people, and there's no rabid anti-Semitism to force us to be Jews. Today a new threat looms: success, Jewry's mass entry into the middle class—"

Dad interrupted, aghast. "Success—that's a failing?"

"Mr. Abel, a story's told about Czar Nicholas the First reproaching the Emperor Franz Josef for emancipating Austria's Jews and granting them citizenship.

Do you know what Franz Josef replied? 'Nicholas, you destroy your Jews your way; let me destroy my Jews my way.' Moses warned that a fat and contented Israel would stop kicking, and it's true. Today we well-off American Jews are slowly assimilating—and not the best of America's cultural values, but its worst. You see what happens at funerals: if it's a plain one, as Jewish law requires, the departed will be eulogized for his spiritual qualities; if it's expensive, the deceased will invariably be eulogized for his material success. But I don't mean to prophesy gloom, Mr. Abel, not on a glorious occasion like tonight's installation. Splendid young rabbis like your son are to me what the rainbow was to Noah: a sign that we will persevere—and indeed be a blessing to many peoples."

When I parked in the driveway beside the lush Beardsley garden, the dean said, surprised, "Is this your temple? Oh, yes—there's the thermometer." He pointed to a nearby nine-foot cardboard thermometer, half inked in red, which bore the legend:

> **TEMPLE EXPANSION FUND**
> Have YOU contributed yet for GOD'S sake?

Rick Adler came running over in a tuxedo, his eyes shining more than when, as chairman of the installation committee, he had suggested staging this evening like the Second Coming, with publicity releases, engraved invitations, printed programs, newspaper articles and, possibly, the gunning down of an archduke. (His choice for guest speaker had been Robert Frost, whom he had given up on only after learning the poet had died since the Kennedy Inauguration.)

I introduced Rick Adler, who exclaimed, "Abentley!"

"Pardon?"

"Bentley." The trustee pointed behind me. "Bentley."

"Tchernichovsky," I whispered, "our guest speaker."

Rick Adler gave me a dirty look. "I meant the automobile." Before I could ask Dad what had happened to his Lincoln, the trustee asked, "Whose Bentley is this?"

"Mine," Dad said.

"It's a beauty. You have taste." Which would have been a nice compliment had Rick Adler emphasized "taste" instead of "you." To me he said, "You should feel honored. Dr. Lipton is here."

"Fine." I explained to my parents and the dean: "He's the rabbi of Hillendale's Orthodox synagogue."

Rick Adler corrected me. "No, no, that's Rabbi Jacobson—and he wouldn't be caught dead inside our temple. Dr. Lipton is a congregant, a psychiatrist, who usually comes to temple only to lecture."

Entering the temple, I was suddenly taken with nostalgia—no, not for Zayda's shul of my childhood, but for the old neighborhood appetizing store. For all kinds of mouth-watering odors washed over us from the lavish smorgasbord that was screened from sight in the lobby.

The dean could smell too. "My nose tells me," he remarked, "your sisterhood has prepared an orgy for the middle-aged."

We were approached by a portly gray-headed woman who stood out in the gathering crowd like an Arab; in this congregation, where life revolved sveltely around forty, she was some two stout decades older.

"Are you the rabbi's mother and father?" she asked my parents. "Oh, you must be *so* proud!" She introduced herself as Mrs. Greenwood, who was living in Hillendale with her son, Jerry, and daughter-in-law, Eve, the president of sisterhood, then took charge of my parents. "Now don't worry about your son one bit," she said. "If you'll tell me what his favorite foods are, I'll never let him go without."

"You say you have a married son?" Mom said, instantly alert. "How did you manage that?"

Before following the women into the sanctuary, Dad drew me aside. "He's such a fine man, the dean," he said. "Find out what size his wife is, and I'll send her a gross of bras."

Rick Adler guided the dean and me through the kitchen to my office, leaving us with the trustees who would be sitting on the pulpit. All eighteen had been assigned pulpit seats until it was pointed out that so many people couldn't fit on the small pulpit even lashed together on tiptoes, and it took only a few hours of discussion to narrow the group down to a seatable number. Dore Redmont, with the starlet's name and a punching bag's build, welcomed me warmly. "Good luck tonight, Rabbi. I'm sure you'll lay them in the aisles." (Well, he meant well.)

Pete Schuster handed me another of his lists. "Now these are the people I want you to thank from the pulpit for preparing the hors d'oeuvres, champagne punch, melon sloops . . ."

I donned my clerical robe, which always made me feel funny because the rabbi of Zayda's Orthodox shul had never worn one; the closest to it in my impressionable childhood had been Batman's cape. So you'll never see me raise my hands aloft in the pulpit: waving those black balloon-shaped sleeves, I'd be afraid of substituting "Jumping Jehoshaphat!" for the benediction.

"Eight-ten, twenty minutes to go, ninety-two people in the sanctuary," Rick Adler announced, popping into my office. "What happened to the carnations for the ushers?"

Nobody knew and he left.

Pete Schuster turned to the dean with a testimonial: "Religion means everything in the world to me. I put in more time running this temple than I do in my own belt business."

"Why?" the dean asked.

"Because I'm determined ours must become the most important temple in the county. So I knock myself out chairing four committees, serving on four more, going after delinquent members, negotiating loans for our expansion fund, reminding the rabbi of things to do . . ."

Too true. My self-appointed adviser on how to succeed in the rabbinate, Pete Schuster is forever telling me how to galvanize the congregation spiritually, never to cross my legs while sitting on the pulpit nor to wear anything that isn't black or blue, and to raid Hillendale's other temple for members. Well, at least he balances a few congregants who, I suspect, regard me as their wicked step-rabbi; they seem unable to say a sentence without beginning "But *Dr. Terman* . . ." Pete Schuster prefers me, praise be; didn't he tell me, "I also had great hopes when your predecessor came here, but he was such a disappointment. He was one of those know-it-alls; he hardly heeded me"?

Dore Redmont sighed. "My ambition is more grandiose. After having made it—which my settling in Hillendale proves—I want to find in temple an answer to: *Now*, what?"

"Huh?" Pete Schuster said.

Rick Adler returned. "Eight-twenty, a hundred forty-nine people here, and they're still coming. Where *are* those carnations?" Exit.

"Yes, we had great plans when Dr. Terman was here!" Curt Langer exclaimed. "If not for him, Dean, we'd still be meeting in the old firehouse. *Irv* was the one who went to the bank president and got us a second mortgage at a full half percent cheaper than any of us could swing it. Now there was a rabbi!"

Dore Redmont shook his head ruefully. "When we were meeting in the firehouse, we didn't need to raise twenty-three thousand every year above our income from dues. At the firehouse we never had to turn the temple into a piggy bank."

Everyone had a comment on that which he believed the others deserved to hear at once. The gist of the ensuing uproar, I gathered, was that some trustees claimed membership never would have doubled if the temple hadn't bought the Beardsley estate, while others maintained that without the Beardsley estate the budget never would have quintupled. Things quieted down, however, when several trustees ended up not speaking to each other. The last word heard was Barney Singer's "Some people just don't realize: the temple is a *business*."

"There's only one difference," the dean commented wryly. "A business is organized for profits, and a temple for *the* prophets."

Rick Adler reappeared. "Too bad we can't install a rabbi every week. We had to move some sweet tables

upstairs to make room for more seats." He checked
his wristwatch. "Okay, line up now."

"Size places?" Dore Redmont asked, but I was too
nervous to chuckle. My mouth was so dry I feared
my tongue would break off like a piece of stale angel
cake were I to move my face.

"Okay, let's go!" Rick Adler marched us out into the
kitchen, where Maurine Levenson was asking, "You
think the herring salad might turn bad with so many
people warming up the sanctuary? Oh, I wish we
were air-conditioned." A sisterhood member, busily
stuffing something into pastry shells, prayed in response, "If only they don't drag out the service."

Pete Schuster held up a manicured hand. "Wait!
People are still arriving."

"What difference does that make?" Rick Adler
asked. "We don't want to get a reputation for starting
our services late. Look, I'm not even waiting for the
carnations."

Barney Singer called for a discussion.

During the debate I slipped back into my office
to pray. Help is what I needed now, and plenty of it,
for I am not what you would call preach-happy. To
tell the truth, even before my experience in Long
Island, I had been leery of sermonizing—no, not
leery; overwhelmed is more like it. Overwhelmed by
preaching, though—this is odd—not by public speaking. Addressing groups I enjoy, and the give-and-take
of questions afterwards exhilarates me because sometimes I don't know my own thoughts till I hear them.
Yet when I get up to preach in a synagogue—mama
mía! The thought of acting as spokesman for God and
four thousand years of Judaism and the prophets and
ancient rabbis and martyrs, it makes me feel—well,

presumptuous. Standing before the Holy Ark with the Torah scroll inside and the Eternal Light overhead symbolizing the Divine Presence, sometimes I can't help thinking that Big Deity is watching me and He's shaking His head, saying, "You have feelings of adequacy, do you, My son?" And all I can think of by way of reply is "Lord, Thou preferest *Billy Graham?*"

"Rabbi?" Pete Schuster was standing in the doorway. "What are you doing back here?"

"Looking for my prayerbook."

"With your eyes closed?" He handed me another list. "Look this over before tomorrow's meeting, will you? It's suggestions for enlivening our Sabbath services."

Enter Rick Adler. "We're five minutes late. Let's get this show on the road!"

Pulling us out of my office, he marched the group through the kitchen and into the crowded sanctuary. Comments trailed us down the center aisle, making me feel like a television set that had come to the temple on approval, which, come to think of it, I had; in June it would be up to the congregation to extend my option. So *that's* why they called this an installation.

As my companions took their assigned seats on the pulpit, I stepped up to the lectern. A hush damped down the congregation, but not my jitters. Sweat ran down my back, collecting in a pool at my waistband. It was a good thing I had prayed before in my office; with all those people watching, I certainly couldn't pray now, during the service. The weirdest thoughts kept surfacing in my brain while I led the congregation in prayer:

Where did I mislay my manuscript!

Who was banging that bracelet, which, from the sound of it, held enough charms to flail a yoke of oxen to death!

If only that man in the first row wouldn't always be three words ahead of me during congregational reading!

Why did that lady in the second row keep staring up at me like Dracula!

Did I accidentally skip a page!

Why was that woman wearing such a low neckline!

How could my mouth be so dry with my body floating in sweat!

If that kid drops those marbles one more time . . .!

She's *still* staring!

My sermon stinks.

Barney Singer succeeded me enthusiastically in the pulpit. With a reddish-brown suit encasing his massive frame, he looked like a spreading chestnut tree when he flung out his sturdy arms and cried, "Welcome, my friends!" He beamed down at his wife and children seated in his shade, then addressed the congregation. "As president of the Hillendale Temple, it is my distinct pleasure to welcome you all to tonight's installation. More about that in a moment; first these few announcements." Twenty-one minutes later he got around to Dr. Tchernichovsky, introducing him at flowery length.

The dean commented to me wryly, "After that build-up I can hardly wait to hear what I have to say." Then he stepped up to the lectern, a majestic figure, whipping his fingers through his creamy white hair. "Such a glorious introduction. I do hope the good Lord was listening. At my age one needs all the references he can get."

The congregation chuckled. I relaxed and stopped

trying to dry my palms on my robe, an impossible task, anyway.

Facing the people alone—without notes—the dean repeated some of his earlier remarks before exclaiming, "Today we have our greatest opportunity in history! For we Jews of America need no longer use up all our lives in making a living or defending ourselves against persecution. Now we can devote ourselves to our ancient covenant with the Lord, enjoining us to be a kingdom of priests, a holy people and a light to all nations ...

"Our purpose on earth is never merely to anoint what is. As sparks fly upward, Jews are born to be gadflies of the soul; licensed skeptics and idol-smashers we have been ordained. Yes, American Jews *do* have a dual loyalty—let us never deny it. We are faithful citizens of the United States, this noble country, and we are at the same time *trans*-Americans, for we are also God's citizens. Indeed, reflecting society instead of ever-refining it would mean our spiritual death.

"This is why Rabbi Abel is joining you now: first, to *teach* you the mitzvos the living God requires of us, because 'the ignorant cannot be pious.' (Do you know, a school is considered holier even than a synagogue? The rabbis allowed a synagogue building to be transformed into a school, but forbade a school's conversion into a synagogue.) Second, Rabbi Abel is here to help you *perform* the commandments, because 'not learning but doing is the chief thing.' Or, as Martin Buber wrote, 'Judaism has no room for a truth remaining abstract, hovering self-sufficiently above reality. Judaism, instead, comprises the whole life: economy, society, state, the marketplace. And where Jews, especially the possessors of power and

property, try to limit the service of God to the sacral
sphere, or limit His authority to words and symbols
—this is where the prophetic protest against social
injustice for God's sake sets in.'

"What kind of rabbi Gideon Abel is, his actions will
soon tell you, just as what you truly believe and
whom you actually worship, your actions will tell
him. Know one thing, however: though Rabbi Abel
is a man of dedication and kindness, intelligence and
good humor, he cannot serve you if you do not assist
him. Your rabbi is not a soloist, and you are not his
audience; he is not a professional Jew, and you are
not amateurs. But together you are a holy congregation, born of Israel's yearning to sanctify this world
for the sake of heaven . . ."

Finally it was my turn to preach in Hillendale for
the first time. No match for the dean in eloquence, I
concentrated on the nitty-gritty, announcing adult
Jewish-education courses (Bible, history, philosophy,
Ethics of the Fathers) and a social-action program to
aid Jews abroad (support of Israel and combat of
Russian anti-Semitism), Negroes at home (new housing, improved schools, guaranteed jobs) and other
fellow Americans (a preschool kindergarten for disadvantaged children, a two-dollar minimum wage).
Several noble causes may have gotten lost in my
diction, for nervousness ejected my words with the
slippery speed of spitballs; surely those who blew
their noses during my sermon missed one project with
every blow.

After the service dozens of people graciously came
over to congratulate me; even more did so when the
smorgasbord ran out of food. There were, however, a
few comments like "Rabbi, I think you're *entitled* to
your opinion" and "After completing all those projects

of yours, Rabbi, what'll you do here *next* year?" and "Marvelous sermon, simply marvelous! Tonight you preached everything I've been telling people for years, and here they've been calling me a crank."

Yet it was now official: crank or no, I was the Hillendale Temple's rabbi, and these people were my congregation, even as it is written in the Song of Songs, "I am my beloved's and my beloved is mine." Hosanna.

✌

——*Rabbi Abel?*

——Speaking.

——*This is Rochelle Levenson.*

——Yes?

——*The niece of Maurine and Jim Levenson from Boston. We met at your wonderful installation.*

——I remember. How are you?

——*Fine, thanks. Rabbi, I haven't seen you since your installation, but I imagine you've been busy.*

——Well, yes. I'm still getting myself organized, and since the temple can't afford a secretary—

——*I wanted to tell you how much I enjoyed your sermon.*

——Well, thank you very much.

——*Dr. Tchernichovsky spoke nicely, but I thought you were far superior.*

——You're very kind, but my sermon was only a paraphrase of his.

——*My, but you're modest.*

——Nobody's ever accused me of *that* before!

——*You're remarkably straightforward, and I won't let you refuse that compliment. Rabbi?*

——Yes?

———*I'd like to see you.*

———Of course. Next Thursday all right? At two?

———*In the afternoon?*

———Well, yes.

———*But I work during the day; I'm not a rabbi. Let's make it eightish.*

———In the evening or the morning?

———*You do have a sense of humor. I prefer a late hour because when I was in Spain this past summer, I got into the habit of eating late. They eat dinner after nine in Spain, did you know that?*

———Really? Well, eight P.M. it is then. Care to tell me now what's on your mind?

———*Oh, I'll leave you to discover that for yourself, Rab. Tell me, how good an explorer are you?*

———Actually I haven't had much experience, so I'll need all the cooperation you can give me.

———*Boy, what a line.*

———What?

———*Gideon, you are one swinging rabbi!*

———Perhaps it would be better—for our relationship to be productive—if you would call me Rabbi.

———*You're very conscious of being a rabbi, aren't you?*

———Well, I am one.

———*Your aloofness now in contrast to your warmth in person and the pulpit. Do all rabbis take the rabbinage so seriously?*

———Rabbinage makes it sound like we live in a hutch. The word is rabbinate.

———*Holy hell, you even take the pronunciation seriously!*

———Well, we all sometimes make mountains out of molehills, don't we? And usually things aren't as bad as they seem, are they? And often asking for help is so embarrassing or painful that one turns on one's counselor—

——*What's with the maxims? You sound like a fortune cookie.*

——Rochelle, what seems to be the problem?

——*Problem? What problem?*

——The problem that seems to be causing the difficulty.

——*What difficulty?*

——Well, where do you think is the area of difficulty?

——*What area?*

——All right now, Rochelle, what's the trouble? Okay, *your* trouble.

——*My trouble?*

——The trouble you want to discuss with me.

——*You think I'm in trouble?*

——I didn't say that. I never said, in trouble. I'm just interested in hearing about the problem.

——*For God sake, what makes you so sure I have The Problem? Or do you mean The Curse?*

——You did call me, Rochelle.

——*Yes?*

——Yes?

——*Yes, what?*

——You did say you wanted to see me, Rochelle.

——*Of course.*

——Well?

——*Holy hell! Doesn't anyone want to see you when they don't have The Problem?*

——What?

——*Don't you ever see girls who aren't in trouble?*

——Of course. Not everyone I see is pregnant out of wedlock.

—*Oh, is that the kind of girl you like to date?*

—*Date?* Did you say date?

—*Yes, date. What do you think we're talking about here?*

—This—a *date?* You *don't* have a problem?

—*My only problem, Rab, is The Rabbi.*

א

SEPTEMBER

You probably don't believe it, but that was the truth I told Rochelle Levenson when I humbly confessed modesty isn't my long suit; as a matter of fact, the one thing they were always hocking me about in Rabbinical Seminary was humility. Just because that's the only virtue the Torah ascribes to Moses—and you know what a big Jew he was—a couple of professors pushed modesty a lot, especially in my direction, so much so I feared flunking out of school for downcasting my eyes at an improper angle. (Not Dean Tchernichovsky, however; his classic remark to a classmate of mine who went around trying to outhumble Uriah Heep: "Bricker, don't make yourself so small. You're not that big.") Even the president of the seminary carped at me at ordination for not scrunching down far enough when he laid his hands on my head; we did not present a humble picture, he said, since he's nine inches shorter than I. "Well," I replied with all the good humor in the world, "you can't bless 'em tall"—which remark he accepted with growl instead of grace.

Happily, nobody at the temple seems to realize that humility is my one and only lack. Oh, occasionally Pete Schuster says, "Rabbi, you're not listening to me again," and Sam Warren tells me, "Not a hundred percent of the congregation approved of your Rosh Hashanah sermon, you know." But nobody's come right out and said, "Rabbi, where the hell is your humility?"

Then came that Erev Shabbas dinner at the Redmont's. Retribution is what they call it in Greek tragedy.

I was delighted to be asked; Rona Redmont, a very pretty blonde, is reputed to be the best cook in the congregation. The three children are bright and sweet and admire my ability to wiggle my ears and thumbs at the same time, a feat they swore Dr. Terman couldn't top. Their father, Dore, is the one who confided to me over matjes herring at my installation, "There must be something dreadfully wrong with a man whose public relations are better than his private ones! I hate my job; I hate working all day on nonsense; I hate peddling people, corporations, products—some of them noxious. Yet what can I do? I can't quit my P.R. firm, when I'm fit for nothing else, not at the age of forty-three with a wife and three children. And I'm making Rona as miserable as myself. She tells me, 'You think there'd ever have been a *Death of a Salesman* if Willy Loman had made sixty thousand dollars a year with stock options?' She's absolutely right too. I'm looking, Rabbi; can you tell me for what?"

Dore must have been good at his job because for someone in the image business, his looks didn't match the image of a public-relations man; he was as plain, dumpy and swarthy as his wife was pert, slender and blonding. Yet he had qualities which made for an attractive man: intelligence, intolerance of cant, and candor—about himself, which is a switch, instead of about others.

I was alone with Dore in the living room, swallowing my first gefilte-fish hors d'oeuvre, when he began anew: "Well, Rabbi? Have you thought of how to save me from my sixty-thou blues? I've been thinking since our little talk, maybe if I got religion, found God—"

Frankly, the man made me nervous. The religious equivalent of the mythical nymphomaniac of every man's dream, Dore, confronting me each time with ultimates alone, made me wonder whether I was rabbi enough for the job. "Why don't you do something like what my mother did," I said, "when her menopause began?"

Dore bridled. "Your mother? Menopause?" He looked mad enough to stone me with Rona's gefilte-fish balls.

Damn! I must learn to speak professionally. "What I mean is, give yourself to a noble cause. My mother, when she got depressed some years ago, she started doing hospital volunteer work. Not just anywhere, but in the Chronic Diseases Hospital; volunteers there are hard to get because the patients are in terrible condition. Since then she's been fine."

"Rabbi, I ask you about religion, God—and you tell me to become a Gray Lady?"

"That's what religion is mostly about—helping others, individually and collectively." Double damn! That was too simple; I must learn to speak more *profoundly*. "That's why I intend for our temple to go whole hog—I mean, with all our hearts—into social action in addition to adult education. If you'll help along—"

Rona and the children entered just then, and Dore said drily, "The rabbi is soliciting me for further temple duty, dear. Tell him what you're doing for our house of God."

"*My Fair Sadie*, the temple's biggest fund-raiser this year," Rona said, then reported on the show committee, which she was co-chairing with Pete Schuster, and summarized the plot. "You see, there's this Reform Jew, Hymie Higgins, who meets this Chasidic Jewess, Sadie Doolittle, selling knishes off a pushcart in Williamsburg, and he decides to teach her to speak like a Yankee so she can open a crêpes-suzette shoppe in Scarsdale. Isn't that clever? And wait till you hear our songs! 'Get Me to the Shul on Time,' 'At the Office Where You Give,' 'I've Grown Accustomed to Her Race,' 'I Could Have Hora'd All Night...'"

This put me in a bind. Could I say to Dore in Rona's proud presence, "I'm certainly not suggesting you do anything like *that*"? I was even afraid to point out—are rabbis supposed to recognize double-entendres?—that the cast would have to be awfully careful in pronouncing "Hora'd," lest ours be the first temple to be closed down by the police.

"Rabbi? Would you join us at the table?"

Gathering around the beautifully set dinner table, with its exquisite white linen cloth and centerpiece of sweetheart roses, we all watched Rona light the

Sabbath candles. She recited the ancient blessing over them, slowly circling the flames with her arms in the mixing motion of my mother, who always gave me the impression that on Sabbath Eve she was rearranging the atoms of the world by hand, improving on their permutations and combinations, and by the time she'd be through praying in silence after covering her face with those same hands, tranquil at last, life would emerge as it would have been had God only had the good sense to consult her in the beginning.

Uncovering her lovely face, lambent in the candlelight and serene, Rona said, "Good Shabbas," and all of us wished each other a Sabbath of peace.

Dore asked me to chant the *Kiddush.* I complied in exceptionally good voice, and we raised our glasses to our lips to drink, an occasion which always makes me feel grateful I'm not a Baptist, when what do I see floating atop my wine?

A big black fly.

First of all, I want you to know I didn't scream, the Marine Corps can take pride. Shaken I was, but outwardly I remained cool as a corpse, watching the fly breast the waves made by my quivering hand. Yet after remaining calm, what was there to do for an encore? Everybody else was drinking up; soon they'd notice I wasn't and want to know why.

"Rabbi, why aren't you drinking your wine?"

See what I mean? That was Rona, a lovely woman whose personal hygiene was impeccable, dressed immaculately herself and the children, kept a spotless home, cooked like an imported chef, and would drop dead with embarrassment in front of her credenza should I point out the fly in my glass—and that would be a great sin. No, I'm not exaggerating too much, for

Judaism teaches that one who shames another in public, it's as if he had murdered him. Moreover, the Talmud declares, "It is better to throw oneself into a burning surface than to humiliate a human being publicly."

What was a fellow to do in a situation like this, where no burning surfaces were handy? That the Talmud didn't say.

Well, I don't know about other rabbis, but I lie; that's another lack of mine. "I don't drink," I gulped. Actually, the truth was only one word away: I don't drink *flies*.

"You don't drink?" The whole family was astonished —even the six-year-old.

"I'm allergic to alcohol." Look, if I tell one lie, I might as well buttress it with a few others to make it look good and not feel lonely.

"Really?" They were aghast. For a rabbi to be allergic to wine is equivalent to a psychiatrist developing an allergy to sex.

"Makes me break out," I said, crossing my fingers.

"But I've seen you drink—every Shabbas in temple after the *Kiddush*," said Dore, the observant Jew.

"I fake it."

"You *fake* it?"

"What I do is this—so as not to void the blessing." I stuck my tongue into the wineglass, praying it wouldn't hit the fly, then yanked my tongue out, straining it through my lips just in case.

"Well!" everyone said, and, "What do you know about that?"

After praising God for bringing forth bread from the earth, we sat down to eat, I rather proud of myself, if slightly nauseated. Sure, I had used up my daily quota of lies, and the Bible forbade the inges-

tion of insects' bathwater, but I had saved the Redmont honor. Now the family would still attend services, adult education and religious school without
thinking every time they saw me: He found a fly in
our wine, I could *kill* that rabbi.

The fruit cup was delicious—fresh too, none of that
canned stuff for Rona, and no fly in it, praise be,
though a watermelon seed gave me a nervous moment. The chopped liver was also superb, not too
much schmaltz, and plenty of onions, one piece so
brown it resembled a you-know-what; by then, however, I could relax. So working on the theory that
people invariably end up believing what they practice, I started listing social-action projects for Dore
to lead.

But he interrupted me to herald the next course.
"Rabbi, if you don't agree this is the best chicken
soup you've ever tasted, better even than you'll be
getting tomorrow at the Evans bar mitzvah, I'll eat
my yarmulka."

Rona said, "Oh, Dore." Yet anyone could see here
was a woman tremendously ego-involved with her
chicken soup.

"Great!" I exclaimed. "Chicken soup was my first
love."

The ten-year-old, helping her mother, served me.
Boy, did that soup smell *good*. Like a good steak,
as my father would say of anything that smelled or
tasted exceptional—whether it was fish, chicken or
perfume. "Like a good steak," he would say, for he
had cast his first vote before eating his first steak.

Swaying in the middle of the soup and setting off
its rich golden color was a royal matzoh ball, as
tantalizing as stretch pants, and fluffy too. Swiftly
my spoon lunged into the broth. At the same moment

I saw something which made my stomach heave. Another fly floated in the matzoh ball's wake.

"Hope you like it," said Rona, the Jewish mother.

Now I couldn't even lie! Who in the world is allergic to chicken soup *also*, coming down with the allergy thirty seconds after his love object is offered him nakedly on a plate? And could I say, "Hey, look who drowned himself in *my* soup; what a wonderful way to go!" Of course not. One word about the fly— no, it wasn't my imagination; the fly was still there, and growing larger, it seemed, from absorbing all that nutritious broth—Rona would die of shame, and her with three young children and *My Fair Sadie* to manage. What about extracting the fly? Yes, I could do that, but where would I put it? The soup had been served in individual tureens, with no dishes under them, so if I parted my fly from its pool, all I could do was slap it down on the white tablecloth for all to see, or shove it in my ear.

There was no out. For Rona's sake, Judaism's too, I had to down the flyed soup. Yet why should that be traumatic when the fly was a good seventy-five inches shorter than I and 190 pounds lighter? Pushing my spoon at the fly, I tried to beach it on the side of the tureen. Alas, Rona used too much schmaltz in her chicken soup, as a good cook should, and the fly kept sliding back. Finally I broke off a piece of matzoh ball, lodged it against the side of the dish, forming a harbor of sorts, and wedged my fly in it.

Dore was watching me like another Jewish mother. "The soup's not too hot, Rabbi. You can eat it."

"Swell." Taking a deep breath, I exhumed a spoonful of fly soup and in one horrible gulp swallowed it.

Rona: "Well? Well? *Well?*"

Dore: "Isn't it *fantastic?*"

"Never tasted anything like it," I said. (Ordinarily I'd have asked for the recipe to give to my mother, but this one probably started out: Take one horse-fly . . .)

"You see?" he exulted. "I told you, Rabbi!"

Rona beamed. "I try my best."

"Next time," I felt like saying, "instead of Irish linen napkins for your guests, better give them fly-paper." It was natural, a snide thought like that. Look what I was doing for the woman, after all, and who would note or long remember?

"Don't let us interrupt with our chatting," Rona said. "Eat, eat."

I plugged away at the soup. Just a little more now, a little bit more; you don't have to finish the damn stuff, just about three quarters of it, then say you want to leave room for the main course and *its* inhabitants.

Six more spoonfuls now—who could bear to look?

Five more . . .

Four . . .

Three . . .

Happy ending coming up . . .

One more only and—HORRORS!

Where the hell was the fly?

Not in my tureen, not any more. The matzoh-ball mooring had broken loose; it floated now immaculately in the middle of the bowl with no speck on, around or under it. And chances were, the fly hadn't flown the soup; the fat in it would have weighed down a B-52. Now *if* the fly wasn't in the soup, and *if* the fly wasn't on the matzoh ball, and *if* the fly was nowhere to be seen, *where* could the fly *be?*

I dropped my spoon and nearly coughed the middle ear out of my head.

Dore and Rona pushed glasses at me. "Drink," they urged.

Drink? In this house, whose liquids all the flies in the state used for lovers' leaps?

The eleven-year-old smacked me on the back too hard, and I sputtered to a halt. What alternative was there? Not all the coughs in the Western Hemisphere would resurrect my fly.

"Rabbi, you've eaten only five eighths of your soup," Rona pointed out. "Don't you really like it?"

"How can you ask?" I groaned. "Your soup, Rona, is an experience."

"My! Nobody's ever called my chicken soup an *experience*." Her eyes sparkled. "You're so appreciative, Rabbi—that's one reason everybody likes you."

Valiantly I finished off the entire watery graveyard. And that's the story: Thomas Becket went around washing the feet of the poor in order to teach himself true humility, I eat flies.

"You got to be *kidding!*" the photographer says to me the next morning, when I forbid his setting up floodlights in the sanctuary in order to take three-dimensional color slides of the Sabbath worship service during which the Evans boy will become bar mitzvah.

I tell him, in all humility, not on his life.

"That's why I'm here—to take pictures of the whole bar mitzvah from soup to nuts."

I explain that one reason for *my* being here is to stop him.

The photographer runs to tell Mrs. Evans on me, the same Mrs. Evans who had originally asked me to conduct the bar-mitzvah service in Mountain Tiptop, a catering hall whose furnishings she preferred to the temple's; besides, it would be more convenient for her guests not to have to traipse from the temple to the hall—what if it rained that day? the hair-dos would be ruined—and she comes to ask me, charmingly at first, to make believe we're all on *Candid Camera;* when I decline, she accuses me of being rigid, authoritarian, Pharisaic and, in addition, a bad sport.

Next, enter a guest to rage that an usher barred her husband from bringing her bar-mitzvah present, a saddle, inside the temple. This is a synagogue, I say, not Korvette's. The woman, insulted now, fishes a charge plate out of her bag to prove she buys at Saks.

Time comes to start the service, and where are the Evanses? Mother is in the ladies' room, fixing her strapless bra; Father is outside, greeting guests; the boy is at the front door, pocketing envelopes like a bookie. When the dramatis personae are finally assembled, we ascend the pulpit.

Stepping up to the lectern, I am momentarily stunned by all the women there whose décolletages suggest they came not to pray to God so much as to vamp Him. As the service gets under way, they start trooping in, all the latecomers, to catch the Evans boy's act. Clickety-clacking in spiked heels, they wave to friends and relations, pointedly avoid those they're not on speaking terms with, admire each other's attire, then sit down with folded arms, not picking up a prayerbook, and ask neighbors who had arrived five minutes before them, When does the bar mitzvah *start?*

Finally the Evans boy gets up to do his turn, chanting a prayer, the blessings, and Hebrew portions of the Bible. I follow with my sermon, to which everyone listens intently so long as I'm speaking about the bar-mitzvah boy and his parents. Through the rest of my talk—about people the guests had never met personally, like Moses and Isaiah—guests adjust their plunging necklines, look at their watches, check the time with a neighbor, inquire about directions to the catering hall and how the food is there.

Later everyone recesses to Mountain Tiptop—decorated in the style of an interdenominational bordello —where the first thing to transfix the eye is the Evans boy immortalized in colored cardboard. That's right, there in the lobby is a life-sized cutout of the bar-mitzvah boy, resplendent in maroon trousers and gold-lamé dinner jacket, and off to one side is the photographer, snapping away at amazed guests being greeted by *twin* Evans scions.

"Just look at those faces!" the father keeps exclaiming. "Just look at them when they see that picture! Isn't that something?"

I ask how much the photograph cost.

"Rabbi, I'm surprised you're so materialistic," says Evans, who can't wait for me to ask again. "One hundred fifty dollars, and worth every penny. Just look at their faces!"

I tell him to send me a check in the morning for three hundred dollars made out to UNICEF.

"Why, of all the nerve!" swears Mrs. Evans, so furious I hurry away before she can hit me in the head with an item the *New York Times* had written up on its fashion page that week, a four-hundred-dollar black crocodile purse designed in imitation of a Gideon Bible.

Entering the Mount Ararat Room, I see laid out there a cornucopian smorgasbord of such vast proportions it looks like the last supper for the whole world, a sight as exciting as a naked girl weighing five hundred pounds. The affair is strictly kosher, so the pike is dyed pink and curled to look like shrimp, beef short ribs masquerade as spareribs, chicken pretends to be lobster, and the egg rolls are genuinely nontref. The centerpiece is a huge six-pointed mold of chopped liver, which, so help me, rings out with the theme song from *Exodus* whenever anybody takes a smear.

I repair quickly to the bar, where someone is saying, "You got any idea how much this affair costs? I inquired for my son, who'll be bar-mitzvahed twenty-two months from now. For two hundred guests—the meal itself is twenty dollars a head. Filet of prime beef costs two-fifty cheaper than filet mignon, but look, if you're going to make a bar mitzvah, you make a bar mitzvah, know what I mean? That four thousand is only the start of it." The man then goes through a list as long as Biblical begats—of gratuities, checkroom, rolling bars, bartenders, birthday cake, orchestra, flowers, valet parking, Viennese Table, personalized color-schemed napkins, candles, gift matches and escort cards, plus sales tax—before concluding: "Grand total—$6,845. And I can swing it too, provided my wife goes back to work for the next twenty-two months."

Arming myself with a triple Scotch on the rocks, I retire to a corner table, to eavesdrop on:

"One thing you got to say about that rabbi. He sure is no speaker."

"You're one hundred percent right. He phumphas."

"That sermon of his, I've heard better on TV from Dr. Gillespie. And did you hear how he mispronounced my father-in-law's name?"

"He never even mentioned how Jack got his company to donate twenty-four goose-down pillows to the temple bazaar. That's a lot of pillows, you know."

"And he certainly doesn't dress up a pulpit, that rabbi."

"He's not so hot at funerals either."

"I hear he's *death* at funerals."

"You think you're being funny? Well, it's not funny to invite all your friends and the boss to a funeral, and they all come away very unimpressed. Embarrassing is what it is. Especially when he calls the corpse by the wrong name."

"Boy, I'm certainly happy I'm a Jew."

"Why?"

"Catholics are stuck with the same priests forever."

I'm considering either slinking away in embarrassment or slugging a few guys with delight when one of them says, "Hell, we'd better not vote him down before *my* son's bar mitzvah, else Rabbi Brun will take it out on Sonny. He's just that kind, you know—a vindictive bastard." Only then do I realize I've mistakenly scaled the wrong peak, which isn't hard to do, since Mountain Tiptop's six caverns process a dozen thirteen-year-old men every weekend.

On my way to the Sinai Room, where the Evanses are making whoopee, I am stopped in the pass by somebody coming out of the men's room. "Steingut," he says, giving me a wet hand to shake, or maybe to dry. "Of Steingut and Romano. We're members of your temple also."

"You are? I mean, that's—"

"Yeah, we belong to loads. You know how it is when you're in catering: you want to give every shul a break."

"Oh, do—"

"But what I want to talk to you about, Rabbi: have

you been telling people to boycott our Mountain Tiptop?"

"Boycott? No. Why—?"

"What *did* you tell your people?"

"Only not to blow a fortune or go into debt for a
four-hour—"

"Mama mía! Are there *more* important days in a
family's life than a wedding, bar mitzvah, sweet sixteen? You tell people not to borrow money to buy a
new car or vacation in Europe?"

"No. But bar mitzvahs and weddings are religious
occa—"

"Look here, Rabbi, I want you to lay off us from
now on."

"Lay—?"

"Or else."

"That's funny. You sound like one of those old
gangster movies."

"Funny? Rabbi, don't you know who owns Mountain Tiptop?"

"You and your partner, Roma—"

"Nah, we're only window dressing. I thought everybody knew that."

"Oh! You mean you're fronting for the—"

"We never say that word. Just remember, there's
more than one way to skin a rabbi," Steingut says.
"*Arrivederci.*" And he vanishes into a crevice.

Looking over my shoulder to make sure nobody's
fingering me, I enter the crowded Sinai Room in
time to hear the band strike up our new national
anthem, "Enjoy Yourself, It's Later Than You Think."
We all sit down at our tables, to work our way
through ten courses to the accompaniment of the
snake, monkey, kangaroo, mule, bunny hop—everything except the golden calf.

For dessert the waiters, dressed in baseball uniforms (the reception's theme is a baseball game because the Evans scion is a Little League biggie), bring in platters of bird cages which hold red parakeets, representing Cardinals, perched beside baseball bats of pareve ice cream. When the cages are raised to a drum roll, the noise panics the birds, and some do on the ice cream what they usually do only on newspaper; the rest fly off, six ending up in screaming women's hair.

As soon as the mess has been cleared away, the master of ceremonies brings on the floor show, a couple of apache dancers who smack each other around in time to their shrieks, and twenty-one people who light twelve candles on a birthday cake larger than a pitcher's mound. The lights are turned off, everyone sings "Happy Birthday" by candle glow; then, carrying a prayer shawl on a red velvet pillow, the Evanses' five-year-old daughter enters the hall. But halfway to the dais she trips on the long fringes, falls on her head and bawls until the sexy band singer pulls her into the ladies' room. Now enter the bar-mitzvah boy himself, in a dugout lowered from the ceiling; scooping up the fallen tallis, he joins his parents at the dais. Together they all light the thirteenth candle as the band segues into a medley of "My Yiddishe Mama," "O My Papa," "Sonny Boy" and "Dayenu" (which means, appropriately, "It Would Have Been Enough for Us").

The woman next to me leans over, wiping tears from her eyes. "Oh, Rabbi! I just *love* ritual."

I cringe.

When the lights go up, the bar-mitzvah boy trots by my table with a bottle of champagne. I warn him, only half in jest, not to show up the next morning in Sunday School with a hangover.

"My father says I don't have to attend any more," he says, "so I'm not."

Feeling like Moses after his descent from the original Sinai, I look around for Tablets to smash. There's a pair, sure enough, atop the birthday cake, and I half rise from my seat when I realize that *these* Ten Commandments are pareve butter cream, alas—shatterproof.

Later, still resentful of having been used as a shill for an extravaganza, I hand the Evans scion an envelope before leaving.

"From you, Rabbi? You shouldn't've," he says, grabbing it.

Maybe the kid's right, for what the envelope contains is a note: "You're going to have to return all your gifts, man, if you don't return to religious school. Because I'll revoke your bar mitzvah and declare you a *boy* again."

My humility jag had lasted all of one day.

א

MAN IN THE HILLENDALE *NEWS*:
RABBI GIDEON ABEL
Meet the New Spiritual Leader of the Hillendale Temple

Q. How do you like Hillendale, Rabbi Abel?
A. It's a lovely community.
Q. And the people—how do they strike you?
A. They're lovely too. So warm and hospitable.
Q. Is it a thrill to be undertaking this your first congregation?

A. Yes, it is. And an enormous responsibility.

Q. *How do you plan to discharge this responsibility?*

A. By demonstrating that Judaism is a study-and-do-it-yourself-and-right-now religion. I've begun our adult-education courses, and I'm planning a comprehensive social-action program. If I believed in slogans, I'd say ours at the temple should be: A Course and a Cause for Every Congregant.

Q. *You haven't mentioned the temple's new expansion program. How does that fit into your plans?*

A. Well, we need it, I guess. On Yom Kippur we didn't have enough room to seat all our congregants, and in two years we'll have to have more classrooms too.

Q. *But what about your temple kitchen?*

A. The kitchen? It's beautiful! Some houses of worship, you can't see the religion in them for all the chopped liver. My greatest ambition in life, you see, was to be the only clergyman in America with no kitchen in his house of God. So when I saw the Hillendale Temple's kitchen—it's just big enough to turn out coffee and cake and that's all—I was delighted.

Q. *You certainly speak your mind, Rabbi. Anything else delight you at your temple—aside from its kitchen?*

A. The children. I'm very fond of them. They're so fresh and responsive. Already they've started to collect clothing for the poor people of Appalachia and to tutor disadvantaged students. And sisterhood is sponsoring a prekindergarten class for needy kids . . . That's the greatest thing

about being a rabbi: the world today is like
some gargantuan civil service, but the synagogue
is still an integral community, small enough to
establish communion with and yet large enough
to benefit society as a whole . . .

א

FALL

SOMETHING WAS WRONG.

I felt it as soon as I entered the temple for the first board meeting of its fiscal year. True, none of the trustees there belled me and shouted, "Unclean," but the message came through nonetheless when one woman approached, saying, "Well, you're young yet, Rabbi. *You'll* learn." Before I could ask, "Learn what?" she had made me a wager, "Oh, but I bet you don't remember my name."

"You win," I said graciously. The woman, one of my five-hundred-odd congregants, gave me such a dirty look and stalked away, heaven alone knows why; did she want to be a loser?

As we all took our seats, Eve Greenwood, the spirited sisterhood president, who is as quick-witted as her mother-in-law is good-hearted, whispered, "I'm on your side, no matter what anyone else says."

"What did anyone else say?" I asked in surprise. She replied, "I mean, I'm with you in what *you've* said." That stopped me; how could I ask to be told what I'd said?

Barney Singer convened the meeting by slapping a J.K. Lasser tax book on the table, then motioned everyone to rise. The trustees did so in unison, for they are a homogeneous group; in addition to sharing similar incomes, homes, automobiles, politics and concern for help—to hear some of the women talk, it's a full-time job just to find a maid and keep her—they're all skirting forty, as if they had been promoted en masse into suburbia from the same grade. The president turned toward me. "Rabbi?" (I had asked not to be addressed by my first name, because does anyone want to be hatched, matched or dispatched by one of the boys? Whereupon Curt Langer had commented with his usual frown, "Dr. Terman insisted we call him Irv. Of course, he was an older man.") "The invocation, please."

Who listens to those spot loyalty oaths? If you were God, would you? All I can remember from auditing a million "O Lord" commercials with bowed head is trying to decide each time whether my shoes needed a shine. Yet I had no intention of tilting at invocations here; who yearns to play Cordelia in suburbia? Neither she nor Big Daddy Lear, I recall, had ended up on the sunny side of the street. So picking up the United Synagogue prayerbook, I read aloud from the ancient rabbis: " 'Try to prevent poverty by teaching man a trade. Try all methods before you permit him to become an object of charity, which must degrade him, tender as your feelings with him may be.' "

The trustees remained standing when I sat down. Some kept their heads bowed while others looked up quizzically, as if waiting for me to say, "Hike."

"What about the invocation?" Pete Schuster demanded, in the manner of a district attorney out to maintain an unbroken record of convictions, which in his case I'd have bet were obtained by the third degree.

"That was it."

"That? But you neither invoked God nor prayed. Why, you never even said, 'Amen'!"

As the group resumed their seats, I explained, "Learning, according to Judaism, is a form of prayer. Therefore—"

Curt Langer, wearing the same nose as Judith Anderson who played Rebecca's maniacally faithful housekeeper in the movie, interrupted, "*Irv* never did anything like that."

Realizing that crying aloud, "Dr. Terman is dead; long live Rabbi Abell!" might be misinterpreted, I said instead, "Suppose we begin future meetings with such readings, then discuss them—"

"Christ!" exclaimed Rick Adler, who had asked after my installation why I had ever entered the rabbinate when my father owned a Bentley. "We'd never get out of temple then."

Barney Singer translated, "What Rick means is board meetings never finish before midnight. Tacking on irrelevancies might be all right for those who can sleep late in the morning"—one guess whom he meant—"but the rest of us can't do that."

"How about starting meetings twenty minutes earlier?" I asked.

A collective groan.

"That's a splendid suggestion, Rabbi," Barney Singer

said. "Only we don't have the time." (That made me feel right at home; Dad was always telling me my ideas were so terrific they would surely be executed just as soon as the Messiah arrived.) The president then cleared his throat and addressed the trustees for twenty-two minutes on our "quality product" (the temple), whose "splendid packaging" and "merchandising" should attract "customers" from the "untapped virgin market" so long as our "clientele" continued to generate "favorable word of mouth" about our wonderful "management." Concluding, he turned to a slightly built, rabbity-looking fellow who was gnawing his fingernails as if they were carrots. "All right now, Sam, the minutes."

"Right, Barney." Sam is Sam Warren, the worrier over the wrong petitions who always seems just about to be befallen by something. Earlier he had congratulated me that a "half-Jew" (as likely a state as half a pregnancy) had been nominated for the Presidency of the United States in 1964, because such things had to be done *gradually*, though Sam himself prayed that nobody with so much as a shot of "Jewish blood" in him ever be elected President, because once in office he might say or do something that not a hundred percent of the American electorate might like, and why antagonize Christians needlessly? Subsequently he had bravely asked why it was that every one of the Six Million hadn't at least died fighting. (Charlie Hecht, a lawyer whose diploma from Auschwitz is tattooed on his left forearm, had given the perfect answer: "They certainly would have, Sam, had they but known their fighting would have reconciled you to their slaughter.")

Dore Redmont passed me a note: "Nothing in the rules says we can't discuss over coffee *after* the meeting—you, me, Charlie Hecht, Eve Greenwood and whoever." A sweet note, but what did the postscript mean? "At the same time we can discuss your public utterances and maybe save you some aggravation."

Sam Warren's minutes reviewed the highlights of June's meeting, when the trustees had discussed, among other things: who would charge the least to fix the furnace, clues as to who was crayoning dirty words on the walls of the men's room, installing a soda machine in the temple and how much to charge per drink, what combo to hire for the President's Ball, whether it was necessary for guards checking admission tickets at the High Holiday services to wear guns, how to remove the cuckoo from the expensive antique clock a congregant had donated for the sanctuary, whether to dissuade the chief founder of the temple, Ed Geldzaler, from resigning from the synagogue after having been denied a fifth consecutive term as president, and, finally, what right the placement commission had to threaten the temple that they would send only one more rabbi, Gideon Abel, to be interviewed since the board had already rejected nine other candidates.

(So! There was a second reason for this shotgun marriage of ours. And it was worse than the first.)

Reports followed from the respective chairmen of nineteen different committees. I felt so *frustrated!* Here on my honeymoon with the temple, I'm eager to consummate our union via adult education and social action, yet how do we spend our evening together? On committee reports! Furnaces! Dirty words! It was as fulfilling as having your bride detail on your wedding night the intimate workings of her digestive tract.

The ways-and-means-committee chairman announced future fund-raising ventures: *My Fair Sadie,* the bazaar, football pool, Cadillac raffle, theater party, memorial plaques, rummage sale, duplicate bridge, carnival, white-elephant sale, cemetery plots, picnic, selling Christmas cards—

"You want to sell Christmas cards," I asked, "in the temple?"

Barney Singer said, "No comments now, please. According to *Robert's Rules of Order,* discussions come later—under New Business." He frowned. "At which time, Rabbi, we'll also discuss some of your other comments."

I almost shouted, "There's nothing to discuss! I plead guilty!" Yes, paranoia was revisiting me. What unspeakable things had I spoken? Why was I to be discussed here in public like cemetery plots and graffiti?

Eventually New Business was reached. The first topic was whether nonmembers of sisterhood should be allowed to join its weekly bowling league, a two-part question, since one woman who wanted to join was Catholic but a terrific bowler. When a vote was called for, somebody said, "Let's first find out what our rabbi advises."

Who knew from bowling leagues? Not I, who couldn't tell one pin from another. "I'm sorry, but I really can't say."

There was a silence which somebody's disappointed "Oh" did not fill; then the vote was taken. Results: Jewish nonmembers of sisterhood were barred from the bowling league, but the terrific Catholic high-scorer was accepted because she couldn't qualify for sisterhood anyway, not unless she converted, which was unlikely since her five children attended parochial school.

The next item was a coed junior-youth group that Maurine Levenson proposed sisterhood form for children nine through eleven. The discussion:

——Maurine, what's the purpose of such a group?

——*It's important for children to make the right contacts.*

——Isn't nine through eleven a little early for making contacts?

——*It's never too early to be making the right contacts.*

——Don't boys and girls that age have different interests?

——*Nonsense. Boys and girls that age are both children together.*

——But preteeners want no part of the opposite sex.

——*All the more reason for encouraging them to mingle.*

——How are you going to get them to mingle?

——*Teach them social dancing together. They'll have to mingle then.*

——And what if they don't want to dance?

——*What if they don't want to eat? You make them.*

This time no questions were directed at me; apparently someone who didn't know about bowling leagues couldn't know about children. "May I say something?" I asked. (Perhaps if I began, as Pastoral Psychiatry 1.1 had taught, with a word of praise before criticizing.) "Certainly you should be commended, Maurine, for your concern with our preteens. But wouldn't it be wiser to limit coed groups to teenagers? Start them socializing at nine, they may very well be going steady at thirteen and getting into trouble by—"

Maurine Levenson interrupted. "You never belonged to a coed junior-youth group, did you, Rabbi?"

"No—"

"Well, maybe if you had, your wife would be a member of our sisterhood," Rochelle's aunt said. "Understand now?"

That did it; a majority voted in the coed junior-youth group.

Not everyone was pleased, however. Nearby Eve Greenwood muttered, "Now my ten-year-old is going to make me buy her that twenty-eight-double-A training bra." Dore Redmont replied, "If your daughter fills the bra with Baby Ruths, maybe *then* my eleven-year-old Robbie will come near her."

Next item, the President's Ball, autumn's biggest fund-raiser. Sam Warren reported that half the tickets remained unsold and appealed for cooperation; otherwise the affair would end up in the red, like the Tumble-in-the-Hay Square Dance last June.

(Why the stress on fund-raising, when the temple could support itself through dues equal to the cost per member, then graduated upward or downward according to one's ability to pay, like income tax? But I said nothing; first I wanted to hear the list of particulars in my indictment.)

Up jumped Pete Schuster, breathing heavily. "All those members who never help out! You have to fight with them to take some lousy tickets to our affairs or to serve on committees—God knows we need people to buy and sell tickets, prepare the food and serve it, clean up afterwards, but they can't be bothered. Yet these are the same ones whose children attend our religious school and who frequent Sabbath ser-

vices and adult education too—but they won't do a
damn thing for the temple. These freeloaders, I'd
like to toss them all out on their cans!" His face now
the color of his tongue, he sat down and gritted his
lips. "I had to get that off my chest. God knows the
temple means *everything* to me." And he looked me
straight in the eye.

Like a barroom tough who challenges every gun-
fighter to a draw, Pete Schuster is plainly seeking to
outrabbi me. The trustee has as many answers as Dore
Redmont has questions, and it galls Goneril-Regan
here that I've neglected to be taught of his ways,
walk in his paths and install him as the power behind
my pulpit. When I refused to devote my Yom Kippur
sermon to a pitch for the temple's expansion fund,
for example, he told me, "One thing about Dr. Terman: at least he knew his place." No smashing success in the belt business—beltless people don't heed
him either, and it infuriates him no end that their
pants stay up—Pete Schuster seems determined to
make it big in the temple, and somehow he's got the
feeling I stand in his way. Don't ask me why, ask
Oedipus.

Sam Warren clapped his hands. "I only wish the
temple had more fantastically dedicated workers like
you, Pete, that's what I wish."

Pete Schuster bowed his red snaky-locked head.
"Thanks, Sam. Thanks very much."

"I shouldn't be at all surprised, Pete," Curt Langer
said, "if the board voted you Mr. Temple this year."

I saw Barney Singer flinch even before Maurine
Levenson exclaimed, "But the Mr. Temple Award
always goes to the president—unless, of course, he
quits the temple, like Ed Geldzaler did."

Why should losing the Mr. Temple Award make a

wealthy, grown accountant wince? Don't misread me now; I think Barney Singer is a nice man—unfailingly cordial and conscientious. He attends as many meetings as I—remember too, this is after putting in a full day's work at his office—and no temple toilet overflows without his rushing right over to unstop it. Still, the president doesn't regard social action as the temple's concern, or adult education as his. In a way he reminds me of the chairman of my college hi-fi club, who knew everything there was to know about tweeters and woofers and stereophonics, but nothing about music. Turned out the fellow was tone-deaf.

Then came the menacing announcement: "Next on the agenda is Rabbi Abel."

Swiftly I girded my mental loins.

"I have here in my hand, Rabbi, a newspaper clipping and a letter." Unlike Senator McCarthy, Barney Singer showed me Exhibit A. "Did the Hillendale *News* misquote you perhaps?"

Was that all? Imagine! Worrying me about an interview in which I had hymned everything but motherhood. "You mean, when I confessed to being so fond of the children here?"

The president scowled. "I mean, when you proclaimed that your greatest ambition in life was to be the only rabbi in America without a kitchen."

"Well, I used a little hyperbole there—for effect —but I'm sure readers got the point, that I'm delighted to be leading a shul like this which places first things first." Could Dale Carnegie have been more winning?

So why all the grumblings? "The point is," Barney Singer said, "our expansion program. Don't you know that what we're expanding this year is not the sanctuary or classroom space, but our inadequate kitchen?"

I was astounded. "The kitchen?" But Pete
Schuster's impassioned plea on Yom Kippur for the
expansion fund had mentioned only "our temple,"
"Jewry," "faith" and "God."

"Certainly. The temple is crippled without a new
kitchen. How long can I ask my girls to do our cooking at home and shlep it to temple for our affairs?
Secondly, I want ours to be a total temple, so a person can live, give birth, bar-mitzvah, marry off his
children and hold his golden wedding anniversary
right inside these hallowed halls. Thirdly, just think of
all the kickbacks from caterers that we're losing."
The orator, unsurprisingly, was Maurine Levenson, organization man, whose husband had complained to
me that the temple is ruining his sex life because
when his wife isn't too tired she's too busy. The executive vice-president charged me now with her elec-
tric-blue eyes. "Rabbi, I think you owe it to our expansion-fund campaign to write the Hillendale *News*
that you were libeled."

"But I wasn't."

"Then say you were misunderstood. A man with
five degrees like you, Rabbi, I'm sure can juggle words
around."

"I wasn't misunderstood either. Well, it isn't my
greatest ambition to become the Carrie Nation of the
kitchen. On the other hand, neither do I set kitchens
above my chiefest joy." A reference there to Psalm
137, to link the board and myself with four thousand
years of Jewish history, affording us all some perspective here, don't you see? The trustees didn't; their
looks indicated they thought I was being snotty. So I
hurried on: "If I'd known the expansion fund was for
the kitchen—But I simply assumed, after Yom Kippur, when we couldn't fit everyone into the sanctuary,

and with the projected increase in schoolchildren—
I *am* sorry."

"Irv told us," said Curt Langer, who if he caught me
picking my nose would surely contend that Dr. Terman did it better, "the kitchen table is an altar to
God."

Anxious to get me out of the kitchen, because I
didn't care for any more heat, I asked, "You mentioned something about a letter, Barney?"

The president held up Exhibit B, a note. "Is this your
handwriting, Rabbi? Did you write Bill Evans' boy
at Mountain Tiptop that unless he returned to religious school, you'd revoke his bar mitzvah?"

Out of the kitchen and smack into the catering hall!
"Well, yes, but—"

"Do you know," Barney Singer continued, "how you
embarrassed the Evanses? Everybody saw you hand
this gift envelope to the bar-mitzvah boy, something
nobody had ever seen a rabbi do before. Naturally
they asked how much it was—I mean, what you had
written. So the boy opened the envelope and read
your note aloud before he knew what it said. Mrs.
Evans tells me she almost dropped dead on the spot
—this after spending eleven thousand dollars on her
affair."

"Eleven thousand—"

Pete Schuster exclaimed, "I never heard of such a
thing—a rabbi revoking a bar mitzvah! Why, it's like
uncircumcising somebody!"

"You all misunderstand." Surely a man with five degrees could explain things to everyone's satisfaction,
or failing that, juggle them around. "That note was
simply my protest—a trifle melodramatic, that I admit
—of the Evans boy's quitting his religious education
on the very day he assumed his responsibilities as a

Jewish adult. It makes as much sense as a bridegroom
going off on a separate honeymoon."

"*You* misunderstand, Rabbi." Barney Singer then revealed that the Evanses weren't quitting the *temple*,
having three younger children in religious school;
what's more, they paid their dues promptly and always contributed to the bazaar.

"That doesn't entitle anyone to empty a religious
rite of meaning." And I declared, "From now on,
I'll refuse to officiate at the bar mitzvah of any child
who won't continue his religious education till confirmation at sixteen."

Edythe Loring (the woman whose name I hadn't
remembered before) burst out, ashen-faced, "Rabbi,
how can you deny our children their God-given puberty rites!"

"Suppose," I replied, "we *raise* the age of Jewish
puberty."

Half of the trustees applauded. But the other half
shouted, until Barney Singer gaveled everyone into
silence. Then he made his own position plain. "We're
not in business here to drive families to join the other
temple. Nor to provoke Steingut into making effigies
of our rabbi in chopped liver, to be eaten at affairs,
as Mountain Tiptop did last week; notoriety like that
we don't need. Let's vote on this matter right now."

"Vote?" I was startled. "This is a religious matter,
and as your rabbi *I* decide what's kosher and what's
a farce."

"Hear, hear!" Dore Redmont cried, and I silently
blessed him.

But several trustees regarded me as if I were a
Christian martyr who had bitten into a lion, while one
mumbled something about June.

God, they were a solemn bunch—more a jury than

fellow Jews uniting with me to sanctify God. "Perhaps now would be a good time to discuss what the function of a rabbi is," I said. "What do you think?"

"It's late," Sam Warren replied, then announced the last item on the agenda, the ladies' room, which Edythe Loring proposed carpeting wall-to-wall, because so many other synagogues and churches did so, and she knew somebody who'd install it whosesale.

Eve Greenwood raised her hand. "I second the carpet motion," the sisterhood president said, and Edythe Loring beamed. "Anything that will make us better Jews."

The howl that went up would have killed NATO.

Barney Singer asked for a motion of adjournment, while Edythe Loring told a neighbor in a stage whisper, "See Eve Greenwood's nose? It isn't hers, you know."

Swiftly I intervened. "What happened to the social-action-committee report? I've drawn up a number of projects for consideration—"

"We don't have a social-action committee," Barney Singer said.

"You *don't?* Well, let's form one now."

"We can't."

I said, "All the other temples have a social-action committee."

"That comes under the heading of New Business," said the president, "and suggestions for New Business must be submitted in writing a week before our meeting. That's *Robert's Rules of Order.*"

Sam Warren wrinkled up his rabbity nose. "That agitator minister who got thrown out by his church started with social action."

Before I could say more, Rick Adler pointed out

that it was already 12:49 A.M., and could I save it
for next time? Well, at least the meeting ended on a
happy note: nobody asked for a benediction.

א

——Pete Schuster, please.

——*Speaking.*

——Oh, hello. How are you? This is—

——*Yes, I know. What's on your mind, Rabbi?*

——Well, I was wondering if the two of us could
get together for a talk—

——*About what?*

——Well, about us. We seem to be at odds, and for
the sake of peace—

——*You're blaming me?*

——No, no. It isn't a matter of assigning blame.

——*Isn't it? I blame you.*

——For what?

——*A whole list of things.*

——Another list, Pete?

——*Packing my four committees with friends of
yours who've been trying to outvote me, usurp my
powers—*

——You've got me wrong. Didn't you complain that
nobody was giving you any help?

——*And ignoring all my suggestions. I bet you never even read my last three notes, did you?*

——Of course I did, Pete. But starting every Sabbath service by blowing a ram's horn, or having
committee chairmen like you give reports in the
middle of the service, or dimming the lights and
ringing chimes while reading the names of the
dead before *Kaddish*—

——*It would put some life into a drab service.*

——Perhaps, but no other congregation in the world does such things.

——*Why can't we be original?*

——Well, I try for originality in my sermons.

——*Your sermons—they're too original. You can find more ways to apply three-thousand-year-old laws to current events—*

——Thank you.

——*That was no compliment . . . and when I ask you to recruit us some new members from among all those who dislike Rabbi Jacobson—*

——Barney Singer agrees with me that it's not quite kosher to rustle congregants away from other—

——*You're always so negative. Barney! All he cares about is balancing books; why, he runs a temple the same way he'd run the city dump. Now when I become president . . .*

א

OCTOBER

I LOVE the kids! Even before the coed junior-youth group's first meeting ended with the boys' rubbing cheese dip into the girls' hair and the girls' pouring punch over the boys in retaliation, I loved them.

Funny, it had never occurred to me at the seminary that of all my congregational duties (I wear so many different hats it's difficult for me at times to find my yarmulka underneath), working with children would be perhaps the most satisfying. (Remember, I'm the one who restrains a homicidal response whenever a congregant says his only reason for joining the temple is, of course, the sake of the children. What ex-Marine wants to be turned into a hairy Mary Poppins!) Yet it is, for with the kids, who resemble their parents the way clay resembles concrete, I can see myself affecting them. Weeks following the monthly family service, for example, children are still quoting my sermons, and at the Oneg Shabbas afterwards *kids* never tell me:

"I don't recall the Bible making such a fuss about civil rights."

"Aren't those Jewish values of yours really rationalizations of defense mechanisms and reaction formations?"

"I should think anyone who acclaims Israel so eloquently would want to live there."

"Well, Rabbi, that's *your* opinion."

Kids are so open to new thoughts and experiences, so full of spontaneity and grace, so I-Thouish. (One embarrassed mother to her son: "You got to remember when you talk to the rabbi, he isn't nine years old like you.") It's wondrous to go from kindergarten through confirmation class and watch, in a few hours, children span the years from early childhood to adolescence, like a Walt Disney nature film with photography speeded up so that flowers blossom in sixty seconds. (On one Sunday morning I can be asked questions ranging from "Are *you* God?" to "The older you become, the more sins you get to do?" to "Was Goldfinger Jewish?" to "*Who* says there's a God?")

My affection for the kids may know a bound or two—the only person who loves everybody is a liar—and one is the confirmation class, which I teach myself. They fluctuate so, these turbulescents: one minute they're out to save the world, the next minute they're reciting in unison, "Hear, O Israel, the Lord our God, the Lord is Two." Or after lauding the prophets for promoting social justice, my teen-agers can suddenly start comparing clothes, bank accounts and bust measurements.

Such materialism distresses those parents who recall their own youth as a time devoted to ideals, causes and poverty. "What do you and your husband talk about at home?" I asked one disturbed mother, an alumna of the thirties' Young Communist League. "Well," she replied, "lately, Acapulco and Hawaii. We're trying to decide where to go for Christmas, and it's hard because we've been everywhere."

There are thirteen in my class, most of whom look forward every session to getting hysterical together. The hormones of adolescent girls must be at least fifty percent giggles, while the boys are always intent to prove anything girls can do, they can outdo three times as loud—how else to explain the hysterics when we study, in *Ethics of the Fathers*, teachings of ancient rabbis like Ben Bag Bag and Ben He He? With the troops so restless, what does one do? Desert them or deport them. So periodically, in conjunction with our study of comparative religion, I take the class to neighboring churches, where my students don't giggle at all—this annoys me; why do they bug only Jewish clergymen?—and the boys can't tip over pews without first unscrewing them.

After attending the local Methodist and Christian Science churches—what impressed the girls most was the red velvet gowns worn by two women Christian Science readers; the boys liked the fact that the services were shorter than Jewish ones—I phoned the Episcopal church for permission to visit.

Its assistant minister, Father Vernon Rutherford, was not nearly as cordial as his colleagues, however, "Suppose you make it some other week," he said, after a long pause which suggested he'd prefer my selecting another century.

I had five successive Sunday fund-raising brunches to attend, I replied.

A longer pause. Then the priest said, "Well, all right. Come ahead, Rabbi, if you really want to."

. . .

Hillendale's St. James Episcopal Church—so wealthy it has *two* nicknames, the Country Club at Prayer and the Cathedral of the Ninety Percent Bracketeers —looked exactly like a fish, even down to a forked tail and glazed blue brick that glistened scale-like in the autumn sunlight.

"Holy mackerel!" one of my kids exclaimed. "It's a fish."

The others giggled, and I scolded them all for their bad manners.

As soon as we entered the church, Rutherford approached, greeting me with the handshake of an overstocked used-car salesman. One teen-ager asked about the unusual shape of the building. The young curate reacted with surprise. "Can't you tell?" he said. "It's a fish, a secret symbol that early Christians used for identifying each other in lands where they were persecuted."

"Christians were *persecuted?*" several kids exclaimed.

Guiding us to seats in the second row—evidently the church too had trouble filling front pews (someday I intend to research why people who clamor for front seats at plays, ball games and prize fights always sit in the last rows of houses of worship; you think things would be different if we also charged admis-

sion?)—Rutherford left us, saying he would be happy
to answer questions afterwards, the liar.

"He's boss," said one girl. The boys agreed because
the priest had asked if they were on the Hillendale
High football team, which they weren't, for, as he
damn well knew, the school had no football team.

Soon the service began—with more people in attendance than at a bar-mitzvahless Sabbath service, I
noted not without envy, but Judaism's been on the
boards twice as long as Christianity, and everyone
knows that attendance invariably slackens during long
runs, which certainly isn't the fault of the show or its
performers. Still, I find a half-empty house of God
demoralizing; it sets me to thinking of Stonehenge,
and wondering can it happen here.

That morning the rector, Dr. Bidwell, was away,
and pinch-preaching for him was Dr. Larrabie, a
cherubic-looking man of about sixty with rosy cheeks,
clumps of white hair and, probably, a ho-ho-ho. I
wished him well when he was introduced, because
my heart goes out to all preachers; there for the grace
of God go I. Now if only the priest would speak on
neither positive thinking (let *God* put you in the
driver's seat) nor the Lord (the way some of these
Christians preach about God, you'd think *they* had
invented Him).

Dr. Larrabie began with a hoary anecdote about a
Protestant minister, a Roman Catholic priest and a
"Jewish rabbi," one I had used myself to a respectful
silence; only this time the minister had the punch line,
not the rabbi. Then—I'm not sure how he got there,
because he sneezed (which made a clever transi-
tion)—Dr. Larrabie began to sell "swelling Revelation," contrasting "the Old Testament God of Law"
(here he made such a face, as if referring to some-

thing not only old but also decomposing under his nose) and "the New Testament God of Love."

"Swelling Revelation shows how, beginning at low ebb with the Old Testament's fierce tribal deity of primitive justice, Jesus force-marches humankind via the New Testament to the heights of apprehending the God who is Love. For example, the Old Testament's legalistic Yahweh pronounces this anathema: 'Cursed be he that confirmeth not all the words of this law to do them.' But in the New Testament our loving Saviour bids, 'Love one another: for he that loveth another hath fulfilled the law.' What low tide! What high tide! What swelling Revelation!"

Yessirree, it was stereotype time in the old bullpit—if Lifebuoy can change from green to gold and Rinso periodically add something new or blue, why can't preachers occasionally switch clichés?—as Dr. Larrabie hippety-hopped from Sinai (*Valley* Sinai, to hear him tell it) a million light-miles up to Calvary, implying that the Lord had given the Ten Commandments to the Israelites by mistake, in the manner of a cosmic Pantspresser mixing up trousers, while the Israelites, for their part, had accepted the Tablets of the Law under the impression they were reservations for two weeks, all expenses paid, at Miami Beach.

Dr. Larrabie continued, "The Old Testament vows, 'The Lord will rejoice over you to destroy you, and to bring you to nought.' But the New Testament warms us with 'God is love: and he that dwelleth in love dwelleth in God, and God in him.'

"The Old Testament's chauvinistic Yahweh loves only Israel, as it is written: 'Ye shall be a peculiar treasure unto me above all people . . . a kingdom of priests.' But in the New Testament, 'There is neither Jew nor Greek, there is neither bond nor free, there is neither male nor female: for ye are all one in Christ Jesus.'

"The Old Testament never forgives, vengefully commanding: 'Remember what Amalek did unto thee when ye were come forth out of Egypt . . . Therefore thou shalt blot out the remembrance of Amalek from under heaven.' But in the New Testament, Paul lovingly implores, 'Therefore if thine enemy hunger, feed him; if he thirst, give him drink.' "

He ran on like that for quite a while, demonstrating the Biblical scholarship of General Motors though, alas, not its taste (Ever hear GM knocking Ford in order to make Chevrolet look good?). To Dr. Larrabie the Bible was a treasure trove of great quotations to plunder out of context.

One teen-ager passed me a note: "Rabbi, are we going to take this sitting down?"

What did the kid expect me to do? Boo? Stamp my feet? Walk out? Start singing "We Shall Overcome"?

Rutherford was now staring at me, and I matched him stony look for stony look. His lips were pressed tight, as if biting off the words "Serves you right, smart-ass, for being so pushy. Couldn't you tell I didn't want you in my church?"

To the bitter end Dr. Larrabie blasted the Old Testament's tribalism, provincialism, legalism, chauvinism, ritualism, primitivism (*bad* Old Testament, it contained every nasty *-ism* except communism, and everyone knows who fathered that) while extolling all of the New Testament's pretty *-ities:* universality, egality, probity, fraternity, spirituality, morality. Correction: Dr. Larrabie did not blast; a gentleman of the old school, he spoke throughout in the genial manner of Barry Goldwater proposing to lob a hydrogen bomb into the men's room at the Kremlin.

Succeeding Dr. Larrabie at the lectern, the curate made some announcements. I waited for the one welcoming my kids and me to the no-contest we had just lost. Sure enough, it came: "We are most happy to welcome to our fellowship this morning several visitors, Rabbi Abel and his confirmation class, who come to us from"—I expected to hear "From Brand X, or the Greasy People's Synagogue," but he played it straight—"from the Hillendale Temple." Incredibly, Rutherford added, "Perhaps Rabbi Abel would care to say a few words to us. Rabbi?" The curate motioned me to take his place at the lectern.

I did so. Was he in for a surprise! (I also, come to think of it, because what could I say?)

"I can't tell you how happy my class and I are to join you today." Now what? Sit down, of course. No! Why should I? They started it. And isn't it the New Testament that counsels turning the other cheek? "It was especially interesting to hear about the theory of swelling Revelation. Because different sets of quotes might suggest another swell theory. For example"—well, here goes brotherhood and the good will of those congregants of mine who are all for having *weekly* interfaith services; but I hadn't been feeling too ecumenical anyway since the first meeting of Hillendale's ministerial association, when I, the only rabbi there, was elected treasurer—"in the Old Testament: 'Thou art a God ready to pardon, gracious and full of compassion, slow to anger, and plenteous in mercy.' But in the New Testament: 'He that shall blaspheme against the Holy Ghost hath never forgiveness, but is in danger of eternal damnation.'

"In the Old Testament: 'The Lord of Hosts is exalted through justice . . . Do justice to the afflicted and destitute, rescue the poor and needy.' But in the New Testament: 'Believe on the Lord Jesus Christ, and thou shalt be saved.'

"In the Old Testament: 'Let the oppressed go free . . . break every yoke . . . deal thy bread to the hungry . . . bring the poor that are cast out to thy house . . . cover the naked . . . hide not thyself from thine own flesh.' But in the New Testament: 'Depart from me, ye cursed, into everlasting fire.'

"Swelling Revelation?"

I'll say this for those Episcopalians: they were a damn polite bunch. Nobody in the congregation raised his hand to cast the first stone, no usher came forward to give me the bum's rush, neither priest took my children hostage; they all sat there quietly, perhaps more concerned with quotations from the *Wall Street Journal* than both Testaments put together. (You suppose, really, that's what brotherhood is nowadays—regardlessness of *all* religions?) Out front my kids were squeezing each other's hands, even the boys, while behind me somebody was huffing and puffing as if trying to blow me down or, maybe, up.

Relenting, I made a stab at graciousness, listing briefly some of the Testaments' similarities: Paul's enjoinder to feed one's enemies was a quote from the Old Testament, as was Jesus' bidding to love God and one's neighbor, for Jesus repeated much of basic Pharisaic doctrine. But the minister's stunt still rankled me so much that what emerged, alas, was the implication that Jesus and Paul were copycats who should be sued for plagiarism, not to mention two thousand years of back royalties. Trying to make further amends, I pointed out that the Testaments' similarities were due to the development of the church, Jesus and most of his teachings out of Judaism.

Double alas! That made Christianity sound like a hand-me-down religion and Jesus merely a nice Jewish boy who had made God.

Red-faced, I resumed my seat. Rutherford continued the service, and soon he was delivering the parting benediction with a probable unvoiced postscript that the Lord need not feel obliged to bless, keep, be gracious and grant peace promiscuously to *everyone* in church that morning. My suspicion was confirmed as my class and I departed; when Dr. Larrabie, standing beside the curate at the front door and shaking hands with congregants who filed by, saw me coming, the last one on line, he changed color and stalked away, leaving Rutherford to lie in wait.

What could I say to the priest? You must come over to *my* place sometime and let me work *you* over?

Rutherford clenched his lips, as if afraid to let his tongue have its head. But he lost out and his mouth popped open, to emit—a snarl? imprecation? anathema? A bark! Which swiftly developed into a full-throated roar. "It was magnificent," the priest sputtered, losing control to a laugh, "the way you shot Larrabie out of the saddle! Are you and your wife free for lunch today?"

A woman's voice called out in response to my knock, "I'm on the phone. Door's open."

I entered the Rutherford home. There was a clatter of giant feet, and before I could so much as say, "Gevaltgeshrigginer!" a hairy heavy-breathing something jumped me and tried to bury my head between my shoulder blades, all the while howling such obscenities that one ex-Marine had difficulty controlling his sphincter as he relived the time Dad had insisted on his five-year-old son's making nice to a neighbor's

dog, who promptly bit his hand. Damn that Rutherford! For revenge's sake he had lured me to the
parsonage to be massacred by a wild beast.

"Beauty!" Enter the Lorelei of that ecclesiastical
deathtrap, probably miffed that my disembowelment
was taking so long. "Beauty!"

Two paws dropped reluctantly from my shoulders,
and now the monster's head reached only to the wild
thumping in my chest. I saw then a hound large
enough to enable a two-hundred-pound desperado to
escape a posse of thirty hard riders.

The midtwentyish woman—a billowy honey-blonde
with a broom in her hand and red harlequin glasses
on her long upswept nose, which gave her a cheerfully
sinister look, like that of a witch who really enjoyed
her work—grabbed hold of the dog's harness. "You're
going to the basement," she said, and I didn't believe
she meant the beast until it was dragged, still howling, out of the room.

After counting my ears with one hand and with the
other wiping animal saliva out of my nostrils, I looked
around the lair. Two living-room walls were lined with
books, and three shelves were devoted to works of
and about Reinhold Niebuhr. That was comforting
because the great Protestant theologian had often acknowledged what he called his long love affair with
the Jewish people.

Reappearing without her broom, the blonde said,
"I *am* sorry, Rabbi. Beauty's so friendly. Did she scare
you?"

"A dog? Scare me? Don't be silly."

She introduced herself as Rutherford's wife, Iris;
me she knew from church that morning, she said without commenting on my performance, which meant she
had not approved. "Vernon will be home soon," she

continued. "He's dropping our twins off at a birthday party, and there was some shopping to do."

Like a scab that insisted on being picked, the question had to be asked. "You didn't like what I did before, did you?"

"Well, it *is* a trifle unusual to have a rebuttal to the sermon right in the middle of the service; it's like hearing the eulogy challenged during a funeral. But that doesn't mean I cared for what Dr. Larrabie did, Rabbi. Anti-'s bore me; all they know is what they dislike. Still—" She hesitated.

"Yes?"

"I guess I'm a creature of order, that's what it is. Like all women. It's men who are the bomb-throwers. You couldn't have done what you did without Vernon's help. I only hope the parish won't think the two of you plotted the ambush. Worse stories have been spread about Vernon, and me too, with less provocation. You know how they run: my clothes are too dowdy or Vernon's are too flashy, he's too radical or I'm a snob, I'm always telling him what to do or we're not speaking to each other at all. Heaven knows it isn't easy being the centerpiece of gossip. Your wife is a fortunate woman, Rabbi."

"I'm not married."

"Yes, I know. Vernon told me. That's why she's fortunate, your wife. Last month my husband didn't spend a single evening at home till I dropped him a note, saying Mrs. Rutherford and the twins would appreciate a visitation. Please don't misunderstand; we're a very happy family. Only, someone marrying a law student doesn't expect to end up a priest's wife. Will you have some sherry, Rabbi? You're too good a listener."

Presently Rutherford returned, amazingly transformed. Ninety minutes earlier he had been half a foot shorter than I, sullen, sallow, skinny, bushy-browed, beetle-eyed, hook-nosed; now anyone could see that the handsome priest was amiable, swarthy, wiry, with deep-set black eyes commanding an aristo-cratic nose, and he had grown a head taller. "Sorry to be so late, but the delicatessen was mobbed. Don't any Jewish housewives cook on Sunday?" He began unwrapping one long package. "Iris had already pre-pared a Virginia ham for dinner, *New* Testament style." Out came a salami. "See? Strictly *Old* Testament kosher. For Passover too, just in case." He grimaced. "Well, now you know why I didn't want you in church this morning. Larrabie's sermons invariably contain a higher crap content than fertilizer. This is one Sunday I was happy the church was half empty— that must have surprised you. Jews take their Sab-bath attendance much more seriously than we do, don't you?"

Could I admit that temple attendance was half of his church's? "Well, when you've been in religion as long as us—" I said. "What's Dr. Bidwell like?"

"Nothing like Larrabie, of course, but he has his silly days too. Take last week—Bidwell attacked the Communists for being atheistic materialists. In a three-million-dollar church full of millionaire parish-ioners, whose vestry has just appropriated four hun-dred thousand dollars for a new entrance and a pipe organ, a thirty-thousand-dollar-a-year priest denounces Communists for worshiping Mammon! Other times Bidwell's preached that Negroes must never flout any law whatsoever and that America should send *spiritual* resources abroad instead of mere foreign aid."

Smiling, I quoted a Chasidic saying which I had used in a recent sermon that I mailed to the *Times*:

"Why do you worry so much about my soul and your own body? Take care instead of my body and your *own* soul."

Rutherford chuckled. "You're lucky, Gideon: Jews excel in social justice and civic virtue—Reinhold Niebuhr says so, which is why he's always tried to strengthen the Hebraic prophetic content of Christianity."

I thought of October's board meeting, when the trustees voted not to form a social-action committee but an investigating committee to see what other synagogues were doing. "True."

"What a disgrace. It took the Supreme Court and Congress to end segregation, while it was initiated by the churches, who also supported slavery. And it was not until 1964's General Convention that the Episcopal Church finally banned the exclusion of Negroes from worship. What's more—"

Iris broke in. "Shall we eat? I think the salami's getting cold."

We sat down at the dining-room table, where Rutherford said grace, then looked at me. "You want equal time now too?"

I laughed and dug into the salad. It was delicious. "Best tuna fish I've ever tasted!"

The Rutherfords looked puzzled. "It's crab meat," he said—I gagged; for observant Jews, crab is the pork of the sea—and she added, "I called our Jewish doctor for kosher do's and don't's and he said I couldn't go wrong with fish."

Happily the phone rang.

Iris nervously watched her husband pick up the receiver, while I shoveled the salad into a roll and stuffed it into my pocket. At first the priest responded with one-word replies; finally: "But it's written. ' 'Tis incumbent to pay heed to both sides at all times, verily, for what shall it profit a man to hear a partial truth and close his mind to the whole.'"

When Rutherford resumed his seat, Iris began, "Was that call also about—"

"How about that?" the priest exclaimed. "People were listening in church today."

Iris dropped her fork.

"That quotation of yours, it's good. Where's it from?" I asked. "It sounds familiar, and yet—"

"I made it up." He shrugged. "Amazing how many arguments one pertinent quote can save you. So when I can't think of one on the spot—"

"Vernon! By now Rabbi Abel has enough on you to get you defrocked."

Rutherford sighed. "My wife's afraid I have a priestly death wish, perhaps because she's already witnessed my lawyerly one." He frowned, and his heavy black eyebrows met on the bridge of his nose. "Gideon? Are you accomplishing a lot with your congregation?"

"It's hard to say. I've only been here six weeks."

"I'm here over a year—*that's* hard to say. I thought I had enlisted in Christianity; instead I find myself inside the belly of the American middle class. It's middle-class concerns, you know, not Christian ones, that rule today's church. That's why Protestants have only one low-income church for every two middle-class ones—don't ask about us Episcopalians—and that's why the churches are still not integrated."

"I see." Rutherford was paraphrasing part of Dean Tchernichovsky's sermon! (could it be that Judaism and Christianity shared failings?)

"Vernon," Iris said, as she served me a platter of cole slaw, potato salad, salami and corned beef, topped with a baked pineapple ring, "must you talk shop on Sunday?"

"I don't often get the chance, Iris. You know Bidwell's concern is the church, not religion." To me: "He helped raise a million dollars for a Protestant church at Kennedy Airport. Because the Catholics built one there. Can you imagine a place less in need of churches? Unless they're using them as giant Saint Christopher medals for praying down planes."

"Really?" I didn't mention the synagogue that was constructed at Kennedy Airport.

"*Aaaaaaooooooooooooooooooooooooooooowwwwwwwwww!*"

Howling *My Fair Lady's* opening line, the monster lunged at me again. But happily this time there was a door closed between us.

"That's only our dog," Rutherford said, perhaps noting me spill tea in my lap, as he started for the basement.

"Vernon! Maybe Rabbi Abel isn't as fond of dogs as you," said Iris, while I dried my fly.

Rutherford paused, turned to me. "I usually romp around with Beauty after Sunday dinner. You mind?"

"Well—" He was such a decent guy, this priest, so straightforward. When would I stop pretending perfection that was the Lord's alone?

"Gideon? Do you mind my bringing Beauty upstairs?"

"No," I said finally, "not if you stuff him first. The fact is, I don't particularly love dogs. You see, when I was five years old—Vernon, Beauty scares the hell out of me."

א

——Who's there?
——*Sam Warren, Rabbi.*

——Be right with you.

——*Can you hurry? It's started to drizzle.*

——Good morning, Sam. How are—

——*You still asleep?*

——Well, I got to bed after four—I did some reading after last night's meeting—and I must have slept through the alarm. What time is it?

——*Seven-thirty.*

——Is that all?

——*That's the time we start out to work.*

——Yes, well, I'm lucky the temple is only five minutes away, aren't I? What brings you here this morning, Sam?

——*Your letter to the* New York Times. *I saw it at the station while I was waiting for the train, Rabbi, and—*

——You mean they printed it? How about that! Sam, it's awfully nice of you to stop by to show it to me. Let's see—

——*Don't you remember what you wrote?*

——Well, sure. It was about Frobusher. And the *Times* printed it? Sam, that's—

——*Terrible, just terrible.*

——What?

——*The letter is signed "Gideon Abel, Rabbi of the Hillendale Temple."*

——What's the matter? They misspelled Hillendale?

——*Rabbi, you have any idea what this means? Frobusher is a congressman in the House of Representatives in Washington, D.C., and you called him "a moral moron and an ethical eunuch."*

——Certainly. Have you followed his votes on—

——*Didn't your experience with the Hillendale* News *teach you anything?*

——What?

——*Rabbi, who empowered you to write that letter?*

——Wait, let's get this straight. You didn't come over to congratulate me, did you?

——*Congratulate you? For issuing a controversial public pronouncement on a United States congressman? Rabbi, a minority group like us can't afford to do that, conspicuously denouncing congressmen. Furthermore—*

——Sam, suppose you let me get dressed before we discuss—

——*You have no idea how shocked we all were to see your letter. Everybody was talking about it at the station. Dr. Terman never did anything like this, and I don't think Rabbi Jacobson even reads the* Times.

——At least let's sit down, Sam. I seem to have lost the drawstring to my pajamas— All right now, Sam, why are you so upset? My letter was only an extract from last week's Shabbas sermon, and didn't you praise it afterwards?

——*I was praising what you said within the four walls of our temple, not something printed on the editorial page of the* New York Times. *God knows how many of its readers are goyim!*

——You think I needed permission to write it?

——*Not to write it; you can write whatever you want. But to mail it! On temple stationery!*

——I don't follow—

——*Rabbi, you are our representative.*

——What do you mean, representative?

——*A rabbi represents his congregation.*

——Oh?

——*We elect you just as we elect our congressmen.*

——You pay my salary, if that's what you mean.

——*Yes, we certainly do. Don't we?*

——Sam, the word "rabbi" means teacher. You suppose a math teacher, for example, "represents" his students? Should he reflect their ignorance of math?

——*Are you calling me ignorant?*

——I'm trying to make the point that—

——*That I'm ignorant.*

——Of course not. Look. A rabbi doesn't speak for Jews, but for Judaism, so our authority originates out of tradition, not from congregations. Rabbis are religious leaders, not cheerleaders.

——*Okay, teach and lead all you want, but in religion. You're meddling in politics here.*

——And morals, Sam? What about morals?

——*What's sex got to do with congressmen!*

——I'm referring to the Civil Rights Bill, the Nuclear Test Ban Treaty, social-welfare legislation, antipoverty laws, foreign-aid appropriations. You know how Frobusher voted on all these issues?

——*Now you're really messing in politics. Rabbi, you're going too far afield.*

——What do you think the prophets talked about most of the time—bar mitzvahs and bazaars? Besides, as you say, I was only talking. What'll be your reaction, Sam, when the board forms a social-action committee next month?

——*Over my— Who says we will?*

——I've got the votes, Sam, a clear majority. What'll be your reactions then, when the temple starts doing things?

——*Doing things? Haven't you done enough already? Families leaving the temple because you refuse to barmitzvah their sons . . . Those kitchen comments. And your speech in the Episcopal church must have set the ecumenical movement back a good two thousand years. Agitating now for open housing and improved public schools and—— Rabbi, that wild-eyed Protestant minister never went* this *far!*

א

NOVEMBER

IT was at the end of the November 12 sisterhood meeting, immediately after Program Chairman Maurine Levenson announced the date of the December meeting, that her face turned white, which, believe me, was a refreshing change from what preceded it in the temple:

". . . And here comes Kay Evans, in a fragile full float of polka-dotted silk organza, dimpled darlingly with handsewn tiger-colored beads over a nude crepe slip . . . and Rona Redmont, gorgeous in a cloud of drifting pale chiffon with a hemline of matching feathers plucked from the tender underbellies of swans . . . Can this be our own Trudi Warren, delighting all eyes in a dangerously low scooped-out gay print blouse and a shimmering skin-tight pair of hostess slacks made of black lace over scarlet satin dotted with tiny pearl seedlings . . . ?"

A fashion show in beaded Technicolor! I had entered my protest as soon as the program was announced.

But Maurine Levenson had an answer ready. "Why *not* a fashion show?"

"In a house of God?"

"It's a *Jewish* fashion show, Rabbi. Sisterhood's modeling the clothes, and they'll be coming from Jewish shops."

(All she had omitted saying was that the models would strut down the runway rendering chicken fat.) "Maurine, I'm not asking you to Buy Jewish or Model Jewish. That's not the point—"

"You want us all the time to *Think* Jewish—that point is better? Well, is there anything un-Jewish about a little fun? You yourself preach how this-worldly and life-affirming Judaism is. 'A person who doesn't take advantage of the legitimate pleasures afforded by this world will have to answer for his neglect in the world to come,' the rabbis taught. Remember?"

Quick study, wasn't she? I trembled to contemplate what would happen to her and my small Shabbas congregation when they learned that it was a mitzvah for a couple to read Song of Songs together Friday nights and help each other to sex. *Nobody* would attend Sabbath services then; they'd all stay home, claiming to be busy performing commandments. Could I prove otherwise? Or deny what for some would be the only mitzvah they were likely to be observing all year? "Maurine, sisterhood has ten general meetings annually. Why spend ten percent of them on what the women shop for all week anyway?"

(You'd have been proud of me: I spoke calmly and with utter dignity, when I yearned to grab her by the ears and shake her and jump up and down and scream, "But I became a rabbi to get *away* from my father's business!")

"Okay, Rabbi, you win. I'll let you choose our next program."

Who says chivalry is dead? "That's very sweet of you, Maurine. I appreciate it. Tell me, what were the girls' top requests?"

"Well, first was the fashion show, of course. Their second choice was a wig party."

Foiled! By a bossy Miss Clairol blonde, who if she wears Treasure Chests surely packs inside them pure muscle. But I'm being unfair to Maurine Levenson, for she chairs even more committees than Pete Schuster, and all the menial work that she hires a maid to do at home Maurine does tirelessly in the synagogue— you suppose this is today's secularized form of penance and atonement? There, unfair again! I resent the fact, you see, that Maurine and her clique play a far greater role in temple life than their men, thereby feminizing Judaism (which traditionally has been adult male-oriented).

And so the fashion show took place, with my warm body in attendance . . . I was the only man present —as in this periodic nightmare of mine where I find myself in a lifeboat filled with a hundred and forty women—except for the Coke man, who paused to refresh himself with the sight of models slinking across the auditorium to an instrumental recording of *Fiddler on the Roof* and Maurine Levenson's intermittently Jewish narration:

". . . And if you want to be a Judith and slay *your*

Holofernes with something subtler than an ax, here's Edythe Loring in a Chinese mandarin evening gown, beaded over a field of stylized flowers bright as a million suns and slit up those zoftig thighs . . . Shirl Rosenman, in plain black beaded hip pants from France—pagan in their sensual appeal, yet Biblical in simplicity . . . Even the Bible couldn't have a word for Gladys Schuster's teenie-weenie iridescent sequeenie bikini—"

Bang! went a dropped case of soda bottles out in the hall.

Gladys Schuster covered herself with hands bigger than her bikini. "*A peeping Tom!*"

(Pray tell, naked lady, what was I?) "Let me take care of it." I stepped out gratefully into the hall.

The soda man, picking up broken empties, leered at me. "*Va-va-va-voom!*"

I waited till beads stopped rattling inside (the dean or Dad should see me now, top spiritual banana at a burlesque show, and I'd plotz) before returning to the auditorium to ogle Shirl Rosenman's benediction—delivered out of plain black beaded hip pants from France, which were garnished by a bare bellybutton. Afterwards, Maurine Levenson announced that the next meeting, on December 16, would have a Hanukah motif—with candle-lighting, present-swapping and an original Hanukah playlet, then said, "How's that, Rabbi?"

Gently I broke the news. "December sixteenth is two weeks *after* Chanukah. This year the holiday begins on November twenty-ninth."

And that, as I was saying before, is when Maurine Levenson turned white. Others gasped.

"Rabbi, are you sure? The twenty-ninth of *November?*"

I nodded. "Don't worry. There are still a dozen more shopping days till Chanukah."

"Our children," Shirl Rosenman exclaimed, "what'll we tell our children?"

Yes, Virginia, there *is* a Chanukah that falls in November. "The children have learned about it in religious school—that the Hebrew calendar, which we use for observing Jewish holidays, is a lunar one, with months of twenty-eight and a half days. Of course, every three years or so we add one entire month in order to—"

"Shirl was referring to Christmas."

"Christmas?" I was surprised. "We're talking about Chanukah."

They all stared at me, surprised in turn.

"Aren't we?" I asked.

Twoscore women shook their heads in such unison that the Rockettes, seeing it, would have dropped dead from envy.

"We're discussing Christmas?"

Heads shook again, up and down this time.

"But what has Christmas to do with Chanukah?"

A collective snort. "What can you expect from a bachelor?"

Finally the explanation came; it must have been the official one, for three women said it in harmony and five others rattled their charm bracelets. "It's our children." Trudi Warren elaborated, "All these years Christmas and Hanukah have been falling at the same time, which means everyone can celebrate something together. But if Hanukah comes in November—"

"Are you telling me you celebrate Chanukah every year in observance of Christmas?" (Back came the rest of my recurrent nightmare: I'm marooned in this lifeboat, the only man amidst a hundred and forty women, all holding a couple of children by the hand, and now I see the name painted on the side of the boat, *S. S. Judaism.*)

"Rabbi, *you* know how hard it is to fight off Christmas," Shirl Rosenman exclaimed, "what with it flooding us over radio, television, school, department stores, starting with Columbus Day already. This year even giving our children a present each one of Hanukah's seven nights—that won't help us in *December.*"

"You mean," Eve Greenwood said, "eight nights."

Shirl Rosenman tossed her Sassoon cut. "I was brought up Reform, so we celebrate seven nights. Of course, for our children's sake we give eight presents."

Kay Evans stood up. "Some of you girls might be interested in the tradition my husband created for Hanukah. Bill dresses up like Father Mattathias, with a long beard and a blue suit with a white Star of Judah on the front, and he distributes presents to our children. They love it!"

Eve Greenwood giggled. "And does Bill color matzos for them during Passover?"

Kay Evans sat down.

"Rabbi?" Gladys Schuster said. "Tell us—if Hanukah comes on November twenty-ninth this year, what should we do December twenty-fifth?"

"The same thing you do when the Chinese New Year rolls around," I said, and perhaps that was a mistake; for all I knew, some sisterhood women set off firecrackers on February second and ran around the A & P dressed up like dragons.

Edythe Loring of the zoftig thighs burst out, "Rabbi, you don't understand. *We* are *mothers!*" She paused for me to salute, and when I refrained, she placed a hand over her even more zoftig heart and saluted herself. "Our children would never forgive us."

You see what Chanukah has become in our time: juvenile blackmail. For this the Maccabees started the first revolution in history for religious liberty? For this they fought and died? For this we eat potato pancakes every year? "Ladies," I said, "you're not obliged to keep up with the Joneses religiously. Do they try to keep up with you?"

"Well," somebody said, "they do read *Exodus* and *Herzog* and *How to Be a Jewish Mother*."

Gladys Schuster came back at me out of the depths of her sequined bikini. "Yours is an intellectual answer, but we parents must deal with our children on an emotional level. Don't you see?"

"How many Christian kids living in the State of Israel," I said, "do you think will be lighting Chanukah candles this November and receiving eight gifts?"

Sudden silence.

Broken by a whispered "That's a *terrible* analogy."

"Why," I asked, "is that a terrible analogy?"

A mutter: "Well, if he doesn't know, I'm certainly not going to tell him."

Shirl Rosenman jumped up, fingering her navel. "Maybe if instead of lighting Hanukah candles for only seven days, maybe if we kept on lighting additional candles every night from November twenty-ninth through January first—how does that strike you, Rabbi?"

"Like a fire hazard. I mean, it wouldn't be in keeping with the true spirit of Chanukah, Shirl."

"Mmmmmm," she said, resuming her seat.

Edythe Loring pointed an excited finger at me.

"Well, *I'm* getting my family a tree. It's an American tradition, uniting us with all other peoples; why make our children second-class citizens?"

"Ah, there's one immediate dividend of being a member of a minority group," I said. "You learn at the start that it's perfectly all right sometimes *not* to follow the majority."

Opening up a second front, Edythe Loring heaved both breasts at me. "Your rigidity is shocking! Rabbi, don't you believe in peace on earth? Don't you believe in good will toward men?" Would she consider her questions answered, I wondered, if I bit that waving finger of hers or into those— "Actually there's nothing Christian about Christmas; it's a pagan festival, marking the winter solstice—I read that in *Time*. So why deprive our children of beautiful evergreen symbols of nature's triumph over winter?"

Clearly these mothers would do anything for their offspring except practice birth control. "You're right, Edythe; Christmas trees are pretty," I conceded, "so pretty I approve of Jews' putting them up during January, February, March and April, when you can get really good buys."

Upshot of the meeting: some nine hundred dollars' worth of clothes were sold, sisterhood made ninety-two dollars in commissions, two dozen women came over to congratulate me, one resolved to postpone her observance of Chanukah till the winter solstice on December twenty-second, Shirl Rosenman bought six hundred Chanukah candles, and Edythe Loring defected from sisterhood, stating in a letter: "It took me four years of analysis to work through my conflicts with an authoritarian father—and now Rabbi Abel's dogmatism threatens to destroy everything. That man is too much of a Jew, and he runs too

tight a temple. Sisterhood simply isn't big enough for
the both of us . . ."

This brought Maurine Levenson on the run to ask
me to pacify her. "Rabbi, if you knew how hard sisterhood works to get members—"

The implication was plain: rabbis were far easier
to come by because they were open stock. "You want
me to tell Edythe I'm not *enough* of a Jew? That ours
is a *loose* temple?"

"Maybe if you convince her you're not *too* Jewish—"

"How do I do that? By blessing her damn Christmas
tree?"

We let it go at that, and Maurine still hasn't forgiven me; after all, you can't hire a new sisterhood
member. So it was that Christmas headed for the Hillendale Temple this year, bringing not peace, alas,
but a swearword.

ℵ

Dear Rabbi Abel,

I happened to be at the temple last Sunday when
the children of the fourth grade were putting on
the assembly program, and I couldn't help but be
impressed by the Wohl child in particular, who
spoke so beautifully and with such impeccable manners. I went over to congratulate his mother afterwards, Cheryl Wohl, who struck me what a lovely
young woman she is, with immense charm, intelligence, personality, breeding and such a tremendous
devotion to Judaism.

Hence this letter. Cheryl Wohl is a divorcee, you
might not know. (The divorce was her husband's
fault, which you also might not know, but everyone

in Hillendale can tell you what a terrible man he was.) I am writing this letter therefore not only as your congregant but also as a friend to suggest in all good faith that the lovely Cheryl Wohl might very well make a very fine life's companion for a rabbi such as yourself.

With all good wishes for your happiness,
A Friend

Dear Rabbi Abel,

You *must* have received my last letter (I sent it registered), so I really can't understand why you haven't acted upon my suggestion to look up Cheryl Wohl. She really is enormously charming, personable, intelligent, highly attractive, talented too (she paints) and with a tremendous devotion to our common religion.

Really, what have you got to lose—except your loneliness and what must be an aching void in your life?

Trusting that what they say about a word to the wise being true—

With greatest sincerity,
A Friend

Rabbi Abel:

What's the matter? Don't you like girls? Is that

why you spend so much time with that goy Rutherford when you can be dating a nice Jewish girl?

Suspicious

Gideon:

Mrs. Cheryl Wohl called me last night to say she's quitting the Temple and ask for her dues back. From the way she talked, it sounded like a personal matter to me, as if she'd had a fight with you. What was it about?

Please let me know at once because I'm sending the Sunshine Committee over to see Mrs. Wohl on Thursday night to try and straighten things out, and it's important for them to know *your* side of the story. I think maybe an apology from you would help.

Barney Singer

א

THANKSGIVING

For Thanksgiving, Hillendale's Episcopal Church joined my congregation in a service at the temple. (We invited several outlying Negro churches and the local Catholic church too, but they had already been booked by other houses of worship.) The turnout was excellent, thanks possibly to Vernon and me inciting our respective groups with "Wouldn't it look *awful* if more of *them* attended than *us?*"

Several new faces showed up, like the couple in front of me at the water fountain who, noting my robe, asked about the Christies in my church.

"Sorry, I don't know them." Hold on—Christie? At the temple? "What are your names, please?"

"Claire and Jack Bernstein," the woman said. "We belong here."

"Happy to meet you. I'm your rabbi."

Don't worry, I hadn't embarrassed the couple, though that was my sincere intention. "Happy to meet you," the man said, "Rabbi Jacobson."

Dr. Bidwell, an aristocratic gentleman with sculptured features and graying temples who looked as if he could model aplomb, opened the service with an invocation: ". . . Teach us now, we pray Thee, never to take our munificent blessings for granted, but to count them daily. Make us appreciate, moreover, that religion's sacred mission is to instill the spirit of God into people's hearts, thereby regenerating them with Thy love, for it is only that love that can transform lives. Indeed, the regeneration of society is God's work alone, while ours is to save souls . . ."

(No wonder Vernon had described his rector as the National Association of Manufacturers given extreme religious unction: "His kind preached about the souls of the poor while opposing poor relief, even as the vast majority of Germany's Christian clergy concentrated on 'spiritual' matters during the entire Nazi period. To listen to people like Bidwell, you'd think Jesus was only Adam Smith wrapped up in a bedsheet. So while the church is dying for want of servanthood and public responsibility, our lay leaders take their cue from the Bidwells and conduct church affairs as if Christ died for our first mortgage. The entire Episcopal church allots for social action the cost of one Coke per member!")

I conducted the prayer service, and Vernon preached, opening with "What on earth is there to be thankful for today?" He followed this with harsh statistics: Negroes, who make up ten percent of the labor force, account for twenty percent of the unemployed and thirty percent of long-term unemployment; the year before, only fifty percent of all Negro men had steady full-time jobs. Meanwhile, the gap between the rich and the poor—nations as well as individuals—continues to widen, and three million children die of starvation every year; by the 1970's a billion people will be starving. Yet the United States allocates four billion dollars to limit food production, thirty-five billion dollars more to explore the moon and only one half of one percent of its gross national product for foreign aid. Vernon then suggested that church laymen train adults and teen-agers for jobs, float low-interest loans for middle- and low-income integrated housing, pair rich suburban churches with poor city ones. Concluding, he appealed for our government to appropriate two hundred billion dollars over the next ten years for the war on poverty and, as it did under the Marshall Plan, allot two percent of the GNP for foreign aid.

My friend's sermon did not please everyone. "Does he think people come to services to get depressed?" Maurine Levenson asked me afterwards. And Pete Schuster remarked, "Rutherford was like a foreign movie without the sex."

Dr. Bidwell fared better. "I just love your diction!" Edythe Loring told him. "Are you from England?"

"Well, not quite," the rector said. "Staten Island, actually."

I was leaving the temple later for Thanksgiving dinner at the Redmonts' when somebody drove up, calling my name. At first the driver looked unfamiliar, but the two lovely girls with him, eleven-year-old Carla and her eight-year-old sister Joy (UNICEF's biggest collectors on Halloween), made me guess he was their father, Sid Frankel, a temple trustee I had

seen exactly three times during the past five months—
once at my interview, the second time on Yom Kippur,
and the third time at a neighboring urinal in the local
movie theater.

"We almost missed you," Frankel exclaimed, "we
were so busy preparing this." He pointed to a tray on
the girls' laps, piled high with a turkey, fresh fruit,
nuts and candy, all wrapped in cellophane and rib-
bon.

Before I could thank him, Carla said, "There's nine
more packages in the trunk."

"Ten altogether," Joy said.

Sid Frankel gave a proud-father smile. "It was their
idea, Carla's and Joy's. My wife and I just helped with
the shopping and cooking, Rabbi."

"I see," I said, but of course I didn't, not yet.

Carla said, "I told them what you said to our class
last week." (What had I said? Clergymen talk so
much that it's easier to keep track of our silences
than our statements.) "Remember how you read to
us from Isaiah and Michael Harrington?"

Joy pointed to the tray. "This is for all the *poor*
people."

Touched, I kissed both girls.

"Rabbi," Sid Frankel said, "would you help us dis-
tribute the packages?"

"Sure, of course. Who are you giving them to?"

"We don't know," Carla said. "We came to ask *you*
who, Rabbi."

"Who to give the packages? Why, to—to—" I
stopped short, stricken. I had no ideal I didn't know
any poor people in the North. The closest I had come
to poverty here was shaking hands once with Sargent
Shriver's millionaire brother-in-law.

"Rabbi?"

I was a perversion of Abraham; he couldn't name ten righteous people in Sodom and Gomorrah to save the cities, because there was only Lot—and here were forty million poor in the Other America, and I couldn't think of ten to save my soul. "Excuse me . . . something I forgot . . . be right back . . ." I mumbled, and dashed into the temple.

What now? Where to look? Whom to call? To ask, "Would you kindly give me the names and addresses of ten poor people? No, this is *not* a scavenger hunt." Eve Greenwood, who taught the disadvantaged pre-kindergarteners, had flown to Aruba for Thanksgiving —Barney Singer! An eight-year resident of Hillendale, *he* would know. I phoned; he sounded as testy as if I had interrupted both his dinner and his nap at the same time. "Frankel made up those packages, didn't he?" he said. "Let him find somebody to give them to."

I can't figure my president out. The temple's hardest worker, he is nevertheless' religion-deaf, as attuned to the still, small voice as to dog whistles. The week before, he wanted me to fire our best Sunday School teacher because her students often left clay behind on their classroom floor. Like Curt Langer is devoted to Dr. Terman, Pete Schuster to his own ego, Rick Adler to appearances, Sam Warren to his fears and Maurine Levenson to reliving her sorority days, the president dedicates himself to the temple organization instead of to Judaism and God. *Who* says the Second Commandment is obsolete?

The police were no more helpful. The cop who answered my call had me spell my name and address first, before telling me, no, the police didn't make it a practice to donate food to Jews on Thanksgiving, and he hung up. I phoned back to explain I wished to *contribute* food, and the cop said he'd call me right

back. He did, but with no information. "You're on the
level," he said. "I figured you for some crank, meaning no anti-Semitism, of course; a friend of mine used
to be a Jew, you know. What happened, Rabbi? Got
stuck with leftovers from some bar mitzvah? . . . No,
how should *I* know anybody who's poor?"

Then—how could I have so quickly forgotten his
sermon?—I called Vernon.

There was a silence at the other end of the phone.
"Well," he said, "those migrant farm workers in the
next town—they're bad off; they get paid below the
minimum-wage level, well below. But they're not
there now, at this time of— Wait! This Negro church
just over the county line, the one I invited to join
our Thanksgiving service—I imagine its minister
could help you." Vernon gave me the church's address,
adding wryly, "Thank God for the Negroes. The people they don't make feel superior, they make feel
good and charitable."

I returned to the Frankels a conquering hero—I
had succeeded in uncovering a lead to one four-
millionth of the nation's poor—and told them of the
Negro church.

Carla exclaimed, "Oh, I can hardly wait to see the
people's faces when we give them the packages!"

"You don't want to hand the packages over personally," I said.

She looked at me with surprise. "I don't?"

"Carla, it's wrong to make people feel ashamed of
their poverty or indebted to you for performing your
duty as a Jew. That's not true tzedakah, *true*
righteousness." Sound selfless, don't I? A semitic Mary
Worth. Well, there's appearances for you, because all
this while I'm thinking of maybe inserting some hal-

vah and stuffed derma into the packages to tip off the recipients that the donors were Jewish.

"Would it be right for us to go along while you delivered the packages?" Carla asked. "We could just stand outside and watch."

(Like Miriam watching from afar over her baby brother Moses!) "Sure," I said. "Know what else you can do? You can write notes saying 'Happy Thanksgiving.' That would add a warm personal touch." Back inside the shul with the children I made sure to hand them temple stationery to write on—well, I conceded sainthood wasn't my glass of tea—to combat Negro anti-Semitism, I told myself before calling myself a hypocrite. Then I phoned Dore Redmont to explain my delay.

"I'm jealous," he said. "I wish my kids had thought of that idea. Hell, I wish I'd thought of it myself."

Thirty-five minutes later Carla brought me the notes. "It took so long because we thought it'd be nicer if each letter was different," she said. I picked up one of the notes and read it:

Dear,

Happy Thanksgiving is what we wish you, a *very* Happy Thanksgiving Day to the whole family. It would be very nice if all your other days in the year were happy also. We sure hope so.

> Love,
> Yours truly

Lovely. But wait now—what happened to the letterhead? I pointed to the ragged edge at the top of the stationery, and Carla said, "Yes, we remembered to tear off the temple's name. Now they'll never be able to trace the packages."

(Do you sometimes suspect, as I do, that God has this secretary who goes around tidying up after Him?)

The children chattered all the way to the Negro quarter—about the packages, how they decided what to include in them, why they chose *gold* cellophane and *red* ribbons—but they fell silent when the Frankel car entered the black ghetto of bleak row upon bleak row of shabby clapboard houses.

"Do people live in those things?" Carla asked.

Joy burst out, "Ten packages won't be enough. We should have made more."

Sid Frankel parked in front of the Zion A.M.E. Church. We got out of the car and entered the building. Nobody was inside; that we could tell at a glance, for the entire church consisted of one room.

"Where do they hold Sunday School?" Carla asked. "There aren't any classrooms."

Joy said, "They don't even have a kitchen."

"Let's find the minister," I suggested. "He usually lives near the church." Luck was with us, for as we stepped outside, I spotted directly across the street a big wooden six-pointed star nailed to the front door of a house. "Look, there he is."

"What would a Christian minister be doing with a Jewish star?" Carla asked as we crossed the street.

I explained that the six-pointed star was called the Star of David, and the minister probably used it because his church bore the name of Zion, a nickname for Israel, over which David had been king and which was a land holy to Christians as well as Jews.

"It doesn't make sense," eight-year-old Joy said.

I knocked on the door—a card in the middle of the Mogen David read: YOUNCER—and it was opened by a heavy-set Negro woman dressed in her holiday best. Introducing the Frankels and myself, I asked if she was the minister's wife.

"Minister?"

"Of the church across the street."

The woman snorted. "You say you a rabbi?"

"That's right."

She pointed at her front door. "Don't you see that Star of David?"

"Yes—?"

"You think a Christian nails up a Star of David like that, for all the world to see?"

"That's what I asked, Rabbi," Carla said.

"*She's* smart."

"Well," I said, "the church *is* named *Zion*—"

The woman chortled. "You think Zion and the Star of David go together like ham and eggs? You a rabbi, and you don't know no better than that?"

Already I was beginning to regret having enlisted in the Frankels' war on poverty. "All right. Why did you put that Star of David on your front door?"

"Why do you think? I don't want nobody here taking us for one of them Christians. We're *Hebrews*. Matter of fact, me and my family are leaving for our temple in Manhattan right this minute."

"Really!" I stopped myself from telling her about the several fine Negro Jews I knew: it would sound too much like saying black was the color of some of my best friends. Instead, I explained my mission, asking if the woman knew people in need, perhaps at her temple.

"We don't take no charity," she said curtly, then directed us to the minister's house around the corner.

The parsonage, it turned out, had a big cross on the door, and something told me that in this instance

the cross had spawned the star. Inside, Reverend
Hobbes, an elderly man with a degree from Union
Theological Seminary framed over his threadbare
couch, said his parishioners could put the ten packages
to good use, and accepted them, thank God; I was
beginning to fear having to bear to my grave these
contemporary marks of Cain.

As we headed back to the car, the Youncers drove
up alongside. "Tell them," Mrs. Youncer said, pointing to her two daughters in the back seat, "don't
Chanukah come early this year? Next Sunday night,
matter of fact?"

Delighted with the gutturalness of the woman's *ch*,
I said, "You're absolutely right, Mrs. Youncer. And a
*ch*appy *ch*oliday to all of you."

Carla expressed my own thought as the black Jews
drove off: "If they belonged to *our* temple, Rabbi,
they wouldn't have to travel all that way to Manhattan."

That night at a board meeting I revealed our
exciting opportunity to be the first integrated shul in
the county—tokenly integrated, to be sure, for there
were very few black Jews.

"Hey, that's great!" Dore Redmont exclaimed.

"A good thing," Charlie Hecht said.

"A fine thing," others echoed.

Maurine Levenson asked, "Do they have children?"

"Four," Sid Frankel said, "all boys."

Sam Warren called for a discussion.

"A discussion of what?" I wanted to know.

"Whether to admit those people into the temple,"
Sam Warren said, he the membership chairman,
whose only question of prospective members, hereto-

fore had been financial, and everyone started to talk at once.

My civil rights experiences down South should have taught me, I suppose, not to expect an immediate overwhelming welcome for the Youncers. Still, some of the comments I heard now shook me:

"But wouldn't they be happier among their own kind?"

"They're so pushy nowadays. Take my maid . . ."

So we had our dicussion, and like most of our discussions on most other topics, the same suggestions were advanced:

——consider the pros and cons (Barney Singer wanted to list on a blackboard the debits and credits of having a Negro family join our congregation).

——appoint a committee (Sam Warren suggested two: one to request a statement of policy from the United Synagogue of America, the Union of American Hebrew Congregations, the Union of Orthodox Congregations, and Hadassah; and the second committee to investigate the Youncers).

——beware of hasty action (Pete Schuster advised us to proceed slowly with all deliberate dilatoriness).

——*"Mah yomru ha-goyim?"* (Rick Adler wondered what people would say, those in the temple and outside, Jews and non-Jews, agnostics and atheists, men of good will and bad, everybody in the United States).

——define terms (Charlie Hecht asked me for an exact definition of a Jew).

——realize the complexity of the Negro problem (Maurine Levenson explained that no temple could be expected to solve a three-hundred-year-old dilemma overnight).

——acknowledge that we were all guilty (Dr. Lipton implicated all mankind in systems that produced the oppression of minorities).

——ascertain why it was that Dr. Terman had never discovered the Youncer family (Curt Langer).

Dore Redmont stood up. "I'd like to ask Rabbi Abel a few questions," he said, facing me. "Rabbi? Did you teach us in adult education that Jewish tradition entitles a person to close a synagogue for letting a wrong go unremedied? Like if children won't support their destitute father, can he state his case publicly in shul and bar all prayers inside until the entire congregation rights that wrong?"

"Entirely correct."

"Does Jewish law further teach that a man's color is one hundred percent irrelevant to anything at all?"

"Correct again."

Dore slammed his fist down on the table. *"Then what the hell are we discussing here!"*

(I could have cheered; that was my student who said all that.) *"So* correct is Dore," I announced, "that if this temple barred black Jews, I'd be forced to resign." Don't worry, I was running no risk. The majority of the congregation would surely support me; besides, at this time of year there was no rabbi available to replace me.

By a vote of thirteen (enough to take pride in) to four (enough to be shamed by), the board accepted the Youncers as members. I could not restrain myself from saying, "It appalls me there were as many as four un-Jews who would blackball Negroes."

"Rabbi," Pete Schuster said, "what makes you think all four voted against the *Youncers?*"

After a sleepless night—you'd think I had just felled George Wallace with a slingshot, I was so elated! Somewhat depressed too; would Pete Schuster never stop regarding me as an interloper on his turf?—I knocked on the Youncers' proud Star of David early the next morning.

Mrs. Youncer opened the door. "You still looking for that heathen?"

(Apparently the woman's interfaith needed work.) "I'm here for another reason," I said. "To invite your family to join our temple."

"Your temple?"

"It would save you that long trip into the city, and you could make friends with—"

"But you're a Jewish temple."

"Certainly. Rabbi Jacobson may not think so, but—"

"I couldn't do that—"

"Oh, don't worry about dues. Whatever you can afford is fine—"

"Impossible—"

"Mrs. Youncer, it's un-Jewish to discriminate against people because they're white."

"Who's Jewish?"

"You have a lovely sense of humor, Mrs. Youncer, so Jewish."

"I'm Hebrew."

"That's why we'd like you to join our—"

"But you're not Hebrews. You're all Goldbergs."

"Of course. You remember: I'm a rabbi, a Jewish rabbi—" Finally it hit me: I was talking "Jewish," and she kept repeating "Hebrew." "You *are* Jewish, *aren't* you?"

"Do I look Jewish?"

"Huh?"

"Rabbi, I been telling you: I'm not Jewish. I'm a Hebrew."

"What is a Hebrew?"

Mrs. Youncer told me: the Hebrews were a Negro sect, somewhat similar to the Seventh-Day Adventists in holding to a literal interpretation of the Old Testament (yet Chanukah, which they observed, and the Star of David were post-Biblical) while rejecting the New Testament and Christianity; according to the Hebrews, each of the six points of the star represented—

But inside of me all this time a voice was drowning out her words, repeating: Gideon Abel is an idiot, an idiot is Gideon Abel—and what will happen when the board hears about this?

As soon as I left Mrs. Youncer, I called Vernon and asked him to join me at the Posh Nosh. I needed a friend to bolster my spirits before that evening's Sabbath service, when I'd be confessing my folly to the entire congregation. Yet when I met Vernon it was difficult to speak. How did one begin? "Hey, guess what kind of jerk *I* am!" Coffee was served, and I was still searching for an opener when I realized that Vernon had hardly spoken either.

I looked up at him; at the same instant he looked up at me. We both said, "What's the matter?"

"You first, Vernon; you're three years older. What's bothering you?"

Scowling, he extinguished his fifth cigarette. "I'm a complete and total fraud."

"You—a fraud? Don't be silly."

"You heard my great sermon yesterday. All those statistics, carefully researched like a brief—to stress the urgency of aiding the poor, the unfortunate. Fifteen minutes later you call me for the names of ten, and I can't think of *one*."

"Well, neither did I."

"You've been in Hillendale twelve weeks, Gideon; I'm here over a year. 'The poor are always with us,' Jesus said, but since He neglected to give Vernon Rutherford a map— Well, now you know the truth about me. When it comes to religion I'm like everybody else: I talk a great game. That's why I'm always bitching how un-Christian Bidwell is, and that's why he disturbs me. Because, God help me, I *am* Bidwell."

"I'd rather be Bidwell than an ass," I said, then related my experience with the board and the Youncers, hoping for Vernon to deny my asshood as I had denied his fraud.

But my friend didn't follow the script. "Don't say the Youncers aren't Jewish," he advised.

"You're telling me to lie?"

"It isn't a lie to say Mrs. Youncer refused to join the temple, is it?"

"But, Vernon—"

"Gideon, it all depends which you prefer: absolution from the congregation for acting hastily, or the opportunity to lead them to other difficult choices."

"That's the easy way out, for me not to tell the truth."

"I don't think so. *You'll* never forgive yourself for jumping the gun; that's not easy. Gideon, why discredit your leadership when it's needed for the future?"

"You're mixing me up. I don't *want* to tell them, so it *must* be wrong—"

"Gideon, haven't you told me of Judaism's stress on community? And you agreed with my criticism of pietistic Christians who concentrate on their own individual salvational navels instead of the good of the group. Well . . .?" He paused to light his sixth cigarette. "Gideon, are you now going to choose a personal emotional release, as I did with all my pious talk? (Remember my describing Pope Pius' outrage if the Nazis had issued the Jews condoms instead of only butchering them?) Or will you save your temple's soul?"

Well, you can guess what I told the congregation. But I bet you can't figure my motive. How could you, though? I'm still not sure myself.

ℵ

My Dear Friends and Fellow Congregants,

As you know, in June the congregation will be voting on extending Rabbi Abel's contract for another term. Now I'm sure that our Temple is as dear to your hearts as it is to mine and that you too want what is best for it. This means, of course, that our Spiritual Leader must be nothing less than the best also, outstanding as administrator, organizer and galvanizer of men. Representing us also as he does to the community at large, we need furthermore a Rabbi everyone respects, gentiles and Jews alike, and not one we have to make excuses for.

I would therefore be grateful to you for communicating to me your feelings as to how Rabbi Abel is meeting our standards, if indeed he is. Please feel free to speak your mind frankly, because your letters will be held in strictest confidence. After all, we both want our Temple to be an inspiring success, and not just another synagogue.

May the Lord bless you ever with His most beneficent blessings.

> With kindest personal regards,
> Pete Schuster
> Chairman, Temple Improvement Committee

Dear Rabbi Abel,

Enclosed please find a carbon copy of my reply to an official Temple query, which asked us in the congregation to estimate your performance thus far as our rabbi. I sincerely hope that my comments herein might prove helpful to you.

> With all good wishes,
> Curt Langer

To the Temple Improvement Committee:

Without comparing Rabbi Abel to Dr. Terman (for it would be unjust to measure a beginning rabbi against a seasoned one), it is my sincere belief that Rabbi Abel shows a good deal of promise. Certainly he tries hard and has enormous enthusiasm (though it does often impel his youthful blood never to stand still, but always boiling to do something). I'm sure, however, that time will settle him down, while experience will teach him that nobody has all the answers by himself alone.

In this connection I recall how often Irv would consult me on issues facing the congregation (which he did *before* taking public positions), so personally interested in each and every congregant was he. Whether remembering everybody's anniversary with handwritten notes of congratulation, or joining men's club for a shvitz at the Turkish bath, or sending Valentine cards to the girls in sisterhood, Irv was always more than merely our rabbi, but one of the Temple Family too, happy with us, like a proud father . . .

א

DECEMBER

I FEEL *awful* about Pete Schuster's letter," Eve Greenwood began. "Imagine, soliciting dirt to bury a rabbi with!!"

"Forget it," I said, for I thought it improper to discuss one congregant with another, or to curse in public. "That isn't why you asked to see me, is it?"

She shook her head. "No." Running her fingers through her long red hair as if trying to estimate how long it would take to pull it out by the roots, she said, "Rabbi, I'm going out of my mind!"

I was surprised. Eve was a very bright thirtyish woman who seemed able to take care of everything except perhaps choosing the right husband. Jerry Greenwood, alas, was no match for his wife in intellect, wit or kindness. "Tell me about it."

"It's my mother-in-law," she said apologetically. "She's driving me crazy."

Mrs. Greenwood? Again I was surprised, for she resembled Eve more than her son. Mrs. Greenwood was the warm-hearted lady who had vowed at my installation not to let me starve in Hillendale, and never reneging, she had sent me a different delicacy every week.

"You see, we live in the same house, all of us— Jerry and I, the children and Mother Greenwood. And she's always baking something for Jerry and the girls, or telling *me* what to bake. Jerry's put on twenty-five pounds this past year alone. And when it rains, his mother's telling him to put on his rubbers; he's thirty-five years old and saying yes. She stuffs the girls with so much candy they'll be lucky to have a tooth left in their heads for their confirmations. Then she's always improving on my recipes or taking the wrong side in an argument— Rabbi, she makes me feel so guilty."

"Why?"

"Because I love her! I really do. No, I mean it. Jerry's mother is so unselfish and giving; she's goodness itself. I'm an ingrate to complain about her. And that's the worst of it: Mother Greenwood is driving me smack out of my mind, and I can't even hate her for it. Because she's a darling."

"How long has this been going on?"

"Twenty-three months now, such a *long* twenty-three months. Since Mother Greenwood lost her husband and Jerry worried about her living alone in a big house."

"Well, that makes things easier. Since it was Jerry's idea for all of you to live together, it wouldn't be rejecting if you found Mrs. Greenwood a place of her own."

"Oh, we couldn't do that."

"Why not?"

"It's Mother Greenwood's home we're all living in."

"Oh."

"You see, Jerry hasn't been doing so well the last few years. A partner of his turned out to be a crook, so he had to start a new business. And living at Mother Greenwood's—she wouldn't take any rent, she's like that—has helped a good deal."

"What about outside interests? Service to the community—"

"She does that. She's a Gray Lady at the hospital, reads to the blind, helps out at Neighborhood House, works for sisterhood, and she never misses a Sabbath service, as you know."

True. Mrs. Greenwood had a better attendance record than Barney Singer, and her comments on my sermons afterwards were certainly more discerning. (She always loved them.) A good-natured, plump, fiftyish woman with loving brown eyes and salt-and-pepper hair, she looked like grandmothers used to look before they discovered stretch pants. "What about friends?"

"In suburbia? Suburbia is a coupled affair—haven't you noticed, Rabbi? There aren't any single people around, and she's too young for the Golden Agers. Besides, I wouldn't want to match lovely Mother Greenwood up with just any man."

I pondered for a while, then concluded, "Well . . ."

"Yes, I've run out of ideas myself." Eve Greenwood stood up. "It's been good ventilating, Rabbi. I'll be going home now"—she grimaced—"where I'll find

Mother Greenwood has bought a dozen more outfits for the girls, who'll be eating sixteen Baby Ruths while she's whipping up more blintzes for Jerry, who's getting to look more like Kate Smith every day."

After Eve left I typed my sermon, swearing anew as my two fingers came up with weird words. And that's when a possible solution struck me. I phoned Mrs. Greenwood. "Can you type?" I asked her.

"I used to," she said. "When my husband opened his first law office I— Oh, excuse me, Rabbi, my cake's in the oven—" She put down the phone, but I could still hear her. "Girls, *girls!* You promised not to eat more than two Hershey bars apiece. Now hide these wrappers before Mommy comes home."

When Mrs. Greenwood returned to the phone, I asked if she'd like to be the temple's part-time underpaid secretary.

"Delighted! And forget about salary. It'll be my pleasure."

She started work the next morning, bringing me a pineapple cheese cake. "People don't have confidence in skinny rabbis," she explained.

A few days later the mailman delivered a parcel addressed to "The Greatest Rabbi in the World, c/o The Hillendale Temple." Accepting it at once, I opened the package to find inside five pounds of Barricini's chocolates, with a card that read: "From a wildly grateful congregant and daughter-in-law."

I called Eve to thank her, and she exclaimed in a rush of words, "You've saved my life! When that darling woman comes home now, she's too pooped to pop Hershey bars into the children or blintzes into Jerry or recipes into me. And yesterday morning, when Jerry and I were having a terrible argument, she was so anxious to get to temple on time she didn't linger to announce which one of us was right. How can I ever thank you, Rabbi?"

But I ended up owing Eve. For Mrs. Greenwood turned out to be a superlative secretary, dedicated (she often stayed overtime), conscientious (she took courses to brush up her typing and to learn speed-writing), immaculate (she removed all the cheese cake spots from my jacket, and the only thing that stopped her from doing the same for my trousers was my refusal to take them off), thoughtful (she brought me breakfast every day because, she said, rabbis shouldn't have waists smaller than Scarlett O'Hara's), efficient (she corrected the English in the letters I dictated), kind (she was always inviting me home for dinner), inspirational (she had better ser-monic ideas than mine), considerate (she wrote my parents every week that I was improving).

In short, inside of one month Mrs. Greenwood was driving *me* crazy. Unwitting saint that I was, I had not solved Eve's problem; I had confiscated it. For now I had to spend more time at the temple than I wished (it embarrassed me that Mrs. Greenwood often came earlier than I and left later); I found myself writing my sermons to please her (how would you like to see someone typing a sermon of yours and wrinkling up her nose?); I started writing out my letters at home the night before, correcting the Eng-lish and memorizing them (so she wouldn't find errors when I gave her dictation the following morn-ing); I was putting on weight (my waist now rivaled Scarlett O'Hara's bust); and each morning I had to explain why a nice Jewish boy like me wasn't mar-ried yet, especially since congregants, she kept saying, don't have faith in bachelor rabbis, even fat ones.

One day in self-defense I asked Mrs. Greenwood,

"How come a nice Jewish girl like you isn't *re*married?"

"Oh, who would want to marry me?" she said, not coyly but matter-of-factly.

"Anyone who's mad about cheese cake, ruggelach, honey cake and a marvelously good heart."

She smiled. "The way men my generation figure: why settle for an old heart when for the same two dollars you can get yourself a fresh one? Their accessories are in such better shapes."

"Since when is fifty-four old?"

"You forget, Rabbi—a man is young as long as he can exercise his passions; a woman is young only so long as she can provoke them."

"You provoked Professor Evans." (A stab of mine at matchmaking. I had invited an old bachelor college prof to dinner, then asked Mrs. Greenwood to join us.) "He talked so much that evening, and he's usually quite reticent."

"He talked, all right. But who understood him? Existentialism, angst, theater of the absurd, hexachlorophene. All I understood was the professor's pauses, the one time he did. He must be a wonderful swimmer, that man; he doesn't breathe."

"What about Mr. Kimmel, the butcher?" (Eve's try.)

Mrs. Greenwood snorted. "I was never so embarrassed. I had changed butchers last month, and Eve brings him home for dinner! That Mr. Kimmel—he's always angling for invitations. That way he sells his meat and eats it too. But enough about me." She pulled out a box from her shopping bag. "Here, tell me how you like these ties for your new blue suit that you should buy."

A few days later, following the morning Mrs. Greenwood had waxed my office floor to surprise me and sewn up the rip in my jacket after I slipped and fell on the newly polished floor, I was tracking an article by Barbara Ward on the underdeveloped nations of the world through brassiere and girdle advertisements in the *New York Times Sunday Magazine* when suddenly the idea struck me: my father's bridge crony, Ben Palmer, the Corset King and, better yet, widower. Of course! I telephoned at once, asking him to join me for dinner the next evening at a congregant's home, and he accepted.

In the morning I said to Mrs. Greenwood, as she was unwrapping antimacassars she had made for the couch in my office, "You haven't invited me home for dinner in a long time."

She beamed. "How about tonight?"

"Fine. Okay if I bring along an old friend?"

In his expensive black silk suit, white-on-white shirt and silver lamé tie, Mr. Palmer, when he showed up thirty minutes late at my apartment, would have looked like a stocky Dun and Bradstreet sweetheart if he hadn't smelled like the Bowery. "I didn't have much else to do today," he explained. "They don't change the movies till Wednesday."

I made him take a package of chlorophyll Chiclets. Then I had to remind him to spit them out when we drove up to the Greenwood home.

"Those weren't mints?" he said.

Nobody ever died from swallowing a dozen Chiclets, I hoped. Still, how many drinks did the man *have* that day?

Inside we were welcomed with joy, warmth and childish resentment—depending on whether the speaker was Eve, Mrs. Greenwood or Jerry. No, I wasn't mistaken about Jerry Greenwood's attitude; on previous occasions he had made such remarks as:

"What's this magic power you have over women, Rabbi? If my wife and daughters aren't telling me how super you are, Mother is."

"I don't have to attend services any more. Mother's always previewing your sermons all week long, and afterwards Eve quotes them."

"Well, Rabbi, what do you hear from God lately?"

A college thrownout and something of a failure at business, Jerry Greenwood was the insecure man's insecure man, never appreciating the fact that anyone with a lovely family like his *is* a success. This I had preached in one pointed Shabbas sermon, and afterwards Jerry told me, "That was a long one tonight, wasn't it?" The kind of man who would envy anybody's having a bigger chip on his shoulder than his own, Jerry resented his wife's ability instead of taking pride in it. Eve, for her part, had refused to become a trustee until the board first offered Jerry a committee chairmanship, whereupon even then he had disparaged the temple for accepting women as trustees. That anyone as sweet and good as Mrs. Greenwood was Jerry's mother led me to believe that gipsies went around switching infinitely more babies in their cradles than people ever suspected.

After we had some delicious canapés, I made the mistake of correcting a mistake of Mr. Palmer's because I wanted him to appear in the best possible light. "You mean you're a widower, not a divorcé."

"Yes, Alice died," Mr. Palmer said sadly. "But Dolores didn't."

"Dolores?"

"My second wife. Your parents didn't tell you?" He sighed. "Maybe because my second marriage didn't last much longer than the Huntley-Brinkley Report. It was annulled right away." He felt called upon to explain, heaven alone knows why. "Dolores was underage."

It was hard to discern who among the Greenwoods gasped the loudest. Me, I merely dropped dead inside of me.

Mr. Palmer offered a footnote. "Every person over fifty tries to recapture his youth. I was only being more literal than most."

Mrs. Greenwood started away. "Excuse me. *Something* must be burning in the kitchen."

"Dolores told me she was twenty-five. How should I know she'd turned her speedometer ahead?"

Mrs. Greenwood paused. "Even twenty-five! You're at least—"

"Twenty-five is what she said. And I was only too anxious to believe her. You see, I was afraid the A-bomb was getting me. And I had to get in my last licks before it was too late."

"Too late for what?" Eve asked.

Mr. Palmer hesitated. "Yes, I *will* have a cigarette." He took one out of a gold case and lit up, while Eve and Jerry made unhappy faces at each other and I cursed Barbara Ward. "Age—that's my A-bomb. The way I feel, Red China may not get me, but cholesterol sure as hell will. Oh, I've been married before, like I said. For thirty-six years. To the same woman. And Alice and I were very happy too—ask the rabbi's parents. But we had married very young, and every once in a while, especially after my two boys married and then Alice died, every once in a while I'd get to wonder maybe I was missing out on something. You must feel it yourselves sometimes, don't you? There's got to be *more* to life than *this*. And

Dolores had everything. Anyone could see that. She used to model my girdles."

"Oh!" said Mrs. Greenwood.

"Mr. Palmer," I interjected, "the new styles in women's fashions—how do they affect your business?"

He never heard me. "Ai ai ai, Dolores! Robbers demand your money *or* your life. Dolores, however, wanted both." A sigh. "Still, those four months were marvelous while I lasted." A chuckle. "She almost killed me, that girl! Intentionally, I think. She acted like she'd read somewhere that if your husband dies on his honeymoon, the bride collects double indemnity."

Mrs. Greenwood, annoyed now, paraphrased, "But ah, my foes, and oh, my friends, she gave a lovely night."

That, thank heaven, stopped Mr. Palmer. "You read Edna St. Vincent Millay too?"

"*You* read Edna St. Vincent Millay?"

"Alice," he said, "used to read poetry to me sometimes. Alice, my first wife."

"That calls for a drink." Tactfully—it was obvious Mr. Palmer was a bit high—Mrs. Greenwood asked, "What would you like, grape juice or vegetable juice?"

Mr. Palmer appeared stricken. "Grape juice or vegetable juice?"

"They're frozen."

"I don't doubt it for an instant."

"We also have a bottle of something I take a sip of when I can't fall asleep. Would you prefer that, Mr. Palmer?"

"What is it?"

"Oh, it's alcoholic. I just don't know what kind; we're not drinkers in this family, and the label fell off last June. But I'm sure it's good stuff; it tastes horrible."

"I'll take it. I'm not particular, I drink anything." Mr. Palmer shuddered. "Anything but frozen vegetable juice."

"I'll help," Eve said. Catching up to her mother-in-law, she whispered, "Isn't he dreadful?"

Mrs. Greenwood looked glum. She said, as the two of them exited into the kitchen. "This is the first night I've ever held my husband's death against him."

Jerry beamed. I had never seen him happier, not even the Shabbas when he told me what was wrong with my last three sermons. Evidently one man's turning out to be poison to his mother was his meat.

"You know," Mr. Palmer said, "your mother is very nice, for a person who doesn't drink." A shrug. "Alice never used to drink either before she married me."

"She became an alcoholic?"

Mr. Palmer laughed. "Only a bartender. At our parties. That's the only time I used to drink myself, when we had people over. We liked to entertain a lot. We used to—" Suddenly he turned serious. "I miss Alice, miss her very much. That's why I couldn't resist the offer of a homecooked meal tonight. Not that I'm crazy about food. I do love homes though. Mine is only a house now, as huge and empty as—as me, I guess."

The phone rang. It was the temple's answering service, asking me to call Dore Redmont. I tried, but his number was busy. When I returned to the living room, the women had returned too, everyone was sipping something, and Mr. Palmer was still going strong.

". . . and then she started calling me a *sexagenarian.*

Who knows where she had picked up such a word? It
made me feel like some degenerate. As if Fredric
March wasn't lots older than me when Kim Novak
married him!"

Eve was surprised. "Kim Novak married Fredric
March?"

"Of course," Mr. Palmer said. "Didn't you see *Middle of the Night* on The Late Show? Funny thing—I
didn't mind when I found out Dolores was selling
everything I gave her. But when I found out she was
also selling what *she* gave *me*— She was only my
wife, a private detective told me later with pictures,
as a sideline."

Mrs. Greenwood, her patience wearing thin, said,
"Oh, are we talking about Dolores for a change?"

Mr. Palmer refused the hint. "You know, to me
Dolores was like—"

"Like a daughter."

"Oh, no. She wasn't old enough to be my daughter.
Dolores was like—well, she was like the sun in the
wintertime: she dazzled more than she warmed. Sex
is a wonderful thing, Mrs. Greenwood, but sex—"

Mrs. Greenwood's patience ran out. "Mr. Palmer,
I'm the kind of woman, when somebody starts talking
about sex, all I can think of is Gimbels."

Mr. Palmer slapped his thigh and hooted. "That's
funny! Like something Alice would have said. She'd
say things that sounded funny on the surface, but
underneath, bloody murder. I don't suppose you could
fix me a Bloody Mary—this drink tastes bloody awful
—no, I guess not. Know something? Alice and you—
you're a lot alike. Maybe that's why I've been running on about Dolores. Maybe I wanted to see how
Alice would have reacted if she'd known, whether

she'd have been ashamed of me." He made a face. "Mrs. Greenwood, it's a terrible thing, growing old ... terrible."

(The outburst embarrassed Eve, Jerry looked disdainful, and I found myself thinking of the poignant verse "O Lord, do not discard us when we are grown old.")

Mrs. Greenwood regarded the man with compassion. "Mr. Palmer," she said softly, "you know an alternative?"

He shook his head. "Would you believe it? I still don't know why I married Dolores! Oh, she was pretty, and she was fun, and she certainly knew how to— But still. There's more to life than that . . . That's what everyone tells me."

Happily the phone rang again. This time it was Dore Redmont, who informed me that the deposit for the new kitchen construction was being handed over that evening; since we both insisted on writing an antidiscrimination clause into the trade-union building contracts, I had to be there to make sure it was done. Lovely! A mitzvah would enable me to escape the house now. It wasn't until after excusing myself that I realized the Greenwoods would still be stuck with Mr. Palmer; I couldn't very well ask for him to be excused also.

Eve and Jerry saw me to the door. "It was very sweet of you to try," she said. *He* said, "Nobody's asking you to try, try again."

Mrs. Greenwood came running out of the kitchen. "Don't worry about your old friend," she said. "What he's drinking now is a mixture of black coffee, tomato juice, vanilla extract and Maalox. He'll be all right." And then she pressed a whole roasted chicken on me. "Just in case you wake up hungry in the middle of the night, you should have something to nibble."

The next morning I beat Mrs. Greenwood to the temple. "I'm sorry to be so late," she said when she finally arrived with my breakfast, "but your Mr. Palmer kept me up till the end of The Late Show."

"I'm sorry too, about Mr. Palmer and his behavior."

"What are you apologizing for? It was thoughtful of you to bring me a dinner date. Made me feel like I was still in the race."

"But the way he spoke and all—"

"Well, he was feeling guilty. And guilt is soluble in alcohol, I've noticed."

"He *should* feel guilty. Imagine—a man his age marrying a twenty-year-old. Or was she seventeen?"

Mrs. Greenwood looked at me as if I were no older than Dolores. "Rabbi, lonely people sometimes do foolish things. Some marry teeny-boppers, others bake cheese cakes."

"You're defending him?"

"Well, I've played his games myself."

"What games?"

"Getting through the day and living through the night—I don't know which is worse. When you have nothing to do with yourself and nobody really your own to do it for—"

I felt sad. "Has it been so lonely for you, Mrs. Greenwood?"

She shrugged. "Two by two they went into Noah's ark, Rabbi, and things haven't changed much since. That's why I let the children move in with me—against my better judgment. Because I was lonely. Jerry told me he wanted to save rent money, and Eve he told he was worried about my living alone. Actually, Jerry moved in because he's always been too close to me. Too close for Eve's comfort, or his own good. It's impossible for two women to share the same kitchen, so how can they share the same man?"

This was getting to be more like a murder mystery every minute. It began as an ordinary conflict between daughter-in-law and mother-in-law, and now it turned out neither of them was the heavy; it was Jerry.

"I'd better get to work now." From her shopping bag Mrs. Greenwood produced a yellow pad full of notes, which she handed me. "Maybe you can use this. It's some research I did for that Israel sermon you're planning." The woman was incredible: maybe I would solve her problem, Eve's, Jerry's and my own bachelor one by marrying her myself. "Oh, yes— mind if I leave on time today? Somebody's taking me to *Hello, Dolly!* tonight."

Several weeks passed, and either Mrs. Greenwood began mothering me less or I had begun enjoying her ministrations more. It did seem, however, she was spending less time in my office, more time in the beauty parlor, no time baking my favorite goodies, some time on a diet, and she even missed one Sabbath service and a day of work. Had she found an outside interest, perhaps male? I hoped so.

Occasionally Mrs. Greenwood mentioned Mr. Palmer, and once she commented, "People think they know everything about themselves by the time they reach middle age. But the trouble is, every new stage of life is another adolescence." And the following week: "Who's ever prepared for widowhood? Finding yourself technologically unemployed. Looking forward to the milkman and the mailman every morning,

anyone to talk to. I'm sure Mr. Palmer never intended to marry that Dolores. But what with being
so alone, his sons having their own families, also running the business now, watching *Middle of the Night*
five times on television and—know something? I
think that movie must have ruined more middle-aged
men than all the prostate glands in New Jersey. Mr.
Palmer only proposed to that girl to see if she'd accept. How could he know she'd take advantage of
him and say yes?"

I assumed then they were seeing each other. It
wasn't likely after all this time she'd be able to quote
him verbatim, not without periodic refreshers. And it
was so. Once Mrs. Greenwood was late for a date,
and Mr. Palmer called me, worried. He phoned back
ten minutes later to say she had finally arrived, explaining apologetically, "We didn't want people to
know we've been going together. My sons would
think I was being debauched again. They don't trust
me since I brought them a stepmother younger than
the Beatles and, worse than that, had to give her a
settlement out of their inheritance. And that Jerry
Greenwood thinks I'm a real bum. He acts like I'm
bent on deflowering the woman."

The next morning Mrs. Greenwood apologized for
not having made me a hot lunch all week, then said,
"Well? Aren't you going to say anything about me
and Mr. Palmer? He said he spoke to you last night."

"Praying is a rabbi's business," I said piously, "not
prying."

"What if I want you to pry? Half the fun of going
out is talking about it afterwards, and I can't talk
about Mr. Palmer at home. Jerry doesn't approve of
him. But then, just between us, I don't think Jerry
approved of his father either."

"You like Mr. Palmer?"

"A lot more than cheese cake, certainly. Lately I've been getting awfully sick of baking."

"Should I start looking around for a new secretary?"

"Oh, don't be silly. Mr. Palmer would never marry me."

I bristled at the slur. "Why not?"

"Because Dolores was twenty years old, and I'm *size* twenty."

"What if he *would* propose? What would you say if he did?"

"If! If my grandmother had had heavy water, she'd have been a bomb."

"Mrs. Greenwood, if you don't answer my questions, I'm going to stop prying."

"Well, I know Eve would live happily ever after if I got married, but the question is, Would I?" She picked up her shopping bag and pulled out my clerical robe, which she had taken home to lengthen without my knowledge. "But it's an academic question, really. I'm working on something now that should settle things for good." And that's all she would tell me.

Three weeks later Mrs. Greenwood invited me to dinner, not at her home but at the Posh Nosh, where Mr. Palmer joined us as her second guest. Neither of us knew the reason for the occasion, and she waited till cocktails were served before enlightening us.

"I want you two to be the first to know—Jerry will probably have a tantrum, so like a coward I'm postponing telling him. I want your reactions first. You see, this is like a rehearsal of sorts and—"

"For God's sake," Mr. Palmer exclaimed, "tell us already!"

Mrs. Greenwood took a deep breath. "I'm moving to Israel. My papers came this morning."

Mr. Palmer gaped.

"You're moving to—?"

"The Holy Land, yes. Why so startled, Rabbi? It was that marvelous sermon of yours that gave me the idea."

"But it was directed at our teen-agers," I said, "to enlist a year of their lives for Israel—"

"Well, even the Peace Corps accepts fifty-year-olds," she said. "And the Jewish Agency assured me that people my age also can contribute—"

"But why?" Mr. Palmer burst out.

"You'll have to read Rabbi Abel's sermon. I'll send you a copy."

"Mrs. Greenwood," I said, "what's the other reason?"

"Other reason?"

"Tell us, Mrs. Greenwood."

She sighed. "Well, I think it healthier all around if I don't live with the children. Eve's a dear, but I'm getting on her nerves. And I'm spoiling my grandchildren; I can't help myself. It isn't good for Jerry either. How can you be a man when your mother's always around to remind you that you're a child? And since they can't afford to move out—"

Mr. Palmer cleared his throat, then spoke hesitantly. "May I suggest an alternative? May I? I have this huge house, Mrs. Greenwood. Move in with me."

She smiled. "I'm afraid the rabbi wouldn't approve of that."

He took her hand in his. "Mrs. Greenwood, I just asked you to marry me."

"*Mr. Palmer!*"

I kvelled with nachas! What, after all, was the very first thing the Lord had done after creating Adam?

He made Eve, of course. And if matchmaking was good enough for God—

"You have to call me Ben now—Ruth." He leaned over and kissed her on the mouth. "Come, let's call the children and tell them—"

"Tell them what?"

"Why, that we're getting married."

She shook her head. "But we're not."

I don't know who was more astonished, Mr. Palmer, or I.

"We're *not* getting married? But a second ago—"

"I was carried away," she said apologetically. "It's been thirty-eight years since anyone's proposed to me, and I was just carried away. Even a woman my age can get carried away—almost. Oh, it isn't that I don't like you, Mr. Palmer, because I do, I do."

"Then why—"

"I am fifty-four years old. No, that's not true; I'm fifty-seven. Mr. Palmer, I am too old for you."

"Too old for me? Hell, I'm sixty-three."

"Dolores was twenty. And she was pretty, and she was fun, and she certainly knew . . . things . . . things I've probably . . . forgotten by now. Mr. Palmer, I just would not stack up."

"Ruth, I don't have such a good memory myself, believe me."

"Marrying me after being married to Dolores—no, Mr. Palmer, I have no desire to be an anticlimax. Besides, I don't love you."

"You don't love me?"

Mrs. Greenwood shook her head ruefully.

"That's wonderful! Marvelous! Beautiful! I don't love you either, Ruth. Now you *must* marry me."

"What?"

"Listen, Ruth, when I asked Dolores to marry me,

I said I loved her—and when she accepted, she swore she loved me too. And we both knew we were lying in our teeth."

"But—but—but—"

"It's different with us. I like you, and you like me— you just said so, didn't you? I have the greatest respect for you, you know that, and I'd be so grateful to you for keeping me company during the long days and lonely nights. Ruth, Ruth, Ruth, *save* me from The Late Show!"

She clasped and unclasped her hands. "I don't know, I just don't know."

"What don't you know?"

"I don't know how we'd get along, and who wants to be bothered now? I mean, starting all over again at my age . . . wedding, honeymoon, new husband, new home, honeymoon . . . Now I prefer talking to— It's too unnerving. I may not be ecstatically happy now, but at least I have my peace of mind."

"Peace of mind? Peace of mind can drive you right *out* of your mind! That's what's wrong with the two of us now. Neither of us have any problems to solve, decisions to make, troubles to worry over. So I marry Dolores, and you run away to Israel."

"That's not so—entirely."

"You know who has peace of mind? A vegetable has peace of mind. Ruth, do you want to marry me and have problems and troubles? Or do you want to be an eggplant the rest of your life?"

"Oh, Mr. Palmer, I don't know . . . I just know I'm afraid . . ."

Mr. Palmer grabbed both her hands. "Ruth, you're fifty-seven, and I'm sixty-three. What in hell do we have to *lose!*"

I tried to slip away in the silence that followed.

But Mrs. Greenwood gripped my arm. "Don't go, Rabbi!" she implored. "Tell me, what should I do?"

"Well, if you ask me—" I checked my counsel though rooting for their marrying. "Mrs. Greenwood, what do *you* think you should do?"

She wailed, "Why does a Jew always answer a question with another question!"

It was the first marriage I'd ever officiated at, and I was so nervous that the florist took me for the groom. To pass the time till the ceremony, I helped set up the wedding canopy and decorate it.

The first guest to arrive at the temple was a lovely olive-skinned Latin type, whose long, wavy black hair made me appreciate that woman's curves could begin from the crown of her head. No relative of either bride or groom, Gina—that was the name on her gold necklace—had been befriended by Mrs. Greenwood at the hospital, she said, where she had recently begun working as a therapist and the bride did volunteer work. She also mentioned giving Mrs. Greenwood the address of an aunt in Rome to visit on her around-the-world honeymoon; no, she was not another blind date for me, alas, because she was Catholic. Such a pity! For Gina was a beauty, with huge eyes that were exquisite mosaics of greens and blues, and not caged in her high-cheekboned face by mascara.

"You have eyes like stained-glass windows," I told her, and isn't it lucky I'm an eye man? How would it be for a rabbi to be a breast or behind man? This way, while girls think I'm looking them so steadily in the eye out of sheer attentiveness, secretly I'm being demoralized.

The girl smiled. "Even your words are flowery." She

touched one corner of the wedding canopy. "It's a beautiful chupah."

The way she pronounced the *ch!* "Are you Jewish?" I asked eagerly.

Remember that poignant scene in *Marty* when the butcher asks the old maid if she's Catholic, because *he's* Catholic and his intentions are entirely above bed? Well, that's not the way it played here, not by a moon shot; making an ugly face at me, Gina snapped, "Are you bigoted?" And she started to lecture me on anti-Semitism.

I burst out laughing. "Hey, I'm a rabbi."

"A rabbi?" The girl was astonished. "But you don't look— I mean, the florist truck outside says, 'Lars Jensen,' and with your hair and then that question—"

"Why does it upset you to be asked your religion?"

"Well, I thought—"

"Would you get so insulted if I asked if you were an American?"

"I'm *proud* to be a Jew, I'll have you know. Where's the ladies' room?"

Presently the wedding party arrived. Lest I conclude that Gina was Mrs. Greenwood's matchmaking tit for my tat, she said to us at once, "The two of you shouldn't get the wrong idea. I think you're both *much* too good for each other."

The ceremony began. My voice kept cracking with emotion as I prayed aloud . . .

Mr. Palmer was also nervous; I imagine that's why he stamped on my foot instead of the wineglass at the end of the ceremony. Then, furtively looking around at his children and grandchildren and his new wife's family, he kissed the bride on the ear, as if to demonstrate he was on his best behavior.

"Mazel tov!" everyone cried.

Afterwards dinner was served, and each of Mr. Palmer's sons took turns toasting the bridal couple. Jerry made a toast too, but not for them. "Here's to Super-Jew, Rabbi Gideon Abel, who steals women's hearts and gives them away with equal ease."

All the Palmers laughed at the jest.

But the bride started toward her son with arms outstretched for hugging. (I knew that's what she intended; how else does one comfort a sulking child?) At the last moment, however, she clenched her hands into fists and pulled them down to her sides. "Dear, you must learn," she said quietly. "Mothers also have to leave home one day."

Jerry forced a smile. "Sure, Mom." He embraced her. "You know what I wish you."

And me? What did Jerry Greenwood wish me? I wondered.

א

——*It's awfully nice of you to come visit, Rabbi.*
——My pleasure, Mrs. Levine. What a great week. Yesterday I officiated at my first wedding, and now you've given birth to my first congregational baby.
——*LeVine.*
——Pardon?
——*Our name is pronounced LeVine. Didn't you know? Rhymes with shine, not sheen.*
——Oh. But don't you spell it—
——*The same way—yes. But our V is capitalized.*
——I see. The baby—how's he doing?
——*Eleven pounds, nine ounces; he's so big the doctor says he could have been twins.*
——That's wonderful. What have you named him?

——Well, Ralph wanted the baby named after his father, Samuel.

——Samuel LeVine—sounds feen. I mean, fine.

——Oh, we're not naming the baby Samuel. We're naming him after Samuel. With an S, you know. We picked Sean.

——Sean?

——You don't suppose people will think we named him after those James Bond movies, do you? But we did want a name that wasn't run of the mill. You understand.

——Of course. Let me see now—Sean's bris will be next Friday. What time—?

——Bris?

——The circumcision.

——Oh, that.

——It's done on the eighth day, and since the baby was born Friday—

——Well, to tell you the truth, Rabbi, we've told the doctor to go ahead and circumcise Sean whenever he feels like it.

——What?

——It's hygienic, we know. But to make a whole religious thing out of it with a ceremony and special Jewish doctor, well—I'd never say this to Rabbi Jacobson of the other temple, because he's so old-fashioned Orthodox—it just strikes me as barbaric. You understand, don't you, being a modern rabbi?

——Barbaric?

——Besides, when we attended Ralph's brother's son's bris last year, as soon as the mohel started cutting away at the baby—I'll never forget it as long as I live—Ralph grabbed hold of his—you know—and keeled over in a dead faint. It was *awful! He almost skewered himself on the doctor's knife.*

——I can get your husband a chair to sit on this time.

——*No, thanks, Rabbi. A bris still seems too voodooish for anyone living in split-level times.*

——Mrs. Levine—

——*LeVine. You're not going to give me a Jewish pep talk now, are you?*

——No, no. I'd merely like to ask a favor.

——*Favor? What is it?*

——Please don't repeat what you just said to Queen Elizabeth.

——*Who?*

——Queen Elizabeth, you know, had all her sons circumcised by the official mohel of the London Jewish community. Now I don't know about Prince Philip—

——*Queen Elizabeth of England?*

——That's the one. Here, you can read about it in this news clipping I happen to carry in my wallet.

——*Imagine that! Queen Elizabeth!*

——Yes, Mrs. LeVine.

——*Well, we want our son to have every advantage; we're very Jewish that way, Rabbi. Suppose I speak to Ralph about a bris, and meanwhile would you keep Friday open for us? We certainly want to start Sean off on the right foot. Oh, I just remembered, Rabbi—next Friday is Christmas Day. Would that make a difference?*

8

WINTER

SOLSTICE

I was in the shower that evening when the phone rang, and the only thing that made me answer it, dripping wet, was my hope that the board meeting had been canceled. Who yearned to discuss whether General Electric or Hotpoint would give a house of God's kitchen more for its money? Besides, I needed to husband my resources for the following night, when the stockbroker who had spoken to the Episcopal church brotherhood the week before would offer tips to men's club on blue chips.

"*Gideon! Oh, Gideon—*"

"Iris? What's the matter? The way you sound—"

"Can you come right over? I'm at Hillendale Hospital."

Hospital? I threw on some clothes and raced to the

hospital, scared. Iris wasn't one to get upset easily. Vernon or the twins—had one of them been in an accident? God, no!

She was sitting in a corner of the lobby, staring at the clock over the information desk. Her face looked so drawn and chalky that I hesitated to approach; I wasn't sure I wanted to hear her news. She saw me, however, and ran over; clutching my hand, she told me it was Vernon. No, there had been no accident, thank God; my friend had undergone a series of tests that day—lately he had not been feeling well, I knew that—and the doctor was operating in the morning to remove part of his stomach.

My voice cracked as I said, "Stomach—?"

"Ulcers, the doctor says. But sometimes ulcers turn— Oh, it's all my fault!"

"What are you talking about?"

"You know how unhappy Vernon's been in Hillendale. He never wanted this kind of church, he wanted to minister to the inner city. Only, I wouldn't let him. *He* heard a call, I *never* did. A future lawyer is the man I married, so I wouldn't let him take a slum parish; why subject our children to slums? He's been eating his heart out ever since. That's what's given him ulcers or—"

"Iris, Vernon never told me he was miserable here, least of all that he stayed on because of you."

"He didn't? Too bad. Maybe if he had told you . . . maybe he wouldn't be lying upstairs now. But he probably didn't want to sound disloyal to me. Gideon, the operation's tomorrow; they'll find out then what it is . . . Oh, how am I going to get through tonight . . .?"

She took me to see my friend. I didn't know what to say—against the white linens, his swarthy complexion

looked green—and Iris forced cheery remarks, so
Vernon led the conversation. He joked about all the
church meetings he could miss now, regretted not
having bought a Christmas tree for the twins, told
Iris not to tell his parents about the operation, and
asked her to bring his Bible, adding for my benefit,
"*Both* Testaments." A deep sigh. "Everything I've
urged on hospitalized people, about God and faith
and prayer—now I get to find out if I really meant
it, don't I?"

The nurse came in to say visiting hours were over.
Vernon kissed his wife and shook my hand, a
formality we hadn't observed since the Sunday we
met. "Gideon?" he said. "Pray for me."

Intellectually I'm offended by the notion that God
must be bribed with prayers before deigning to heal
the sick and relieve the oppressed. *The Song of
Bernadette* always infuriated me with its implication
that the Lord couldn't care less for those who didn't
acknowledge Him king of the hill. Yet I replied in-
stinctively, "Sure, Vernon. Of course." No, God doesn't
need our prayers; we do.

A Gray Lady approached Iris and me in the hall.
"Oh, my dear, is it true? I just heard they're operating
on Vernon tomorrow. But it isn't *cancer*, is it?"

Iris gulped. "Of—course—not."

"Oh, that's a relief," the woman exclaimed. "Cancer,
when you're opened up, it spreads something awful—
the air hitting the cells, you know. Oh, my dear, I'm
so glad it isn't cancer!"

Iris burst into tears.

Without pausing to step on the Gray Lady's tongue,
I hurried Iris to her car. "It isn't what that woman
said," I kept repeating all the way home; she would
say, "Of course not," and then we'd switch lines.

She started to prepare dinner for her seven-year-old twins, while one asked if Vernon was at another meeting and the other wanted to know why all the kids on the block had their Christmas trees up and decorated for two weeks now, when *their* fathers weren't priests or even Episcopalians. But she dropped the first plate she handled. It broke, and she cut her hand picking up the pieces.

"We're all eating out," I announced.

Mark and Luke whooped. I asked where they wanted to eat, and the boys cried together, "Chinese!"

We drove to Kublai Khan's Nationalist. While the family was being seated, I phoned Barney Singer to say I'd have to skip the board meeting that night.

"But we're discussing the new kitchen," he said.

I'd explain at the men's-club meeting, I told him, then joined the Rutherfords without removing my overcoat; in my rush to the hospital I had left my apartment without a jacket, tie or belt. I ordered for the four of us: dinners for the boys, Jell-O for Iris, tea for me. It was good that the children were with us: she wouldn't let herself break down in front of them, and their fight over who had more noodles distracted her; it was bad too, for the boys resembled their father so much one couldn't look at them without thinking of Vernon in the hospital.

"I remember once telling you," Iris said, playing with her dessert, "how shocked some ministers' wives are to discover their husbands have weaknesses, like ordinary men. But not me. I was different—because I had married a law student. Yet when the doctor told me Vernon might have—" She checked herself. "Character weaknesses I was prepared for, but not this. My first thought was: It can't happen, not to a clergyman. God wouldn't *allow* it."

Poor God, He gets it in the neck every time. If only He didn't let Himself be publicized as all-powerful. But he probably had His pride, like everybody else. The Lord guides us in living a good and creative life—only an ingrate would demand He do anything. I couldn't say this to Iris, of course, not now. Besides, at this moment I myself didn't accept it.

"*Do* it, Rabbi."

"Do what, Mark?"

"Wiggle your ears."

"And your thumbs, Rabbi."

"Okay." Would you believe it? Nothing I had learned in divinity school had stood me in such great stead in the rabbinate as having been born double-jointed and loose-scalped.

"Having a good time, Rabbi?"

Sam Warren was standing beside me. I stopped in the middle of an intricate double-wiggle to introduce Iris and the twins.

"Say, who you voting for, Rabbi? Hotpoint or General Electric?"

"What? Oh, the meeting. Well, neither. I'm not going tonight."

"You're not? But it's such an important meeting."

Iris intervened. "Don't miss your meeting on my account, Gideon. You don't have to stay with me." Which was a mistake.

Sam Warren's eyes opened wider than Little Orphan Annie's, as his eyebrows raced for his hairline.

I couldn't very well explain, not with the children there. Besides, it would seem I was granting Iris some kind of favor. "I can't go tonight. But I'll see you in temple on Shabbas."

Sam Warren threw me a look which clearly stated, You don't come to my meetings, why the hell should

I come to yours? (I know that's what he was thinking, because a few weeks earlier his wife had told me, "Roberta never invited us to any of her parties; why should we attend her funeral?")

After Sam Warren left, Iris said, "I can manage now. You really should go to that meeting."

"Oh, my congregants can get along without me." Not to give the game away, I added, "For one night."

The Rosenmans descended upon us. "I thought that was you, Rabbi," Shirl said. "I told Max here, but he said, 'It couldn't be the rabbi, not without socks,' and I explained that that was the height of fashion now, no socks, among college boys."

So I was also sockless. What would Shirl Rosenman think when she found out I wasn't wearing underwear either? "I was in such a rush—"

Iris tried to help again, alas. "It's my fault. I called Rabbi Abel before and he's so obliging—"

"Isn't he though?" Shirl said, and Max commented, "I see you go in for Chinese food, Rabbi, spareribs and all."

"Only Chinese tea. They make swell tea, the Chinese. I believe Rabbi Jacobson *also* drinks Chinese tea." I stood up. "Would you excuse us? We were just leaving."

On our way to the cashier Rick Adler hailed me, and I only had myself to curse for not having remembered that Chinese restaurants outdraw synagogues every day of the year except Yom Kippur. "Mind if I ride to the meeting in your old green thing, Rabbi? It would save me a trip. I could give my wife the car now."

I flinched. "Sorry, I'm not attending the meeting. Something important came up. I mean, something *more* important. I mean, something *even* more important." I couldn't change my mind now if I wanted to, which I didn't. What, trustees would want to know, had been pressing enough to keep me from the meeting that became *un*-pressing as soon as everyone saw me dining out on spareribs in public alone with a married woman and wiggling myself? Now if only Iris would *not* say—

"Go, Gideon. You don't have to keep me company any more."

For centuries mathematicians have been talking about the perfect circle; Rick Adler's mouth now formed it.

"Maybe I'll stop by later," I said. "The meeting will probably be going hot and heavy till after midnight, like always."

Rick Adler regarded me coolly. "Sorry you think we blabber too much, Rabbi."

We left.

"Gideon, want to know the truth?" Iris said. "I'm glad you're staying with us tonight. It helps." That made all the gossip that was sure to follow worthwhile. It also eased my embarrassment to discover in front of the cashier that I was not only without a jacket, tie, belt, socks and underwear, but also with no wallet. So when I asked Iris for money, I pretended nonchalantly not to see the Rosenmans, Adlers and Warrens pretending not to see her hand me ten dollars to pay the bill.

I drove the Rutherfords home—all the way the twins nagged about a Christmas tree, worse than Edythe Loring—and dropped them off there, saying I had to pick up the rest of my clothing. Returning to my apartment, I finished dressing and got my billfold, then went out looking for a tree; it would cheer the kids, and decorating it would help Iris pass this long night. I found a mart in a lot off Main Street—its enormous size implied there were more Christians in the world than I had ever realized—and asked the proprietor for a nice tree.

"Nice trees is all I got, mister," he said. "What color?"

"What do you mean, what color?"

He pointed to an assortment of pink, white, red, blue and green evergreens. "Where you been living, mister—in a monastery?"

"Well, I'm a rabbi, you see—"

"A rabbi? No sh—" He checked himself. "Really?" He shook his head. "Boy, this ecumenical thing is really something, isn't it? I can't go to church any more without tripping over a bunch of Protestants or Jews there. You have no idea how hard it is on my priest; he can't use his old sermons any more."

"The tree is for a sick friend—"

The man smiled. "That's what all my Jewish customers say." He held up one finger. "Hey. You being a rabbi, you should know. How come Jews have holidays thirty and forty days long?"

"No Jewish holiday lasts that long."

"Are you sure? Every night for a month now this Jewish neighbor of mine is lighting candles in her window; tonight there were twenty-five candles there. Which doesn't bother me, except this Rosenman woman gave her son his twenty-fourth present in a row last night, and my kids are calling me a Catholic cheapskate."

A traditionalist in religious rites, I decided on a green fir tree instead of a dyed synthetic, and the proprietor helped me tie it—the biggest tree there—to the roof of my car. "When you rabbis go in for something," he remarked, "you really go all out."

"Why, you look *exactly* like Rabbi Abel! Anyone ever tell you that?"

It was Kay Evans, of course, Christmas shopping. God, I hate small towns. You can't blow your nose without people noticing, debating its necessity and commenting on your style. They always knew whose relative I blind-dated, with how much success, and they were still asking me about Rochelle Levenson. I said, "The tree is for a friend—"

"A *sick* friend?" Kay Evans asked.

The children hugged me when they saw the tree— what a sad holiday for them without their father at home—and tears filled Iris's eyes. But putting it up would present a problem, since the tree was taller than the house. I hacked off a few firry feet (learning in the process that there are such things as pine-needle splinters), and the four of us stood the tree up in the living room, then decorated it with tinsel and foot-high figurines of angels. Around the base Iris arranged the nativity scene, with the Magi, animals and onlookers. "Vernon buys me a few of these every year. Aren't they lovely? This year he—" She stopped.

I asked for the star to put atop the tree.

"I'll hang it up," Iris said.

"Sure. I understand. You should put up the Star of Bethlehem yourself."

"You think I don't want an unbeliever tainting our star?" She almost smiled. "I just don't like chancing your falling off the ladder. What would your congregation think of a rabbi who broke his neck while trimming a Christmas tree?"

"If that's your only reason," I said, ascending the ladder with the star in my hand. "It's less risky for a man to hang than a mere woman."

"Please be careful, Gideon," she said.

Reaching out from the top of the ladder—my hand was two feet from the treetop—only then did I realize that Christmas trees are shaped like triangles, not rectangles, but after all, this was my first Christmas tree. Down I climbed from the ladder, pushed it closer to the tree, though not two feet closer because the thick branches blocked me; then back up I went. Now only nine inches or so wide of my mark, I leaned over nearer, with the twins cheering me on and Iris again cautioning.

Seven inches to go . . . three . . . I stretched myself just a little bit farther.

"Let's help Rabbi," Mark said.

I smiled—they were such adorable kids—then gasped as the ladder began to wobble.

Iris clapped her hands. "All right, into bed now. We can't have you knocking down the rabbi."

The boys resisted, Iris insisted, with me silently rooting for her, and they left the room after bidding us good night, they were such well-mannered children —so well mannered they even stopped to say good night to their dog, which since my first visit was always locked away in the basement when I came over; they were a most considerate family.

"Sweet dreams, Beauty," the twins said.

It replied with a howl that was much too clear and far too close; evidently good manners dictated that one must never say good night through a closed door, and when the boys had opened the basement door Beauty bounded past them into the living room. Spying me, the beast howled the equivalent of "Long time no see!" and lunged to complete what he set out to do at our first dialogue, knocking the ladder out from under me.

"*Beauty!*"—that was the last thing I heard Iris cry

as, below, a wide-open drooling mouth rose to meet
me—"Be *careful . . .*"

ℵ

——*How's your head, Gideon?*
——Fine, thanks, Barney. It wasn't a concussion,
after all.
——*That was a nasty spill you had. Lucky the dog
broke it.*
——Good old Beauty.
——*I'm surprised he didn't bite you, your landing
on him like that.*
——Well, it seems I scared *him.*
——*And Reverend Rutherford—how's he doing?*
——Thank God it wasn't— I mean, the doctor said
the operation was a complete success. Vernon
will be home in two weeks.
——*Good. I explained to Doug Bettleheim that
that was the reason you didn't visit him in the
hospital—you were all banged up yourself.*
——Doug Bettleheim? In the hospital? What's the
matter with him?
——*A stone in his bladder. And he was put out you
didn't visit him, especially when he heard you
were on the same floor that day, seeing Reverend
Rutherford.*
——Why didn't the Bettleheims call me, like Iris
Rutherford did?
——*Doug was sure somebody would tell you. You
didn't know, Gideon, did you? I mean, just between us.*
——No, Barney, I didn't. I'll visit Bettleheim tomorrow.

——*Well, he's home now.*

——*Oh?*

——*He was just there overnight. He passed the stone right away.*

——Then I hope to soon have another chance to visit Bettleheim in the hospital.

——*There are a few other things, Gideon, I want to discuss.*

——Yes, Barney?

——*The new temple kitchen, for one. The contractor is ready to start building—only we don't have enough money to finish. And some people say the reason we don't is because of you, because you never supported it in any sermon or temple bulletin column. Why, you never so much as mentioned the kitchen. People find that odd, you being our spiritual leader.*

——What could I say about a kitchen?

——*When we were considering this old Beardsley estate, Dr. Terman compared our buying it to the Maccabean recapture of the Second Temple.*

——I'm sorry, Barney. I honestly can't think of anything appropriate.

——*Well, doesn't the Torah recount at length the building of the Tabernacle?*

——Yes, but the Tabernacle housed the Tablets of the Law, Barney, not a walk-in freezer.

——*All right, if that's the way you feel about it. Gideon, there's another thing that needs discussing—our Sabbath services.*

——Yes?

——*Only seventy-four people attended last week.*

——There were eighty. Well, I also counted.

——*You probably included the Shapiros and the*

*Goldins, didn't you? But they're way behind in
their dues. And those two strangers aren't members, they just came in off the street.*

——Oh.

——*What's worse, attendance has been decreasing.
Take the last four services: eighty-nine, eighty-
seven, seventy-nine and now seventy-four. I'm
not counting the family service—that always
draws over two hundred, since the children like
you—or last Sabbath, when a hundred and
eighty-six people came because they heard you
almost killed yourself trimming a Christmas tree.*

——You think I ought to fall off ladders more often?

——*I'm serious now. Gideon, you're just not drawing at Sabbath services. Yet business is booming
at all our other affairs. The Sisterhood Gourmet
Supper was a sellout, so was the Father-and-Son
Dinner, the Valentine's Day Darlings' Dance is
half sold out already, and when that stockbroker
spoke to the men's club, even the women came,
and I don't know how many Christians. So evidently people are dissatisfied with Sabbath services; it stands to reason. If more people were
satisfied, we'd be drawing more people.*

——I guess so. It works that way with *Bonanza.*

——*There! That's another thing I want to talk to
you about.*

——What?

——*Your sense of humor. It rubs people the wrong
way sometimes. Not me, understand, because I
always enjoy a little humor; it's important, I
think, whatever your religion. But at the last
board meeting, after Curt Langer got through
telling you exactly the way Dr. Terman ran
things around here, you said, "Thank you very*

much"—which was fine, very polite. But why did you add, "Mrs. Danvers"? You have no idea how insulted Curt got, hearing his masculinity impugned. He's a married man, you know, with four children and a pregnant wife.

——That wasn't my intention. Mrs. Danvers was Rebecca's devoted housekeeper in—

——*Well, that's very nice, but not everyone understands your Biblical references. And at that same board meeting, when after the success of our special services—the birthday service, anniversary service, Sisterhood Sabbath, Men's Club Sabbath, Young People's Sabbath—when Maurine asked you to come up with ideas for more special Sabbaths like that, you suggested a Witches' Sabbath. Really, Rabbi.*

——I was only trying to point out that the Sabbath itself is reason enough to attend services.

——*Well, evidently the message hasn't been getting across. Here we're talking of enlarging the sanctuary because it's too small to hold the entire congregation on the High Holidays; yet it's never more than thirty percent full on ordinary Sabbaths. Why is that, do you suppose?*

——Good question. After all, the congregation *invited* me to preach to them; how would they like it if *I* didn't show up?

——*Well, you're paid to be there. Which reminds me—there's something I want to ask you, Gideon. It isn't public knowledge yet, but that director we hired for* My Fair Sadie—*he's quit to do an off-Broadway show. Worse, he won't give us back our fifteen hundred dollars—*

——You were paying him fifteen hundred dollars?

——*The temple show is always our major fund-*

raiser, so it has to be professional, to keep people coming back every year. Well, we remembered your degree in the drama and— Gideon, would you take over the direction for us?

——*Me? Direct My Fair Sadie?*

——*We don't have the money to hire another professional. And there's this to consider: if the show doesn't open, we'll have lost so much money I don't know how we'll be able to keep paying your salary.*

——*Barney, you know what you're asking? You want me to go over to the enemy.*

——*What enemy?*

——*My Fair Sadie! Thirty-five people are involved in that damn show, and they rehearse so often they can never attend services or adult education. You want me to aid and direct my biggest competitor?*

——*But, Gideon, you know our financial troubles; we rely on the proceeds from the Coke machine to pay our phone bill. Don't forget that the temple is, after all, a—*

——*Yes, I know, a business. But people work so hard at keeping it solvent they never have time to use it for religious purposes. Sometimes I wonder why they joined in the first place! Why did you join, Barney?*

——*That's a very personal question.*

——*Sorry.*

——*Not that I mind telling you, Gideon. It's an obligation, I feel, to contribute to the community. For years I devoted myself to general charities like the Community Chest. Until I realized that not once had any of the non-Jews in those organizations ever invited my wife and me to their homes for social reasons. I was good enough for heading drives because of my contacts with Jews, who are far more charitable than other groups—that's statistics—but otherwise they wanted no part of me. So I turned to the temple, hoping to be of service to people here. That's the real reason, Rabbi. I'm sure you don't believe any of Pete Schuster's stories. He's been slandering me because he wants to be president himself next year, that egomaniac. Because he can never join anybody, he's always trying to beat them. But what's all this got to do with your attracting more people to services?*

——Well, maybe if I understood the congregants' motivations—

——*That's what we're trying to do, Gideon—motivate members. The telephone squad is reminding them to attend services, I'm appealing to their loyalty to the temple, the ritual committee is involving more people and cutting down on the Hebrew, we're expanding the refreshments served at the Oneg Shabbas. So you see, Gideon, we're doing our part.*

——I appreciate it, Barney. Though after checking around, I find that we draw better at services, percentage-wise, than most synagogues. Seems that we Jews, who gave prayer to the world, may have given it away; we who led peoples into religion may be now leading them out.

——*Well, you could help by doing something about your sermons.*

——What about my sermons?

——*For a change, can't you preach on things that people don't feel quite so strongly about? Or maybe if we lined up some guest speakers, like David Susskind—*

——Barney, there's something else we can do. Instead of sermons, what if we had lectures, followed by discussions after services?

——*Lectures?*

——Yes, I could lecture on Friday nights, and later we could sit around and discuss. It would be a real learning experience.

——*Look, I'm trying to boost your popularity, Gideon, and you won't let me. Springing lectures on the congregation! And when I give you the chance to take over something as important as* My Fair Sadie——

——Barney, I have no choice. The rehearsals conflict with adult education. I'd have to drop my whole program to direct the show.

——*Still and all, twice as many members are involved in* My Fair Sadie *as in adult education. And you know our annual meeting is only a few months away, when people will be voting on Dore Redmont's proposal to give you a four-year contract.*

——Oh, I don't care about any four-year contract, Barney.

——*You don't? Why not? The other rabbis do.*

——Because they're family men. To me a yearly contract is just as good. I only want to do a good job each year.

——*Gideon?*

——Yes?

——*I hope you won't take this as an insult, but——*

——What is it?

——*You're no businessman. Oh yes, Gideon, before*

I forget—Curt Langer is going into the hospital next week for a tonsillectomy. Now be sure to visit him.

——Yes, Barney. I'll accompany you.

——*Oh,* I'm *not visiting Langer. We aren't that friendly.*

⌘

JANUARY

Nᴏʙᴏᴅʏ can accuse my congregation of not being as modern as tomorrow's war. Jesus, according to the New Testament, drove moneychangers
out of the Second Temple, and what drove us out
of the Hillendale Temple was George Bernard Shaw
bastardized. When *My Fair Sadie's* cast began meeting nightly—throwing themselves into rehearsals with
the feverishness of performers intent on crashing the
big time, Temple Emanu-El on Fifth Avenue—all
nonthespians were forced to congregate in private
homes for the duration, except on the Sabbath.

My sole contact with the show came when Dore
Redmont insisted that Rona, the co-chairman, have
me judge the suitability of one of the songs:

All I want is a colored maid
Who doesn't vanish when she's paid;
I'll not find her, I'm afraid,
Though wouldn't it be mazeldik!

A maid who doesn't chase the men,
Who takes her day off and not ten—
Let her even be Zen!
Oh, wouldn't it be mazeldik!

Oh, so mazeldik relaxing without travail,
I would never budge till Saks
Ran its first summertime sale.

Someone to care for the family
Who will not run off on a spree
And doesn't envy me—
Mazeldik! Mazeldik!

I ruled the song out, then offered a substitute of
my own. (The way sales were going, this was my
chance, as a lyricist, to reach ten times my audience
as a preacher.)

All I want is a home somewhere,
Far away from the Negro lair—
No integration scare . . .
Oh, wouldn't it be suburban!

Lots of problems I could escape,
No more Negroes trying rapes
And getting into scrapes—
Oh, wouldn't it be suburban!

Oh, so suburban sitting absopositively quiet—
I would never budge till summer
Brought its annual race riots.

There we could live so happily
With not a trace of bigotry,
Because it's Negro-free—
Suburbia! Suburbia!

Pete Schuster, Rona's co-chairman, called for the
inevitable discussion, which resulted in my song being
replaced by a new one, "Mrs. Fish's Knishes Taste So
Delicious." Why? Because several people charged my
song with being anti-Negro, anti-Semitic, lewd, all
three, or none of the above but so preachy it would
damage ticket sales.

Alas, Dad was right: you can't wise up all of the
people all of the time. Now in the middle of my
freshman year here, I'm realizing that there's nothing
I can do or say—or *not* do or *not* say—without one
of my hundreds of bosses taking exception or umbrage
or muttering darkly about June, not because it rhymes
with moon but, rather, with screw'im. I'm beginning
to feel like the man in the Talmudic tale with two
wives—one old, and the other young; the old one
kept pulling out the husband's black hairs while the
young one pulled out all his gray hairs, until the poor
guy ended up bald.

Not that all is bleak; far from it: there are many
lovely Jews in the congregation. It's just that Gresh-
am's law infects me too; at times the few bad Jews
here drive all the good ones out of my mind. Still,
though the *My Fair Sadie*-niks outnumber those congregants involved in adult education and social action, there are enough to make me feel like a rabbi.

Take Dore Redmont, for example. At the temple's New Year's Eve Frolic, he told me soberly, "I never felt happier than when pushing through that vote for the Negro Jewish family, because I never stand up that way for principle in my P.R. firm. How could I? I'd be out on the street in no time. All this while, you know what's been making me so miserable? The feeling I was constantly missing out on opportunities without even knowing what they were. That made me feel guilty. For wasting myself. I wouldn't have turned alcoholic, but I'd have found *something;* when a man's looking, he's bound to find. But now I feel some small sense of purpose, having discovered there's a people I belong to and mitzvos to accomplish. So I put in my forty stupid hours a week at myth-making, then take the money and run to try to accomplish things with the rest of my life. Because one thing's suddenly become clear to me: people become what they do."

Only a few weeks old, Dore's social-action committee was meeting for the fifth time—in Charlie Hecht's home that night—to map out campaigns for open occupancy, the improvement of public schools, a survey of job opportunities, job training, a negative income tax, the Israel bond drive, the combat of Russian anti-Semitism, safe cars, restrictions on gun sales and more. "Aren't you proud of us, Rabbi?" Dore exclaimed. "We're coming up with as many causes as the new temple kitchen will have appointments!"

During the meeting, Vernon phoned to ask me to stop by his house afterwards and look over his Sunday sermon. "Iris agrees with the gist of it," he said, "but she thinks maybe it's a little too rough and should be toned down."

"Sure thing. And I'll bring you *my* sermons. Maybe

you can give me endings. I'm still having trouble with my third acts."

"Gideon, use this last sermon of mine, and you won't worry about endings ever again—only a new beginning."

Vernon was kidding, of course—wasn't he?—but I was serious: it isn't easy, you know, to knock off two good sermons a week. Edward Albee established a world-wide reputation on the basis of two one-acters even before *Who's Afraid of Virginia Woolf?* and here we poor clergymen must compose their equivalent every week of the year, then preach to the same audience each time—and look what overexposure did to Milton Berle and Lassie. Worse yet, we usually preach to sanctuaries that are two-thirds empty. You have any idea what that feels like? As if you've stumbled into the fabled lost graveyard of the pews, the place where sermons go to die.

I left Charlie Hecht's around midnight, while the others lingered over coffee and cake, and drove to the temple to pick up my unfinished sermons. As on every Thursday night, I mused about their efficacy. Most clergymen consider preaching their main duty, maybe because it takes some eight hours to come up with a good sermon, and anyone who's expended that much time doesn't like to think the hours could have been better spent paring toenails. Let Billy Graham boast that his preaching has changed men's lives—after all, that's his racket. Me, I rather suspect preaching resembles dropping aspirin tablets from the top of the Empire State Building in the hope they'll fall into the open mouths of people on the street below on their way to Ohrbach's with headaches. Ever know a clergyman to walk a block to *hear* a sermon?

The temple was dark, the *My Fair Sadie*-niks having departed, and I made my way by the red light of exit bulbs through the hall and kitchen to my office. Opening the door, I flicked on the light switch and—

"*Oh . . .!*"

The couple on the couch reacted to the light as to a movie director's "Cut!" In the middle of making nice, the woman threw her hands over her face, the man disentangled himself, she screamed out like one dispossessed, he whirled around—and it turned out to be not a foreign movie after all. I beheld Pete Schuster with friend.

"*Sonofabitch!*" he cried, jumping to his feet.

Though I appreciated that fate was being addressed, not I, nevertheless the Marine in me automatically lashed out at the chairman of four different committees. Lashing was easier, more satisfying too, than explaining at length that a married trustee does not behave like this at the scene of his noblest temple-waving speeches. Almost as quickly I realized that my blow, a karate chop aimed at his windpipe, could very well kill the man—hardly sporting and rather awkward; what could I do with a dead Pete Schuster? —so I pulled my hand up short in mid-swing, changing its angle to a slap, which maintained enough momentum to spin him around like a corkscrew and send him sliding across my desk.

Something of Pete Schuster hit an open drawer, and he disappeared with a clunk over the far corner.

The woman was still screaming, so loudly now you'd have thought her virtue was being wrested from her petal by petal. Who was she? It was impossible to tell, for she kept her face covered, her hair was standard Miss Clairol blonde, and she was wearing basic black.

Scarier though than her screams was the silence emanating from Pete Schuster, parts of whom were dangling in the wastepaper basket. Had I executed him by mistake? I rushed around the desk and bent over him. He was stunned but breathing, thank God, through a bleeding nose, and his left cheek was bruised. Suddenly something blushed by; looking up, I saw the woman hightailing it out of the room.

Now what?

I could tattoo a scarlet letter on Pete Schuster's nose, then drop him on his front doorstep. Yet what good would that do? After all, there were his wife and children to consider.

Stepping into the adjoining kitchen, I soaked my handkerchief in tap water, then returned to wipe the blood off the man's face. He groaned, picked a paper clip out of his ear, opened his eyes, saw me, passed out again, or probably only pretended to while he tried to think up a better line than "You realize, of course, you just lost my vote for the four-year contract."

"Hello. Anybody home?"

I jumped and Pete Schuster quivered as the temple door slammed shut.

"Rabbi?" Now steps were heading through the hall toward my office, which was the only room lighted. "Is that you?"

Fly! Away! I couldn't let anyone walk in on this: Pete Schuster on the floor, and his tie and a brassiere entwined on the couch like a family crest. No, it wouldn't do for word to get around Hillendale that as a special fund-raising feature, the temple ran midnight orgies. Besides, there was always the possibility that I had jumped to the wrong conclusion; maybe the blonde on my couch had been Pete Schuster's wife, and the two of them were merely trying to invigorate their marriage by romancing in new surroundings, as prescribed by the *Ladies' Home Journal.*

I darted to the threshold, turning around to close the door behind me.

"No, don't do that!"

"Oh!"

"I didn't mean to scare you, Rabbi, but it's dark as hell out here." It was Dore Redmont. "What are you doing in temple now?"

"Picking up—sermons—on my way—Vernon—"

"Everybody else gone?"

"What?"

"From rehearsal. I thought I'd get Rona and go out for a bite— Say, I never realized you were that much taller than me, Rabbi." He pointed to my stained handkerchief. "Bloody nose?"

"Uh-huh. Dore, how about us going for a cup of—"

A sudden noise behind me startled the two of us.

"Didn't you say everybody had left?" Before I could stop him, he stepped into my office.

I didn't follow him inside. What good was it? I had tried to shield Pete Schuster, why I'm not sure, but it was no use now.

A gasp. Moments later Dore stumbled out, looking shorter than when he had entered, now that I was no longer standing on my toes to block his view. "You hypocritical bastard!" he cried, and ran off.

Not until Dore's car roared away did I collect my wits; even then all I could manage was "Who? Me?"

I stepped back into my office, ready to clobber Pete Schuster again and repent afterwards. But one look around and my arm wilted. For all I saw was:

the couch, the brassiere and tie, a dress and jacket, the new window the board had finally installed, now wide open, and no Pete Schuster.

Gevalt! Dore thought he had caught me in flagrante delicto. Now I had to clear myself, and before morning, before Dore talked to Rona and she shared the gossip delicto with all of Hillendale.

Dashing outside to my car, I sped to the Redmont house so fast I beat Dore there. His Thunderbird was not in the driveway, where he usually left it; only Rona's station wagon was in sight. To make sure he hadn't been driving her car that night, I checked the motor to see if it was warm, and to my astonishment nobody popped up to inquire why the rabbi of the Hillendale Temple was going around at one o'clock in the morning feeling radiators.

I returned to my green thing to wait and aggravate. Of all the people to have stumbled into the temple before, it had to be the writer of this song for my fair Sadie's father, Rabbi Doolittle:

> So you founded
> Ev'ry shul in Passaic;
> If you're Judaic,
> Show me.

> Don't say you're religious
> All through and through;
> If you're a Jew,
> Show me.

> "A Jew at heart"—
> That's so bromidic;
> If you're Semitic,
> Show me.

Of social action
Don't be skittish;
If you're Yiddish,
Show me.

Pious don't speak,
Just do, do, do;
If you're He-brew,
Show me.

Don't wait till the Messiah or de Gaulle comes
To show you exactly how;
Show me now!

It was after four, closer to five, when Dore finally drove up. His Thunderbird came roaring down the street, bobbing and weaving as if through heavy traffic, only his was the only moving object in any direction. I ran over as the car stopped on his front lawn.

Dore swore at me with a hundred-proof breath. "Adulterer!"

"Let me explain—"

"From my rabbi I don't want explanations. Explanations is what I hear every day of my life from people doing rotten things. From my rabbi I want inspirations. Now will you get the hell out of here before—" He burst into tears.

There seemed nothing wrong with Dore's crying: it was that kind of night. I felt like crying myself. Only when he stopped crying as suddenly as he had started did I begin to wonder: Why was *he* crying if *I* had committed adultery? And how did he know it was adultery? I'm single, and the woman was gone.

"Dore, listen for two minutes." He said nothing.

That encouraged me to jump into the car beside him. I started talking even before closing the door and didn't stop till I had recounted every detail, omitting only Pete Schuster's name.

Dore said, "You expect me to swallow that?"

I threw up my hands—figuratively. Actually, my heart sank down into my small bowel, where it sat in mourning for me.

"You forget I'm in the business of creating lies, believable lies, and never have I heard a more incredible story. I expected better from a man with six degrees."

"Five, just five," I said, wearily opening the car door.

"Wait." Dore reached over and grabbed my throat. "Your tie!"

He was good and drunk. Here I'm aggravated to death, and he's concerned with my haberdashery! Or was it my garroting he had in mind? I pulled away. It was Friday morning, almost dawn now, and I still had my Shabbas sermons to complete and lady's wear to bury.

Dore jumped out of his car and ran around it to head me off, babbling all the while. Suddenly his words came through: "You're wearing a tie now, just like before, but before there was also a tie on the couch. Nobody wears two ties! Maybe you're telling the truth!"

Saved. By a tie. I should have felt elated, I suppose, thanked Dore for his faith in me, maybe even sat down on the grass right then to write an article for the *Daily News:* "Justice *Does* Triumph!" But I resented having been placed on trial; that made me a loser from the start.

"Swell," I said. "Good night." Yet several loose

threads remained untied. "Dore, what makes you think the woman was married?"

"The dress. It's a chorus costume from *My Fair Sadie*. And since all the women in the chorus are sisterhood members—"

"And why did you go out on a drunk?"

"I didn't go on a drunk. I went to a bar, but the bartender kept asking me with every drink, 'What's the matter, pal? What did your wife do to you?' What could I say? 'It isn't my wife; it's my rabbi. I caught him with another woman.' I mean, it was ridiculous. So I left and drove out to Westport, just me and Jack Daniel's."

"And the tears just now? Why tears?"

Dore's answer didn't come readily. He turned away before speaking. "In my business, Rabbi, there's nobody to trust or respect, not even yourself, *especially* not yourself. And outside of Rona, there's only one other person I've trusted and respected. You, Rabbi."

I felt—I'm not sure what. At five o'clock in the morning it's hard to feel anything.

"Look, I'd better get inside. I called Rona from Westport; she was hysterical. The maid told her I'd gone to pick her up at the temple a few minutes before she'd returned, and the poor thing thought I'd had an accident. I guess I did at that. What a night . . . Well, see you in temple, Rabbi. Rabbi—that's a lovely word, you know that?"

It was five-thirty by the time I got back to my office to tidy up. I put the dress in the storeroom with the other show costumes, hung up the jacket and tie, and went looking for a manila envelope to stuff the brassiere in before taking it away to burn. Then I saw it: on the other side of the couch, an alligator handbag.

It was easy now to identify Pete Schuster's partner,

who had cost me a night's sleep and two sermons. All I had to do was open the bag and look inside.

But was it right? I wasn't sure. For what purpose? I wouldn't drum her out of sisterhood. To preach at her? It was more important for her to condemn herself. To scare her into behaving in the future? Anyway, she'd think I knew her identity; surely it would never occur to her that I *hadn't* looked inside the bag.

So I didn't. Retrieving the bag, I stuffed the bra inside—Dad would have been pleased; it was a Treasure Chest—hoping the woman had reached home safely. The way my luck was running that night, she might have been killed on the way by a pygmy's poisoned dart, and the police could start an investigation which would turn up charred belongings of hers bearing my fingerprints. Automatically I wiped my prints off the bag, wondering whether to rinse out the bra too before I burned it. And then I saw them on the clasp; so big, so golden, they were impossible to miss—initials: RR.

No wonder she had been hysterical when Dore phoned.

RR: Rona Redmont.

ℵ

"Next Saturday Mrs. Rutherford and I leave this church for Chicago's Urban Training Center for Christian Mission, and so I take for my text this morning First Corinthians twelve: four through six: 'Now there are varieties of gifts, but the same Spirit; and there are varieties of service, but the same Lord; and there are varieties of working, but it is the same God who inspires them all in every one.'

"Why am I leaving Hillendale for a different means of service? In brief—because it's impossible to tell

---

St. James Episcopal Church

The County's Most Spectacular Church
Famous for Its Great Architecture

Rev. ALISTAIR F. BIDWELL, D.D., Rector

Sunday: 11 a.m., Holy Communion and Sermon

Preacher: REV. VERNON RUTHERFORD

"Religion in America"

The Friendly Church of Hillendale

---

from people's actions who are the churched and who
the *un*churched; because churches with a hundred
twenty million members exercise so little influence on
domestic affairs, international relations and social
change; because the church becomes something other
than a church when it ceases generating values and
merely sanctifies those of society.

"The tragic fact is that today's typical church, as
segregated by class as it is by race, has restricted
itself to the sidelines of life—to the suburbs, the
familial, the domestic, the private, the sentimental,
the leisured. Ministers, who have trained to offer
witness in the world, spend their days supervising
social activities and catering to egos. For parishioners
want their minister to do everything except change
them, regarding him as the plastic statuette on their
Protestant dashboard, whose purpose is to give people
some sort of identity, soothe their anxiety and never
shake them up.

"Indeed, this is the function of religion in America

today: *to don't.* That accounts for its overwhelming material success: the institutional church is supported precisely because it *is*, for the most part, irrelevant, inoffensive and purposeless.

"Is it any wonder that today more than a third of newly ordained ministers don't enter the parish ministry—they choose instead the public sphere of causes over the private sphere of symptoms—while half of the young people leave our church never to return?

"What is needed today are new ministerial modes for all the structures of society that shape most lives. We need ministers trained in housing, automation, economics, race relations, drug addiction, alcoholism; we need ministers to work out of storefronts and apartments, in industry, business, penal reform; we need ministers to influence banks to grant mortgages and home-improvement loans to slum residents; we want ministers to speak out on the Cold War, Red China, Vietnam, the Middle East.

"God, remember, created the world, not religion.

"What is a church but a way station in time, where people come to be charged with their mission to live for each other and reconcile themselves in God? The church is not the billion dollars spent every year on building new houses of worship to serve as comfort stations for the bored housewife and the tired businessman. Rather, to quote Henrik Kraemer, the church is 'the interfering community'—a launching pad for, in the words of our Rabbi, 'the setting at liberty of those who are oppressed.'

"One thing I know as surely as I know that God lives: a church that lives to itself, preoccupied with survival and self-service, will die by itself—as it so deserves . . ."

FEBRUARY

REMEMBER that god-awful Evans bar mitzvah? Well, the Margolin one, which was celebrated the Shabbas after Vernon's departure, nearly wrecked me altogether.

Sandy is the name of the boy, very withdrawn and scrawny, with the look of an island castaway. In class and at services he strands himself in the farthest seat of the last row, his tentativeness suggesting he might decide any moment to disembody himself entirely—portrait of the loser as a child. It's impossible to engage him in conversation, for his favorite responses are "Uh-uh," "Uh-huh" and "Mmm." Three words are the most I've ever coaxed out of him at one clip, and they were "I don't know," preceded and followed by a shrug, like body-English parentheses.

Several months before his thirteenth birthday, I called Sandy to my office to ask him to check with his parents on a bar-mitzvah date. This time the boy responded: with tears. Yet even they looked unsalted and dehydrated.

"Sandy, what's the matter?"

The boy wiped at his eyes.

"What's bothering you?"

"Nothing."

"Why did you get so upset?"

"I don't know."

"Something to do with your bar mitzvah?"

He shrugged.

"You do want to become bar mitzvah, don't you?"

The boy's eyes opened wide. "All my life," he said.

My lessons with Sandy soon revealed the trouble: he couldn't read the required Hebrew Biblical texts, not a word. Well, maybe a word, but that word he never read the same way twice in succession; the vowels (dots and dashes in Hebrew) were always mispronounced, and any two consonants that resembled a third were mistaken for a fourth. After a month, I told the boy the obvious: "Sandy, you're not trying."

"I am."

"Do you ever study your haftorah and maftir?"

"Every night."

"That's hard to believe."

"But I do."

"I'll have to speak to your parents about—"

The boy started to cry; that he did well.

"Okay, I'll give you another week. But only one."

I asked Sandy's religious-school teacher about him —there was something not quite right—and she said, "But didn't you know? Sandy's blind."

"Blind?"

"Oh, I don't mean totally blind. Legally blind. That's probably the reason he never says a word in class, though he does write nicely. In public school they give him books with extra-large print. Didn't you see those thick glasses he wears?"

Who notices glasses and braces on children any more than minks and wall-to-wall carpeting on their parents? The next day I asked Sandy why he hadn't mentioned his poor eyesight.

"I don't know."

"Here I've been bawling you out for something that isn't your fault. I'm sorry, Sandy. How bad are your eyes?"

He shrugged.

"What exactly do you see—rather, what part of the Hebrew don't you see?"

"The vowels. The *a* looks like the *ah*, and the *ah* looks like the *aw*, and the *aw* looks like the *eh*, and the *ee* and the *o* I can't see at all."

Who would have guessed the boy had so many words in him? Hurray for the Hebrew vowels. Helping him now was easy: I had a photographer blow up the texts to three times their regular size. In one week Sandy was reading his first three haftorah verses correctly.

"Why didn't you tell me about your eyes to begin with?" I asked again, after congratulating him.

"I was afraid."

"Afraid? Of what?"

"My bar mitzvah."

"What about your bar mitzvah?"

"You'd stop it."

"Why would I do that?"

Shrug. "I don't know." Shrug.

Within a month Sandy could read all his Hebrew

selections and chant them nicely. His next assignment was to compose an original speech. (I am a great believer in original talks, ever since my own bar mitzvah, when the rabbi gave me a canned speech to memorize, and bright sonofagun that I was, I memorized it so well that when I recited a phrase in the concluding paragraph: ". . . on this great day of my becoming a man of responsibilities and duties in the eyes of Jewish law . . ."—which phrase appeared in the first sentence of the talk, automatically I started the whole speech all over, while the people out front began whispering—they had never heard a broken bar mitzvah before—and I can still remember my growing terror as that same phrase loomed once more, and unable to recall what came after it, I feared never being able to end the speech, but repeating it again and forever, like the mills at the bottom of Davy Jones's locker that forgot how to stop grinding out salt.)

I was expecting some difficulty, a speech of twenty-five words or shrugs. But Sandy brought in a fine talk based on the rabbinic dictum: "If one destroys a single person, it's as if he had destroyed the entire world; if one saves a single life, it's as if he had saved the entire world." The boy wrote of his desire to become a doctor, which is what his mother wanted him to be (where had I heard that before?) because, he said, a person who is good only to himself is a good-for-nothing. In his conclusion he promised to continue attending religious school after bar mitzvah (alas, ninety percent of Jewish boys don't, while many families quit their synagogues upon returning from the reception) and expressed his filial appreciation in a way that made me wonder whether to revise it:

At this time I'd like to thank my parents for all they've done to me. My father and my mother have been very good and patient, which I appreciate very much. I know I have disappointed them sometimes, but I will attempt with all my might in the future to disappoint them not as much. I want them to be proud of me as a son, person, Jew and American, and I promise to try. When you're number two hundred, you try harder.

The last sentence was an excessive tribute to me, which, unhappily, revealed that Sandy's self-esteem had risen because he felt liked by me, a thought that in the long run would prove harmful. He had exchanged one wrong notion, his being a disappointment because he felt unliked, for another wrong one, his being worthy only because *I* liked him. So I suggested he add to the speech a few paragraphs about the Biblical verse that tells us all men are created in the image of God, and the next session we'd discuss them. "Sandy," I concluded, "I'm proud of you. Your speech is exceptionally good."

"You like it? *Really?*"

"Very much. Some of the English needs to be corrected, but that's usual. Here where you say, 'The temple is a special place, a holy place, a quiet place. Other places are quiet, like the beach in winter with only the sea gulls skipping waves, but temple quiet is *quieter*, quiet enough to hear yourself think and make plans as well as pray'—that's fine. But we'll have to substitute a word in this sentence, 'The words I hear in temple are *wordier*.' Sandy, you have such fine thoughts, how about speaking up more and sharing them with us?"

Shrug.

For his first scheduled rehearsal on the pulpit Sandy called in sick. He missed the second one too; when he didn't show up for the third, I phoned his house. He answered on the first ring, as if he's been sitting beside the phone.

"Oh, is it today?" he said.

When Sandy arrived I took him into the sanctuary and reviewed his cues for reciting a prayer, the blessings over Scriptures, the textual readings and, finally, his speech. I asked the boy to begin. Very pale and thin and clammy-looking, he approached the lectern as if it were a bull, he the bullfighter and the empty seats out front a crowd cheering—but for the animal.

From my pulpit seat behind him I said, "All right, go ahead."

The boy said nothing.

"You can start now."

Not a syllable.

"Sandy?"

Silence.

Annoyed, I stepped up to the lectern, where I glimpsed the boy's now beet-red countenance. Eyes popping, nostrils dilating, cheeks bursting, it looked as if all his features had panicked and were trying to flee.

"*Sandy!*"

His face caving in before a sudden downpour of tears, the boy darted out of the sanctuary.

I raced after him and grabbed him at the front door. "What is it? Tell me."

But he broke away and ran out of the temple.

I dashed to my office and dialed Sandy's home with a shaking finger. That horribly contorted face! Had he suffered a seizure? What was with this boy anyhow?

Mrs. Margolin, answering the call, made me fear that what was wrong was Sandy's genes, for she said, "What are you talking about, Rabbi?"

"The bar mitzvah—"

"Whose bar mitzvah?"

"Sandy's bar mitzvah—"

"Bar mitzvah?"

"That's right, your son's bar mitzvah, twenty-seven days from now."

"There must be some mistake. We're not having any bar mitzvah."

"You do have a son, Sandy? Small, thin, glasses, brown hair, mole on left cheek—"

"Yes, that's my Sandy," Mrs. Margolin said. "But I don't understand. We decided long ago Sandy would not be bar-mitzvahed."

I lectured the mother on the value of bar mitzvah, while every couple of minutes she responded, "I *agree*, Rabbi, I *do*." (She was such an irritating woman.) Finally, when I let her, she elaborated, "Rabbi, we would love Sandy to be bar-mitzvahed; you don't have to convince me. But how can he? Sandy's a terrible stutterer."

"Stutterer? Impossible! He's never stuttered— Oh." That's what had happened. "Well, just once—today."

"He doesn't always stutter, only in front of groups or when he's tired or nervous or ill at ease, which I'm afraid is most of the time. He'd been seeing a psychologist in Chicago before we moved here last June, and—"

"Why did you have him prepared for bar mitzvah if he can't go through with it?"

"*I* never asked you to prepare him. Why, we never even consulted a caterer."

"You gave me the date. No, Sandy did." And I had

automatically started his lessons, as I did with all the other boys entering their teens. "But why is it I never heard him stutter till today?" Then I realized: until now the boy had hardly spoken to me.

Mrs. Margolin replied: "You make him feel comfortable, Rabbi. Sandy's always talking about the long discussions the two of you have together."

The bar mitzvah was out of the question—on the pulpit Sandy didn't stutter; he simply couldn't open his mouth—unless I taped his recitation and played it back at the Sabbath service while he lip-synched it. To make sure—the bar mitzvah clearly was important to him—I called his former psychologist in Chicago, and he said, "I wouldn't want to rule out the bar mitzvah, no. Sandy's never felt himself the equal of other boys. His vision is poor, though that's not the cause of his stuttering. He can't play ball with other boys as a result, he's smaller than the others, he doesn't speak well. Now if a bar mitzvah is *also* denied him, that would be still another blow for a boy who thinks himself without a single accomplishment."

"But if he stutters—"

"Rabbi, doesn't the boy's part in the proceedings consist of singing?"

"To a great degree, yes—chanting."

"Well, then, maybe things can be worked out. Sandy doesn't stutter when he's singing. Many stutterers can sing without difficulty—don't ask me why, there's so little we know about either the cause or cure of stuttering—and Sandy is one of those."

"But, Doctor, boys *without* problems get nervous at their bar mitzvahs. Hell, *I* still get nervous during services. Even if Sandy can sing okay, won't he freeze up when he has to sing in public for the first time?"

"There is a risk of that, yes. Yet either way there's a risk. If the bar mitzvah is canceled, Sandy will be crushed; if it proceeds and he freezes in front of everybody, he'll be humiliated. On the other hand, if he is bar-mitzvahed successfully it will be an enormous boost, money in his emotional bank, so to speak, to draw on when he feels frightened or inadequate."

"What do you advise, Doctor? Should we chance it?"

"It's hard to say. What do *you* think, Rabbi?"

There's nothing like a counselor counseling a counselor: What do you think I should *do*? I don't know; what do *you* think you should do? *I* don't know; what do *you* think?

I called the Margolin family to my office to tell the parents in front of Sandy that he knew his Biblical portions as well as any other bar-mitzvah boy in history, and to tell Sandy in front of them that there was no religious necessity for him to go through with the ceremony.

"I want to be bar-mitzvahed," the boy said.

I related the history of the bar mitzvah—how it began among the Jews of Germany in the fourteenth century to celebrate a boy's assumption of religious responsibility, which he could do then because an intensive study of Bible and Mishnah had familiarized him with the mitzvos, or commandments, that were his obligations to perform—and confessed that since few thirteen-year-olds today underwent a comparably thorough Jewish education and since Jewish life in America was being devastated by today's bar mitzvah, which has become the literal as well as figurative end of most of Jewish education (with the result that most Jews are frozen with a child's-eye view of Juda-

ism, which evaporates as soon as the eighty-two percent of Jewish youngsters enter college), I favored
postponing all bar mitzvahs till eighteen—when adolescent turbulence subsides, his status crystallizes, and
emotionally and intellectually he is ready to study
and appreciate religion on a mature level—or even
twenty; in any event what was important in Sandy's
case, far more meaningful than a ceremony anybody
could undergo with a few months' training, was his
mature decision to continue his religious training.

When I concluded my speech, Sandy said, "I *have*
to be bar-mitzvahed."

Neither Abraham, Isaac nor Jacob had undergone
a bar-mitzvah ceremony, I pointed out, nor Moses,
Isaiah, nor Judah Maccabee.

But Sandy's standards were higher. "Please, Rabbi.
I *got* to."

Mrs. Margolin voted against it, admitting that she
had been told there was some connection between
her pressuring the boy and his stutter, while Mr.
Margolin voted for it because for generations all the
boys in his family had been bar-mitzvahed. Both decided to leave the resolution to me, and all I could
come up with was "I just don't know."

Sandy burst out, "Where's your f-f-f-faith?"

That line was the clincher, for each of us inter-
preted it in his own way: Don't you have faith in
God? (Mr. Margolin.) Don't you have faith in *faith?*
(Mrs. Margolin.) Don't you have faith in *me?* (Me.)

So back into the sanctuary to practice Sandy went,
relinquishing his speech and prayer. Happily, after
many stumbling starts and snags, he sang his portions well enough to get by. If only the boy could do
as nicely at his bar mitzvah, standing defenseless in
front of hundreds of people . . .

Nineteen days before BM-Day, Sandy called me excitedly into the sanctuary. "I've been practicing. Listen." He recited his speech and prayer—haltingly and stammering syllables beginning with *b* and *p*, but he made it to the Amens. Then: "I want to speak too."

"Sandy, let's not press our luck."

"*Please*, Rabbi—"

"It's not a good idea. No."

"I *got* to."

"We'll see."

To help Sandy with the prayer and speech I opposed his delivering, I substituted different words for all those with syllables beginning with a *b* or *p*— "mother and father" for "parents," "synagogue" for "temple," "this day" for "bar mitzvah," "Aunt Jane" for "Uncle Paul"—and eliminated all references to me, since the only substitute for "Rabbi Abel" was "Spiritual Leader Gideon." Moreover, acting on a tip from my cram course on stuttering at the library, I read the speech and prayer in unison with Sandy endlessly.

The rehearsals continued, longer than *My Fair Lady's* or even *My Fair Sadie's*. By now I was spending twenty hours a week with Sandy—from six o'clock, when religious school let out, till the start of meetings or adult education, and most of Sunday. (Devoting a proportionate amount of time to the rest of my congregants would mean a total of eight thousand working hours a week, which wouldn't be at all bad if I were paid by the hour.) Yet that was one reason for my becoming a rabbi: to enter into meaningful I-Thou relationships, and twenty hours a week was as person-to-person as you could get; did Romeo see that much of Juliet before killing himself for her? Still, I was getting awfully tired of sending out every night for hot corned beef sandwiches that were delivered always cold and never lean.

Fifteen days to go now, and all was going almost like the preparations for a normal bar mitzvah, when one evening Sandy, rehearsing for the thousandth time, easy, sputtered to a halt. What now? Another surprise? The boy came up with a new one every month; I expected him any day to surprise me again, maybe change into a bat and fly away.

"I didn't mean to interrupt, Rabbi. I was looking for my hammer." It was the caretaker. Sandy had seen him enter the sanctuary, and that was enough to silence him. What would he do with hundreds of people watching?

We had to start all over—now *I* refused to forgo the prayer and the speech, for his obsession had become mine; if Moses could make a go of it with *his* stutter, why not Sandy?—this time dragooning as a representative audience the caretaker, stray sisterhood members, the soda-machine man, the delivery boy from the delicatessen. After a few days Sandy could speak before all kinds of uninterested strangers, who couldn't wait to escape. But ten days to go till BM-Day, I sneezed—and Sandy froze again.

I conceded for the both of us. "Look, Sandy, we're dropping the prayer and the speech. That's final."

"I want to speak."

"Sandy, it's not worth the risk."

"I *got* to."

"You don't want to be worrying throughout the ceremony about sneezes. Then there are always people coming in late, making noise, talking—"

"All the boys speak."

"Not all. Most bar-mitzvah boys don't speak; they just chant their portions."

"Why do they speak here?"

"Only because I make them."

"Why do you make them?"

"Just chanting is kind of mechanical; the speech is creative, makes them think—I mean—"

So back into rehearsal it was, while I rambled around the sanctuary, sneezing, coughing, hiccuping, rattling candy wrappers, stamping my feet as Sandy spoke. The boy got used to all this—with eight days till BM-Day, but then a fire engine came screaming down the street, and that was the end of the speech.

Two days later I brought in a transistor radio, switching from one rock-'n'-roll station to another with the volume turned way up high. I also broke paper bags, sneaked up on the boy and yelled in his ear, and stepped on his feet. Sandy himself got into the spirit of things by stuffing jelly beans into his mouth as he talked, a candied Demosthenes.

And it was working. Four days till BM-Day, Sandy delivered his speech and prayer perfectly, though it embarrassed me to be caught by Barney Singer throwing Silly Putty at a bar-mitzvah boy while he spoke earnestly about God. The next day, on his own, Sandy restored his deleted references to me, but he never made it to "Abel"; between "Rab" and "bi," sure enough, he got stuck.

I thanked Sandy for his sweet thanks and excised them again. Peace of mind is what I needed, not appreciation.

"I want to say it," he insisted. "You've spent more time with me than anybody else besides my mother, and she spends too much time with me."

But I forbade it absolutely—even when the boy showed me he could say "Rabb-i Abe-el"—out of fear that by now every bone in the camel's back had been splintered by the last thousand last straws.

Two days before BM-Day, Mrs. Margolin called to ask if we were really going ahead with the bar-mitzvah. I said yes, and she said she'd now get busy on the phone, inviting people to the service, which she hadn't yet done in order to make it easier on Sandy if he had to back out. "Sandy will do all right, won't he?" she wanted to know.

"From your mouth," I prayed, "into God's ear."

Came the Shabbas of the bar mitzvah—surely the most unusual in the annals of contemporary Jewish history in the United States, for it was being held without the blessing of either printed invitations or caterer ("Don't you know affairs have to be arranged at least ten months in advance?" Mountain Tiptop had told Mrs. Margolin, when she called them the day before. "You some kind of greenhorn, lady?")—and Sandy came to temple an hour earlier for his last rehearsal. Not that he needed it; I did. The night before, it had come to me in a nightmare that Aaron had been delegated by Moses to do his speaking for him precisely because of his stutter.

As I watched from the last row of the sanctuary, Sandy stepped up to the lectern—angled, like my pulpit chair, to enable me to see his face during the service. Suddenly there was no more reason for apprehension, only panic. The boy had opened his mouth, nothing had come out, and he had vanished behind the lectern. I blinked twice—what had happened *now?* we had rehearsed everything that could possibly occur, omitting only the outbreak of World War Three—then dashed up to the pulpit.

Sandy was lying on the floor unconscious, like a sacrifice.

The first thing that sprang to mind, to be perfectly honest, was not to revive him. Instead, I gave serious consideration to fainting myself. After all these months, after all the effort and hopes and coming so close, the bar mitzvah would have to be canceled. Maybe the show must go on—because producers hate like hell to give refunds—but not a bar mitzvah, not with an unconscious boy.

When Sandy came to, I led him into my office, where I gently told him of the cancellation. There were better things in life to drop dead for than a bar mitzvah.

"I'm all right," the boy said.

"You looked all right—stretched out on the pulpit."

"You *can't* stop my bar mitzvah *now*."

"Sorry, Sandy. My mind is made up."

"I didn't eat any breakfast this morning or supper last night, I was too nervous. That's why I fainted, not because of the bar mitzvah. I didn't stutter up there; you saw: I didn't stutter once. I just fainted, that's all. Because I'm starved."

It sounded logical. I myself felt light-headed from not having slept or eaten since my dream about Aaron.

"Rabbi, have just one hour's more faith," Sandy said.

I gave in for the last time (who would ever be able to unearth that poor camel now from beneath all those straws?), when my inclination was to do what they did to the theater during the Restoration:

hang up a sign outside the temple saying: CLOSED ON ACCOUNT OF THE PLAGUE. Well, at least the kitchen was on our side; its refrigerator yielded us leftover sponge cake, pickled herring, egg salad, tuna-fish croquettes, gherkins and pastry shells. Then all we had to do was sit around and tell each other how all right everything was going to be, just like in *The Song of Bernadette* . . .

Finally the service began, and an odd one it was. Nobody came late, everyone took a seat without greeting anybody, opened his prayerbook and followed the service intently; there was not a single whisper. The unusual deportment unnerved me; it was like leading services in a wax temple. And was it *safe?* Silence was one thing Sandy and I had never rehearsed; could the boy function without noise, sneezes, exploding paper bags, tossed putty?

Finally it came, time for Sandy to stand up, step to the lectern, and debut with his prayer, from which I had also eliminated every syllable beginning with a *b* or *p*. I broke into a cold sweat, to which the gherkins and greasy tuna-fish croquettes contributed nauseousness, as the boy rose from his seat and walked up front. God help him . . .

Sandy opened his mouth. I heard nothing. Yet his lips were moving. Then, like the time lag between hitting yourself on the thumb with a hammer and the coming of the pain, I heard the boy *speaking*. I had been so fearful of silence that silence is what I heard. Beautiful syllables were falling from his lips, joining into beautiful words; the words formed phrases; the phrases became sentences, then paragraphs; the paragraphs added up to a prayer, and Sandy was finished.

The congregation heaved one great sigh along with

me. Relaxing, I wiped my forehead—there was time to tense up again before Sandy's speech—because now he would be singing. The Torah scroll was taken out of the Ark, uncovered, unrolled, blessed, read, and then someone with my voice called out, "*Ya-amod ha-bochur ha-bar mitzvah, Shlomo ben Binya-min;* let the bar-mitzvah young man arise, Sanford the son of Benjamin."

Sandy grabbed the little silver hand from me; clutching it like a dagger, he pointed to his place in the Torah scroll and sang out the blessings. Good! Now for the chanting of the Biblical verses. Again he sang out—*very* good!—and I felt so happy that— What was this?

The silver pointer was no longer moving from right to left over the Hebrew scroll, but up and down as if Sandy were reading a Chinese laundry ticket. He had lost the place—I knew another surprise was due —and between my despair (the boy would freeze-freezefreeze*freeze*) and his frenetic waving (upand-downupanddownandnowcrissandcross) I couldn't find the place for him.

Yet Sandy was still chanting his portion, correctly too. No, he wasn't looking at the scroll at all; he was singing it from memory. Hadn't he rehearsed it more times than his own name?

Crisis 139 over, next came the chanting of the chapter from the Prophets. That too was accomplished well, until something—a dozen of them— went rattattatting on the floor out front. "My pearls!" a woman exclaimed.

The entire congregation turned around and said in unison, "SSHHH!"

Without missing a beat—what were pearl drop-pings, compared to my boxing both his ears during rehearsals?—Sandy continued till the end of the haftorah. Then he sang the final blessings.

All that remained now was the speech. Sandy stood up straight in the pulpit, spread his legs apart for better balance, licked his lips and swallowed a few times to relax his throat muscles, fixed his gaze on a spot I had marked on the back wall to keep him from being distracted by eyes, then began talking, slowly and loudly. We had rehearsed so much that his speech came out mechanical, as if it were being delivered by Ken doll to Barbie, but every word was distinct.

In the congregation, people were clutching their hands or a neighbor's, nodding with nachas whenever he finished another sentence. Mr. Margolin had tears in his eyes, and Mrs. Margolin silently mouthed every word along with her son, and when he got to the part about his parents she pressed a handkerchief to her lips.

Finally, after a journey of only five months, came the last sentence in the talk. Sandy had completed everything—splendidly.

So why wasn't the boy returning to his seat? Why did he remain standing in front of the lectern? Was he *now* going to change into a bat and fly away? Sandy opened his mouth, and out came additional words, familiar ones but unrehearsed: "At this time I want to thank also my very good friend who worked so hard all this time with me so I can speak just like everyone else on this great day—"

For a moment, just for a moment, I was touched. How sweet. What's lovelier than doing a kindness anonymously and then being found out? Then it struck me: how terrible! The one time Sandy had spoken that line—

"I mean, of course, Rab—" Sandy froze, his jaws

locked together as if in a battle to the death, and most likely it was my fault for terrorizing him about the *b*'s and *p*'s. *No no no no no no no!*

I jumped to my feet, and just as quickly—at such a moment who could remember that when turning my chair to face Sandy at the lectern, I had placed it catty-corner to Barney Singer, who always sat on the pulpit with his legs spread out as if he were watching the Army-Navy game on television?—I fell forward on my face.

Not a sound from the congregation at first; everybody was probably busy poking a neighbor, asking, "Am I seeing things, Gertrude, or did the rabbi just topple off his chair dead drunk?" All answers must have been affirmative, for six seconds later—it was really too much to expect people *not* to—they burst out laughing.

Poor Sandy! Unaware of what had happened—of what I, his very good friend, had done to him on this great day in his life—he was sure to think the congregation was laughing at him. Could all those months of practice end like this?

Reaching up from the floor, I grabbed the boy's right leg.

Startled, Sandy turned and looked down, seeing me sprawled there like a bum in the gutter. "*—bi Abel!*" he exclaimed.

Shlomo, the son of Binyamin, had completed his speech and bar-mitzvah rites, hallelujah.

א

——Hi, Dore. How are you?
——*Fine, Rabbi. Gee, I feel awful.*
——What's the matter?

——*I mean, about the mix-up. Here I invite you to the house for dinner, and at the last minute Rona remembers this long-standing date with her sister.*

——That's all right, Dore. We'll make it another time.

——*You must get awfully tired of eating here at the Posh Nosh.*

——Not me. My childhood dream was to marry a delicatessen owner's daughter.

——*That makes me luckier than you. Because my dream came true.*

——What was it?

——*To get filthy rich. If it hadn't come true, I'd have chased that dream all my life without realizing how empty it was.*

——You may be right, Dore. When I was dreaming of becoming a rabbi—

——*Yes?*

——Well, it hasn't turned out as expected. My being here doesn't seem to make that much of a difference to the congregation. If I disappeared down an open manhole, probably nobody would notice—not till their son's bar mitzvah or their own funeral.

——*You just happen to be all wet, Rabbi. You've accomplished so much here. Take the religious school. Sandy Margolin and the rest of the kids —they love you. And since most people join synagogues for the sake of their children—*

——It's funny: my father's generation worships God with the hearts of their parents, and this generation worships Him with the hearts of their children.

——*Rabbi, in my business when even ten percent*

of the audience responds, that's a fantastic suc-
cess. And you've had dozens of successes here.
——I have?
——*Count me one of them. I don't know where
I'd be today without you, Rabbi.*
——Your involvement in adult education and social
action—they *have* pleased me, Dore, very much.
If only more members followed your lead—
——*I was referring to something else, Rabbi. Like—
well, what I just told you about Rona's forgotten
date with her sister—it wasn't true.*
——It wasn't?
——*No. You see, Rona still can't face you, not yet—*
——Dore! You know?
——*Ever since that night. Rona saw us together out
front and assumed you'd told me everything. So
as soon as I set foot inside the house—*
——But I didn't know till an hour afterwards that it
was Rona. Not till I found her handbag.
——*I see. But if you had known before, Rabbi,
would you have told me?*
——Well, no. What good would it have done,
Dore? I was hoping that her shock and guilt . . .
I was hoping that would help the both of you.
——*It did, Rabbi. But you know what helped most
of all?*
——What?
——*You. Your attitude—it never changed toward
Rona. From the way you treated her after that
night, nobody could have guessed that she'd—
Anyway, that's why I took her back finally. You
set me the example. We're going to make it too,
Rona and I.*
——I'm glad, Dore. You have no idea how glad—
——*So I don't want you getting discouraged. From*

*where I sit, you're the greatest rabbi in the whole
world.*

——Are you including Brooklyn and the Bronx too?

——*There are only a few areas that could stand
some improvement.*

——Oh?

——*Like maybe it wasn't such a good idea to spring
that sixth-grade exam in Jewish beliefs and practices on the board; they resented it, especially the
seven trustees who flunked. Why couldn't you at
least have marked on a* curve? *And proposing
a new dues system based on ability to pay in
order to eliminate fund-raising—don't you know
the only thing two Jews will ever agree on is
how much a third Jew should give to the temple?
And then—*

——What happened, Dore? From one swell rabbi,
all of a sudden I've become Public Enemy Number One.

——*See what a good educator you are? Always a
word of justifiable praise before offering criticism,
didn't you teach us that? Mind you, Rabbi, these
aren't my own criticisms. But some members have
made them, and you should take note—*

——Meaning?

——*Look, June is only a few months away. Why
don't you lay low till then? Forget about Vietnam,
for one thing—*

——Lay low? You *do* think I'm Public Enemy
Number One.

——*I only want your convictions to take a vacation, that's all. They could use the rest. You're
always giving them such workouts.*

——Oh . . . because the congregation will be voting on that four-year contract for me.

——*Rabbi, this has nothing to do with any four-year contract.*

——It doesn't?

——*No.*

——Then why do you want to muzzle me? You, my best student and social activist.

——*Rabbi, some vital things we have to take on faith. Isn't that another wise thing you taught us?*

א

SPRING

AFTER Mrs. Greenwood's wedding I *had* to see Gina again. Didn't we meet cute enough, after all, to warm the typewriter of any Hollywood screen writer? You remember: if Rock Hudson goes shopping for pajama bottoms, Kim Novak is sure to be there trying to buy only pajama tops; or they bump into each other during an electrical blackout in New York; he thinks she's a boy, and she mistakes him for a girl, so they decide to room together at the Y.

But Gina didn't share my feeling of inevitability. The first few times I tried to date her for my one free evening of the week, she was busy, then at Grossinger's or the Concord, and finally—it was almost Passover now, the time for reading Song of Songs, and there's nothing more depressing than to read that exquisite book to a synagogue full of people or to yourself alone—she hemmed and hawed.

"What's the matter? Don't you want to go out with me?"

"Well, you being a rabbi, it would be sort of like dating God—"

That accounted for the girl's reluctance: I awed her. How *about* me?

She continued, alas: "—since I'm not sure I believe in God—I mean, you think a Christian Scientist would date a doctor?"

"If they're both Jewish, why not?"

The girl laughed, and agreed to see me.

Gina's mother, a stocky grandmotherly woman who looked a lot like Sydney Greenstreet just before he discovered the Maltese Falcon in his hand was a fake, beamed when her daughter introduced me. "It's a honor to meet you, a real honor," Mrs. Sitomer said. "Now how do you like your rice pudding? With raisins or without?" The entire Marine Corps couldn't have stopped her from sitting me down at the kitchen table for a snack even though I was taking Gina out to dinner that evening. "Eugenela likes without; she's modern. Barnard girl, you know. Scholarship. Some head on her shoulders. And isn't she beautiful?"

"*Eugenela?*"

Gina made a face. "My legal name is Eugenie, after Eugene V. Debs. Mama was one of the early organizers of the I.L.G.W.U. Lucky she was a socialist and not an anarchist, else I'd have ended up Vanzettila."

Mrs. Sitomer served me a salad bowl full of rice pudding. "On the right is without; on the left, with. I figure you should taste both—even people who ain't crazy for raisins like my with; it's my mother's recipe from Russia, and she was some cook—so next time you should be able to make a intelligent choice."

It was no use, long experience with my own mother told me, to point out it would take all the Children of Israel who had participated in the exodus from Egypt to consume so much rice pudding in one sitting. I dug in. "Delicious."

"How can it be delicious without nothing?" Mrs. Sitomer said, and emptied a pitcher of cream into my bowl. "Now you'll taste what good is." But before I could, she pulled up the left sleeve of her dress. "You know skin?"

"Skin?"

"Here, give a look." She showed me red scales encrusting her arm. "You see? Splotches."

"Mama! He's eating."

"He's used to it, Eugenela." To me: "And on my back too, splotches. Itches something awful. If my back was my nose, I'd never sleep; the whole day I'd be sneezing."

"That's a shame," I said.

"You're a very sympathetic person for a professional, you know that? That's real nice. Well, what do you think?"

"I'm sorry, but I'm ignorant about skin."

Mrs. Sitomer patted me on the shoulder. "At least you admit it. You have any idea how many doctors I went to didn't know skin but never told me? Big men too. All they did was take twenty-five dollars—that's how big they were; twenty-five dollars used to be my month's salary in the shop—but when it came to curing my condition, there was nobody home. You ever hear such a thing? If somebody brought me a dress to make and I didn't know how, would I have the nerve to charge twenty-five dollars for making it? So where can I go for my splotches? You know?"

"No, not offhand. I don't get to see many splotches—"

"What do you specialize in?"

I smiled. "That's a good question, Mrs. Sitomer. I wish I did have a specialty, but the way things are today I'm supposed to be a jake-of-all-trades."

"Oh, a general practitioner," she said, and I chuckled. "Well, you're nice not to charge me twenty-five dollars for hocking you such a chainik. What am I talking about? House calls are double the price, and doctors don't even make them. But eat, eat, finish the pudding. I got a nice piece knubble carp I want you should try."

Sitting down to dinner afterwards, while still picking raisins out of my teeth, I finally caught on. Gina had introduced me as Dr. Abel, and Mrs. Sitomer had taken me for a physician. Why, I asked, hadn't she corrected her mother's mistake?

"Well," Gina said, "I want Mama to get to know you first as a human being."

"A human being? In contrast to what?"

"I mean, before telling her you're a rabbi. You see, Mama doesn't go for religion; she calls it the television of the masses. Synagogues to her are settlement houses for the rich, and rabbis overpriced camp counselors for adults . . ."

To accommodate Gina on subsequent dates, I acted like a human being, at least when picking her up at her mother's Brighton Beach apartment. And graciously she returned the accommodation by taking an interest in Judaism after I called her my fair shiksa.

"The first thing you can teach me is," she said, "what exactly is a shiksa?"

The week before *My Fair Sadie's* opening—did I forget to mention that I had taken over the show during its final throes of rehearsals, when it fell apart, raising the specter of having to refund five thousand dollars' worth of tickets?—I spoke to Gina about Milton Steinberg's *Basic Judaism*. And never did I enjoy adult education more, perhaps because never before had I delivered a lecture while holding hands with a beautiful greenish-blue-eyed adult.

"Since you're so intelligent, so eager to learn," I sighed after kissing the girl good night, "soon as you finish reading the Steinberg book, we'll go right into the Song of Songs."

On Tuesday evening I went to take Gina to *My Fair Sadie's* opening. About to knock on her door, which was partly ajar, I heard voices inside raised in dispute, and hesitated.

"Eugenela, I don't trust that Dr. Abel one bit. Tonight I'm going to ask him some questions."

"Questions?"

"A mother has a right to question fishy men taking out their daughters."

"What's fishy about Gideon?"

"It isn't fishy I know more medicine than him?"

"Oh, that. Just because Gideon doesn't like to talk shop—"

"You know why he doesn't like to talk shop? Because he doesn't know shop. Listen, Eugenela, I was telling him about Bertha Goldstein, how much aggravation ileitis is giving her, and her with two small children to take care of. And your Dr. Abel says Bertha Goldstein and her husband should go talk things over with their rabbi, maybe *he* can straighten out their marriage."

"So he misunderstood—"

"Misunderstood? Know something, Eugenela? Your Dr. Abel—I don't think he's a *dentist.* Know something else? He's a goy. Even Mrs. Silverberg remarked, who should know because her cousin's daughter married one. Platinum-blond hair like that shiksa Harlow, skinny and undernourished, no nose, and the same name as that Russian colonel spy, who was no Jew, thank God. Who ever heard a Jewish boy should be named Gideon? And what Jew talks about religion all the time? Your other dates, nice Jewish boys, never do. And over my dead body will I let you marry a goy, you hear me? What are you laughing about! You think it's so funny, running around with a fake-doctor goy?"

I knocked on the door.

Gina opened it at once. "Oh, hello, Gideon." She pointed to the pail in her hand. "Garbage."

"Dr. Abel," Mrs. Sitomer said, "we were just talking about you."

Gina said, "I'll be right back." She darted into the hall toward the incinerator as I entered.

Mrs. Sitomer scrutinized me like trustees interviewing rabbinical candidates. "Hmmm."

"Well, Mrs. Sitomer, how was shul this Shabbas?"

She regarded me suspiciously. "What kind question is that?"

"Nothing special. I just wanted to say something—Jewish."

"*Du redst a gazinta Yiddish?*"

"Pardon?"

"I asked if you spoke *Mamaluschen.*"

"Yiddish? No, I'm afraid not."

She nodded. "Figures."

"But I'm fluent in Hebrew, the language of the Bible."

"Uh-huh."

"*V'ahavto l'rayacho komocho*. That's Hebrew. For 'Love thy neighbor as thyself.'"

"Smart fella. You know Hebrew is Greek to me."

"By the way, how is Mrs. Goldstein? Is her oleitis any better? It must be very difficult to take care of her family when she's so sick with oleitis."

"It's ileitis," Mrs. Sitomer said, "Doctor."

"Oh, is it? Well, that's wonderful. I mean, *i*leitis is less serious than *o*leitis."

Gina returned. "Did I miss something?" she asked brightly.

Mrs. Sitomer looked grim. "Not yet."

I said, "Why are you so concerned about my being Jewish?" Both women were startled. "Well, I overheard you."

"Because, Mr. Eavesdropper," Mrs. Sitomer said, "no girl marries somebody she don't date."

"Mama! Who ever said anything about marriage?"

"Figures. Marriage he's not interested in, only skin and girls."

"I am, Mrs. Sitomer. But why are you so insistent on Gina marrying within the faith?"

"Aha! Then you *aren't*. A Jew wouldn't *ask* such a question."

"A Jew should be able to give an answer, Mrs. Sitomer."

"Foolish question."

"Why is it foolish?"

"If you were a Jew, you'd know why."

"Mrs. Sitomer, when's the last time you attended a synagogue?"

"What's that got to do with anything?"

"When, Mrs. Sitomer?"

"Synagogues are for old people with nothing else to do and suburban all-rightniks."

"What Jewish practices do you observe? Which holidays? Do you read the Bible or other Jewish books?"

"Who's asking questions here—you or me? *My* intentions are honorable."

"I want to see how you differ from a non-Jew. Is it blood that makes you different?"

"No, not blood, but you're warm. Soul. There's a Jewish soul born out of the Jewish experience. But you wouldn't know about that."

"You mean, Jewish souls are holier than Brand X's?"

"I'll say one thing for you: you have chutzpah! But you wouldn't know about that either."

"Chutzpah is what a man has who murders his parents, then requests mercy from the court because he's an orphan."

"You know, because Reston in the *Times* wrote that in his column once."

"And James Reston isn't Jewish."

"Who says Reston isn't Jewish? A man with a soul like that! Don't you read his columns?"

"Okay, if Reston *weren't* Jewish, would you let your daughter marry him?"

"He's already married."

"But if he weren't married, and if he weren't Jewish—"

"If! *Ven mein buba zul huben beitzim, volt zee gevain mein zayda!*"

"What does that mean?"

"Never mind. In English it comes out—not clean."

"You know, Mrs. Sitomer, you still haven't made clear to me—"

"There, *that's* why I want my Eugenela should marry Jewish. A Jew has respect for parents, honors gray hair. Not like you, bullying me like a Cossack."

Gina intervened, laughing. "Mama, it's time to tell you the truth. You're absolutely right; Gideon isn't a doctor."

"Aha!"

"Mrs. Sitomer, I'm a rabbi."

"A what?"

"Mama, I didn't say so to begin with, because you're just as prejudiced against rabbis as you are against gentiles. How one person can be both anti-gentile and anti-rabbi at the same time I don't know, but—"

"A rabbi? I don't believe it! What kind rabbi looks like a goy?"

"It's true. As a matter of fact, Gideon is taking me to his temple tonight for the first time."

"Wait a minute, wait just a minute! He's taking you to his temple?"

"That's right, Mrs. Sitomer."

"On Tuesday night? You wait right here, I'm calling the police."

"Mama!"

"There's no services in any temple this late on Tuesday night."

"Mrs. Sitomer, it's not a service I'm taking Gina to. It's—it's—well—"

"Yes? Yes? Why are you taking my only daughter to a synagogue if not for services?"

"Mama, Gideon's taking me there to see a show he directed."

"So! A rabbi is taking a beautiful girl to a empty shul on a dark night to see a show that *he* directed. Did he also promise you a part in it? Modern girls today, they all think they're smarter than their own mothers. *Where's the phone?*"

How does one prove he's Jewish, let alone a rabbi? I took off my jacket and rolled up my left sleeve to search my biceps for tefillin imprints to show Mrs. Sitomer. Only then, after examining the rest of my arm for needle marks, would she grant me custody of her daughter.

Gina, who hadn't yet learned about phylacteries, regarded me with suspicion on our way to Hillendale when I explained they were scrolls of Biblical verses encased in small boxes, which observant Jews fastened to their heads and their left arms, every weekday morning before prayer, by means of long, thin strips of leather, as reminders to love God with all one's heart and mind. "Long, thin strips of leather? Like whips?" she asked, and I regretted having told her my nickname for the show, *My Fair de Sade* (because the three solid weeks I had given to it pained me).

Barney Singer welcomed us in a state of euphoria: "Isn't it marvelous to see the temple packed? Biggest crowd we've had here since the Yom Kippur Night Ball. Isn't it *marvelous!*"

Suddenly I felt depressed.

Sandy Margolin came running over. In addition to having grown and gained weight since his bar mitzvah, he now started conversations. "I've changed my mind about being a doctor," he said.

"How come?"

"I'm going to be a rabbi."

"Great!" I punched him in the arm. "I'll save all my sermons to sell you at half-price."

Sandy laughed, something he had also learned to do since his bar mitzvah.

I was buttonholed by Ellie Prinz, a tough cookie of a congregant, who was high on my Love Thy Neighbor Nevertheless list. "You must talk to my son," she told me. "He wants to go off to Israel for a year."

"Wonderful!"

Ellie Prinz gave me a look that would have killed anyone who hadn't been vaccinated by dozens of dirty ones. "I want you to talk him *out* of going."

Rick Adler, attired in a carnationed tuxedo, announced that the show was starting, and Gina and I took our seats on the aisle as the lights dimmed. Immediately she began squirming, pulling at the skirt of her blue-sequined green angora sweater dress, whose colors matched those glorious eyes, and yanking up its turtle neck.

"What's the matter?"

"The way my neighbor's eyeing me," she whispered, "something of mine is either too high or too low."

Leaning over, I introduced Gina to Maurine Levenson, beside her, as the curtain arose on Sadie Doolittle selling knishes in Williamsburg and crying, "Aaaooowww *vey!*" when somebody accidentally knocks them out of her hand . . .

. . . Two hours later, the curtain fell after Hymie Higgins' singing of the show's biggest hit, which was, deservedly, Eve Greenwood's parody:

I'm joining a shul in the morning.
Dunning me, the building fund'll begin.
My head starts to ache!
Such sacrifices I make!
But I'm doing it for my kin.

For my son's getting bar-mitzvahed in a few years.
And my in-laws vowed to pay the tab.
Pull out all the stops
For dear old grandpops!
We'll throw a reception that's fab.

Rabbi Abel says we can't duck
Confirmation;
But with a little bit of luck,
Before then he'll go to another shul in the nation!

I'm joining a shul in the morning.
Duplicate bridge I will now have to play,
Support its bazaars
And raffles for cars.
For God's sake I'm joining the temple today!

The audience gave the cast an ovation, which they had earned if only for their seven months of preparation that neither snow, rain nor adult education had kept them from. Suddenly the cast began to applaud the audience, as Russian troupes do—only, it turned out they weren't applauding the audience, but their director. Hands pulled me out of my seat and up on the stage, where I received a standing ovation. For the first time that year I had done something that all five hundred of my bosses approved.

The crowd quieted down, expecting a speech, but all I could say was "Thank you." Then I hurried back to Gina, grabbed her by the arm and propelled her out of the temple, disengaging myself from those who besieged me with offers to direct their organizations' *Goys and Dills, The Manomanischewitz from La Mama,* and the like.

Inside my car, Gina remarked, "Your congregation is certainly fond of you."

"Yes, they consider me the Gower Champion of the rabbinate." I said no more till we reached a diner, where I apologized for my long silence.

She smiled. "That's all right. My father used to say, a person who doesn't understand another's silences won't understand his words either. Me, I don't listen to words so much as to pauses and inflections. For example, Sandy isn't so much interested in the rabbinate as he is in adopting you to be his spiritual father—and you accepted him. Another for instance— one woman's voice told me her feelings for you are more than congregantly."

"Only one?" I smiled in disbelief. "If you're so smart, tell me, why couldn't I respond to the applause before?"

Gina sighed. "For the same reason I don't enjoy hearing I have eyes like stained-glass windows."

She was such a joy, this Gina, so perceptive, warm and bright. But I didn't fall in love with her till after picking up a morning paper at the cashier's stand. Next to the *Times*, I couldn't help seeing a tabloid's front-page photograph of a girl, about twenty years old, lying in the street—was she asleep?—while an older woman crouched over her. No, the girl couldn't have been sleeping, for grief contorted the woman's face; alas, the caption reported that the girl had jumped out of her apartment window to her death when the mother failed to restrain her. Horrible!

Halfway back to Brighton Beach, for no apparent reason, Gina suddenly began to cry. Startled, I pulled my car to the curb, asking what had happened. Unable to control her sobs, she couldn't speak coherently; all I heard was something about disgusting human beings. Finally, quieting down, she told me she too had seen the front page.

"Horrible tragedy," I said with a shudder.

"That horrible photographer! Can you imagine anyone taking that picture? Focusing his camera to get in every gory detail, walking around those poor people to snap them from the best angle, all the while the mother's crying her heart out—but how could any *normal* person snap such a picture to sell to newspapers? And what normal people would want to *look* at it!" Again she burst into tears.

No, this was more like a Russian movie: the girl's sensibility is what attracted me. Sliding my arm around Gina, I pulled her toward me.

"*No!* Don't—"

I pressed forward.

"No, don't *move!*" I hesitated, and she explained, shamefacedly, "My contact lenses—I've cried them out of my eyes."

We spent an hour searching for the lenses, which were so tiny they might have been clinging to any of Gina's long hairs or those of her form-fitting angora sweater, so each had to be examined, delicately, one by one. And by the time we found the lenses—in the hollow of her warm, pulsating throat—Gina's face was dry to my lips, and I no longer cared that her unique stained-glass eyes were falsies.

ℵ

Dear Vernon,

That makes us even: I miss you and Iris and the kids too. Worse yet, next Christmas where can I put to good use all my tree-trimming experience?

Your Mission's recent "exercise" sounds kind of C.I.A.-ish—sending you to spend a week in a Chicago slum with seven dollars and no identification "to teach you about the down-and-outers and survival." Yet if that was the idea, why not have you live like that for a week in suburbia? It's far easier to learn to eat your heart out when everybody around you is eating high off the hog.

You may have started a trend hereabouts, did you know that? One of the priests at Saint Mary's up and quit too; only in his case he quit the Catholic Church as well. Some of his reasons, as reported in the press: "The Church has become an impersonal, dehumanized corporation which no longer embodies the living reality of Christian presence. . . . it's an outmoded pseudo-political structure more concerned with authority and procedures than with truth and people . . ." *Everybody*, to quote the sage James Durante, is trying to get into the act of religion! Hallelujah.

Me, I've been having some second thoughts myself. Seems what I'm doing in Hillendale is symbolizing ethnic togetherness, like a Jewish Queen Elizabeth. A master of religious ceremonies for specific occasions is what I am, the living sign that God's in His heaven—and He'd damn well better stay there. All's right so long as I sanctify, glorify and magnify, but when I specify—! God knows it isn't easy being a prophet on a payroll.

I've considered leaving the temple for work in some charity. But I'm no organization man; I still prefer people. I also thought of following my grandfather's example and going off to Israel, until I realized it's impossible for me to live there as a rabbi. The Orthodox monopoly of Israel recognizes neither

Conservative nor Reform rabbis; we are to the Israeli rabbinate what Red China is to the United States: not there. So here I stand; I can do no other.

We pause now for a happy announcement: I got me a girl! (Please ask Iris to forgive me; she'll understand.) Can't describe her in less than a dozen pages, and since I still have two sermons to complete—

Write! Soon! Sooner than that!

My love to the mishpochah,
Gideon

א

APRIL

S AM Warren was bemoaning to the ways-and-
means committee his failure to stimulate be-
quests—"Nobody's put the temple in their wills yet,
and all those members who fly so much won't even
name us the beneficiary in their flight-insurance pol-
icies"—when Charlie Hecht summoned me to the
phone. It was dead, however, when I got there. Who
had called?

Charlie didn't know. "She wouldn't say. She just
asked for you; even that was hard to catch because it
sounded like she was crying."

For thirty minutes I waited near the phone, but the
woman never called back. The only other call that
evening was for Jerry Greenwood, and it didn't upset
him, though he did leave the meeting at once.

Subsequently Barney Singer gave pointers on his

specialty, taxes. "The thing to stress always is the business advantage of contributing to the temple. Show people how to be religious and business-wise at the same time. Because you can deduct the full value of religious donations, regardless of their appreciation. For example, you own a stock which cost you five hundred dollars, say, and now is worth a thousand; if you sell the stock and donate the thousand dollars to the temple, that money is deductible, but you must still pay a capital-gains tax on your five hundred dollars' profit. But—now listen carefully—if you donate the *stock* to the temple, you still deduct the thousand dollars, but you avoid the capital gains entirely. See the business advantage?"

Strange! Dad never called Treasure Chest a business (to him it had always been something of a religion); yet to my president, as he was constantly reminding everyone, this house of God is a business. And while Treasure Chest's officers dwell on the product, new trends in bras and the latest theories about breasts, the trustees had spent four nights in a row with the closest thing to God my partner's imprecation when I had reneged at bridge at a men's club meeting.

"Or let's say you're a manufacturer. Well, when you contribute merchandise to our bazaar, you can deduct its retail price, which means you profit a third or more right there. And if instead of donating, say, ten thousand dollars in cash, your corporation gives us ten thousand dollars' worth of merchandise (whose real cost to you is only five thousand dollars, remember), then your contribution costs you nothing at all, because you're giving our plant the five thousand dollars you'd have had to pay in corporation taxes anyway."

Damn! Well, how would *you* feel, spending five years in divinity school only to wind up junior administrator of the Hillendale Plant? You suppose a graduate of the Harvard Business School, like Barney Singer, for example, would relish landing a job where everyone talked constantly about death, never taxes?

"Any questions?"

There were dozens, all from people impressed with his tax expertise, who asked about personal-income-tax loopholes, and by the time he answered them all—it would be unfair to refrain, because he had become president to serve people, Barney Singer said, distributing his business cards—it was midnight, and the meeting was adjourned till the following week.

Early the next morning I was awakened by a phone call from Eve Greenwood.

"How's the daughter-in-law of the bride? Where are they now—?"

"Rabbi, I have some news to tell you—"

"What—?"

"Bad news. Jerry's mother—she—she—"

"*Eve*—"

"—died last night in—"

She kept talking, but I heard nothing. Mrs. Greenwood—Mrs. Palmer—dead? God in heaven! "Then it was *you* on the phone last night."

"Yes, Rabbi. Mr. Palmer had just called and I didn't know who to turn to, what to do. So I phoned you, before realizing it would be better for me to tell Jerry myself. So I hung up—"

"I'll be right over."

"Oh, would you? I'd be so grateful."

My eyes burning with unshed tears, I sped to the Greenwood house. Perhaps if I hadn't introduced Mrs.

Greenwood to Mr. Palmer, perhaps if they had never married, perhaps if they hadn't taken that trip around the world—

"It's so good of you to come," Eve kept saying, mistakenly assuming *I* was there to comfort *her*.

"What happened?"

"I told you on the phone. A stroke. All of a sudden."

"Jerry—how's he taking it? Where is he?"

"You didn't hear me before? I drove him to the airport last night. He didn't have to go to London—Mr. Palmer was bringing her back—but you know how close they are—were." Eve wiped her red eyes. "I loved her, I really did, like my own mother."

She served coffee, and we sat without touching it as we reminisced about Mrs. Greenwood Palmer. Thank God Eve never said the stroke had been God's will; I couldn't bear that thought. Surely it's more religious to believe in a limited good God than in an omnipotent Heartbreaker.

"Jerry will be back tonight with the—" I steeled myself, but Eve never completed the sentence. "The funeral will be tomorrow, I suppose."

Returning to my office, I reread all of Mrs. Greenwood Palmer's post cards, the Book of Psalms and the thirty-first chapter of Proverbs, before starting on the eulogy for what would be my most trying task as a rabbi; never before had I officiated at the funeral of somebody close to me. By the time I finished writing —about the lovely woman who was born in a Russian shtetl, came to America as a child, grew up on New York's Lower East Side, left high school as a teenager to work and bring money into the house, married early, helped put her husband through law school, raised a family—I had twenty pages of notes which would have to be cut to four. Then I called Gina and broke the terrible news to her.

In the evening Mr. Palmer came to my office directly from the airport. He talked for two hours about his late wife, punctuating every few minutes with "Don't forget to say *that* at the funeral." Wiping his eyes, he said, "I didn't love her when we got married, you know that, Gideon. But I did by the time we got to Athens. Such a *remarkable* woman! To her everything in the world became *we*. It wasn't 'I Ruth' and 'you Ben'; from the start it was 'we.' In Israel it was 'Isn't it beautiful what we Jews have accomplished in our tiny country?' Even in Greece, it was 'we Athenians.' Because, she told me, Western civilization is the child of Jerusalem and Athens. Who knows from civilization, and who cares? But I loved how she incorporated everything around her. Gideon, say *that* at the funeral." His voice cracked. "And now I'm only an I all over again." Suddenly he burst out, "It wasn't *my* fault Ruth died. The doctor said it was an accident—a cardiovascular accident, he called it. Couldn't be helped; it would have happened in Hillendale too. Please say *that* at the funeral."

"I know, Mr. Palmer. Dr. Lipton told me the same thing." I had called him that morning to relieve my own feelings of guilt. "Nobody's blaming you."

"Jerry is. In London and all the way back on the plane he never said one word to me. Would you talk to him, Gideon, report what the doctor said? And tell him I loved his mother. She was so remarkable."

The Greenwoods weren't home when I called that evening; a neighbor directed me to the funeral chapel, which was packed with visitors (even though Jewish law forbids condolence calls prior to the funeral, while mourners are still in a state of shock, ill equipped to receive them) and the chatting—about golf, bridge, vacations, children's summer camps—gave the mortuary the sedately festive air of a cocktail party whose first guests had not yet gotten stoned. And then, chilled, I saw her: up front inside an elaborate bronze coffin atop a flower-bedecked dais, Mrs. Greenwood Palmer lay exhibited beneath a pink spotlight.

A man emerged from behind a rubber tree to greet me. "Rabbi, glad to see you." It was Goldwyn, the undertaker, who for business reasons belonged to ten times as many synagogues as Maimonides had. "Your eulogy at the Grossberg funeral was a real highlight, I want you to know. And everybody there thought you look exactly like Harry Belafonte, isn't that something?"

I asked where Jerry Greenwood was.

Goldwyn lowered his voice. "You're not going to start anything now, are you, Rabbi? About closing the casket, I mean."

This was not the time, I said, but he knew Jewish law required that the dead be treated with dignity, not displayed in coffins like store-window mannequins.

Goldwyn frowned. "It's a casket, not a coffin. And if we close it up, how can anyone see how beautiful it is inside and all the workmanship?"

According to Jewish law, I said, people were to be buried in plain pinewood boxes.

"My God, you're talking communism! A wooden crate for a beloved mother? It violates the Seventh Commandment. Besides which, Greenwood drives around in a Cadillac, and you want his only mother buried in a Volkswagen?" He proceeded to explain that the United States was a democracy, where money meant nothing when a loved one passed on, because far more important was showing respect in the proper fashion, thereby discharging guilt—

Excusing myself, I sought out Jerry Greenwood. He was sitting in a corner of the room, sunken-eyed and gray-faced, barely responding to condolences.

"Jerry? Let's go someplace quiet to talk." (I should have said something about being sorry, but could sorry cover the loss of his mother?)

I led him into the clergyman's room off the main chapel, where he turned to face me. "What do you want?"

"If there's something special you want said tomorrow—"

"Tomorrow?"

"At the funeral."

"What about it?"

"The eulogy for your mother. I talked with Eve and Mr. Palmer, but you, as her son, being so close to her—is there anything you'd like me to say tomorrow?"

"*You?* You're not burying *my* mother."

"What—?"

"I've asked Rabbi Jacobson to officiate."

※

London

Dear Rabbi,

We think you're in the wrong profession—you should have been a matchmaker. You're better at it than Hello, Dolly! Yes, we're very happy, thank you. (In marriage, I suspect, Like triumphs far more often than Love.)

Our best regards to Gina, that lovely girl. And when are we going to dance at *your* wedding already?

See you next week—

Loads of love,
Ruth and Ben Palmer

א

MAY

THE first time I saw Caleb was at the church-and-synagogue sing, which featured the choirs of all Hillendale's houses of God—this was three moons *after* Brotherhood Month; now I ask you, isn't that progress? Happily too, not only were the hymns beautifully rendered and the public-school auditorium crowded, but here a dozen houses of worship had assembled with nobody's congratulating himself or the others once during the evening on having apprehended the most elusive of -hoods, brotherhood. It was almost enough to convince you of that other -hood, God's Father-.

After the musical program, Dr. Bidwell, chairman of the evening, invited questions from the audience about the various faiths, their practices and beliefs.

238

The queries were all polite, even the one inquiring how the three branches of Judaism differed. Rabbi Jacobson, answering, was also polite: "The difference between Orthodoxy and the other two is like the difference between day and night," he said, but that was all.

When a lithe young Negro up front stood to ask the next question, Reverend Hobbes, who was sitting beside me (he's the one who finally took those Thanksgiving turkeys off my conscience), exclaimed softly, "No."

The youth spoke up in a throbbing bass, so loud he seemed to be wired for stereo. "What kind of *farce* is this? So many churchmen haven't gathered under one roof since the Council of Trent, and what do you do? You sing. While my people are dying!"

Dr. Bidwell reddened. "Young man, if you don't have a question—"

"Oh, I got a question, baby, a million of 'em," he retorted, and Reverend Hobbes winced. "*Why* did the churches convert the slaves to keep them subservient? *Why* did the churches focus Negro attention on the afterlife to keep us docile? *Why* did the churches start segregation in this country? *Why* did the Southern churches unanimously endorse the Civil War? *Why* are the churches today still shot through with racism? *Why* have the churches always sinned against my people?"

Reverend Hobbes clasped and unclasped his hands as Dr. Bidwell replied sharply, "But the churches *have* supported freedom rides, sit-ins, the March on Washington, civil rights legislation—"

The Negro sneered. "They were only getting on the bandwagon, baby. Even Republican and Democratic party platforms were always more outspoken on race than the churches. And just look at them today: still more segregated than any whorehouse in the country, still not using their enormous wealth and economic power to end slums and get us jobs and a decent education. Your churches are as morally bankrupt as the rest of society, and I say the hell with them all."

Dr. Bidwell, losing his British accent along with his temper, cried, "Young man, there's such a thing as good manners. If you were a Christian, if you were anything, you would know that issues must be discussed with courtesy and a civil—"

"You want us to die politely—isn't that it?" the Negro shouted back. "Well, go screw yourself, baby!"

The audience gasped. Reverend Hobbes jumped to his feet. "Caleb!" He rushed to the podium. "You must excuse the speaker for his intemperate—"

The youth roared, "Don't you *dare* apologize for me! Not to white bastards!" And he dashed out of the auditorium.

The assembly broke up almost immediately. Nobody could think of anything to top that outburst, I suppose, unless it was to kick Dr. Bidwell in the head.

I went over to Reverend Hobbes, who remained alone at the podium. He was trembling.

"Don't let that last speaker bother you," I said. "There are people like him in every congregation."

Reverend Hobbes's voice trembled too as he said, "Caleb is my son." (The look on his face reminded me of Zayda when he discovered that his children no longer observed the Sabbath; a year later he left for Israel.)

Caleb appeared one week later in, of all places, my office. Without knocking on the door, he strode in, saying, "I'm Caleb Hobbes. *You* remember, the party pooper." He snorted. "These brotherhood binges are too much. Like some guy hitting the sack with the same chick for two thousand years, and all he does every night is declare his love for her without once scoring. Makes you suspect, to say the least, the guy's intentions."

I asked him to take a seat.

"You also disapproved of my 'intemperance,' didn't you?"

Yes, but was that fair? How did I react that Sunday in Vernon's church? Yet I had been provoked. Well, wasn't silence sometimes more provoking than words? True, but I didn't respond out of hate. But why assume Caleb Hobbes's passion was hate? Had he said anything, after all, that Vernon hadn't said before? Still— "What did you hope to accomplish, Mr. Hobbes? You think you can goscrewyourself people into aiding the freedom movement?"

The fellow stood up. "Well, that answers my question, baby."

"What question, Mr. Hobbes?"

"Don't patronize me, baby," he snapped. "Everybody calls me Caleb."

I smiled. "And what would you have said had I called you Caleb? Tell me, what's the question?"

He shifted from one foot to another, then back again, so full of nervous energy he seemed to be running on electricity. "I want you to join in picketing a slumlord who lives on Peachtree Lane. That is, baby, if you ever join things besides sings."

Funny guy. Here to make a request, nevertheless he wouldn't stop insulting me. "Suppose you give me the details—sweetheart."

Caleb told me—in the same roar he had used in

the auditorium; he was either deaf or wished to deafen—of one Ev William, who owned fourteen tenements, which he was milking dry, and Caleb had documentary proof. William's houses had scores of violations that he never remedied. It took up to eighteen months to bring him to court; even then the court treated him so leniently, fining him less than fifteen dollars per violation, that it was cheaper to pay the fines than to make repairs. For the courts never jailed more than a dozen slumlords a year, and with the housing shortage so acute, the city could not vacate William's buildings and board them up; there was no place to relocate the tenants. Caleb therefore wanted to shame the slumlord, whom he had traced through a dozen dummy corporations, into rehabilitating his buildings. Publicly identifying him as a slumlord, the youth thought, would do the trick.

Shall I tell you the truth? My first reaction was: Thank God William isn't Jewish. (His name had not appeared on the membership committee's untapped-market list.)

"Well, baby," Caleb concluded, "are you with us? Or against us?"

"Let's talk a little more, sweetheart."

He flared. "*Don't* call me sweetheart."

"Don't call me *baby*; I have a name. Besides, from the way you talk, I'd guess you're a college graduate. Aren't you?"

Caleb scowled. "Smart man. Yes, I'm a college grad—and one who'll matriculate till his thirty-sixth birthday. Whitey isn't going to turn *this* black man into mercenary cannon fodder. Well, baby—Rabbi? What's it going to be?"

"Let me see one of William's houses first. I can't be hasty."

"Behold: one gen-u-ine slum! Hur-ry, hur-ry, hur-ry, be the first of your race to get in on the ground floor!"

So saying, Caleb pushed open the front door of the five-story tenement at 34 Halifay Street. He played with the latch. "Behold, no lock, designed to make the premises all the more inviting for addicts and winos." And waved a hand overhead. "Behold, no light bulbs, to foster that romantic atmosphere for prosties eager to turn quick tricks in the hall." And pointed a finger upward and sideways. "Behold, ceiling and walls with matching holes." And nodded at the filthy floor. "Behold, no janitor for the last four months." And touched one of the upright uncovered iron spikes along the stairwell. "Behold, no banister, the easier for playful children to make shish kebab out of each other." A kitten brushed by my leg in the dim hallway as Caleb concluded, "Now for the denizens of the deep-pressed."

He showed me through a few apartments—introducing me as the Miseries' Inspector—and it was hard to tell whose reaction distressed me more: those tenants who bombarded me with complaints about clogged toilets, inoperable refrigerators, uncollected garbage, lack of heat and hot water, rotting walls, shattered windows, exposed electrical wiring; or those whose apartments contained the same violations but who never complained at all, accepting them as their due. To think that people lived like this in the richest, most powerful nation in the world.

I felt nauseated and ashamed.

The fifth apartment's occupant had just admitted us when her baby started to cry. Going to a half-open closet, the woman climbed up on a chair in front of it, then lifted the infant out of a basket on the top shelf.

I couldn't restrain a chuckle. "That's a funny place to keep a baby. Why put him up there?"

My question seemed to surprise the mother; she looked from me to Caleb, then back at me, before saying what evidently was common knowledge: "We got rats."

I remembered the furry animal that had brushed by my leg before, in the dark hall—then it *hadn't* been a kitten—and shuddered. Turning to Caleb, I said, "Let's go. I've seen enough. *Too* much."

"Can we pick a picketing date now?" he asked, on our way out of the building.

I delayed my reply till we reached the street, then said, "I want to be fair. Will you show me those documents?"

Caleb snickered. "What good are documents if you're blind? But okay. I'll have them sent to you."

The next day a folder marked "Willev Enterprises" arrived special delivery at the temple with a notation from Caleb: "Here's *integrated* proof—everything's in black and white." But I was in over my head as soon as I opened the folder. How could anyone whose major contact with legal documents had been his birth certificate evaluate such material?

When Caleb called me that evening, I told him I had forwarded his papers with a letter of explanation to—

He cut in. "Stalling again, baby?"

"It's necessary to check these things with a lawyer—"

"But a lawyer prepared that file, a *black* lawyer. You need whitey to tell you it's kosher, right?"

A few days later Charlie Hecht phoned. "It's true," he said. "Willev's profits are unconscionable. The corporation is making four times the normal returns by writing off building-violation fines as business expenses. Actually, the government is to blame here, for allowing slumlords full depreciation—on an accelerated basis yet!—though they never maintain their buildings. Well, Rabbi, what are you going to do?"

That's what Caleb wanted to know when he stopped by the temple the next day and learned Charlie Hecht had corroborated him.

"Why so anxious to get *me* on your picket line?" I asked.

"Because black pickets are a drug on the market today; no newspaperman covers us any more unless there's a fresh angle. Now if we got white middle-class clergymen to picket one of their own, we'd make TV and every paper in the country, maybe inspire other clergymen to follow suit and scare other slumlords into fixing up their rattraps. Dig?"

"What other clergymen will be picketing?"

Caleb looked at me with feigned surprise. "Does that matter, Mr. Minister of God?"

I flushed. "No."

"I'll tell you this much: if you join the picketing, that'll mean one hundred percent of the clergymen I invited are cooperating. Well, Rabbi?"

Sure, I was reluctant. The seminary hadn't educated me to be a vigilante. "Let me contact this William, tell him of the picketing. Maybe that will persuade him to do what he should. Your goal here is to get him to repair the buildings, not simply to picket—right?"

Caleb smiled a smile that was darker than anybody else's glower. "Okay, baby. I'll give you enough rope."

Why did I take such abuse from this guy? I felt responsible, of course, for the horrible way those people at 34 Halifay Street lived; isn't our High

Holiday confession, listing more sins than any one human being could ever commit, always said in the first person plural? Moreover, I admired Caleb's single-minded devotion to justice for his oppressed people. The fellow was embittered, sure—wasn't he entitled?—but he overacted his toughness, a certain sign he was overcompensating for a good heart too bruised for him to let it show.

I wrote William, care of Willev Corporation (his Hillendale phone and address were unlisted). He didn't reply. Registering my next letter, I called when there was no response. But his secretary had the gall to deny there *was* an Ev William!

Caleb phoned, a few days later. "I can hardly wait," he said, "to hear this month's excuse."

"Okay. Name the date."

For the first time Caleb seemed at a loss for words. "Christ!" he swore, finally. "You're really going to picket!"

What else could I do? There was no moral alternative. To justify my action, to myself as well as to others, I made my own picketing sign, printing on it the Biblical verse: "He hath oppressed and forsaken the poor; he hath taken a house and will not build it up. Because in his greed he suffered nobody to escape, therefore his prosperity shall not endure."

Gina, seeing the sign, remarked, "Why, that sounds like something Mama would say." She smiled. "Who would ever have guessed the Bible was so socialistic?"

The afternoon before picket day, Caleb stopped by the temple to hand me a big placard. I refrained from showing him mine; clearly he regarded his as a bond uniting us in our common cause, for as he presented it to me his gaze never left my face.

"Caleb, I certainly appreciate this. It's a fine—" I looked at the sign and saw:

YOUR NEIGHBOR

WILLIAM EVANS

IS A

SLUMLORD

William Evans?

"What's the trouble, Rabbi?"

I barely got the words out. "You told me *Ev William.*"

Caleb shrugged. "A mistake. I thought Evans was his first name and William his last. Sometimes it's hard to tell with Jewish names, you know?" His eyes searched my face. "Why? Does it matter?"

Only if it mattered for a rabbi to picket a member of his own temple. Dumbly I shook my head.

"See you tomorrow on the picket line. Oh, did I tell you? You're the only clergyman I invited. You should feel honored."

As soon as Caleb left, I looked up Evans' office number in the temple files—yes, it was that of Willev Enterprises—and phoned him. This time the secretary put me through immediately.

"Rabbi? You want to know about my contribution to the kitchen fund, I presume—"

Quickly I revealed the reason for my call—Evans

sucked in his breath sharply—then asked why he hadn't answered my letters.

"They sounded like practical jokes, all being addressed to a nonexistent Ev William. Besides, everyone knows I live on West Drive, not Peachtree Lane."

"Just as long as I got to you in time. Can we get together tonight to discuss—"

Evans cut in. "I have nothing to discuss with you, Rabbi."

"Your houses, the violations. I'm sure you know nothing about them, being so busy with all your other enterprises, but to the people living in tenements like 34 Halifay—"

"Rabbi, have you checked all your other congregants' enterprises to make sure they're a hundred percent pure?"

"What?"

"Well, till you do, *my* business is none of *your* business, understand? Don't think I'm going to let you spoil things now the way you spoiled my bar mitzvah. Who set you up as judge over me anyhow?" And he hung up.

The phone began to shake; no, it wasn't the phone that was shaking, because it stopped when I returned it to its cradle. My hand was shaking, and not only my hand, but my entire body. I never knew that rage could give a sober person the D.T.'s. In a cold fury— make that a hot fury; now I was sweating too—I called Western Union and sent off a telegram to Evans, telling him it was one great shame that Judaism doesn't practice excommunication. The operator read the message back to me as regretting that Judaism doesn't practice decapitation, and I let it stand.

The phone rang. When I picked it up, my hand was still trembling so much I waited before speaking, because my voice would be shaking too.

"Hello? Hello? That you—?"

I let Evans have it; for all his victims I gave it to him. How could a *Jew* be so callous to human suffering!

"Who do you think you're talking to?"

Such chutzpah! I told Evans of my tour of his filthy building with the rats and no superintendent, the broken toilets and exposed wiring, the busted refrigerators and no heat, the rotting walls and filthy—

"*Gideon!*"

I worked Evans over some more, pointing out that the cost of his son's bar-mitzvah party could easily have paid for 34 Halifay's rehabilitation—

"Gideon, this is your father."

"Dad?"

"What's going on there?"

"Well—a little disagreement—with a congregant—"

"A *little* disagreement? What do you say to members during a major one? Or do you simply fire off an H-bomb?"

I told Dad the whole story—up till Evans' last words: "Who set you up as judge over me anyhow?" —and bless his Jewish heart, he volunteered either to join the picket line or to donate money to have 34 Halifay Street repaired, or both. Yet when I began to thank him, he stopped me.

"Don't thank me, Gideon, because then I'll only have to call up Evans and thank him."

"Thank Evans? For what?"

"You'll see, Gideon, you'll see."

What did he mean? Dad wouldn't tell me.

Dore Redmont stopped by my apartment early that evening to ask, "Are you *crazy*, Rabbi?" Before I could enter a denial, he rushed on: "You can't picket Evans. Know what he's doing? Trying to oust you from the temple. He called me today to help him."

Evans' move was obvious. He hadn't called Dore for help—everyone knew we were friends—but to get him to pressure me. "I told you before, I don't care about any four-year contract."

"Rabbi, we're talking now about a *one*-year contract."

"What? Oh, but the great majority of the congregation are fine, decent people, and they're with me."

"Rabbi, fifty percent of the congregation would march on Cairo if you asked them to. Probably sixty percent. Maybe even seventy percent—"

"Well, then—"

"But according to our constitution, you need a vote of seventy-five percent—"

That shook me. "Seventy-five—?" (Now I remembered why Evans' words had sounded familiar. Who set you up as judge over me? That was the line that had impelled Moses to drop his princeship and beat it out of town after smiting an Egyptian slumlord.)

"—and that's hard to get under *normal* circumstances. Look, five to ten percent of the congregation hated you even before you set foot in Hillendale, just as the same percentage loved you then too; who can explain some people's reactions to father figures and God images? Another five to ten percent wouldn't know, much less care, if we had installed Popeye here as our rabbi. So that leaves between five to ten percent who'll be deciding your election, when it's your luck to be running against Peter Perfect. In an

ordinary election a nominee is matched against somebody who also has faults, but here people will be
voting you down now, and later start thinking about a
replacement, who will have flaws but not the same
ones as yours; if he does, he can be got rid of just as
easily. On rabbis it's always open season. Don't you
know that?"

"Dore, you're asking me not to picket Evans—"

"I'm begging you, Rabbi—"

"—not because it's wrong, but because it's impol-
itic."

"What's the difference?"

"Dore, people are always telling me I push integration so hard because I don't own a home of my own,
whose value might decline. And here you want me to
think of a paying job first?"

"I want you to think of all of us here who love you,
and yes, I want you to think of yourself too. What's
wrong with that? You think Hobbes is thinking of
you? Picket Evans tomorrow, and the majority of the
congregation will cheer, sure; they too despise these
rotten slumlords. But there's bound to be some members who'll wonder who's next. Rabbi, there's a great
big business world outside this temple, and some
of the things some members do in that world aren't
exactly kosher—that includes me—and if they start to
worry that soon you'll be indicting them too—"

"Goddamnit! Shouldn't a house of God have standards? Why allow somebody like Evans inside a
synagogue? Rotary and the Boy Scouts have qualifi-
cations for membership; why shouldn't we?"

"That sonofabitch Hobbes!"

"Dore!"

"Oh, I'm not cursing him because he's black; I'm
cursing him because he's a bastard. *That's* all right,

isn't it? Look what he's done to you; he's placed you in an impossible position."

"It isn't Caleb's fault. He even gave me the chance to back out by telling me the slumlord's Jewish. Caleb only acts tough; he's really—"

"If Hobbes tipped you off beforehand, it was for some devious reason. Look what he pulled at the sing. Was that rational? Or productive? And how did William Evans ever turn into Ev William? Or West Drive into Peachtree Lane? Hobbes knew from the start Evans belonged to this temple. And didn't you just tell me you're the only clergyman he asked to picket?"

A call from Barney Singer interrupted us; Evans had gotten to him too, of course. "Your picketing would force everyone to take sides," he exclaimed. "It would split the entire temple."

Justice, I said, comes first.

"Gideon, I'm no bigot. But this is different. How just is it for a rabbi to wash dirty linen in public by naming a prominent temple member as a slumlord?"

Everyone knows, I said, that the Jews, far more than any other group in America, have consistently supported civil rights.

"How many people you think would remember that, once a rabbi denounced a congregant for slum-profiteering? Gideon, you can't picket Evans. Haven't groups seceded from synagogues before over things as small as a skullcap? Wait there. I'm coming over to talk to you."

Dore implored me to heed Barney. But was the social-action-committee chairman being any more Jewish than the president, whose first allegiance was to an organization, or, for that matter, than Curt Langer, who was emotionally tied to one rabbi? "You're more concerned about my welfare than Caleb's because you like me and not him. Dore, didn't I teach you better?"

Was there ever a nobler speech? Yet as soon as Barney reached my place, I surrendered Caleb's phone number. Astonished? Well, don't be. Once my fury was spent, I had no stomach for picketing Evans. No, I didn't fear losing my job—the rabbinate I've never considered a mere job—just as I didn't regret sending that telegram. It's simply that denouncing evil is one thing; it's something else altogether to publicly identify it in the person of someone with a wife and four innocent children, who would suffer for sins not their own. If I could not bring myself to expose Pete Schuster's adultery or the fly in Rona Redmont's soup, how could I now shame the Evans family?

Dore got Caleb on the phone. Instead of asking about what had puzzled us, however, Dore began to holler: "Do you know what you're doing, Hobbes? Do you? You're going to get Rabbi Abel fired, that's what you're doing. And his successor would never be half as involved in civil rights—"

"That's not fair!" I grabbed the phone away from Dore to apologize to Caleb, and we both heard his throbbing voice: "Who the hell cares what happens to Rabbi Baby? No honky white devil is my concern except as a *tool*."

"Caleb!"

"That you, baby?" Hobbes said without embarrassment. "The same Rabbi Bountiful who tries to erase a lifetime of guilt with ten Thanksgiving turkeys? You want to know what happened to one quarter of one of them? I'll tell you. My father kept it for us—a man like him with three college degrees but black, so he's condemned for life by the clergy placement office to a one-room church which doesn't pay him enough to buy a decent Thanksgiving meal—but I threw it into the gutter. Nobody's gaining absolution that easy!"

"Those turkeys weren't mine. I explained to your father. Two little girls here wanted to—"

"Forget it. I'm interested in one thing now. Are you joining us tomorrow? Or do you have a previous engagement to deliver Easter bunnies to other unfortunates?"

Dore had been right: Caleb was a sonofabitch. "You," I cried in a roar to match his, "can go to *hell!*" I slammed down the receiver.

"Didn't I tell you?" Dore said, while Barney Singer shook my hand in relief. "Hobbes knew all along Evans was your congregant. That's why he hid his name from you. Understand now?"

Not at all. If Hobbes had been so eager to enlist my aid, why did he reveal Evans' name prematurely, enabling me to withdraw? And even after I had agreed to join him, why wouldn't he stop insulting me? It didn't make sense.

That night I could not sleep. Half the time I tossed in bed, excoriating Hobbes for his Machiavellian manipulations; afterwards the people at 34 Halifay Street kept me awake, complaining about busted toilets, rotting walls, no janitor, the rats. If I chose not to humiliate the Evanses, who would suffer? Not Hobbes, but the blameless tenants. That momzer! Here I had gone far out of my way, and did he give a damn? *You* heard: "Who the hell cares what happens to Rabbi Baby? No honky white devil is my concern except as a *tool.*" And such hate spewing out of him, triggered by a loving gesture of two sweet children. Hobbes wasn't embittered; he had been poisoned. Maybe God had the antidote; I certainly did not. Nobody would blame me for not picketing. (How many knew the situation, anyway? Without Hobbes's forcing it on my attention, I'd never have known about it either.) And look at Dore, who respected me; my change of mind had elated him. No, *nobody* but Hobbes would condemn me—not even that baby on the closet shelf—and Hobbes was a gen-u-ine hundred percent bastard, as callous in his own way as Evans. No, nobody but that damn *Hobbes*.

And myself.

Two blocks away from the elegant Evans estate, I heard Hobbes's blaring voice leading a chorus in: "William Evans is a slumlord." Yet when I parked near Evans' fourteen-room house, I saw that Hobbes was using no mechanical amplifier; he simply had turned up the volume on his own thundering basso profundo.

I took out my placard—the Biblical one, not Hobbes's, for his had been given to an instrument, not to a person—and joined the twenty shouting picketers, positioning myself behind the mother who had to hide her baby in a closet. She was my bond here.

Hobbes broke off his chant to exclaim, "What are you doing here, baby? I never expected *you* to show."

The expression on his face—no joy at seeing an ally alighted there, only sullenness—finally solved the mystery of Hobbes's actions. The solution was too obvious to have occurred to me. "You never *wanted* me to come. Did you? Even though you needed me—"

"What are you talking about? Baby, you're full of—"

Scowling, he stopped short, hesitated for a moment, then turned to a companion. "Phone the papers and networks again. Tell them now we have a newsworthy story: 'Rabbi Pickets His Own Congregant.' That should bring them running." Yet for the first time since we met, his voice sounded low and colorless, almost uncertain. Was it possible the mystery's solution had never occurred to him either? Did powerlessness corrupt too?

Well, at any rate Caleb Hobbes didn't tell me what to go do to myself. That, also, was progress.

א

——*Rabbi?*

——Yes?

——*Oh, did I wake you?*

——No, no I've been up for *hours*—

——*You can come clean with me, Rabbi. This is Eve Greenwood.*

——Eve. Why didn't you say so in the first place? And why wake me so early in the morning?

——*I couldn't wait to tell you the good news.*

——What is it?

——*Well, last night we held our final meeting of the sub-rosa committee*—

——Sub-rosa committee? I never heard of *that* one.

——*You weren't supposed to. Because you're its total agenda.*

——Me?

——*Yes. The last few weeks we've been polling the congregation about renewing your contract*—

——What?

——*also proselytizing borderline cases to vote for you and the Right.*

——Really? You've been doing that?

——*Not just me. There's Dore, the Margolins, Charlie Hecht, dozens of people; ours was the most popular committee ever. Because, as it turned out, you're getting eighty-one to eighty-five percent of the vote. Mazeltov!*

——No joke!

——*It's true. Know what is a joke? Your picketing of that creep Evans, it did cost you votes—five, to be exact. But it won over nine undecideds. How about that?*

——I don't know what to say. You've done all that for me?

——*No, Rabbi. We've done it for us.*

——You're sweet, Eve. I'm very grateful. Frankly, the Evans affair did have me worried. Not getting my contract renewed after my first year in the rabbinate—that would have been . . . humiliating.

——*There's one thing—*

——What is it, Eve?

——*Something crazy—a couple of families are splitting their votes, like the wife will be voting for you and the husband against—*

——You mean Jerry? That was to be expected.

——*You have no idea how ashamed I feel. The way Jerry took a dislike to you, what he did at his mother's funeral. It made me feel terrible. And now, voting to fire you—*

——Forget it, Eve. After all, I do have eighty-five percent with me.

——*You do, Rabbi, but I don't. All I have is Jerry. Oh, I suppose after fifteen years of marriage, I should have learned to accept his limitations. But when he starts arguing with me and I com-*

pare him to a man like you—Rabbi, don't you ever get married at eighteen.

——I promise, Eve. But you have to promise me something too.

——*What is it?*

——Don't ever discuss me with Jerry. If you two must argue, let it be about something important in your marriage.

——*A rabbi is important to a marriage when the husband always throws him up to the wife as the other man. Not that Jerry's wrong about my feelings for you, Gideon— Oh, I didn't mean to say that! I never wanted you to know I— Good-bye—*

א

JUNE

THINGS have a way of working out, don't they? Not only was Caleb proven right in exposing slumlords—the ensuing publicity shamed Evans into selling nearly half his slum holdings and repairing the rest—but Dore's fears for my future in Hillendale had been polled wrong. The contractual meeting held no nervous stomach for me now, since justice would be renewed for at least another year.

Even the night before the meeting ended happily, when I joined a colleague, a psychologist and a marriage counselor in a panel discussion on marriage at another synagogue. Mine was the finest presentation of the group, I admit; you could tell from the women's sighs when I proclaimed marriage a religious art form, how they nudged their husbands and the way husbands glared at me.

Following my talk, I answered a dozen questions to perfection, before one lady called out, "Rabbi Abel, your wife is *such* a lucky woman."

"Well," I said, and called for the next question. "Is she here tonight, Rabbi?"

I twitched my head spasmodically to indicate either a negative or that something had got stuck in my ear which kept me from hearing the query. "Since there are no further questions—" I said, and sat down.

The woman had to persist. "How long have you been married, Rabbi? I mean, to have gained such understanding about women and marriage. You look so young."

I didn't lie; there was no time, for Rabbi Schwartz rushed to my debacle. "Oh, Rabbi Abel is a bachelor," he said. "Couldn't you tell from his talk?"

The women took the news slightly better than the fall of Adam, except for those who had nudged their husbands before and were now being punched back.

"*A boy!*"

"*Aha!*"

I hastened to say, "Surely you all don't think one must always speak from experience, do you? My good colleague, Rabbi Schwartz, for example, preaches a great deal about sin, yet he doesn't indulge *every* day."

They didn't buy that. I received no more questions from the audience, only dirty or amused looks and the impression that the psychologist on the panel who had mentioned impotence before would soon be called on to prove his. After the meeting (coffee and cake were served, of course; a thousand years hence archeologists will dig up today's synagogues and churches, and finding all our refrigerators, ovens, coffee urns, hot plates and Danish pastry, will conclude that we in the twentieth century worshiped cafeteria-style) five husbands gave me the lowdown on marriage.

"You can't learn about marriage from books," one said.

"That's right," another agreed. "It's nothing like *Fanny Hill*."

But, as I said, things turned out deliciously. For I realized on my lonely drive home the reason for my hymeneal. Of course: I wanted to get married. After my broken engagement I had hesitated to commit myself again, but this time I was sure; Gina was the girl for me. So I called her for a date for the night after the congregational meeting.

"But that's a weekday night," she said. "Don't you have a meeting?"

"I'm skipping it. There's something I want to ask you."

The following evening, when I arrive at the meeting, after composing my spontaneous acceptance speech, I suspect at once that the sub-rosa poll contained some errors. Dore Redmont must be one; I see Rona pick up the anonymous family ballot with a sidelong averted glance at me, and I know that unless Dore himself fills out their ballot, there's .7 percent down the drain. No matter—even without the Redmonts, 84.3 percent is still with me (113.5 families versus 19.5, with the seven undecideds apportioned proportionately).

True, Bernstein, whom I haven't seen since the Thanksgiving interfaith service, comments, "Dr. Bidwell never proposed a raise in dues at his church."

Since Bernstein is doubtlessly a con voter anyway, I tell him, "Okay, so join the low-priced spread."

Barney Singer, a silver-plated *T* in his hand, calls me aside to ask me to present Pete Schuster with this year's Mr. Temple Award.

How do I get out of this? By suggesting an *A* for Pete Schuster instead? "You do it, Barney. I've already promised sisterhood to make the presentation to the raffle winner of the free weekend at Grossinger's."

The president shakes his head. "I don't understand you. It's always hardest for you to do the easy things."

After the meeting is called to order, I read from Henry Slonimsky: "The assertion of God in a godless world is the supreme act of religion. It is a continuing of the act of creation on the highest plane. . . . That is true religion: to insist on God in a God-forsaken world or rather in a world not yet dominated by God, and thus to call Him into being."

Barney Singer comments, "Thank you, Rabbi. Nobody, I'm sure, will ever accuse you of talking *down* to us." He presents the Mr. Temple Award to Pete Schuster, whose ineffable contributions to the shul this past year, he declares, manifested the greatest qualities of heart and mind, head and hands, body and soul, his inventory omitting only Schuster's kishkes and loins.

With a catch in his voice, Mr. Temple accepts the award in the name of Hillendale, the synagogue, his wife and God, whereupon a photographer snaps his picture for the Hillendale *News*, the congregation applauds and Gladys Schuster weeps—which leaves only the Lord to be heard from. Then he takes over the meeting briefly while the evening's first vote is taken, for next year's officers and trustees.

There is no discussion, only a call for a show of hands, and Pete Schuster jubilantly announces, "For president, it's Barney Singer again! By unanimous vote!"

(You'd never guess, would you, that Singer had run unopposed on a single slate. Or that he had made a deal beforehand with Pete Schuster, guaranteeing him the Mr. Temple Award provided he wouldn't challenge Barney for the presidency.)

The president, touched, thanks everyone for the heartwarming vote of confidence, adding, "I've always tried to guide myself by a proverb on this ashtray that I keep on my desk as an eternal reminder: 'Use the talents you possess, because the woods would be silent if no birds sang except the best.' Now I'm not the best singer there is (except in this congregation, of course, because that is, after all, my name; get it?), I don't know so much about Judaism, and I'm not that religious. But I assure you all of one thing in all humility: I'll do the very best job I can. Because it's a rare privilege to serve you. I therefore accept this mantle of leadership for the greater glory of the Hillendale Temple and Jewry."

If you think mixed emotions are elbowing me throughout this meeting, you're not wrong. For that's the state of communications between my congregants and me: mixed—half the time I don't know what they want from me, the other half of the time they don't care for what I want of them. A doctor exists to cure the sick, an accountant is to find tax loopholes, a dentist fixes teeth, a lawyer takes money away from one sonofabitch in order to give it to another sonofabitch, or so Vernon told me—but with rabbis everything goes. Each member has his own peculiar concept of the ideal rabbi, which makes my vocation much like playing Hamlet before an audience of English professors; have you ever met a Jew who doesn't consider himself an authority in three areas of life: his own business, show business and shul business?

How then is a rabbi to gauge his effectiveness? Effectiveness? Hell, it's hard to tell if the congregation is marking you present. All year long now I've preached essentially one sermon: that religion is a demand and God the challenger, who obliges us to set ourselves and the world aright. Yet how many got the message, when no requirements whatsoever are demanded of congregants? And so religion inevitably ends up the name people give their own biases.

No more than Vernon's church needed him, alas, does my temple need me. For there's a growing Jewish community in Hillendale, devoutly middle-class, with a sizable number of school-age children, fecund parents, lots of churches and plenty of upcoming affairs. And if you think I'm jealous of the new temple kitchen and carrying on a fierce sibling rivalry with its contemplated walk-in freezer, you're right.

"The first order of business is a proposal to add a steam room to the temple, which can be constructed at the same time as the kitchen for a few extra thousand dollars."

I assume it's a steam room for corned beef and vegetables—to complement the walk-in freezer—until somebody tacks on a request for showers and a masseur. Following the defeat of both proposals, Charlie Hecht outlines the adult-education committee's plans for next year's expanded educational program, which will include weekly Sabbath Eve lectures and discussions in place of sermons. Then Dore Redmont reports on his committee's activities in promoting no less than thirteen important social issues. ("Dore for God!" cracks Pete Schuster, patiently projecting his own ambition.)

This makes me feel, after all my misgivings, like a gold-plated ingrate; now I regret not having invited my fair Gina to the meeting to shep nachas along with me from Charlie Hecht's and Dore's reports, a rain-in-Spain sort of climax. Sure, the synagogue has weaknesses and the rabbinate limitations, but what doesn't? Where can one better invest his life than in continuing a magnificent four-thousand-year-old heritage, inculcating values in children, setting goals for adults, combating injustice, alleviating cruelty, asserting dignity, confronting people with the living God? My batting average needed improvement, but at least part of the congregation (like sisterhood, which runs the preschool kindergarten; the youth group, which tutors disadvantaged kids; Dr. Lipton, who's organizing a neighborhood health center in Harlem; Charlie Hecht, who contributes his legal services to an antipoverty agency; a college senior, who applied to rabbinical school; the nineteen regulars who never miss adult education; Dore's social-action committee, not to mention the sub-rosa committee), at least they know I'm in there swinging. Well, you know how it is: life, even for clergymen who urge the counting of one's blessings, is like sitting on a tack; you don't usually spurt to your feet, shouting "Hallelujah" over the unpunctured state of the rest of your bodily terrain.

When Barney Singer announces that next on the agenda is my contract renewal, I leave the room, as he had earlier requested, in order to make it easier on nit-pickers. "Suppose we go at this in a businesslike fashion," the president says, and I repeat along with him: "Suppose we list now on one side of the blackboard Rabbi Abel's debits and, on the other side, his credits." (Yes, I pause behind the door to listen, partly out of nostalgia; this is how I came in—at my interview, remember?)

Pete Schuster clears his throat. "Since we owe first consideration to our beloved temple and what's best for it, I'll start the ball rolling. Now according to all the letters I received, scores of members oppose retaining Rabbi Abel because: one, he's too young and immature; two, he has a negative attitude toward everything; three, he draws more flies than people at Sabbath services; four, his personality is abrasive and ungodly; five, he couldn't inspire a sardine; six, his reputation is terrible—"

An uproar breaks out inside. (Me, all I can think is: Forgive him not, Father, for he knows damn well what he's doing.) Barney Singer gavels it down. "You'll all get your turn to speak, so please . . . Courtesy is due Mr. Temple, don't you think? I'm sure Pete doesn't enjoy saying these things. But we must go about this chore scientifically."

Pete the Ripper thanks the president but says no more. He doesn't have to; there are others to pick up the knife.

Sam Warren: "What disturbs me about Rabbi Abel is his taking a stand on everything under the sun, even moon shots and their cost. He's only a rabbi, after all, not the Secretary of State or Defense. There are lots of things people agree on; why can't Rabbi Abel ever find the consensus in something? He's much too controversial."

Shirl Rosenman: "Exactly. I joined the temple for peace of mind, but all Rabbi Abel gives me is constant headaches. I resent his trying to make me feel guilty every time some Hottentot on the North Pole stubs his toe. He never gives us the spiritual uplift a rabbi should. Only guilt and *more* guilt."

Rick Adler: "It's true. Rabbi Abel is not the least bit inspiring. And have you seen that green jalopy he rides around in?"

Some people laugh, others boo. Barney Singer raps his gavel. "Please, *please*."

????? ?????: ". . . . Proposing to make the temple self-sustaining through graduated dues! You can bet the rabbi wouldn't be so liberal with his own money if he had to work for a living."

???? ????: "Speaking of liberal, you know why Rabbi Abel's so liberal about Negroes and integration? Because he's a bachelor. Personally, I don't think we should be led in the race thing by somebody who has no daughters."

????? ?????: "Hy has touched on something vital here. Rabbis must be married. Else how can he counsel people with sex—I mean, marital problems? Not that I even know anyone with sex—I mean, marital problems, but it's vital to have ourselves a rabbi who's experienced."

Cheryl Wohl: "Who would want to marry Rabbi Abel? He's so cold and unfriendly—no personality. It's no wonder he has to resort to prostitutes. Yes, I said prostitutes. From what I've heard from people whose neighbors told them—"

"Objection! Objection!" It's Charlie Hecht for the defense. "Mr. Chairman, you can't allow such slander from the floor. It's entirely unfair and prejudicial to my client—I mean, Rabbi Abel."

"Really, Charlie," Barney Singer says, "This isn't a court of law, just friends trying to do what's best for our temple. But okay, no more charges; from now on let's stick only to our opinions. Go ahead."

???? ????: "Well, I believe Cheryl. All the anonymous letters the board's been getting—about the rabbi running around with Negresses and other gentile girls, his orgies after adult education (I myself have seen the light burning in his office many times after midnight), why he doesn't date any more girls from the congregation, his illegitimate child—I'm not saying they're *all* true. But where there's that much smoke, you know. Didn't the rabbi propose introducing a sex course for teen-agers?"

Charlie Hecht: "Objection! Objection!"

"Sustained," Barney Singer cries. "Let's have no innuendoes, please. Anonymous letters are not scientific. Go ahead, Doug."

Doug Bettleheim: "This is no innuendo—because I was there—laying in a tremendous bed of pain at the hospital. And did my rabbi ever come to visit me? He did not. What did he care about those stones in my bladder, and how I was passing them? For all he cared, I could have choked to death."

???????? ????????: "And he has no sense of the sacred either, Rabbi Abel. You should see him training bar-mitzvah boys. I stopped off at the temple once for a Coke, and what do I see but the rabbi busting paper bags and blowing a horn in the bar-mitzvah boy's ear while he's chanting—imagine."

"How can you say that?" Ben Margolin shouts. "If you knew what Rabbi Abel did for my son, Sandy—"

"You want to say something to the rabbi's credit?" Barney Singer asks.

"You bet!" Ben Margolin replies. "My wife and I don't have the words to tell about the change that's come over Sandy since the rabbi—"

The president interrupts. "Well, that's fine, admirable—glad to hear it. But would you hold it till we get to the other side of the blackboard? Go ahead, please."

????? ???????: "About bar mitzvah—what right does Rabbi Abel have to hold our children here for ransom, blackmailing them into continuing till confirmation in order to get bar-mitzvahed? This is America, isn't it, the land of the free choice?"

Ralph LeVine: "Speaking of America, how dare our rabbi oppose our government's policy in Vietnam? I don't want a dove for my rabbi—*or* a chicken."

????? ?????: "You're nuts. Rabbi Abel is a hawkish apologist for American imperialism. Has he called for America's immediate withdrawal of our mercenaries in Vietnam? Well, has he?"

A tumult of outcries . . .

Barney Singer gavels them down, shouting himself hoarse. "Let's have no more talk about Vietnam. It's much too complex an issue; most people feel exactly the way I do about it—confused. Remember, we're here to vote on a rabbi, not foreign policy. Yes, Mr. Steingut?"

Steingut: "Speaking objectively—I belong to so many shuls it doesn't matter to me who your rabbi is—the word of mouth about Abel at all my Mountain Tiptop affairs is something terrible. He's giving this temple such a bad name. A regular Jewish Typhoid Mary is what he is."

Goldwyn: "Exactly what I've heard at my funeral home. People would rather not die than be buried by Rabbi Abel. That's the truth. Look what happened at Jerry Greenwood's mother's funeral."

Eve Greenwood: "I want everyone to know *I'm*

voting for Rabbi Abel! Because he's an extra-
ordinary—"

"Order in the court," Barney Singer exclaims. "Let's
calm down, take matters in turn, without rebuttals.
Otherwise we'll be here all night. Please—"

Eve Greenwood: "But all this slander—"

"You'll have your turn, Eve, very shortly. Be patient," the president says. "Okay, Ellie. And let's all be
pleasant now, shall we?"

Ellie Prinz: "Pleasant? About that man? I told him
to dissuade my only son from going off to spend a
year in Israel—who knows if he'll ever come back?
Instead, Rabbi Abel tries to convince me to give
my only son my blessings. Well, if Israel is so vital to
Jews, like our Jewish champion here keeps telling us,
why doesn't *he* settle there?"

????? ?????: "Some Jewish champion. What does he
do in his spare time? Trims Christmas trees. I'm sure
it was no dog but God Himself who pushed him off
that ladder—"

?????? ??????: "Even so, that doesn't excuse him for
his shenanigans at the Episcopal church. Getting up
in the pulpit and quoting their own Bible at everyone!
My Episcopalian friends were so insulted."

Curt Langer: "Barney, I think I can sum up what
everyone's been saying. Rabbi Abel is just no Irv Terman—that's all there is to it."

Let's see, that makes twenty out of 140 against me
—sure, I'm counting. Yet even if all the undecideds
vote me down, over eighty percent still favor me, so
there's nothing to worry about.

Maurine Levenson: "He has no temple spirit, Rabbi
Abel. He gave us absolutely no cooperation in our
expansion-fund drive—no personal letters, no pep
talks, not even a contribution. And he refused even to

deliver the invocation at the kitchen's cornerstone-laying ceremony."

Edythe Loring: "I never would have joined this temple if I'd known you had a rabbi here making it *so* Jewish. Extremism in the pursuit of Judaism, I distinctly believe, is a vice."

"Anybody else?" Barney Singer asks, whereupon I begin to wonder. Wonder, not worry. Jerry Greenwood, Bill Evans and Bernstein would swell the total to 24.5 "No" votes, but what of the five whom my picketing had alienated? None of the Evans backlashers had spoken up—no doubt they were ashamed to—and maybe there were *more* than five of them; had everyone told the sub-rosa committee the truth? Now I regret that in a try for an appearance of saintliness I had refrained from asking for my opponents' names—

"Okay, that does it for Rabbi Abel's debits," Barney Singer says. "Suppose we start now on his credits."

People *applaud!* I am immodest enough to feel pleased. Relieved too, if you must know; for a while this meeting was shaping up like the prelude to a disembowelment.

"Please, please, no demonstrations. This is not a political rally," the president says. "And let's be brief. We have so many other important items on tonight's agenda. Pete? You want to speak now *for* Rabbi Abel?"

Pete Schuster: "No, not for him. For brevity. I think we can dispense with further discussion. At this late date, nobody's decision will be affected in the slightest by comments. I therefore move for an immediate vote."

Shouts and catcalls.

"Ladies! Gentlemen! Everyone!" Barney Singer

pounds away with his gavel. "Let's settle this in the parliamentary way—by a vote. My own feeling is that eliminating anything at this point would be a godsend; it's already almost midnight. Okay now, who thinks they need to hear more about Rabbi Abel before making up their minds? Raise your hands . . . Okay, those who don't need testimonials . . . Well, I guess Pete was right. Let's go ahead with the vote on retaining Rabbi Abel . . ."

While the secret ballot is tallied, I think up a new acceptance speech—on the order of "With malice toward eighteen percent . . ."—until Barney Singer announces the results. Only 30.5 voted against me! That means I won almost eighty percent of the vote, or about what the sub-rosa committee had— What's this now? Only 83.5 voted for me?

What *happened*? Some twenty-five families were absent from the meeting. I knew that, but—

"Recount! Mistake!" Dore Redmont shouts. "You didn't include the seventeen proxy votes!"

"Of course not," Pete Schuster says, then reads from the temple constitution an article that disallows proxies in rabbinical elections.

"But Sam Warren assured us," Ben Margolin cries, "proxies are valid."

"We're responsible only for what the constitution says, not Sam," Mr. Temple states and rereads the article, adding, "I guess your sub-rosa committee didn't think of everything, did they?"

Pandemonium!

The loudest yeller is Charlie Hecht: ". . . and moreover, I challenge the vote of Steingut's partner at Mountain Tiptop, Romano. How can he vote on our rabbi when he's a Catholic and belongs to Saint Mary's?"

Sam Warren shouts back, "I'll have you know Romano was our first member this year to pay his dues."

As Barney Singer calls for a discussion the door bursts open, and the sub-rosa committee skitters about me like scalded cats. Dr. Lipton runs into my office to phone the absentee members, Dore Redmont dashes into the phone booth to call his proxies. Both swiftly emerge, however; somebody has misplaced the key to the lock on the office phone, and the coin slots in the pay phone are full of chewing gum.

So the two of them, plus Eve Greenwood, Charlie Hecht, the Margolins and a dozen others, race off to make calls, but their cars conk out on the way because, according to what we learn later from mechanics who tow them away, just that night some kid had poured sugar into the gas tanks, and though some do get to phones, by then Romano's vote has been invalidated and another vote taken (in which Barney Singer again doesn't participate, because, he explains, his role is like that of the Vice-President in the United States Senate, who votes only to break ties) by then—

Now is the time to worry. Yet when I start, already it's too late. Yes, that's right; my fair laity had fired me.

§

——*Hello?*
——Oh. Hello, Mrs. Sitomer. This is Gideon Abel.
——*I thought you were dead.*
——No, just—well, busy. How are you?
——*So you really were a rabbi, after all.*
——Yes. May I speak to Gina?
——*Now I believe it because I hear you got fired.*

——Is Gina home?

——*Why were you fired?*

——Mrs. Sitomer—

——*And why did you stand up Gina last month? Personally, I'm glad you did, but was that nice?*

——I had to get away—suddenly. But I sent Gina a telegram—

——*She bought a new dress yet.*

——There were reasons, Mrs. Sitomer—

——*What reasons?*

——I'll explain to Gina.

——*I got a right to know. Who's got a better right? But you don't have to tell me because I'm not letting my daughter run around with no defrocked rabbi anyway.*

——Rabbis don't get defrocked. I'm still a rabbi.

——*Where?*

——Where what?

——*Where are you still a rabbi?*

——Well, I don't have a congregation, if that's what you mean.

——*What do you have?*

——All rabbis don't have congregations. Some write, some teach, some work for charities or other worthwhile organizations—

——*So what do you do?*

——I—well—I'm in business.

——*Business? What kind of business?*

——Well, it's my father's business.

——*And what business is that?*

——What difference does it make?

——*I'm curious what kind of business defrocked rabbis go into.*

——I'm not defrocked. I was just—

——*Yes?*

——Unsuited. That's it: I was unsuited.

——*If your business was a legitimate business, you'd have told me by now.*

——Goodbye, Mrs. Sitomer. I'll write Gina.

——*You don't have to go to all that trouble. I see the mail first.*

——Why are you so prejudiced against me!

——*A rabbi was bad enough, but a rabbi drop-out . . . Anyway, my Eugenela is going with somebody now, and I don't want you should spoil anything. He's a labor-union lawyer, and not disbarred.*

א

SUMMER

THERE's more to brassieres than meets the eye; the average woman, all she's interested in is putting one on, and the average man cares only for tearing one off; people just don't appreciate what goes *into* brassieres. No, these witticisms aren't mine; they belong to Treasure Chest's sales manager, who's teaching me one phase of the business while employing much of temple vocabulary: institution, service, long-range growth, promotion, plant expansion, inspiration, make an impression. The biggest switch here is the four-letter-word explosion, from Love and Laws to: hold, mold, slim, skim, pare, bare, push, tush, et cetera. Yes, I left Hillendale the morning after the annual meeting, because I guessed, after being fired, the congregation didn't want me.

Good old Barney Singer stayed in character to the end—out of focus as the president of a house of God and in the saddle as an accountant. When I called to tell him where to pick up my keys and two hundred dollars some members had given me for the Cadillac raffle, he said, "But if you leave before August first, we'll have to prorate your month's vacation and deduct five days' salary."

The day after my return home, Dad gave me—without one I-told-you-so, for which I blessed him—a business card reading: "Gideon Abel, Vice-President, Treasure Chest." I accepted it despite the salary's being almost four times my temple honorarium, or enough to endow any kitchen. Not to be outdone, my mother put a catalogue from Columbia University's medical school under my pillow for me to sleep on, along with a feature article from the *New York Times* about Joseph Coleman, the president of Maidenform Bras, who, it turns out, is also a *doctor*.

"Wouldn't you consider it a sign," Mom asked me, "that Maimonides, a rabbi, and Coleman, who's Maidenform, both got medical degrees?"

Engaging in ladies' undergarments full-time, I felt at first like a paid fetishist. To overcome my manly embarrassment, I forced myself to spend a week going from department store to department store, stepping up to counters and asking strange saleswomen for an assortment of brassieres, not an easy thing to do when half of them reminded me of my mother and the other half of old girl friends, and all of them wondering aloud over my purchasing, then returning so many bras of diverse sizes. (One lady wanted to know if my memory was that bad, another asked if my wife was on a diet or out of town, a third inquired just how much I dated, a fourth reported me to the store detective.) But after a week of wallowing in brassieres, I could finally look upon them dispassionately, as if they were nothing more than pairs of skullcaps sewn together.

That accomplished, there were no further adjustments to make. A year at the temple had accustomed me to business meetings, and Treasure Chest's were briefer, always to the point, exclusively about the product, and best of all, nobody felt impelled to testify what brassieres and breasts meant to him personally and how grateful he was for the honor of bringing them together for the greater glory of mankind. Add to that a forty-hour week, a four-room apartment with three terraces and a view of six bridges, Fifth Avenue's New York Public Library's excellent Jewish Room close by, plenty of time for myself, no bitching by customers, no factions in the office, no gripes from executives that any time spent on my studies was taken out of their mouths—and who could ask for anything more?

Yesterday, for example, my father told me what my congregation voted down. "Gideon," he said, "I'm proud of you."

"What for?"

"That name of yours for our new false-bottomed girdle and your slogan—they're the talk of the industry. The results of the Chicago test run just came in. We got eight percent of the market. The Philadelphia test with a different name and slogan never did better than four percent. So it must be you who made all the difference. This means already you've earned your entire year's salary."

I was incredulous. "With just seven words?"

"You of all people, Gideon, should appreciate the power of the word. 'Fanny Hills'! That doctorate of

yours in English finally paid off. And that slogan—
'There's *bold* in them thar Fanny Hills'—brilliant!"

My rabbinical training made me confess, "Actually,
Dad, I think both the name and the slogan are a
little on the vulgar side. No, a lot."

"You don't like it?" Dad was taken aback. "Why
suggest it then?"

"Well, I was joking at the time. How should I know
your sales manager would take it seriously?"

"Joking?" Dad's face turned as pink as Pete Schuster's tongue. "Gideon, one thing you got to understand: business is serious business. Yet creative too,
just like art or literature. Only difference is, instead
of with words and pictures, we create with dollars
and cents and underwear, utilizing the same imagination, style, innovation. It's creative to manufacture
a false derrière, it's creative to promote it with a good
name and a catchy slogan, it's creative to capture
eight percent of the market at the very start. You
see that, Gideon?"

I sighed. "Frankly, no."

Dad smiled indulgently. "Well, you're young yet.
You'll learn."

That made me feel right at temple. Congregants
used to tell me that all the time, and it will probably
end up carved on my tombstone:

Here lies

GIDEON ABEL

He'll learn

Otherwise, my job has only one annoyance: people
at work are constantly asking about my switch from
the rabbinate to Treasure Chest, as if I were Norman
Vincent Peale taking a vow of poverty. I could answer them all with "Well, I'm still in the uplift busi-

ness, aren't I?"—but that's too flip. So I try for dignity-
cum-pathos by presenting nosey bodies with a copy of
a recent resolution of the Central Conference of
American Rabbis:

> We are deeply disturbed by the fact that an in-
> creasing number of rabbis have suffered improper
> and unjust dismissal from their pulpits. These all too
> frequent actions reflect a growing spirit of aliena-
> tion between the laity and the rabbinate, which
> eventuates in great personal tragedy to rabbis, se-
> rious injury to the morals of the community, and
> harm to the growth of the movement.
> We therefore recommend that a special com-
> mittee be appointed to study and to report in de-
> tail to the next convention on the cause of this
> situation and to recommend appropriate action.

Coincidentally, the *New York Times* has broken
out into a rash of articles—one even made the front
page—about dozens of Christian clergymen being
fired by their churches. Happily, the Hillendale Temple's interfaith-lovers had kept in smart ecumenical
step.

ℵ

——*Gideon!*
——Hello, Gina.
——*What are you doing here at the hospital?*
——Your mother has you guarded tighter than
  Rapunzel. She won't let me write you or phone.
  I waited outside your apartment house half of
  August—
——*But I was away in Europe.*

——Mrs. Goldstein with the ileitis finally told me.

——*That's too bad. I mean, that she told you.*

——Gina, I'm sorry about canceling our date on such short notice.

——*It wasn't the canceling that bothered me or even the new dress I bought; it was the way you did it. In a telegram—so cryptic it sounded like the FBI was after you. Why couldn't you have seen me, called me? I thought there was something between us, Gideon.*

——There was—is.

——*Is there? Then why didn't you come to me?*

——I was—well, you see—

——*I know what happened, Gideon. I called the temple, and whoever it was who answered the phone told me. But why didn't you tell me?*

——All year long people have been coming to me for help, comfort—

——*And you were too proud to come to me.*

——Proud? Gina, I was ashamed. I couldn't talk about it then.

——*Gideon—*

——And I don't want to talk about it now. I want to forget the whole thing—and concentrate on us.

——*Us?*

——You know what I mean, Gina.

——*I used to. Gideon, my father often said a good marriage is when a man can come home and say to his wife, "They beat me today," and she says, "It's all right," and then it is all right. Gideon, when a woman doesn't feel needed—*

——Yes, I know, Gina. I know now all about needed; Hillendale gave me a diploma in it. It was wrong of me to withdraw—

——*Where are you now?*

——Where?

——*Your new congregation.*

——Congregation? Well, I don't have one. All rabbis don't have congregations. Some teach, some write, some work for organizations—

——*Where are you teaching?*

——I don't. Well, Sunday School.

——*What do you do the other six days of the week?*

——Your mother didn't tell you? I told her when I phoned—

——*No. Mama doesn't even speak against you any more, not since she fell in love with this labor lawyer I've been dating.*

——Oh? Who is he?

——*Somebody who says my eyes remind him of the color of the lines on a legal-size yellow pad. The horizontal lines, I presume.*

——Is that why you cut your hair? He likes it short? I like it long.

——*Short hair is cooler in the summer.*

——How often have you been seeing him?

——*When did you disappear?*

——That many weeks?

——*Oh, let's not play games, Gideon. Mama loves my labor lawyer; I don't. Tell me about you. What are you doing now?*

——Well—

——*Why so hesitant?*

——I've gone into my father's business.

——*Business? You? And isn't you father in—*

——Gina—

——*—ladies' underwear? Oh, wait till Mama finds out you're a boss now!*

——Gina, there's a rabbinical-association resolution I want you to—

——*What?*

——Skip it.

——*Gideon?*

——Yes?

——*Are you happy?*

——I'm successful. I'm a vice-president already, with only one boss, and he's on *my* side. What's more—

——*I seem to recall someone telling me that the great use of a life is to spend it for something which outlasts it, that what man is he ultimately becomes through the cause he's made his own.*

——You didn't give me a chance to finish, Gina. I was saying that last month I read more than I did the whole year at Hillendale; I can study, now that I no longer lead a congregation. I work on different causes, teach Sunday School and—

——*Gideon, I know brassieres will outlast us all, but are they what you want to* become?

——That's not fair.

——*Fair? Is it fair what you did to me? Stuffing me with all your religious books, turning me into My Jewish Lady. You know why I don't go for that labor lawyer now, when I liked him well enough four months ago? Because since meeting you I can't approve of somebody who works for this union that's as rapacious as any of Mama's old-time bosses. And then this doctor I was seeing, when I saw his feeling for medicine was a mechanic's—talking about organs and cases and never persons—Gideon, you've spoiled me for everyone else.*

——Great! Gina, you don't want anyone else now. I'm here.

——*You're here, Gideon, but is it you? In bras-*

*sieres? Know something? I think you've spoiled
me also for you . . .*

ℵ

"Are you free for lunch today?"

It was Dean Tchernichovsky on the phone, and before I could stop myself I had told the truth. "Yes."

I met the dean at his office—he had been in Israel
most of the summer—and we walked downstairs to
the cafeteria, a long way to fidget. After the dean
thanked me for Dad's sending his wife three dozen
brassieres of the wrong size and I promised to exchange them, I resorted to chattering about the rumor
that *Time* magazine had chosen God its Man of the
Year, despite His reputed death.

"It's significant," the dean commented, "that belief
in God is nowhere listed as one of the Bible's six
hundred thirteen commandments; actions, our tradition teaches, prove one's belief. When man appears
before the Throne of Judgment, the ancient rabbis
said, the first question asked of him is not 'Do you
believe in God?' or 'Did you pray to Him and perform
ritual commandments?' but 'Did you deal honorably
and faithfully with your fellow man?'"

We went through the cafeteria line, then seated
ourselves at a table, as I wondered how to explain
myself. But before I could begin, the dean said, "The
placement commission told me you were taking a
sabbatical. Usually sabbaticals come every seventh
year, but since everything else is so speeded up in
this modern world, why not sabbaticals too?" I relaxed, and the dean, whipping his fingers through
his tousled white hair, continued throughout lunch to
speak about God and not me, thank Him.

"Perhaps during the childhood of the human race, people could not face the truth about God's imperfection. But today they must be told: God is now only *growing* toward omnipotence, just as people have only just *begun* to be religious. Therefore, when God's justice and love are in eclipse and, impotent, He can do nothing but weep, it is up to us to take over for Him, offering the Lord our faith and strength in return for His continuing light and support . . .

"All this is the merest guesswork, of course, for faith has never been more than a working hypothesis. Yet the believer stakes his entire life on this glorious hunch about God—that He indeed lives and needs us —and what is heroism but acting as *if* something were true in order to *make* it true!"

א

——— . . . *Gideon will be here later. He always spends Shabbas with us . . . Oh . . . Who is she? . . . no, I'm not interested in what her father's worth . . . But who is she? . . . Well, I can't promise. Give me her name and number . . . All right . . . Goodbye.*

———Hi, Mom.

———*Gideon. I didn't hear you come in.*

———Who was that? On the phone.

———*Just some mah-jongg player.*

———You must have an awfully good memory.

———*Why?*

———You didn't write down that girl's number. I never thought I'd live to see the day my own mother would stop force-feeding me prospective daughters-in-law.

———*To tell the truth, Gideon, I'd just as soon you*

didn't date right now. It's liable to end up badly.

——What do you mean, badly?

——*Marriage. Oh, I want you to get married, of course, but not while you're with Treasure Chest. The daughter of Fetching Stretchpants who'd marry a brassiere vice-president might not make such a good wife for—say, a medical student.*

——You never give up.

——*Look, even if you never practice, the education is a good thing. What can it hurt, a medical education? The worst thing is, you'll have six degrees instead of five. Gideon, if you ask me, it's a pity.*

——I'm not asking you. What's a pity?

——*A person like you, who works so lovingly with people, burying himself in bras—its.*

——That's the trouble, Mom. I can't work with people. I don't get along with even seventy-five percent of them.

——*Gideon, I remember your weekly visits to Chronic Diseases. The patients still talk about you, they loved you so.*

——That was different; nobody paid me to visit Chronic Diseases. Dad was right: the only good rabbi is a self-employed rabbi—the way it used to be centuries ago, when rabbis supported themselves at trades. But suppose we change the subject for a change. Who was the woman who called? Maybe I'll try her stretch-pants girl.

——*I thought you were going with that Gina.*

——No more.

——*What happened?*

——Nothing.

——*Nothing?*

——Everybody in the world knows what I should

do! Like you love medicine, Gina wants to see me
crucified on still another congregation.

——*Well, anything is better than its. Take your
father and me. The money we don't need, the
vacations he doesn't take, the fancy style I don't
care to live in. All I can say for Treasure Chest
is, it keeps your father busy; it's like his being
president of a temple. But you, Gideon, with
your feeling for* people—

——For crying out loud!

——*I'll say one thing more, and that'll be the end of
it, Gideon, for now. Did you ever look at medicine this way? A doctor, when his patients disagree with him, they* leave.

N

Since the dean never questioned me about leaving
the congregational rabbinate, when we met for lunch
the third time I told him of my Hillendale experience,
relating it dispassionately, as if it were another man
of God altogether who had got bushwhacked, because I didn't want pity, no pity at all, just a comforting word maybe, like "Those bastards."

Dr. Tchernichovsky listened attentively, and when
I had finished he commented, "Well, you know what
the great nineteenth-century scholar Malbim said
when people asked why he went from pulpit to pulpit: 'Tell the truth and see the world.'" He added,
"But the Midrash reminds us, Abel, that oil is improved only by beating."

"My story doesn't disturb you?"

The dean sighed. "Only because it isn't new. It's a
serious problem today in all houses of worship—
minister-congregation relations. And it's not always

the congregation's fault. Last week, for example, when Fleisher died in Philadelphia, Axelrob left his shul to replace him—at twice the salary of his Connecticut synagogue—and here it's September, and all available rabbis were hired by last June."

"Good. Now a temple will know how it feels to be fired. You know what kills me, Dean? All those people who voted me down—not one of them was even religious."

"What about those who voted for you?"

"Well, most of them weren't religious either. But who is nowadays? You know what houses of worship are today: parent-teachers associations of the Sunday School."

"That's the way it is, Abel: man's religion is of his life a thing apart; 'tis a clergyman's whole existence. Do you think, however, theatergoers care passionately for the drama? Still, there is this saving grace: in a house of God, congregants are there for the minister to get at."

"You mean, before they get him?"

"Really, Abel, when you think about it, it's amazing a rabbi accomplishes as much as he does. Remember, a rabbi doesn't mediate between man and God, nor can he promise anyone heaven or threaten him with hell. His authority derives from his personal virtues, which are taught only through example. Yet a teacher influences all eternity, I believe that; he never knows where his teaching will end. Just because a rabbi deals in nothing so tangible as diseases cured, law cases won, sales made—"

"Dean, you know how congregants think? The rabbi is hired to be religious—their vicarious Jew—and that lets them off the hook."

"You think you had a worse time of it than our

first rabbi? Moses, you recall, started out so disgusted with his people he smashed the Tablets of the Law. Yet he ended up blessing them before his death."

"Yes, but nobody voted to fire Moses because his ass was sixteen years old and green. Dean, you want to know my greatest success at the temple? I directed a show there, *My Fair Sadie*, which netted four thousand dollars, and everybody called me a champion rabbi. For directing a play. I used to do the same thing in college every month, and all they called me there was a drama major."

"Is it total victory you were after, Abel? In one year?"

"What?"

"Abel, in our vocation, success is measured more by dedication than achievement. There is such a thing as the *success* of failure. God Himself gains strength from our failures, I devoutly believe, so long as they are undertaken for His sake. So long as man struggles, so long as God struggles, so long as man and God both grow through their shared struggling—well, that's as much as we can hope for in this world. Yet that should be enough to see us through to the next battle, and beyond."

"Dean, are you telling me I was a bad rabbi?"

"Not at all. In my desk are over one hundred letters from your congregants, which came to the seminary— apparently you left no forwarding address—and I don't imagine all of them wrote to express delight with your departure. There's also a scroll petitioning your return, which, according to a notation, every child signed, including one who promised not to write on any more walls, whatever that means. No, Abel, you weren't a bad rabbi. You were an illusioned rabbi—*that's* bad. Because illusions go before despair, and despair is the cardinal sin; hope, you see, half creates its own objectives. But do you know what's worse even than despair?"

I was afraid to ask.

"Self-pity is worse, Abel. Self-pity is a nice place to visit; it's like a warm, wet diaper. But who would want to live there? After a while it begins to stink."

Always a word of praise before that damned crusher.

The dean reached out and touched my hand. "By no means is that my last word to you, Abel. This is, the Talmud's: 'If a rabbi is popular, it is not because the people love him, but rather because he does not reprove them.' Doris Day is popular, also well-mannered, soft-spoken, innocuous, relentlessly cheerful. But I would never want Doris Day for my rabbi. Abel, I prefer *you*." His hand gripped mine. "Have you forgotten? I am seventy-seven years old now, and you are my rainbow."

א

——That rabbi of yours ought to be shot!
——*Gideon!*
——Today's Rosh Hashanah sermon of his, Mom— it was immoral.
——*What was the matter with it?*
——Didn't you hear him, Dad? Talking about the importance of law, and then, in passing, taking a slap at Negroes for rioting, without explaining any of the underlying causes.
——*When did he do that, Gideon?*
——*While you were dozing, Sol.*
——*The new air-conditioning system in the temple —it's wonderful, Lena.*

——That sermon was a disgrace.

——*Then I'm glad I was dozing. If it was such a lousy sermon——*

——It wasn't lousy. It was harmful, vicious——

——*Gideon, I've never heard you talk like this. I wish you'd stop——*

——Mom, that rabbi was distorting Judaism. Law is important, certainly it is, but he should have been teaching congregants *Pirke Avos:* "The sword comes into the world because of justice being delayed, because of justice being perverted and because of those who render wrong decisions." That's what he should have preached, your miserable rabbi.

——*Gideon, it's time you got married.*

——My God, you too, Dad?

——*I notice it's always the bachelors who are such firebrands. If you were a family man with a wife and children, you wouldn't constantly be running a temperature about everything—and you'd probably accomplish more good too.*

——My father has become a Marxist of love, an erotic determinist!

——*Who? What?*

——It's because of those brassieres of yours.

——*Ours, Gideon. Treasure Chest is ours now. Oh, yes, speaking of ours—the shul has asked me to read the Book of Jonah at services on Yom Kippur. Would you like to read instead of me?*

——Oh? Usually the board gives the Jonah reading to its president, the shul's greatest scholar, if it has one, or the congregation's biggest giver. Which one are you, Dad?

——*Well, I contribute some.*

———But so much? Why? After all your own criticism of the temple's shortcomings—

———*Well, when somebody invents something* better
than the synagogue, I'll give to that instead.
Gideon, what about it? Want to read in my
place?

———I'd love to. Jonah is a favorite of mine; too bad
most people think it was written by Walt Disney.
But that sermon today. If a doctor operated the
way your rabbi preached, the congregation could
sue him for malpractice, and collect.

———*No question about it, Gideon. You'd be far*
superior.

———You mean, up there in the pulpit, Mom?

———*As a surgeon.*

———You're pushing again.

———*Yes, but did you notice, Gideon? You've*
stopped overreacting.

———*Now, Lena, you cut that out. Leave my vice-*
president alone!

———For crying out loud, will you both stop!

———*We're sorry, Gideon. You know what we want*
for you. Only one thing. We want our only son
to be happy, that's all. If you're happy we're
happy. What else do parents live for?

※

She was standing at the door, awaiting my return
from the office, as I now constantly fantasied, for my
apartment was too big to live in all by myself, and my
new color television set made me lonelier still, its
commercials insinuating that I was a sex-for-nothing,
while the programs reminded me that I didn't have
anyone even to beat up . . .

"*Gideon—*"

No fantasy this time! It was Gina, forlorn in her clipped hair, inside the lobby of my apartment house. Braiding her fingers together, she stammered, "I came to ask forgiveness before Yom Kippur—isn't that required?—for my sin."

"Sin?"

"Losing faith in you . . . Forgive me." She began to cry. "Oh, Gideon, I've been so unhappy—"

I pulled her close, my soft benediction. "Me, I've felt like a dybbuk with nobody to inhabit."

"—and even if you do stay with Treasure Chest, knowing you, I'm sure you'll be manufacturing the most . . . *humane* bra in the world."

Intoning her name like an invocation, I squeezed her to me.

"My contact lens, it's in your ear—"

"—Gina Gina Gina Gina—"

"Oh, yesyesyesyes!"

"You'll marry me?" I kissed her.

She pulled away and gulped for air. "Gideon," she gasped, "you certainly don't *kiss* like a rabbi . . ."

א

. . . And God saw the works of the people of Nineveh, that they turned from their evil way; and God repented of the evil which He said He would do unto them; and He did it not. But it displeased Jonah exceedingly, and he was angry.

And he prayed unto the Lord, and said: "I pray Thee, O Lord, was not this my saying, when I was yet in mine own country? Therefore I fled beforehand unto Tarshish; for I knew that Thou art a gracious God, and compassionate, long-suffering, and

abundant in mercy, and repentest Thee of the evil.
Therefore now, O Lord, take, I beseech Thee, my
life from me; for it is better for me to die than to
live."

And the Lord said, "Art thou greatly angry?"

Then Jonah went out of Nineveh, and sat on the
east side of the city, and there made him a booth,
and sat under it in the shadow, till he might see what
would become of the city. And the Lord God prepared a gourd, and made it to come up over Jonah,
that it might be a shadow over his head, to deliver
him from his evil. So Jonah was exceedingly glad
because of the gourd.

But God prepared a worm when the morning rose
the next day, and it smote the gourd, that it withered.
And it came to pass, when the sun arose, that God
prepared a vehement east wind; and the sun beat
upon the head of Jonah, that he fainted, and requested for himself that he might die, and said: "It
is better for me to die than to live."

And God said to Jonah, "Art thou greatly angry for
the gourd?"

And he said: "I am greatly angry, even unto death."

And the Lord said, "Thou hast had pity on the
gourd, for which thou hast not labored, neither madest
it grow, which came up in a night, and perished in a
night; and should I not have pity on Nineveh, that
great city, wherein are more than sixscore thousand
persons that cannot discern between their right hand
and their left hand . . .?"

א

——Dr. Tchernichovsky? This is Gideon Abel. Am
I interrupting your supper?

——*No, no. On Yom Kippur night I wolf everything down. How was your fast?*

——Fine, fine. Dean?

——*Yes?*

——I read Jonah in shul today—

——*Oh? And "Art thou greatly angry"—still?*

——That's why I'm calling. About that congregation in Connecticut, the one whose rabbi left them in the lurch—how hard up are they? I mean, is the congregation desperate for a rabbi?

——*Desperate enough. There are no rabbis to be had at this late date.*

——So desperate they'd accept certain conditions in order to get a rabbi?

——*What kind of conditions?*

——Oh, I don't mean a big salary—

——*That condition I feel certain they'll accept.*

——Conditions like: required attendance at adult education, no fund-raising, a cause for every congregant, seventy-five percent of the cost of each bar mitzvah and wedding reception and funeral must be donated to charity, bar mitzvah at eighteen, ethics in business, the rabbi not be required to attend every cat-hanging—things like that, Dean.

——*Abel, Abel. I'm beginning to wonder if you're not too idealistic for the rabbinate. You left out the most important condition of all.*

——What's that?

——*The first condition to lay down is that only fifty-five percent of the voters need approve the rabbi's contract. Eisenhower was elected to the Presidency of the United States by fifty-seven percent, and that was considered a landslide.*

Anyway, ask for fifty-five percent—and settle for sixty-five percent.

——Oh. I see what you mean. Maybe I ought to follow Maimonides' example and become a doctor, after all; doctors don't have to play the percentages.

——*Medicine is one of the noblest of professions, that's true.*

——Dean? What do you advise me to do?

——*What do you think you should do, Abel?*

——Well—

——*Bearing in mind that a rabbi's obligation is to learn, and to teach, so as to bring about what he affirms—*

——I could take some med courses, I suppose, on the side—

——*Nu, Rabbi? What shall I tell the placement commission tomorrow about that Connecticut temple? "Whom shall I send, and who shall go for Me?"*

——Okay, Dean—for the sake of heaven. "Here am I; send me."

א

W9-BIT-872

With one quick twist,
he shoved her face against the wall

"Move and you're history," the intruder said, pulling Julianna's hands behind her.

That voice. She knew that voice.

Swiftly, big deft hands patted her down, moving under her arms, sliding around to her breasts, then down between her legs, at which she felt a familiar pull low in her stomach. He clicked on the light and yanked her around.

His eyes went wide. "Jules?"

Five years and he still looked the same. Same cobalt-blue eyes that crinkled around the corners whether he was smiling or not, the same lean, hard features that said he was a man's man—a man with a purpose—and always in control. Qualities she once thought sexy and desirable.

He was so close she felt his heat. His familiar scent made her blood rush. And if the look in his eyes was any indication, he felt the same. But then, lack of desire had never been their problem. In the end, desire hadn't helped the marriage. She hated what they'd done to each other in the year before the divorce.

Things that would stay with them forever.

Dear Reader,

I'm delighted to bring you another COLD CASES: L.A. novel and again delve into the inner world of law enforcement—a world that's always intrigued me. While career choices took me in another direction, I did enroll in my city's civilian police academy. Little did I know that the six-week class would spark the idea for this miniseries.

Husband and Wife Reunion is the last book in the series, but it seems perfect to end with Luke's story. It's about second chances, and don't we all wish we could do some things over? But even when given the opportunity we don't always make the best choices. I believe true character is revealed by the choices we make when our personal risks are the greatest. Detective Luke Coltrane is a man who has hit rock bottom. He's lost his son and his wife, alienated most of the people he loves, and it nearly cost him his job. But he's on the mend and determined to put his life in order, starting with his relationship with his father. But he never expected to run into his ex-wife, Julianna, back home in Santa Fe. That's one fence he knows he can't mend. To do that, he'd have to take the greatest risk of all…and open his heart to love.

Luke and Julianna have been through a terrible tragedy. In order to find love and commitment again, they must overcome nearly insurmountable odds. I didn't know until I wrote the end of this book whether they'd be able to do it or not. I'm happy with the outcome and hope you enjoy Luke and Julianna's story.

I always like hearing from readers. You can write me at P.O. Box 2292, Mesa, AZ 85214, or e-mail me at LindaStyle@cox.net. For upcoming books and other fun stuff, visit my Web site at www.LindaStyle.com and www.superauthors.com.

May all your dreams come true,

Linda Style

HUSBAND AND WIFE
REUNION
Linda Style

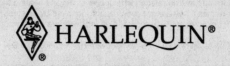

HARLEQUIN®

TORONTO • NEW YORK • LONDON
AMSTERDAM • PARIS • SYDNEY • HAMBURG
STOCKHOLM • ATHENS • TOKYO • MILAN • MADRID
PRAGUE • WARSAW • BUDAPEST • AUCKLAND

If you purchased this book without a cover you should be aware
that this book is stolen property. It was reported as "unsold and
destroyed" to the publisher, and neither the author nor the
publisher has received any payment for this "stripped book."

ISBN-13: 978-0-373-71361-5
ISBN-10:   0-373-71361-4

HUSBAND AND WIFE REUNION

Copyright © 2006 by Linda Fensand Style.

All rights reserved. Except for use in any review, the reproduction or
utilization of this work in whole or in part in any form by any electronic,
mechanical or other means, now known or hereafter invented, including
xerography, photocopying and recording, or in any information storage
or retrieval system, is forbidden without the written permission of the
publisher, Harlequin Enterprises Limited, 225 Duncan Mill Road,
Don Mills, Ontario, Canada M3B 3K9.

All characters in this book have no existence outside the imagination of
the author and have no relation whatsoever to anyone bearing the same
name or names. They are not even distantly inspired by any individual
known or unknown to the author, and all incidents are pure invention.

This edition published by arrangement with Harlequin Books S.A.

® and TM are trademarks of the publisher. Trademarks indicated with
® are registered in the United States Patent and Trademark Office, the
Canadian Trade Marks Office and in other countries.

www.eHarlequin.com

Printed in U.S.A.

Books by Linda Style

HARLEQUIN SUPERROMANCE

923–HER SISTER'S SECRET
977–DADDY IN THE HOUSE
1062–SLOW DANCE WITH A COWBOY
1084–THE MAN IN THE PHOTOGRAPH
1155–WHAT MADELINE WANTS
1243–THE WITNESS
1281–HIS CASE, HER CHILD
1323–AND JUSTICE FOR ALL

Don't miss any of our special offers. Write to us at the following address for information on our newest releases.

Harlequin Reader Service
U.S.: 3010 Walden Ave., P.O. Box 1325, Buffalo, NY 14269
Canadian: P.O. Box 609, Fort Erie, Ont. L2A 5X3

For Courtney and Connor,
You are the stars that light up my life.
I love you both.

My sincere thanks and appreciation to all the people who contributed to the research for this book, and all the books in the COLD CASES: L.A. miniseries—the professionals with the Los Angeles Police Department, the city of Los Angeles Chamber of Commerce and the Orange County RWA members who so generously shared their expertise about the City of Angels.
Many thanks to my editor, Victoria Curran, for her guidance and uncanny ability to see the essence of a story.
Since this is a work of fiction, I've taken some liberties with facts where needed.
Any errors are solely mine.

CHAPTER ONE

"YOU CROSSED THE LINE. You're going to regret it."

Julianna Chevalair listened to the distorted digital-ized voice, heard a click and then the dial tone droned in her ear.

She swallowed around the tightness in her throat, closed her eyes and waited for the next message. The recorder had indicated there were three.

"If you don't stop, I'm going to stop you."

Her heart raced. She'd ignored the caller's earlier e-mails warning her to stop writing the story, and the second installment was about to run in the magazine's next issue.

A moment later, the next call started. As she listened, the hairs on the back of her neck stood on end. A chill ran up her spine. Hands shaking, she clicked off in the middle of the message.

How had he gotten her number?

The Achilles' Heel received dozens of crank calls, letters and even more e-mail messages from readers who didn't like some of its stories. But this was new. She'd never received a phone call at home before. And the two e-mails she'd gotten prior to leaving San Francisco had definite threatening undertones.

It creeped her out and she'd jumped at Abe's kind invitation to stay at his ranch outside Santa Fe. Now the decision seemed even more right. No one knew where she was, not even her editor. Her ex-father-in-law's ranch was the last place anyone would expect her to go.

She heaved a sigh, fell into Abe's recliner, its leather soft and cracked with age, and switched on her laptop. When she finished the piece she was working on right now, she'd be done with the series about a little girl's abduction and murder in Southern California.

It was only one of many she'd written about missing children who'd met the same fate. And someone wanted her to stop. She bristled at the thought. If anything, he'd made her even more determined to complete the series. She'd never give in to a coward who made anonymous threats. She'd finish the story even if she had to go somewhere else to do it. But she *would* finish.

She pulled up Word on her laptop, went to the last page of the story and typed in, "If you recognize anything about the individual profiled in this article—if you know *anything* about this case, call the LAPD, your local FBI office or 1-800-CRIME TV. Help us take this killer off the streets before he harms anoth—"

A noise outside made her sit up straight as a soldier. She stopped typing. She was used to city sounds, but here in the desert, in the stillness of the night, every small noise seemed magnified.

Listening, she heard nothing more. Okay, she was

jumpy because of the messages, but that really was silly; the calls had gone to her condo in San Francisco two thousand miles away.

Abe had complained about a family of javelina disturbing his chickens; maybe that's what she'd heard. He'd had trouble with coyotes, too. It certainly wouldn't be a visitor at two in the morning—Abe didn't have visitors any time.

She smiled, thinking of the old man sleeping in the back wing of the sprawling adobe ranch house. Besides being her ex-father-in-law, he was a friend, a surrogate father who'd taken her in, no questions asked. Abe might be cranky and more stubborn than a donkey, but she loved him dearly.

Except for the soft light of an old faux oil lamp across the room and the glow from the laptop screen, the rest of the house was dark. No lights were on outside either since Abe insisted on conserving energy. He called himself thrifty. Others called him cheap.

A coyote bayed in the distance, its lonely howl a faint echo in the vastness of the high desert, reminding her how far they were from Sante Fe. Yet, here, she felt a peace she never enjoyed at home. The air was so pure that sounds traveled for miles, the sky so clear, she could see the Milky Way, like a road of sparkling light against a velvet black backdrop. She hadn't seen the stars like that since she was a kid and had taken a trip with her mother in their VW bus to Arizona.

Julianna hauled in a deep breath and kept on typing, the keys clicking loudly in the quiet.

Another sound…from the kitchen. Her fingers stilled

as the doorknob rattled and her heartbeat quickened. Was someone trying to get in? She heard a crash and the doorknob clattered again.

She pulled her cell phone from her briefcase. They were so far out in the boonies, it would take forever for anyone to get there, but she punched in 911 anyway.

Nothing but static. Then somewhere between the crackles, she heard a voice. She rattled off her name, Abe's address, her cell phone number and that she thought someone was breaking in, hoping whoever was on the other end had heard her.

She should wake Abe. But shouting for him wouldn't do any good because the old man took out his hearing aid at night and he was deaf as a post without it.

Her heart pumped like a piston in her chest. Her gaze went to Abe's rifle in the gun rack against the far wall. She crossed the room, found the key to the case and took out one of the rifles. The wood on the butt felt smooth under her fingers, but she'd never handled a gun in her life. She'd probably shoot herself.

What the hell. It was protection. She opened the drawer and scooped out some rifle shells. All she had to do was put them in and pull the trigger. She'd seen Abe do it before.

She pocketed two shells, then, gun against her chest, edged down the hallway toward Abe's room to wake him. He knew how to shoot. Besides, what was she going to do? Force a burglar to leave at gunpoint? Tie him up for the police? How long would it be before they arrived? *If* they arrived?

With each step, she tightened her grip on the weapon. She couldn't imagine who would break into an old man's house in the middle of the night when he had nothing worth stealing. It could still be an animal searching for food. In California she'd heard of bears and bobcats wandering into homesteads. She was going to feel pretty silly if that's what it was.

But animals didn't rattle doorknobs. She heard a dull thud and before she could react, the door to the hallway creaked open. A large male form appeared, shadowed in the opening.

Oh, God! Adrenaline coursed through her. She raised the gun, butt end up, and mustering all her strength, smashed the man on the head.

He grunted…but he didn't keel over.

Oh my God! She dropped the gun and turned to run. Fingers dug into her shoulder and in one quick movement, he shoved her face against the wall and pulled both her hands behind her.

"Move and you're history," the intruder said, his voice low and raspy.

That voice. She knew that voice.

Swiftly, big deft hands patted her down, moving under her arms, sliding around to her breasts, then down between her legs, at which she felt a familiar pull low in her stomach. He clicked on the light and yanked her around.

His eyes went wide. "Jules?"

Words stuck in her throat. Abe had assured her there wasn't a chance in hell she'd run into her ex. Frowning, she flung off his hands and rubbed her arms where he'd manhandled her. Then she saw him reach for his head. He was bleeding. Scowling and bleeding.

"You coulda killed me."

She stiffened. "That was the intent. I thought you were a burglar. Most normal people don't come in through a window, y'know."

Blood trickled down his forehead and she realized how hard she'd hit him. "Geez, I'm sorry, Luke. Here, let me get something for that."

As she turned to go, he grabbed her by the arm. "What are you doing here?"

"What am *I* doing here? I think I should be the one asking you that question."

"This is my father's house."

"Well, I'm here by invitation. Abe told me you hadn't been here for a year."

A puzzled look crossed his face. "It couldn't be that long."

She shrugged. "That's what he said." She could tell Luke felt guilty about it. Luke was never good at hiding his reactions. If he was irritated you knew it. If he was happy, you knew that, too. Angry, you *really* knew it. But he kept his thoughts, his reasons behind the emotions locked inside.

"Yeah, well, if it's been that long, then he'll be pleased to see me."

"Not with you dripping blood all over his floor." He seemed to have forgotten about his head and was staring at her instead. She gave him a shove, urging him down the hall to the bathroom. "Let's do something about that cut." Once inside the tiny room, she pulled a wash-cloth from the linen closet and moistened it under the faucet. "Here, this will help."

He took the cloth and, looking in the small mirror above the old cast-iron sink, applied it to his forehead.

Five years and he still looked the same. Same cobalt eyes that crinkled around the corners whether he was smiling or not, the same lean, hard features that said he was a man's man—a man with a purpose—and always in control. Qualities she'd once thought sexy and desirable.

"Your hair is different," he said, still looking in the mirror, but gazing at her.

"Different than what?"

"Than before. No ponytail." His eyes narrowed. "What *are* you doing here?"

"Is that important?"

"Still good at answering questions with a question, aren't you?"

"And you're still good at thinking everything is your business when it's not."

A tight smile lifted his lips. "Touché."

With that one small concession, an uncomfortable silence fell between them, a silence laden with recrim-inations and guilt. Their divorce had been inevitable, filled with heartache and pain. The hurt was so great, she couldn't be around him and vice-versa. She'd even moved from L.A. to San Francisco to lessen the chances of running into him.

In the confines of the small bathroom, he shifted his

stance and lifted one foot to the edge of the tub, effectively imprisoning her between his leg and the sink.

He was so close she felt his heat. His familiar scent made her blood rush. And if the look in his eyes was any indication, he felt the same. But then, lack of desire had never been their problem.

In the end, desire hadn't helped the marriage either. She hated what they'd done to each other in the year before the divorce. Things that would stay with them forever.

"Okay, here's a question you can answer. How's my father?"

She shrugged. "You know Abe, he wouldn't admit to anything even if he were inches from death's door. Personally, I think he'd be a lot healthier if he stopped smoking."

"Fat chance of that."

"I know."

"So let's quit the sparring and you tell me what's up with the visit."

She sighed in resignation. He wasn't going to give up. "Your father invited me for a vacation. I needed one." She crossed her arms. "Now it's your turn."

"I'm taking a couple weeks off. And since I hadn't seen Pops for a while, I thought I'd check how the old rooster was doing."

"*You're* taking time off?" He never took time off.

Just then she heard a loud banging at the door. "Oh Geez. I called the police. That's probably them."

They went into the living room. Spotlights flashed through the window, rotating red and blue, lighting up the room like a nightclub. Another percussion of knocking rattled the house. "Sheriff's department. Open up."

She crossed the room and threw wide the door. A tall man in a black hat stood in front of her. His badge said he was indeed the sheriff.

He peered inside. "I'm Sheriff Ben Yuma. I received a call."

Julianna flipped on a light switch next to the door. "I'm sorry, Officer. I called because I thought someone was breaking into the house, but I was wrong."

The sheriff glanced at Luke. His dark eyes narrowed.

"Luke Coltrane, LAPD," he said, pulling out his shield. "I came to see my father, forgot my key and decided to use a window."

The sheriff brushed a hand across his smooth chin, assessing both of them. "With bad results, I see."

"I was protecting myself," Julianna countered. "Well, I thought I was anyway."

"What the hell is going on here?" Abe's gravelly voice resounded.

Julianna turned. "Abe, what are you doing up?"

Luke gave her a pointed stare, a slow smile tipping his mouth at the corners. "Question with a question," he said under his breath, as if proving his earlier point.

She wanted to laugh, but held it back. He knew exactly how to get to her. Make her laugh and she'd forget everything. But not anymore.

Ignoring him, she glanced at Abe. Though Luke loved his father, there'd always been tension between them. In five years of marriage to Luke, she'd never figured out exactly why. Luke had always passed it off as his father being too hard on him, making him feel he couldn't do anything right. She'd always thought there was more to it.

When Abe saw Luke, he looked surprised at first, but then his mouth turned down, his expression dour. He acknowledged the sheriff and then turned back to Julianna. "I'm up because someone's making so much racket it's impossible to sleep. And that's saying a lot since I can't hear worth spit."

Julianna crossed to Abe and placed a hand on his arm. "There's nothing to worry about. I thought there was a burglar and called the sheriff. But it was only Luke, so everything's okay and you can go back to bed. We'll talk in the morning."

"We will not." Abe made his way to the couch and eased onto the sagging cushion. "Sheriff, you want to arrest someone?"

"Someone?" The sheriff glanced at the only other people in the room. Luke and Julianna.

"I invited one person to stay here. The other is a stranger to me. And apparently he broke into my house."

Luke's nerves bunched. Okay, that was his dad's way of getting back at him for staying away so long. He had to admit it had been awhile, so he probably deserved whatever lambasting he got. Still…his dad was irritating the hell out of him. "Fine. I'll leave right now."

For a fraction of a second, Luke thought his father seemed a little crestfallen. But the reaction quickly passed.

"If that's what you want, then go," Abe said gruffly.

What Luke wanted was a soft bed. After driving six hours from L.A. to Phoenix and another six to Santa Fe, he was dog-tired. But his old man wouldn't be satisfied until he had it all.

Abe wanted Luke to grovel *and* apologize. "I came to see you, why would I *want* to go? Why don't we let the sheriff get on with his business and we can talk about everything in the morning."

The sheriff shifted his feet, crossed his arms. "You got a problem with that, Abe?"

"I got a big problem standing right in front of me."

The sheriff frowned. "So do you want me to arrest him?"

Luke groaned. *Another nutcase.* "For what reason?" he asked incredulously.

"Whatever reason I want." The sheriff shrugged and smiled, his teeth bright white against bronzed skin. "We do things differently out here than in the big city."

Great, just what he needed. His father's wrath and a rogue sheriff who didn't give a rat's ass about procedure. And then there was Julianna. Dear Jules. He cleared his throat. "Fine. Arrest me if you want. Otherwise, I'm outta here." He turned to leave.

"Suit yourself," Abe spat out. "Never could stick anything out."

Luke edged toward the door, primed for a comeback, but then, for the first time since his father entered the room, Luke noticed how frail he seemed. He'd lost weight, and his face looked gray and haggard, the lines deeper, more like canyons instead of crevices. "Okay then," Luke said, "if it's up to me, I need a good night's sleep. I'll leave in the morning."

Abe scoffed and with great effort tried to rise from his seat on the couch. Julianna hurried over, but Abe waved her off, then took hold of the armrests and laboriously lifted himself to his feet. "I'm going to bed."

The sheriff tipped his hat. "Seems everything's okay here, so I'll be on my way, too."

That left Luke alone with Julianna. The woman he'd once thought was the center of his life. The woman whose very presence pounded in another sharp reminder that he'd lost everything that had made life worth living. A reminder that he'd failed her and their marriage.

"I'm turning in, too," Julianna said, her voice oddly quiet. "I'm in the back bedroom, so you'll have to take the smaller one."

"Fine with me." Only he knew there wasn't a chance in hell he'd get any sleep with her in the next room.

CHAPTER TWO

THOUGHTS OF JULIANNA had kept him awake for a while, but it was the nightmares about the kidnapping that woke him a mere three hours after he'd gone to bed.

He rolled over, sweat pouring from his body, sheets drenched.

As Julianna's face loomed in his mind, muscles cramped in his chest. The death of their son had created a chasm between them and destroyed their marriage. Seeing Julianna brought it all back in spades.

He had to go. No matter how much he wanted to mend the rift with his father, he didn't know if he was strong enough to stay in the same house with Julianna. It had taken him too long to get back on track. He couldn't jeopardize everything he'd accomplished.

For nearly four years, he'd gone through the motions of living. He went to his job, he went home and went to sleep, but not before consuming copious amounts of alcohol to speed up the process. He'd alienated his father, put his friends at a distance and had been within a hair's breath of losing his job.

Life might not be everything he wanted, but at least

he was among the living again. His job and his friends were all he had.

The sharp ring of his cell phone surprised him. He was used to calls at any hour when he was in L.A., but he hadn't expected to get them here. "Coltrane."

"I need some information," Captain Jeff Carlyle's rough voice blared. The captain had seen him through some tough times. Luke owed him a lot.

"Sure. What's up?" Luke had been working on two high-profile cases before he left L.A. The missing congressional aide, Michelle Renfield, who they suspected was dead, and the latest Studio Killer case, a serial murderer who specialized in killing porno flick stars near the location where their latest movie had been shot.

"It's Thorpe."

"Figures." Congressman Thorpe was the prime suspect in his aide's disappearance three years ago. Thorpe was suspected of having an affair with her and though they'd found no conclusive evidence of his involvement in her disapearance, Luke hadn't let up on his investigation. But Thorpe didn't like anyone messing with his life and he'd let Luke know it. "What's his problem now?"

"His attorney's threatening a lawsuit. Says you have a vendetta, that you've prejudiced the public with your investigation and that it's detrimental to his upcoming election."

"I thought my taking a vacation was supposed to help, get me out of sight for a while. Besides, Thorpe should've thought about that when he seduced a sixteen-year-old and forgot he had a wife."

"She was twenty."

"She wasn't when he met her. He's a predator." Luke's grip on the phone tightened.

"Okay, I know how you feel about it. But the reason I called is to make sure there's no question on procedure if Thorpe's attorney goes ahead with the suit."

"None whatsoever." He might be aggressive in his investigations and quick to jump on things, but he was thorough.

"I also wanted to tell you I'm putting St. James and Santini on the case."

Luke's nerves tensed. He'd worked his guts out on this case and now because some politician threatened to sue, he had to give it up?

"It's not permanent," Carlyle said. "And they've both got full loads right now."

That meant the assignment was only for looks. No one was really going to work on it. "I'm on it again when I get back, right?"

After a long pause the captain said, "Sure." Then he asked, "How's your father?"

"He looks terrible."

"Well, you've got two weeks, or longer if you need it. I just wanted you to know." Carlyle clicked off.

Luke felt satisfied. The captain knew Luke would be pissed if he came back and found the Renfield case had been pulled out from under him. It didn't matter if Jordan and Rico actually worked the case or not.

That Thorpe's attorney had the gall to file a lawsuit burned Luke's ass. Thorpe had the kind of connections that might help him if he was ever arrested and brought to trial—only the congressman wasn't about to let it go that far. He wanted to be vindicated now and a lawsuit would probably guarantee it if no other evidence turned up.

Yeah, well, Luke didn't give a damn about anyone's connections. With every fiber of his being he believed Thorpe was responsible for the disappearance of the young aide. If the evidence showed he was right, the congressman was going to jail.

Whether he was reelected or not. As far as his having a vendetta—if seeking justice for murder victims was a vendetta, then yeah, he did have one. And the sooner he got back to L.A., the better.

Only in this case, justice would have to wait. He had to first assess his father's health and see what he could do to help him while he was here. Maybe find him a hired hand—someone who could stay at the ranch. And when his father discovered that plan, all hell would break loose.

"Good morning," Julianna greeted Luke when he came in from outside. "Out doing chores?" She busied herself making coffee, trying not to look at him.

"Funny," he said, letting the kitchen door slap shut with a bang.

"Well, you know there's plenty of work to do around here. Too much for your father." She scooped some coffee into the basket.

"I noticed. Everything seems to have fallen apart since I was here last."

"He could use some help."

"He could easily afford to hire someone."

"You mean if he wasn't so stubborn and didn't think he could do everything himself."

He paused for a moment, as if considering what she'd said. "Yeah. While I'm here, I'm going to see what we can do about getting him help."

"Good idea." But she hoped that didn't mean he intended to stay for long.

Luke sat at the old oak table, wearing only a white T-shirt and faded jeans, his sandy sun-bleached hair still wet from the shower. He smelled of fresh soap and shampoo, and just looking at him made her breath hitch. Still. After all these years.

"Weren't you cold out there without a jacket?"

"I'm tough," he said, smiling.

She turned and retrieved a pan from the maple cabinet next to the harvest-gold stove that had one door half hanging from its hinges. Even though she had her back to Luke, she felt his gaze boring into her.

"You never did answer me last night," he said. "What brings you here?"

She turned, leaned against the counter. "I answered you. I said I was invited and I came."

He arched his brows without commenting. It was obvious he didn't believe her and his smug know-it-all attitude annoyed her. "I don't need a reason to visit someone I care about."

Luke had been gone most of the time they were married so she doubted he had any idea she'd developed such a close relationship with his father, or that they'd become even closer after the divorce.

"I could ask you the same thing. What's the *real* reason you're here?"

He shrugged. "I don't need a reason to see my father."

"And when did that become important?" The second the words left her mouth Julianna regretted them. Abe didn't get along well with people in general. She also knew the distance in Abe's relationship with Luke hurt Luke a lot—but just like his father, he was too stubborn to admit it.

"I'm sorry. I shouldn't have said that." She turned away. "But…can you at least tell me how long you're staying?"

He shrugged. "It depends."

She heaved a sigh. If he wasn't going to leave, then she would have to. Just talking with Luke made her anxious. Made her remember too much. And her only defense seemed to be anger. She wasn't proud of that, but there it was. "Well, don't let my presence be a factor in your decision. I'll be leaving soon."

"You're not going anywhere," Abe's voice boomed as he came in and joined them in the kitchen. "What kind of nonsense is that?"

The scent of hazelnut coffee wafted through the room and she noticed the pot had stopped burbling. She reached for the old chipped mugs, brought them to the table and poured them each a cup. "I've been thinking it might be…easier if I go. Besides, I have more investigative work to do on the next series and—"

"Well, you just stop that kind of thinking, young lady."

Julianna had to smile. She didn't want to hurt Abe's feelings, but if Luke stayed, she had no choice.

Luke leaned back in his chair, raised his arms and clasped his fingers behind his head. "You can both stop worrying. I've got to get back to L.A. Something has come up."

She raised her chin. Of course. The job. The job that was more important than just about anything. But she'd swallow her tongue before she'd say it. If it meant he'd leave, she was grateful.

Abe coughed. "I'm going to work on the fence out on the line."

"What's wrong with the fence?" Luke asked.

Julianna glanced at Abe.

"Someone keeps tearing it down."

"Really. Why would anyone do that?"

"Duke Hancock wanted that piece of land for years, but I told him I wasn't going to sell. Now they want it again."

"Duke died twenty years ago, Dad. And who are *they?*"

Ignoring his son's question, Abe went on. "The fence is destroyed. The cattle can run right through."

"You haven't had more than a few head of cattle for years, and that's not even where they pasture." Luke gave him a look of exasperation.

Abe scoffed. "It needs to be fixed."

"Okay. I'll go out with you to help on the fence," Luke said, then caught Julianna's gaze.

For a moment, she couldn't look away. His eyes were still bluer than Paul Newman's. Intense. Sexy.

"Okay with you, Jules?" He smiled.

A wide white smile. Her heart stalled...in the same way it had when she'd first met him at that environmental rally where they'd been on opposite sides.

And apparently her recent lack of male companionship was making her hormones shift into overdrive. "I'm scrambling eggs. Anyone else want some?"

Luke looked surprised. "You learned how to cook?"

Dammit. She wasn't going to acknowledge Luke's gibes. That's another way he got to her. He knew it and she knew it.

"No one needs to wait on me," Abe sputtered. "I can make my own breakfast. Been doin' it for years."

"I know you can, Abe. But since I'm making eggs for myself, it's no big deal to toss in a couple extra. I'd appreciate it though if I could have the kitchen to myself for about fifteen minutes."

Both men rose. Abe went down the hall toward the bathroom and Luke headed for the living room.

As she watched Luke walk away, an unexpected sadness washed over her. She swallowed back a sudden lump in her throat. After getting the eggs from the fridge, she leaned wearily against the door. What was the matter with her?

Was it being together again with Luke and Abe, like the old days? Was it remembering the love she and Luke once shared? The love. The heartache. The loss.

After three years of grief therapy and finally learning to live in the present, she'd thought she could handle just about anything. But now she felt as if she'd tumbled backward in time as all the memories, all the emotions she'd tried so hard to forget, roared to life once again. She thought she'd resolved all that. Had she only been fooling herself?

Maybe. But she couldn't slide back into the abyss that had been her life. She'd worked too hard to make herself into a whole person again—even though a piece of her would never mend.

She strengthened her resolve and went to the stove.

Seeing Luke again had thrown her off balance. That was all. She'd get over it. She'd carved out a comfortable niche for herself at the magazine. She had a great loft condo in the heart of San Francisco. Her life was good. She cracked an egg into the bowl with so much force it splattered everywhere. Her life was good, dammit.

Except for the loneliness. And right now, she felt more lonely than ever.

But going back home wasn't an option.

LUKE FINGERED THROUGH the magazines piled in the corner of the living room. He didn't remember his father being much of a reader. It was probably why Luke wasn't. That and the fact that he never had time. When he was off duty the last thing he wanted was to read about more crime and world problems.

Most of Abe's magazines were about ranching, except for one called *The Achilles' Heel*. Recognizing the name of the national magazine, Luke was surprised that Abe even had a copy. Hell, he had a whole stack of them. Luke picked one up and flipped a page. Most of the titles had a liberal slant, taking jabs at anything and everything that might be fair game.

Odd, because Abe was the biggest redneck around. Flipping another page, he saw Julianna listed on the masthead as a regular columnist. Ah, now it made sense.

He'd heard Julianna was doing well, but since she'd moved to San Francisco after the divorce, that's all he knew. Reading her brief bio, he felt a moment of pride over her success.

And then sadness. He missed what they'd had before everything went haywire. He missed having a family to come home to.

He dropped the magazine back in the pile. What they'd had was long gone. She'd made that crystal-clear the day she walked out on him, saying the only way she could find herself was to start a new life.

Instead of staying to work things out, she'd run away. He'd been willing, but she hadn't.

It'd stuck in his craw ever since. No, he didn't need reminders, and as soon as he got his father straightened up, he was outta there.

"Better come and get it if you want to eat," his father said as he passed Luke on his way to the kitchen.

Luke followed Abe, watching the uneven gait in his step, saw the gray in his thinning hair. When had his father gotten so old, so frail? "When was the last time you saw a doctor, Pops?"

"Don't need no doctor. I'm not sick."

They walked into the kitchen together. The aroma of

sizzling bacon and fresh coffee made his mouth water. Julianna had set the table and was dishing up the eggs.

"Everyone needs a checkup at least once a year. Especially someone with high blood pressure."

"I go when I'm sick. And it's nobody's business when I go and when I don't."

Luke walked over to the counter, refilled his coffee cup, then raised the pot to the others. Julianna said, "Yes, please," and his father grunted his response. When Luke finished pouring, he put the pot on the table on a trivet and sat.

The tension in the air was so thick you couldn't cut it with a sharp fillet knife. He felt more uncomfortable sitting here with his father and Julianna than he did scoping out a crime scene.

But his discomfort didn't keep him from noticing how little Julianna had changed in the last five years. She was still slim and toned, and her flawless skin looked even more perfect framed by long, wavy chestnut hair. Silky hair that always fell in his face when she was on top. "You still jog?"

She nodded. "Abe, Luke's right. You really should get a checkup. Everyone needs to do that once in a while."

Luke smiled at his dad with satisfaction, glad that Julianna had supported him.

Ignoring both of them, Abe mumbled around a mouthful of eggs, "If you're going to fix the fence with me you better eat and quit talking."

Luke nearly dropped his fork. It sounded almost as if his father was asking for Luke's help, something he had never done before. Whenever Luke had offered in the past, he got shot down. Maybe there was hope for them yet. "Sure. I'm only going to be here until tomorrow, so we should get as much done today as we can."

Abe's head jerked up. "If that's all the time you got, then we might as well forget it. It's a two-day job at best."

Luke fought another smile. His old man sure knew the art of manipulation. "I'll stay until it's done. If it's done today, I'll leave in the morning. If it takes another day, I'll go home after that."

But he was going to do everything he could to finish in one day. Besides needing to get back to L.A., he wanted to focus on the life he had, not the one he'd lost.

"Fine. Getting the fence fixed is all I care about."

Julianna gently touched Abe's arm. "Luke will help and it'll get done," she said, always the calm one. With her mediating skills, she should've been a diplomat.

She turned to Luke. "Got a big case to get back to?"

He chewed some toast and finished with a sip of coffee. "Always."

"I heard more on the news about congressman Thorpe's aides, and Thorpe didn't seem happy about it. Is he a person of interest?"

"He's more than interesting to me. The guy's a weasel who thinks he can use his political influence to derail the investigation."

"That's why you're going back?"

"That and a serial killer on the loose."

Julianna's face went white.

Oh, man. Insert foot into mouth. Again. Though he'd

long ago separated his personal life from his job, Julianna didn't know how to dissociate. He should've remembered that. "What about *your* career?" he said, changing the subject.

"Uh…it's good." She pushed back the hair from her eyes and tucked it behind one ear. "I'm a regular contributor for a magazine. *The Achilles' Heel.* I like it and it pays well."

He knew it was more than that to her. Writing was a part of her, something she *had* to do. And the liberal magazine was the perfect venue.

"How is Starr?"

She looked surprised that he'd asked. "My mother's fine. Still the same. Stumping for one cause or another. The environment, PETA, stem-cell research." She smiled. "All good causes."

"Still a hippie at heart, huh?"

"That she is. She thinks it's the seventies, and that she's still twenty, and actually, she doesn't look much older."

"And your sister?"

"Lindsay's married, has two children and lives in London. As far away from Mother as possible."

Luke nodded. "I can understand that." He remembered the strife between Julianna's sister, the yuppie, and her mother. Julianna on the other hand, had been Starr's protégée.

Jules's mother and her ability to suck her daughter into her causes had been another sticking point in Luke and Julianna's relationship.

"Unfortunately, my sister's far away from me, as

well. I rarely see Ally and Devon, my niece and nephew."

Julianna would miss that. She'd always loved children. They both did, and he'd been deeply disappointed when she refused to have another child after Michael. He was surprised that she hadn't married again. He wanted to ask her about it but didn't want to open old wounds for either of them.

"Kinda the way Luke thinks, too," Abe said. "Wants to be as far away as possible."

Luke shoved his plate away and leaned back in the chair. "I moved because I was given an opportunity. You didn't want Grandpa's house, remember? That's why he gave it to me." Even though the house on one of the much desired canals in Venice Beach was worth double what the ranch was at the time, his father had turned it down, refused to move to California. Luke suspected Abe didn't want to be beholden to his father-in-law in any way. That and the fact Gramps never thought Abe was good enough for his only child and wasn't afraid to say so.

"You can come out and stay with me any time you want."

"And who would take care of things here?"

"Hire someone. You need help anyway. Then you can come and go as you please."

Abe shoved his chair back and rose to his feet. "I'm not going anywhere and no stranger is going to come in here and take over. Now let's get to work."

Julianna stood and began clearing the dishes. "So, get out of here, you two. I've got to write."

That figured. She was just as intense about her work as he was, only she'd never seen it that way. "What kind of a story are you working on?"

Her brown eyes expanded. "Uh, just a series. I do an installment once a month."

Gazing at her, he barely heard a word. He'd forgotten how pretty her eyes were. Big brandy-colored pools that drew him in, made him want to get closer.

But her evasiveness put things in perspective. In the past, when he'd asked about what she was writing, she'd couldn't wait to share her ideas. Now, it was obvious she didn't want him to know.

Why should she? She hadn't wanted to share *anything* in her life for five years. Maybe she was sharing those things with someone else now? For all he knew, she could have a live-in lover.

"What's the series about?"

She looked at Abe.

"We need to get cracking," Abe said. "We're wastin' sunlight. You can chitchat later."

The lines around Julianna's mouth softened, apparently relieved that Abe had ended the conversation.

And that made him even more curious. Okay. He'd play along. For a while. "I'm with you, Pops. Just let me grab a shirt and a hat."

In the hallway on the way to his room, Luke's cell phone rang. He recognized his partner's number. "Yeah."

"Luke, it's Jordan."

"Hey, bud. What's going down?"

"I wondered if you heard from the boss?"

Luke shifted the phone to the other ear while he pulled on a faded denim shirt. "I did."

"Did he tell you it's the chief who's pushing to take you off the Thorpe case? I heard Carlyle told him to stuff it, in so many words, but—"

"I talked to him. It's no big deal. I can't leave here yet anyway. My father isn't well and I've got to get him some help."

"Bring him here. California has some of the best physicians in the world."

"Great idea, but he's dug in. He'll never leave. And… he has a guest."

"A guest?"

Luke hesitated. "Julianna."

Jordan let out a long blow of air. "Whoa. That's a surprise."

"You telling me."

"What's she doing there?"

"I don't know, but I'm going to find out before I come back."

"When's that?"

"Tomorrow or the next day for sure." Luke started walking back to the kitchen to catch up with his dad.

"Okay. Let me know." Jordan was one of Luke's best friends, and also one of the finest detectives in the Robbery Homicide Division. While Luke often operated without a partner, he'd worked with Jordan on several cases recently.

"I'll call you when I get back."

"Good."

"How's the better half?" Luke asked.

"Laura's great. Today she hired someone to stay nights at the shelter for her so she and Caitlin can move into my place after the wedding. Don't forget, you've got a job next month."

Luke smiled. Jordan could've picked any one of their friends to be best man, Rico or even Tex. But he'd asked Luke. "Not for a second."

As he reached the kitchen doorway, Luke said goodbye and clicked off. Julianna stood only inches away and gave him a knowing look. The one that said he couldn't leave his job for more than five minutes. "That was Jordan. Remember him?"

Julianna's eyes lit up. "Of course. How is he?"

"He's getting married next month."

Mouth open, Jules put a hand to her chest in surprise. "Really! I never thought that would happen." She smiled, showing an expanse of even, white teeth and very kissable lips.

"I'm the best man." Jules had always liked Jordan and for a time they'd all been really close.

"I'd be surprised if you weren't."

The pleased look in her eyes switched to wistfulness. Was she thinking of their wedding? She'd once said it was the happiest day of her life.

"Please give Jordan my best," she said, and then hurried away.

She left him standing there, feeling as if one small moment from the past had somehow brought them closer. But then he could just as easily be misreading things. He did that a lot with Jules. Whenever he'd been sure he knew what she thought or wanted, she'd been on another wavelength altogether.

But there was no denying that something had passed between them. He just didn't know what the hell it was.

He headed out the back door, glanced around for Abe, who was nowhere to be seen. The old reprobate had probably taken off without him. Luke strode to the barn. As he went inside, the familiar scents of hay and manure took him back to a time when he couldn't have imagined ever leaving the ranch.

The mare was gone, but Balboa stood in his stall and nickered softly at Luke. When Abe had downsized, he'd kept two horses and five head of cattle, just enough to stay busy, but not too much to handle.

Luke talked softly to Balboa before saddling him up. "Hey, big guy. It's been a while." The golden palomino nuzzled him, apparently remembering they'd been inseparable once upon a time. He wished other parts of his life were that easy to resurrect.

He mounted the stallion and headed for the line, not having a clue where the fence was broken. He figured it was at Stella Hancock's property line, otherwise Abe would have no reason to complain about her long-dead husband.

He sat straight in the saddle and took a quick breath of fresh mountain air, a nice change from the smog and gasoline fumes of downtown L.A. Even the salty ocean breezes at his home in Venice were a respite from the pollution that hung like an ochre cloud over the rest of the city.

Out here, he could breathe. The scent of piñon pine teased his senses, reminding him of a time when life was simple and uncomplicated, a time when the only thing he'd cared about was what he was going to do that day.

His mother's sudden death when he was thirteen changed all that. She'd been the peacemaker, she'd held the family together. Clearly something he and his father had no desire to do once she was gone.

Back then his father always blamed Luke's bad behavior on adolescence, but it was more than that. Something he'd long since put out of his mind. He'd never approached his father about it, but he'd always thought Abe knew that Luke knew—and neither wanted to open that door.

One thing was certain, his mother's death had changed his life forever.

He nudged Balboa to a canter. He hadn't thought about that in years. He preferred physical activity over thinking. But being here, seeing Jules again, had him thinking more than ever. Love complicated everything— and losing everything you loved made life intolerable.

When they'd lost Michael he'd soldiered on for Julianna's sake. But when she left…there wasn't any point to anything. He'd hit bottom.

The anger he thought he'd buried a long time ago burned in his veins. Bitterness rose like bile in his throat. Never again would he let himself feel so much. If he didn't feel, he couldn't hurt.

JULIANNA WENT INTO the den to do some research for her next story. *If* she could concentrate. Luke had said he'd be there only a day or two. God, she hoped so. He was too intense. Too probing. She was on tenterhooks every time he entered the room.

One day she could handle. Couldn't she? All she had to do was maintain her distance, keep her mind in the present and stay focused on the end result. Luke going back to L.A.

She'd made a quick decision not to tell Luke about the story because she knew the subject would upset him. She knew that as well as she knew her deadlines. It would simply make the time he was here even more strained. He already suspected she hadn't just come simply because Abe asked her to. As intuitive as Luke was, if she told him about the story, he might connect the two. And if he knew she was being threatened, the cop in him wouldn't let it go. He'd have to take action.

There was no way she could tell Luke. But she had to tell Abe about the phone calls.

CHAPTER THREE

BY THE TIME Luke reached his father, Abe had already taken out the new roll of barbed wire and was trying to fasten it to the fence by himself. "Couldn't wait a few more minutes?" Luke dismounted and strode over.

"Can't wait forever. I'm not getting any younger."

"Not getting any easier to get along with either."

"One of the few good things about getting old. You can say what you want and the hell with what anyone thinks."

Luke couldn't remember a time when his father didn't say what he wanted or ever cared what anyone thought. But he wasn't going to stay that long and he needed his father's cooperation if he was going to hire someone to help out. Getting Abe to accept that help was going to be the tough part.

"We need to shore up the posts first," Luke said and walked over to one that was tilted at forty-five degrees.

"It'll straighten out with the wire on it," Abe countered.

Luke let out an exasperated breath. He knew he should just agree with his dad and then get out of there. "C'mon, let's do it together."

That seemed to agree with Abe and they both started

working on getting the post upright. And while they were somewhat sympatico, Luke said, "I know Jules isn't here just because you asked her to come."

His father turned and looked at him. "Is it such a hard thing to believe, that someone would actually want to be here with me?"

"No, Dad. Of course not. You have company all the time, don't you." No matter how hard he tried to be nice, his father made it impossible and Luke couldn't seem to hold back his sarcasm. But then it wasn't likely he'd hurt the old man's feelings anyway. Nothing fazed his father. And he usually gave out more than he got.

"People never did take to me, like they did your mother," Abe said. "And when she died, it was hard to be nice to anyone."

Including me. But this time, Luke bit back the words. He'd come here to make amends with his father and dammit, he was going to. "I know you missed her. I did, too."

"I still do."

The softness in his dad's voice might've made Luke think he actually meant it. "So why are *you* here?" Abe said. "I know you didn't come to keep an old man company."

Luke smiled, hoping to ease the tension. "But you're wrong. That's exactly why I came. I had two weeks vacation and I thought it a good opportunity for us to… to reconnect."

Abe snorted, then as if he hadn't heard a word, walked to the next post and started righting it.

Yeah. Luke sighed. Had he hoped for a different reaction? What Luke wanted didn't mean squat when it came to his father. Never had. "So, getting back to Jules. I know she likes you and all that, but what's the other reason she's here?"

"Ask her, not me."

"I did. She won't tell me."

"Shoot. If you'd kept in touch with her, you'd know why she was here."

Keep in touch? Where had his father been all this time? Julianna didn't want anything to do with him. It was her decision and he'd respected it.

"And if you hadn't bailed on the marriage, she probably wouldn't be here at all."

Picking up the roll of wire, Luke gritted his teeth. Tension crackled in the air between them. Luke started attaching the end of the wire to the first post. "Dad, that was five years ago. Long enough for you to quit harping on something that's over and done with."

"She was the best thing that ever happened to you," his father grumbled.

Yeah. He'd thought so, too. "Like Mom was the best thing that ever happened to you?" Sarcasm laced his words.

Slowly Abe turned, his eyes narrowing to slits. "Yes, like your mother."

He'd hit a nerve. He'd spent a lifetime wanting to say that and trying not to. And now that he had, he didn't feel any better. "Julianna may have been the best thing for me, but I wasn't the best for her. I doubt she'd agree that there'd been anything good between us."

Abe spat on the ground and grumbled, "People don't always say what they mean, you know."

Yeah, he knew. He saw it in his job all the time. People lied to save their butts. But Julianna wasn't a liar. She'd meant every last hurtful word. Every time he thought about it… Hell, dealing with both Jules and his father, his head felt about to explode.

"Things happen," Abe said. "Good stuff, crappy stuff. It's called life. If love is there, it's there. People go on."

"Dammit. It's a dead subject, Dad. Now why don't you just tell me why she's here and be done with it."

Abe grabbed the roll of wire Luke held and yanked it away. "I told you. It's not my place. Ask her yourself."

Luke released his grip before the wire cut his hand. Then suddenly Abe spat out a string of cuss words. His face went ghost-white, his lips blue. He staggered back, grabbed his chest and sank to his knees.

Shit. Luke dropped the roll.

"IT'S OKAY, MARK. I'm finishing the story and that's that. I'm in the safest place I could be, under the circumstances."

"But you can't stay there forever."

She sighed. "I know. Once the story is done—"

"What makes you think this lowlife will stop bothering you when you're finished?"

"That's what his threats are about. He doesn't want me to finish, so if I do, he's lost."

"I think you're wrong. It could make him even more incensed that you didn't listen."

That was true. So far it had. "Look, Mark, I'm not going to live my life in fear because of some jackass. No one is going to tell me what I can and can't do when it comes to my writing." Her temper flared at the thought.

"Well, I can."

She stifled a laugh. "Right." Mark was such a cupcake. He'd given her free rein after only a month on the job. And she was careful not to abuse the confidence he had in her. "You'll see. It'll be business as usual after the last installment."

"Damn, I hope you're right. Because otherwise I'm going to feel responsible."

"So, what else is new, *Dad?*" Mark wasn't much older than her own thirty-two years, but he acted as if he was sixty sometimes.

He chuckled. Finally.

"I'll be in touch." As she hung up, Julianna heard something bang outside. She glanced at her watch. Luke and Abe had only left a half hour ago, it couldn't be them.

Just as she went into the kitchen, Abe burst through the back door, Luke right behind him. "What's wrong?"

"Nothing a little good sense won't fix," Luke said.

Abe waved him off with a hand covered with a blood-soaked cloth.

"Oh, you're hurt!"

"Just a little cut. I've had worse. No big deal."

"When did you last have a tetanus shot?" Luke asked.

Abe shrugged.

"That's what I thought."

"That's enough, you two. What we need right now is a first-aid kit. Do you have one, Abe?"

"Under the sink in the bathroom," he grumbled, then quickly added, "But I'm not going to get any shots."

"Can you get it, Luke?" Julianna asked as she lifted Abe's hand to see the damage. "What were you doing?"

"Nothin' I don't do all the time. I just got distracted."

As Abe answered, Luke returned with the kit and handed it to Julianna. She went to work, cleaning the wound, a gash about two inches long. "You really should see a doctor. It might need stitches."

No response.

"While you're taking care of that, I'm going back out to finish what we started." Luke motioned with a tip of his head that Julianna should follow him outside.

"Hold the pressure on it, and I'll be right back, Abe."

Outside on the porch, Luke stood with his feet apart, arms crossed over his chest. "He wasn't distracted," Luke said, keeping his voice low. "He looked unsteady on his feet, as if he was dizzy or something. Then he fell. But he wouldn't tell me what was wrong. Maybe while I'm gone you can find out. I think he needs to see a doctor…whether he wants to go or not."

Julianna saw the concern in Luke's eyes. For a tough cop, he felt things intensely, though it wasn't always easy to tell.

"I'll see what I can do." Before she could go back inside, Luke placed a hand on her shoulder.

"You're going to have to tell me why you're here, because we both know it's not just a visit. I don't have any desire to pry into your personal life… I mean if it's something like you've had a fight with your boyfriend or whatever, just say so and I'll butt out. But if it's something else and it involves my father, then I need to know." He stared at her, determined. "Besides, you know I'll find out one way or another."

The skin on her arms prickled. "And what does that mean?"

He shrugged, but didn't let her go. "I'm a detective."

Annoyed, but knowing he meant what he said, she pulled away. "Okay…it's personal, so butt out." She stalked back inside. It wasn't exactly a lie. It *was* personal…and if telling a tiny untruth meant he'd leave her alone, so be it.

After she finished cleaning Abe's wound and bandaged it as best she could, she said, "So, how about that tetanus shot? I'll be happy to drive you."

"Nearest doc is in a little clinic outside Pecos."

"Fine. Let's go." Before he could protest, she said, "Oh, one other thing."

He glanced at her.

"I received a couple of voice-mail messages on my home phone. Threatening messages."

"The bastard," Abe spat out. "It's a good thing you're here then."

"I was thinking of going somewhere else."

"Nonsense."

She sat on a chair next to him and clasped his good hand. "It's not nonsense. If there's any chance I'm in danger, then my being here puts you in danger, too."

Abe squinted. "Why do you think you'd be any safer someplace else? No one's going to find you here. And if they can't find you, that keeps us both safe. Right?"

She shrugged. "I don't know. I took precautions, but I can't be sure it was enough. I couldn't bear it if—"

He held up a hand. "I won't hear of it," he sputtered. "You leave, you'll have the same problem. This is the best place and that's the end of it."

Julianna smiled, then gave Abe a long hug.

"So, let's quit jawing and get that shot."

"I'll leave a note for Luke."

She started to help Abe get up, but he protested.

"Tell him we're going to the grocery store. He doesn't need to know we went to the clinic."

"I'll write the note however you want it." Luke would know where they'd gone. He was a smart guy. Someone who could unravel puzzles in a flash, who understood people at a glance. And he hadn't believed for a second she was there on vacation. But what difference did it make to him why she was there?

If he'd just finish the fence, hire someone to help Abe and then go home, she'd be fine. But from the determined look she'd seen in his eyes, she had an awful feeling that wasn't going to happen. Luke would hound her until he found out what he wanted to know.

THAT NIGHT during a very late dinner, Luke told Julianna and Abe about his progress with the fence. "But there's still more to do," he said.

Luke didn't ask why Abe's hand was bandaged differently and Abe didn't offer that they'd gone to the clinic. Julianna talked about the weather, of all things, simply because she wanted to get through the meal without any further references to why she was there.

So far, so good, she thought as she brought dessert to the table, a pie that she'd picked up at the grocery store after Abe had his hand stitched and had grudgingly submitted to a tetanus shot.

"Good pie," Luke said.

"Thanks to Sara Lee."

"Pot roast was good, too." Luke forked another piece of pie and brought it to his lips.

Her eyes fastened there, on his mouth, the little indentation in the middle of his top lip.

"I don't remember you cooking much before."

Maybe that was because he was never home at dinnertime. She and Mikey had eaten alone most nights. "I learned a thing or two when I had an exchange student living with me for a while. Actually the student was doing an internship at the magazine and somehow I ended up with her at my house."

"You have a house?" Luke looked surprised.

"A loft condo. No upkeep, and someone else does all the fixing."

He nodded. "Not a bad idea. At my place there's

always something going wrong." His bluer-than-blue gaze caught hers. "But then, you know that."

Her pulse quickened. Was he still living in his grand-father's house? The house they'd shared?

"That's why I didn't want that place," Abe grumbled. "Too much fixin'."

Both she and Luke turned to Abe. Then Luke said, "And there isn't here?"

"It's different," Abe said gruffly. "There's mem-ories here."

Julianna sighed. There *were* memories—both here and at the house in Venice Beach. She couldn't believe Luke was still living there.

"The ranch has memories of all kinds," Luke said. "Some good, some not so good."

Abe's chair scraped on the tiles as he abruptly rose to his feet. "I need to feed the horses, and then it's time for me to turn in."

When Abe was gone, she carried some dishes to the sink. "The doctor gave your father a tetanus shot and put five stitches in the cut." Luke was right behind her with the dessert plates. Close. She moved to the side to put the dishes in the dishwasher.

"Good." Luke scraped off a plate and handed it to her.

"He said Abe should come in for a checkup."

Luke gave a dry laugh. "I don't have to guess what the old coot's response to that was, do I?"

"Right. But I think someone really needs to make sure he goes. He hasn't seemed like himself since I got here."

Luke leaned on the counter, watching as she finished

up. She felt sweaty all of a sudden, unnerved to have him so close. It seemed odd that they were talking about Abe as if they were still married.

"If you could work some of your magic to get him to agree, I'd be indebted," he said.

The soft plea in his eyes touched her. She put the last cup into the dishwasher, added soap, pushed the button and started the machine. "I'll see what I can do. But right now, I've got work to do."

Luke's gaze followed as Jules walked away. She'd seemed nervous—as if she couldn't wait to get away from him. If he didn't know better, he might think... But hell, she was probably worried that he was going to ask again why she was there. And truth was, if she hadn't left, he would've.

Repeatedly asking the same question was one way to wear someone down. He did it with suspects all the time when he thought they weren't being truthful. While Jules might not be lying, something was definitely wrong. She jumped out of her skin every time the phone rang.

Walking into the living room, he heard the kitchen door slap shut. His dad coming back inside. Abe had said he was going to bed, and though it seemed early for that, his father'd had a busy day what with the fence and the doctor and all. Luke felt tired, too, but he knew it was more mental exhaustion than physical.

As he reached the worn-out couch, its worst parts covered with a red-and-blue Southwestern serape blanket, he inhaled the familiar scent, a mixture of cigarettes, Old Spice and old man. He glanced around. Nothing had changed. Nothing in the house and nothing with Abe.

Though he'd come here with the idea of smoothing out his relationship with his dad, he could see now it was a bad idea. Abe was too set in his ways. More importantly, his dad didn't care about mending anything between them. And now, in addition to finding hired help, he had to get Abe in for a physical.

He couldn't leave until he had those two things under his belt. He hoped Jules would help. She was good at getting people to do things without them realizing it.

An image of Jules immediately popped into his head. An image of how she looked today, not the one he'd carried for the past five years. She looked more mature, more comfortable in her own skin, and she was every bit as beautiful as he remembered. Just watching her had made his blood run hot…made him remember what it was like to feel something.

Something other than duty and responsibility.

And Jules was the last person he should be thinking about like that. He reached for a magazine. *The Achilles' Heel*. What the hell. Reading might get his mind on something else. He flipped it open. The title of the article practically leaped off the page. "Missing."

He read a couple paragraphs. Turned the page. What the—the story was about a little girl who'd been abducted fifteen years ago in Los Angeles. Renata Willis. He tossed the magazine on the pile and picked up another. Another story with the same theme, but a different child.

Anger rose from the dark well inside him, the place where he'd buried his feelings. How long had she been doing this? A sharp, heart-stabbing pain drove into his chest.

How could she!

CHAPTER FOUR

SOMETHING WAS WRONG. Luke had kept his distance all day, barely grunting when Julianna or his father asked a question. Would he like coffee? Grunt. Aren't you going to have breakfast? At least that one had gotten a grumble that she thought was a "No thanks. Gotta get to work."

He'd left immediately and, since he'd been gone all day, Julianna suspected he'd long since finished the fence. "He can't still be working, can he?" she asked Abe as they finished up dinner. "It's getting dark."

"Luke can take care of himself."

"I know he can, Abe. But for him to be gone so long, something could've happened. Aren't you worried just a little? Curious maybe?"

"Nope. I learned a long time ago that Luke doesn't need anyone to worry about him." He glanced at her from under his brows. "And I think you seem more worried than necessary."

Julianna stared at him in surprise. Abe never talked about anything personal. Never once had he mentioned the divorce. "I don't know what you mean."

As he smiled, the crevices in his face deepened and

she saw a glint in his faded blue eyes. Eyes that reminded her vaguely of Luke's. "You know what I mean." He rose from the chair and then raised his hands in the air. "But then I'm an old man and you probably think I don't know what it's like to be in love."

She did a double take. "I…I'm not…there's nothing—"

"It's okay. No need to explain."

Sheesh! What did Abe think? That she'd been pining away for Luke for five years?

JUST AS LUKE WAS finishing up the fence, he heard a noise behind him and turned to see Stella Hancock astride a pinto that looked as old as she was.

"Hello, Luke."

He tipped his Stetson. "Mrs. Hancock."

"How are you? It's been a long time."

Luke drew a breath, then shifted his stance, feet apart, arms crossed. "I'm fine." He didn't ask how she was and instead said, "I'm surprised to see you out here. You ride out very often?"

She smiled and the fine wrinkles around her eyes fanned out. For a woman who'd spent most of her life on a ranch, she'd aged gracefully. Most ranch women were well weathered by the time they were forty.

"No, I came because I heard you were fixing the fence and I wanted to know how Abraham is doing?"

When he didn't answer right away, she added, "I saw your wi—Julianna at the grocery store yesterday. She told me your father had hurt his hand."

Luke looked away. Jules had met the Hancock woman once when they'd come to visit when they were first married, and she'd been impressed that Stella had run her own ranch after her husband passed away. Luke didn't think it was a big deal, not when you had her money. She might run the place, but other people did the work.

Coughing, Luke grated out, "He had a couple stitches, that's all."

"The last time I saw him in town he didn't look well."

Annoyed that he was even talking to this woman about his father, this woman who'd— Luke stared at her, willing her to get the drift and go away. "I'll take care of whatever is bothering my father."

He saw her wince a little, but she quickly recovered, then said, "That's good to hear. He needs someone right now." Then she pulled on the reins, made a clicking sound and rode away.

What did she mean by that? And how did she know what his father did or didn't need? As far as Luke knew, she and his father hadn't had any contact for years. Maybe he was wrong?

Climbing onto Balboa again, he took a minute to survey the land, a vast span of nature at its best. Just east of the Sangre de Cristo Mountains, the landscape was made up of rolling hills and piñon pine. Mountains and streams surrounded the valley and as a kid, Luke had always thought he lived in a magical place, a utopian paradise. What did he know?

His mother had loved it here and he remembered riding with her often, to picnic or fish or just to soak up the scenery. The land reminded Luke of her. Beautiful in its simplicity, yet strong enough to withstand the elements.

In the end, cancer had taken his mother at too young an age. But she'd seemed at peace with herself. Unlike him, her faith had held her in good stead. He'd gone the other way, damning whatever forces had taken her from him so soon. And then later, took Michael. And Julianna. If there was a God, he wasn't doing his job.

No, he didn't have the kind of faith his mother had. Why should he?

He touched Balboa's side with his heel, but the stallion wasn't in any hurry to return. The horse probably didn't get enough exercise with only Abe to take care of things, so Luke took the long way back to give the stallion a workout and on the way, he stopped at a shallow creek to let Balboa drink. He dismounted. Except for the burbling sounds of crisp clean water over the smooth rocks, it was so quiet he could hear himself breathe.

Balboa suddenly rose up and whinnied. "What? What's wrong, boy?" The horse snorted and jerked away, spooked. "It's okay," Luke soothed, stroking the animal's neck and scanning the area to see what had scared him. "It's okay, big guy."

As he took in the property on the other side of the creek, on the hill he spotted an animal on the ground. Very still. "It's okay," Luke reassured his mount and stroked him again. He tethered the horse to a tree and made his way across the creek, rock by rock.

It was a calf. But what was it doing out here alone? Was it sick? A few more steps and he knew the animal was dead. He didn't want to get too close, but he had to know what had happened. As he moved closer, he saw a pool of blood under the animal's head. The calf's throat had been cut.

On instinct, he reached for his weapon and swung around. Only he wasn't carrying and felt like an idiot. He was standing in the middle of a pasture with a dead calf and he'd reacted like he'd been ambushed by the Mob.

Maybe the captain was right, his nerves were shot and he needed the vacation more than he realized. Even though he'd covered numerous crime scenes, the coppery odor of blood, the scent of death, made him cover his mouth with his hand. He never got used to that. People who thought police were immune to gruesome scenes were either misinformed or stupid.

He rode Balboa back to the ranch at a gallop and twenty minutes later, after unsaddling the stallion and brushing him down, he walked into the kitchen. It was quiet, so he headed down the hall and tapped on Abe's door. "It's Luke, Dad. I need to talk to you." Without waiting for an answer Luke opened the door.

"What's wrong?" Abe was sitting in his favorite chair. On the table next to him was a photo of Luke's mother. The room reeked of stale tobacco, even though Julianna had persuaded Abe long ago to quit smoking in the house. She hadn't wanted Michael exposed to secondhand smoke.

Luke pulled an old oak chair up next to his father's and turned on the lamp. "Sitting in the dark for a reason?"

"You get the fence fixed?" his father asked.

"Yep. I did. But I came across a dead calf on the way home. Down by the creek."

"Dead?"

"As a doornail."

"One of mine?"

Luke nodded. "Had your brand. And…it looked like its throat had been slit."

Abe drew back, his face turning red as he glowered at Luke.

"Any ideas?" Luke asked.

"Yeah. Get me my gun."

"No, I mean any ideas who might've done this?"

His father shifted in the chair. "Someone who doesn't like me, I guess."

Well, that took in half of San Miguel County. "Anyone in particular?"

Abe shook his head. "Could be kids. Teenagers thinking it's fun to wreck people's property."

"This isn't just property, Dad. That calf was a living animal, part of your stock. It's more than vandalism. It's animal cruelty."

Abe took a moment, then said, "I'll take care of it."

Luke crossed his arms. "How?"

When Abe clammed up, Luke bolted to his feet. "I'm going to call the sheriff," he said, turning to leave.

Before Luke got out the door, Abe said, "I said I'd take care of it. I don't want you calling anyone."

His father could be so damned bullheaded sometimes. But maybe it was kids out raising hell. Instead of doping up on meth or heroin as some teens did in L.A., the youngsters here found their fun in other ways.

When he'd lived here, there wasn't anything like this going on. A little vandalism maybe, but nothing so sick. No, whoever had done this had a twisted mind...and no respect for life.

Luke strode into the living room and looked up the sheriff's number. He didn't care if Abe wanted him to call or not. The dispatcher answered, then said the sheriff was out, but he'd be there as soon as he could. Two hours later, Ben Yuma was at the door.

"Twice in one week," Yuma said. "Nothing serious I hope."

"I think it is, but if you ask my dad, you'll get a different answer." Luke went back to tell Abe the sheriff had arrived, but his dad was asleep in front of the TV. Odd. Luke turned off the TV, then filled in the sheriff on what had happened.

"So," Luke said. "You know the area, the locals and their crimes, do you have any idea what's going on here?"

"None yet. I'll have to take a trip out there. There have been similar incidents on other properties. Some ranchers think they're connected to the corporation that's trying to buy up the land around here to build a spa resort."

Abe hadn't mentioned anything about that.

"Others say it's kids. Rich kids with nothing better to do."

"Rich kids? When I went to school here, most ranch kids had to scrape by."

"There's been a big real estate boom in the past few years, spreading out from Albuquerque and Santa Fe. Condos, planned communities, people with money."

"Whoever did this, rich or poor, they've got some real problems."

"True," Yuma agreed. "I'll be back tomorrow morning to take a look."

When the sheriff left, Luke headed for Julianna's room.

THE KNOCK on her door made Julianna jump. She checked her watch. 10:00 p.m. It wouldn't be Abe, and that left only one other person. "Hold on," she said, "I'll be there in a minute." She saved the story on her laptop, closed the cover and went to the door, opening it a few inches. Luke stood with one arm resting on the door frame.

"We need to talk," he said.

Her heart thumped. "What about?"

"Abe."

She expelled a silent sigh of relief. "Okay. Just give me a minute."

"Sure. I'll be on the patio."

He'd always liked the outdoors, the fresh air, at the beach or wherever. Closing the door, she quickly threw on the pink zip sweatshirt that matched her sweatpants, and then slipped on her flip-flops. She took a quick peek in the mirror. Plain. She'd always been plain. Nothing like her classy sister. She ran a comb through her hair, then dabbed on a bit of lip gloss before realizing the futility. What did she think? That the gloss would somehow transform her into something she wasn't. Dammit, she'd come to grips with her self-image a long time ago. So why were the old insecurities resurfacing now? What the hell, she dabbed on some blush, too, and then headed down the hall.

At the back door she saw Luke sitting outside on a bench. She stopped to look at him. So handsome, so… masculine. Instantly, she remembered how she'd felt being the other half of the couple people whispered about and said, "What is he doing with *her?*" She'd always wanted to feel his equal, like they belonged together. She'd tried hard, but it never quite came together for her.

But when she and Luke were alone, he always made her feel beautiful, as if he saw something in her that others didn't. Something even *she* didn't see. She realized later it had been easy to forgive a lot in their marriage because of those stupid insecurities.

The door creaked as she went out. "Hey."

"Hey," he said, then indicated the place next to him on the bench. He wore jeans and a black sweatshirt and was sitting near the beehive-shaped chiminea in the corner. A crackling fire radiated warmth and the pungent scent of cedar, instantly conjuring memories of better times. The first time she'd met Luke's dad. The Christmas they'd spent here when she was pregnant. Memories she didn't have time for anymore. Luke wanted to talk and that's what she was going to do.

But as she lowered herself to sit next to him, she sensed something was wrong. "What's up with Abe?"

"That's what I want to know. Has he said anything to you about problems on the ranch?"

She shook her head. "No, but he did say he thinks Mrs. Hancock wants him to sell his property."

Luke shifted uncomfortably, as if she'd hit a nerve. "Sheriff Yuma was here a little while ago and mentioned something about a corporation trying to buy up land for a spa resort."

"Do you think someone approached Abe about it? And maybe Mrs. Hancock, too?"

"Could be."

"If she comes by again, I'll ask her."

"No need. Pops wouldn't sell to anyone for any amount of money."

"So, why was the sheriff here again?"

"I called him because when I was out on the line, I found a dead calf."

"Oh, that's awful. But why call the sheriff?"

"The calf's throat was slit."

"Oh, my." Goose bumps rose on her arms. Had the caller found her and was this a warning? "What did the sheriff say about it?" There's no way anyone could possibly know where she was. With help from Patrick, the private investigator she used as a resource, she'd effectively disappeared. Except for calling her editor once a week, she had no contact with anyone else.

"The sheriff said there's been some vandalism at other ranches and they suspect some high school kids may be involved."

She breathed a sigh of relief. That made more sense. "But killing a helpless animal? That's sick."

"I know. Sociopaths are sick. And they start young. Usually with small animals."

The thought made her shiver. She rubbed her arms. "Does Abe know?"

"I talked to him before calling the sheriff."

"How's he feeling?"

Luke shrugged. "With him, you never know."

"I do. I can tell when something bothers him. It's subtle, but noticeable. I see it every time he talks to you."

"Yeah. Well, I've been bothering him since I was thirteen. That's nothing new."

"What I mean is that I can see it bothers him that you two don't get along."

He gave her a sideways glance. "You take up psychiatry somewhere along the line?"

She smiled. "I have learned a few things in that area, but no, my knowledge of your father is based on years of watching how he reacts when you say something that hurts him."

"I don't say things to hurt him."

"Not intentionally, but some of the things you say, do hurt him."

"Well, I'm not going to debate your sixth sense when it comes to my dad. And I'm not going to monitor my words either. He and I have never understood each other and we probably never will."

"So, why are you staying? I thought you were leaving as soon as you could."

Wearily, he leaned against the post behind him so he was facing her. "Things changed."

"Like?"

"One…my dad seems…not himself. Two, I need to find him some hired help, and three, the dead calf. I wouldn't feel right about leaving until those things are resolved." His gaze narrowed as he turned to look at her. "I'd also like to know why you're really here," he said softly. Teasingly.

There it was again. The question that wouldn't go away. She cleared her throat. "When I spoke with your father before I decided to come, he sounded a little flat, depressed almost. I thought maybe my visit would cheer him up." That part was true. She had felt Abe needed someone, if even just another person in the house. He was alone too much.

"Getting help for your father would be wonderful. And it would give him someone to talk to. It has to be hard being alone all the time."

"You'd think. But that's the life he's chosen. He doesn't like too many people." Luke grinned, then touched the sleeve of her shirt. "Except for you."

Julianna's heart warmed at the comment. "He's been the father I never had. Even though I haven't seen him too often, we've stayed in touch."

Leaning back on one elbow, Luke rubbed a hand over the stubble on his face. By the end of the day he always had more than a five o'clock shadow. "I didn't know that," he said, his voice still low, reflective almost.

She shrugged. "No reason you would."

"Well, like I said, there are things I have to do before I go."

"I don't think there's anything you can do about the calf other than let the sheriff handle it. If it is vandals, he'll do something about it."

"But there have been other incidents, so I'd like to know what he's doing about it before I go."

She looked down. "So, when *are* you leaving?"

His eyes sparkled with mischief. "Can't wait to get rid of me, eh."

She laughed, feeling her cheeks flush. "You found me out."

Luke's expression softened. "I always liked the way you laugh."

He'd never told her that before. Hearing it now made her more self-conscious than anything. Sitting here with Luke was a dangerous place to be. She looked away. "I didn't do that very often during the last part of our marriage, did I?" Their last couple of years together had been so bitter, so filled with pain.

"No. But you had good reason." He reached out for her.

Even though his touch was tender, she felt her muscles tense and launched to her feet. "I…I need to go in. I still have work to do."

He stood almost at the same time, then stepped in front of her, effectively blocking her way. "What's the rush?"

She placed one hand on her hip, hoping she looked cool and calm—even though her insides felt like they were in a meat grinder. "You heard me. I have work to do."

"Really?" His voice seemed lower, huskier. He stroked her cheek with his fingertips.

Her blood rushed. "Yes, really."

"You look like you need to relax."

Her heart thumped so hard she was certain he could hear it. "Nighttime is when I work best. Besides, I have a deadline to meet."

He frowned, his mouth forming words that didn't come out, as if maybe they were too difficult to say. "What?" she asked.

Squaring his shoulders, he said, "I'm still wondering why you left me."

Oh, God. Her throat constricted. "Luke. Don't. Please." When he just stood there, she said, "You...you know why."

"But that's just it. I don't. I know what you said when you left, but I know there was more to it. And it's been eating at me for five years."

Her voice was barely a whisper when she said, "I can't get into all that again, Luke. I just can't."

"Was it me? I couldn't blame you there."

Her head came up. "Oh, no. God, no. It wasn't you, Luke. I promise." His drinking hadn't helped, but that wasn't it at all. On instinct, she rested her hand on his arm.

He looked at her hand, then placed his other one over hers.

Tears welled, but she pushed them back. She'd gone through therapy, learned how to live with her grief over losing Michael, thought she'd learned how to live with the breakup of the marriage. So why was she such an emotional mess?

Finally, she managed, "I can't do this, Luke. I've moved on. I hoped you had, too." She pulled herself up to her full five feet six inches. "Now please let me go."

Tears burned behind her eyelids as she walked inside, trying desperately to hold herself together. Trying desperately not to turn around and rush into his arms.

CHAPTER FIVE

LUKE WATCHED Jules walk away, his jaw clenched, his fists kneading his thighs. If it wasn't him, then what the hell was it?

People who loved each other were supposed to stand united and support each other when bad times came. People who loved each other didn't run away and destroy everything good that they'd built together. Maybe she'd never loved him. Maybe the wonderful relationship he'd thought they had was a bunch of garbage. He'd convinced himself of that more than once.

And now, seeing the pain in her eyes as she ran inside to escape him made him feel even worse. He'd brought up things that hurt her. Damn. He banged the wood railing with the flat of his palm. He was like a fox in a chicken coop, tearing things apart because *he* wanted something. Because *he* needed to know. God, he was a jerk.

He stomped inside and on the way to his room hesitated outside her door. He wanted to say he was sorry for hurting her. But the hurt was already there. Sorry didn't change anything.

Tomorrow. Tomorrow he'd apologize. Tell her he'd

never bring it up again. Then he had to get outta here. Go back to work. Work was what he did best.

In his room, he punched in his partner's cell number. "Yo," he said when Jordan answered. "What's happening?"

"That's what I was wondering. When are you coming back? I've got a good lead on the Renfield case."

Luke's pulse quickened. "Does Carlyle know? He didn't want me on it until after the election."

"No. But I'm not doing anything to stir the pot as far as Thorpe's concerned."

"How good is the lead?"

"It's hot. I tracked down an old friend who'd heard Thorpe threaten to kill Michele Renfield."

"Who's the friend?"

"Betsy Stephens. Renfield's former college roommate."

"So why haven't we heard about her before?"

"She said she was questioned way back but nothing ever came of it. And in the back of her mind was the thought, if her friend disappeared, so could she."

"So, what changed?"

"She said she was cleaning out some of Michele's things and found something. An ultrasound photo."

"Renfield was pregnant?" *With Thorpe's kid?* Luke's nerves vibrated with excitement. All his instincts said Thorpe was guilty as hell and Luke wanted to get him so bad he could taste it. He hated politicians who thought they were above the law. Now they had motive and if they could get this girl's testimony... damn. He had to get back to L.A. "I'll be back the day after tomorrow. It's a full day's drive and I have to clear up some things here first."

"So how's it been?" Jordan asked.

"My dad needs help. I'm going to try to take someone on before I leave." Then he'd plead with Jules to get his father to a doctor. And she'd be overjoyed that he was leaving.

"That's good. But I meant how are you managing with Julianna in the same house?"

Luke rubbed the stubble on his chin. "No big deal. The past is in the past."

There was a hesitation on the line before Jordan said, "Yeah? So that's what you tell yourself."

Annoyed that his partner had him pegged, Luke gripped the phone tighter. "Yes, it is. But I fully understand your thinking. You have this pie-in-the sky philosophy that love conquers all, and because you're about to be married, you can't understand why everyone doesn't feel the same way. But take my word for it, in my case, love doesn't conquer anything. The past *is* in the past. It's done. Kaput. Finito."

Jordan coughed as if choking on what Luke had said. "Yeah, okay. Whatever you say."

"I'll call you when I get close to home."

When he was finished with the call, Luke stripped off his clothes and headed for bed. Dammit. The past was in the past. Except he kept seeing how Jules had looked when she came out and sat beside him tonight. She'd smelled clean and fresh and he longed to feel her in his arms again, to be as close as they'd once been.

The fat yellow moon and the brilliance of the stars had reminded him of all the other times they'd sat together simply enjoying the night.

Times he needed to forget. *Done. Kaput. Finito.*

THE NEXT AFTERNOON Julianna was taking a break from her research and making lemonade when she heard a noise outside. After taking the sheriff out to see the dead animal this morning, Luke and Abe had disposed of the carcass and then spent the rest of the morning working around the place. Though Abe had come in earlier, Luke was still in the barn.

Last night after she'd gone to bed, her emotions warred with her needs. She wanted to go to Luke and try to explain, but she knew going to his room wouldn't end well. She hadn't been with a man for six months, at least. Not since her one attempt at a relationship—post-Luke—fell apart. And right now, her hormones were working overtime. Getting too close to Luke could be a dangerous proposition. In more ways than one.

Luke was comfortable. She knew him, knew how to please him. He knew how to please her. But to do that would be misleading. He'd think it meant more, and even if it did, it wouldn't be fair to either of them. Because nothing would change.

Luke was probably staying outside so he wouldn't have to see her again. She couldn't blame him. Every time he'd tried to talk to her she'd cut him off.

She poured the lemonade into a large thermal container, placed some cookies she'd made into a Ziploc bag and headed for the barn. Luke was inside, replacing the hinges on the side door and didn't seem to hear her come in. Wearing jeans, a blue denim shirt and his Stetson, he looked the typical rancher. A far cry from the perfectly groomed, designer-suited detective she'd once been married to.

She knocked on a wooden box to alert him she was there. When he looked up, she said, "I made some lemonade." Putting both the cookies and the container on the box, she motioned for him to come and get some. Then she'd get the hell out of there.

Luke untied the bandana around his neck and wiped off his forehead. He seemed surprised to see her. "Sure. Thanks. It's hot in here."

"But it's nice outside." A crisp fall day and the sun was shining. She handed him a glass and saw his hands were covered with tiny cuts.

"Where's Abe?" Luke asked.

"Taking a nap."

"Great. Good time for me to call some people about the job. I'm calling a couple guys I know and see if they can recommend anyone, and I put a help wanted ad in the local paper."

Luke took a cookie, and then after another swig of his lemonade, said matter-of-factly, "I'm sorry about last night. I was out of line."

She glanced away. He shouldn't be apologizing. She was the one who'd fled. She was the one who couldn't explain herself. An irony that hadn't escaped her. A writer who couldn't express herself. How sad was that?

But then the only time she had the problem was when she was with Luke. "It's okay. Let's just leave it alone. Okay."

His gaze caught hers again. "Deal. If I can hire someone, I'm leaving tomorrow morning, so I want to do as much as I can today."

She felt the tension in her shoulders ease. "Well, if you need anything, if you need my help—"

That got a raised brow.

"Okay," she said. "I know I'm probably the most unmechanical person around, but I am good at helping if I'm told what to do."

He smiled, then picked up another cookie. "Great. I do have something I'd like you to help me with."

"Oh…okay." She hadn't really expected him to take up her offer.

He walked over and sat on a bale of hay, then gestured for her to have a seat, too. She sat on the bale opposite him, pulled up her feet and sat cross-legged. The scent of hay teased her senses, dredging up a long-ago memory of the time they'd made love in the hay loft. She wondered if Luke remembered.

Luke took one last sip of lemonade, then said, "It's about my dad. Since I'm leaving tomorrow, I won't have time to get him to see a doctor, but he needs a checkup."

"And you were wondering if I'd convince him to go."

He nodded. "That's it. I know it's asking a lot. He can be stupidly stubborn when he wants to be." He gave a half laugh. "Which, now that I think about it, is all the time. At least when I'm here. You might have better luck asking him after I leave."

"I'll be happy to do what I can. But you know—with Abe—there are no guarantees."

"If you can't, then we'll have to go to plan B."

"Plan B? What's that?"

"I don't know yet, but there'll be one if this doesn't work."

"If what doesn't work?" Abe hobbled inside. He looked at Julianna, a scowl on his face. "You scared the living crap out of me disappearing like that," he said. "You shouldn't leave without letting me know where you're going."

Luke glanced at his father. "Why?"

"She knows why," Abe said.

Julianna looked at Luke. "It's nothing. Really."

"Well, now that I know you're together, I'm going back to do some figuring on the books." He started to leave, then turned back and said, "Don't scare me like that again, young lady. It ain't good for an old man."

She smiled affectionately. Abe had been extra watchful of her since she'd told him about the voice-mail messages. She jumped off the bale, walked over and gave Abe a hug. Of course he'd be worried. "I'm sorry," she said. "Promise I'll be more thoughtful."

When Abe was gone, she gathered up the things she'd brought, but Luke stopped her with a hand on her shoulder.

"You want to explain?"

She slipped from under his hand. "It's nothing really. Abe is overly concerned about me."

"That's easy to see. But the question is why?"

She crossed her arms, hugging herself. Then she shrugged.

When she didn't say anything, he said, "You might as well tell me because now that I know there *is* a reason my father's worried about you, I'm not about to let it go. And you know I can find out just about anything."

"Not this time." She didn't like his attitude...or being told she had no choice. Despite that, she knew he *wouldn't* quit until he did find out. Luke was a detective. But if he cared at all about her, he wouldn't spread the news she was hiding out, either. Maybe it would be okay. She dismissed the thought as quickly as it came. Knowing Luke, he'd call out the forces, the media would hear, Mark wouldn't like the publicity and she'd never finish her story.

He gently took her by the arms and sat her on the hay bale again. "Please tell me."

Maybe it would be better to tell him something. Something that would make him back off. She settled herself on the bale, then palms up, she said, "It's just that I received a couple nasty e-mail messages from some creep who didn't like the article I was writing. That's all."

Luke pulled back. "That's all."

She nodded.

"You're hiding out."

"Not hiding out exactly. Just taking a vacation to finish the last installment of a series."

Luke knew Julianna wasn't the kind of person to run from idle threats. It had to be more serious than that. "What didn't he like?"

"He didn't say. He said he wanted me to stop writing about missing kids." Almost as the words left her lips, his eyes darkened—and she knew. She should never have mentioned what the story was about. But just as quickly, he reined himself in.

"Or what? Did he threaten you?"

"I can handle it, Luke. People write letters to the magazine all the time." She stood, her back straight as a board.

"I'd like to see the messages," he said.

"I see no reason for you to get involved."

Luke gritted his teeth. She never saw things from his perspective, only her own, which in this case was clouded by her need to shut him out. "Sorry. That doesn't cut it. You're involving my father. That gives me more than a passing interest in knowing what you're getting him into."

He stood at the door blocking her way. "If my father is involved, I'm involved. Whether you like it or not."

Her mouth pinched. Her hands clenched at her sides. He felt as if they were in a war of wills. But if she knew him at all, she knew he wasn't going to back down.

"Okay!" she said. Then with a hint of resignation in her voice, "When you finish here, I'll pull up the messages."

He placed a firm hand on her arm, urging her forward. "Let's do it now."

Walking to the house, Julianna bristled at Luke's demands. She shrugged off his hand. So, big deal. She'd show him the messages and that would be that. What was he going to do? Tell her to leave? This was his father's house, not his.

Abe was waiting for her on the porch, pacing back and forth.

She glanced at Luke. "Give me a minute will you."

When he just stood there, she added, "Alone. Please."

Luke looked at his dirty hands and grungy clothes. "I'm going to take a quick shower. Then I'll be back."

When he was gone, she turned to Abe. "What's the matter, Abe?"

Abe stopped his pacing. "Did I screw things up?"

She forced a smile. "No, you didn't screw things up. I'm sorry I worried you." They went inside together.

"You sure?"

"Sure. I was going to tell Luke anyway."

Abe rubbed the gray stubble on his chin. "That's good. Keeping secrets is foolish. They always come out somehow."

"No more secrets, Abe. I promise."

It must've been a satisfactory answer, because then Abe said he was going to go take a nap. She'd noticed he was taking a lot of naps lately. "Are you okay?"

"I'm fine. I get this tired feeling once in a while, that's all." Then, he stood straighter, as if bolstering himself up. "Old men get tired easier than the young studs, you know." He winked at her.

"Not you. You can outwork anyone your own age— and most younger men as a matter of fact. I've seen you do it."

"I like how you think, young lady. Maybe you can talk some sense into that son of mine."

She frowned. "About what?"

He sent her a look that said she should know what. And unfortunately she did. "No, Abe. Luke and I are divorced. We've been divorced for five years. We've made new lives for ourselves. It's better this way."

On his way out, he said, "Maybe you've made a new life, but I don't think Luke has. And that can only mean one thing."

She didn't want to hear it. "Go, take your nap, Abe. I have things to do."

Abe left and she headed for the den. Sitting at the old oak table, she pulled up the first e-mail message and got the creeps all over again. What was it about the story that threatened this guy? He had to be threatened somehow, otherwise why was he so adamant that she stop writing it.

She left the message on the screen and picked up one of her research books, her muscles tensing as she read the title. *Killing for Sport: Inside the minds of serial killers,* a necessary resource for the articles she was writing. It was important to know her subjects.

No sooner had she sat in the chair to start reading, than Luke returned. She got up and went to the desk and showed him the first message. The least threatening message. "Stop the articles about Renata Willis or you'll be sorry."

"And the other?" Luke glanced at the book in her hand. His face went ashen. She saw a muscle jump near his eye. "Nice reading material," he said through gritted teeth.

She tossed the book on the chair, then pulled up the next message. "Stop now or you'll be next!" Both messages were signed with a star at the bottom. Reading it again, a chill jagged up her spine. She'd been shocked when the first message had come, and she'd been a little scared when she'd read the second. Then something in her rebelled. Scared or not, she'd never acquiesce to threats.

She had notified the San Francisco police but all they did was write a report. That's all they could do, they'd said, and if she didn't like the heat, she should get out of the kitchen. Their attitude made her even more determined to finish the series.

As Luke read the message his body practically vibrated, the veins on his neck bulging. "You think this is nothing?" he spat out.

She pursed her lips. "The magazine gets nasty letters all the time."

"If you didn't think it was so bad, why did you go into hiding?"

"I didn't go into hiding. The opportunity to get away presented itself, and it seemed a better idea than doing nothing. A precaution—sort of."

He pointed to the book. "How can you read that stuff?" He snatched up the latest edition of *The Achilles' Heel* and shook it in her face. "How can you *write* this stuff?"

Julianna stiffened. "The same way you can keep working in Homicide."

His expression switched from anger to insult. "It's different. I'm helping people. Trying to find some kind of justice for victims and their families."

"And what do you think I'm doing?"

He shook his head. "I don't know. I honestly don't know."

"The stories I write are about victims who've been forgotten. Their cases closed because the police can't find the perpetrators. I'm telling the public that these children and their grieving families shouldn't be forgotten. I'm a constant reminder that these killers are out there, ready and willing to kill some more. By keeping the stories in the public eye, maybe someone somewhere might do something. Maybe even the police."

He winced at the comment, then squared his shoulders. "You know damned well a cold case is only shelved because there aren't any viable leads. If there were the police would be on it."

She chewed on her bottom lip. She'd hit a nerve by questioning his precious job. "Keeping the story alive is important."

"And your life isn't? Putting yourself in the line of fire for a story…how smart is that?"

She shrugged. "It's what I do." She hoped she sounded more confident than she felt.

Raking a hand through his hair, Luke spun around. "Then you need police protection."

She gave an ironic laugh. "Right. I tried that. But the police in San Francisco don't hand out protection to every woman who's been threatened or harassed. You of all people should know that."

"Yeah," he said on a sigh. "Well, then, you should stop writing the stories."

Her mouth fell open. "Excuse me?"

"The solution is simple. Stop writing the stories."

She gave a huff of indignance. "I'm not going to stop writing the stories. I can't do that. I need to finish the series." She turned away from him, her muscles drawing tighter and tighter. He had never understood her passion for writing, and he'd never grasp why she had to write these particular stories. If he could, he'd never have stopped looking for Mikey's murd— She caught herself midthought.

Don't. Just don't. Her pulse suddenly pounded in her ears. "Besides, no one would ever think to look for me here. I haven't told anyone. Not my editor. Not even my mother."

The sharp ring of Luke's cell phone interrupted. Why was she not surprised?

Luke pulled out his phone, glanced at the number of the caller, saw it was Jordan and then walked a few steps away before he answered.

"Yeah," Luke said, keeping his voice low.

"Just checking on your ETA. I'm going to make an appointment with the new lead on the Renfield case and I want you to be there."

Luke felt the usual rush of adrenaline. He needed to get back. He had a job to do. But…if he left, there'd be no one to protect Jules. Dammit. He couldn't leave her here alone.

"Some things have come up. You'll have to do the interview without me."

It was quiet on the other end of the phone for the

longest time. Finally Jordan asked, "Something wrong with Abe?"

"No, something else. I can't talk now, but I need a favor."

"Sure—what's up?"

"A cold case." He searched his brain for the name of the child in the story. "Willis…Renata Willis. Pull it for me, will you? Then I'll get back to you as soon as I can."

Jordan agreed and Luke hung up. Julianna was incredibly naive if she thought there was no danger. It was obvious the articles had triggered some kind of hostility in the person who wrote the messages. She had to know that.

But why? What bothered this person so much he, or she, had to make threats? That's what he needed to find out.

He walked over to where Julianna stood by the window. It was dark now and there was nothing to see outside, but she stared out anyway.

Standing behind her, he said, "Tell me about the other threats."

She pivoted around to face him. "What other threats?"

"There are more, aren't there?"

She closed her eyes, rubbed her temples with two fingers. "If you're going to nag me until you find out, then yes, there were a couple of phone messages. I picked them up from my voice mail the night you arrived."

He touched his forehead where there was still a mark from her bashing his head with the butt end of the gun. "So that's why you reacted so violently when I came in. You were scared."

She pushed him away and went to sit on the couch. "Yes, I was scared. I thought you were a freaking burglar."

As he turned to look at her, he couldn't help the grin that formed. "Yeah. I guess you did."

He saw a tiny grin tip the corners of her mouth. "You have to admit, that night is kind of funny in retrospect," she said.

"Don't try to change the subject." He went over and stood in front of her. "What did the recorded messages say?"

"Just more of the same. You can listen to them tomorrow. Right now I'm tired and I'm going to bed."

She rose to her feet and as she started to walk away, Luke placed a hand on her shoulder. "Now. I want to hear them now."

CHAPTER SIX

SLEEP WAS AS ELUSIVE as Julianna's answers to Luke's questions. He kept thinking about the voice-mail messages. She'd told Abe about them, but she hadn't told him. And he was the one who could protect her.

He'd been taken aback when she showed him the e-mail messages, but the calls were serious threats. Whether the police did anything or not, the calls needed to be documented with the San Francisco police. Julianna would know that. She wasn't stupid.

But she'd always been unpredictable. Just when he thought he knew what she was going to do, she threw him for a loop. Which was why he had a bad feeling that she might not be telling him the whole story.

He remembered the first time he saw her across the room at Bernie's, the local sports bar where Luke and his buddies hung out whenever they could watch a game. He'd been a beat cop when they'd met, on the cusp of promotion to detective.

For him, it'd literally been lust at first sight. But she'd been with another guy and they'd left before he could find a way to introduce himself.

A week later he'd arrested her at an environmental rally that had turned into a riot. So started their tumultuous relationship. And it had been that way ever since.

The thought made him smile. Despite everything, she still made him smile. She'd affected him like no other woman ever had, and from the moment they'd met, he'd wanted to get her into bed. When he fell in love with her, the desire only intensified…and no matter how many times they'd made love during their marriage, each time was as exciting as the first.

He wondered how it would be now to feel her body against his again. She had the smoothest skin he'd ever felt. His pulse quickened, blood rushed to his vital parts. But he knew the danger of giving in to desire with Jules. He'd only open himself to more pain. He couldn't do that again. Not even if she was willing. If he did, he might never recover.

He checked the clock on the night table. 2:00 a.m. It was pointless to stay in bed when he couldn't sleep, so he pulled on a pair of jeans and headed for the living room. On the way, he grabbed a Coke from the fridge, noticing some Bud Light next to the soda. Jules must've bought the beer because his dad wouldn't be caught dead drinking light beer.

In the living room, he set his drink on the end table, clicked on the lamp and dropped into the worn leather recliner next to it. The chair had been there since Luke was a kid. Even though it was his father's favorite, his mother had threatened to torch the behemoth more than once.

He glanced at the pile of magazines next to him and his stomach knotted. He didn't want to read about missing children, but to know what was going on with Jules, it was something he had to do. He picked up the latest issue of *The Achilles' Heel,* and as he read, he could see why the caller might've been disturbed about the story. By putting all the facts and the interviews from the victims' families together, it gave a more complete picture. A human interest story that put faces to the cold statistics and made the tale more compelling.

And from his experience in working with criminal profilers, she'd described the traits of a serial killer perfectly. If the person making the threats was the murderer, he might believe she could expose him.

In another part of the article, she'd stated her theory about the connections between several similar crimes, even indicating she knew the names of criminals with the same M.O.

Whether she realized it or not, she'd made herself a perfect target.

"Couldn't sleep either?" Jules's low sexy voice came from behind, making him jerk to attention.

He chucked the magazine back onto the pile upside down. "Something like that."

She came around and sat on the couch across from him, curling her legs beneath her. She was wearing a tight-fitting yellow top with barely-there straps, and loose yellow pajama bottoms with pictures of a cartoon bird on them. Tweety Bird, he remembered, her favorite. "So, what do you think?"

"About what?"

"The story. You were reading my story, weren't you?"

He raised his hands. "Guilty. But I didn't finish, so I won't be drawing any conclusions."

"Conclusions about what?"

"Whether the story's good or not."

"That's not what I meant. I thought maybe you'd find it interesting. Compelling. It's supposed to be compelling."

He shrugged. "I found it disturbing. In more ways than one."

She frowned, then said, "That means I've done my job. It made you think."

"It did that. It made me realize how serious the threats are. It made me think there's a lot of anger in your words." *Anger and pain.* Every word dripped with the pain of a parent who'd lost a child.

"It's a sensitive subject." She closed her eyes and leaned her head against the red-and-blue blanket covering the couch. When she opened her eyes, she looked directly at him. "Sensitive yes, but nothing I can't handle."

"You can handle a serial killer?"

She sat upright. "You don't know if he is."

"You profiled the guy perfectly. He could think you know more than you do."

She ran a hand through her hair, then with a shake of her head, flipped the long locks back over her shoulders. "Good. I wanted to wake people up. If I've done that, I've succeeded."

"So, where did you get your information?"

Her eyes sparkled. "Are you questioning my resources?"

"No, I'm just curious how you know so much."

"I don't know any more than anyone else. I've just put it together in a different way. In each case I write about, the profiles are composites garnered from the experts who wrote them. The rest is public information and interviews."

"You've been goading him."

"That wasn't my intent."

"But it's the result. That's why he's threatening you."

"So why didn't the police do anything when I told them? They thought I was a hack wanting publicity."

"I don't know, but I think you need protection, and if I'm going to help you, I need to know everything."

"I'm not asking for your help. And if I need protection, I'll…I'll call the police."

"The police are already here." He wanted to smile, but it was important she knew how serious this was. "In addition to letting your local police know, we need to contact the FBI. But…it might be more effective if I'm the one who calls."

She hesitated, stood and then paced in front of him.

"You can't blow this off, Jules." Luke felt his blood pressure rising. "Or are you just burying your head in the sand like you used to?"

She stopped dead in her tracks and glared at him.

He held up a hand. "I'm sorry. That was uncalled for. It's just that…I can't sit by and do nothing."

"Luke." She turned to him. "Please let it be. Whoever is making the threats thinks I'm in San Francisco."

Her words didn't fit her demeanor. She seemed edgy, more so than before. Maybe what he'd said was getting to her, but she couldn't…wouldn't admit it. Another of her traits he knew so well.

"I can't let it go. You may be putting my father in danger." He cleared his throat. "And *you* are definitely in danger."

Her expression went from obstinate to resigned.

"Abe knows about the calls and he insisted I stay. But if there's any chance it might put him in harm's way, I'll leave."

Luke rubbed his chin. "No…no, I don't think you should."

She turned, came over, snatched his Coke and took a long swig. She shifted from one foot to the other. "First you want me to leave. Now you don't. Make up your mind."

Ideas started falling into place. "I think if we take the right precautions, you might actually be safer here. Especially with me as your bodyguard."

"For once I agree with you. But not about the bodyguard part. I truly don't believe anyone could track me here. No one knows. I left no trail. I even used a different name on the plane."

"What name did you use?"

"I bought a fake ID from a reputable source who got it from someone else who got it from—"

"So someone else knows your fake name."

Frowning, she said, "Okay, maybe so. But it's some-one who doesn't have a clue who I am. Too many people in between."

"But he knows the name and could track it, or give it to someone if they asked."

She whirled around. "Only if he wanted to be arrested. Believe me, fake IDs aren't the only illegal thing he traffics in. Besides, how would anyone know to even contact him?"

"You found a way."

She shook her head. "Someone else got the I.D. for me. I'm safe. Believe me."

Safe, maybe. But not a hundred percent. "Okay. Let's leave it at that. We don't know what anyone knows for sure, but to be safe, we have to assume they know ev-erything and be prepared. Once I notify the FBI, I think we should talk to Sheriff Yuma as well."

"Even though nothing has happened?"

"Even though. I'll make the calls from my cell."

"Then what?"

"We need to take steps to find out who sent the mes-sages." He caught her gaze to see her reaction. "Deal?"

She hesitated. Then, finally she said, "Deal," and she reached out to knock knuckles the way they'd always done.

Luke smiled. Funny how some things came so natu-rally.

Yet other things seemed so foreign. She did seem dif-ferent now, but he couldn't put his finger on exactly what. Maybe it was simply the fact that she was older, wiser. More confident. More beautiful.

"I'm going back to bed. Don't strain your eyes reading in the dark."

"I don't read. Remember."

Julianna left the room feeling as if she'd achieved some measure of success. Once she sent off the last installment in the Willis story, she was off to London to visit her sister—and work on her next story. The only glitch was that she had to put up with Luke until he left. And now, she had no clue when that might be.

She carried her laptop into the bedroom, sat on the bed and flipped to her working file. But the words on the page might as well have been written in Russian. All she saw was an image of Luke's face, which now seemed embedded in the forefront of her brain. If only she could hibernate until she finished. Keep Luke out of her sight.

We. Everything he said was *we*. It looked as if he was involved whether she wanted him to be or not.

But his staying was a two-edged sword. Whenever she was around Luke, she couldn't stop looking at him, and when she wasn't looking at him, she was thinking about him. His mouth. His eyes. The muscles in his back that moved sensuously under her fingertips when they'd made love. She couldn't remember how long ago that had been, and yet, the image was as fresh as if it had been last night.

Forcing herself to focus, she typed a couple paragraphs, but when she finished, she knew it was crap. She switched programs to her calendar and noted the imminent deadline for the last installment and the date she was leaving for London. Then she typed in a reminder that she had to convince Abe to get a physical.

Sweet Abe. She hoped he was okay. Sometimes he was in good spirits, but other times he seemed to flag. He was also coughing a lot, and his energy level certainly wasn't what it used to be. But then he was getting older; he had to be seventy.

Abe had been over thirty when Luke was born, while Luke's mother had been a few years younger. Luke had idolized her and Julianna had always wished she'd had the opportunity to know his mother. She might've given Julianna insights into the man who still remained an enigma to her.

But none of that was important now. Luke wasn't a part of her life anymore, and barring any unforeseen incidents, they'd both go their separate ways. She should be happy about that, but instead, she felt sad. Spending time with Luke had been both disturbing and oddly comforting. She couldn't deny that his presence made her feel safer.

But safe was a relative term. She might be safer physically—but not emotionally. Since Luke had arrived, there'd been moments when the past seemed so vivid, she felt as if they were living it all over again. She'd heard that sometimes people fall back into relationships with an ex-spouse because it's more comfortable than finding someone new. She could easily imagine herself with Luke again, for just that reason.

But she was a realist. The reasons she'd left were still there—and always would be, no matter what. He'd married her because she was pregnant. She'd never really known if he truly loved her or if he'd felt obligated to marry her. Living with that uncertainty had made her insecure and needy. When he spent more time at his job than at home, it reinforced her worst fear.

After Michael's death, there was no reason to stay. She'd had to leave.

THE NEXT MORNING as Julianna was making breakfast, Abe came into the kitchen. Luke was working outside somewhere and later he was going to interview a man he might hire to help Abe.

"Morning, Pops." During her marriage to Luke, Julianna had taken to calling Abe *Pops,* as Luke did. It seemed silly to change that even after the divorce. He'd always been the father she never had.

"I'm not sure it's good," Abe said as he lowered himself onto a kitchen chair.

"Oh, I bet you'll perk right up after some coffee."

"Maybe. Right now I feel sluggish." He coughed a couple times.

Julianna looked at him in surprise, her mouth half open. Abe would never admit to feeling ill. Maybe he didn't consider "sluggish" the same as being sick. "Well, what strikes your fancy this morning. Pancakes or French toast?"

A knock on the door startled both of them. As she

walked over, Julianna saw a shadowy form through the sheer curtains over the glass of the door.

Opening the door, she was surprised to see Abe's neighbor standing there. "Hello, Mrs. Hancock."

Abe made a noise in the background, as if clearing his throat. Julianna ignored him and said, "How nice to see you."

"Nice to see you, too," the older woman said. "But please call me Stella. I came to see how Abe is doing."

Puzzled, Julianna looked at Abe, who waved her off, indicating he didn't want to talk to anyone. She stepped outside and closed the door behind her.

Julianna stared at the woman, not sure what she meant.

"His hand," Stella said. "When I saw you at the store, he'd injured his hand."

"Oh...oh, yes." Where was her head these days? "His hand is doing well, but he seems a little under the weather this morning, probably a flu bug, and he really shouldn't see anyone until we know for sure."

"Of course. I wouldn't want to bother him," Stella said, but the disappointment in her eyes was almost palpable. Brown eyes that looked as if the color had faded over the years, and once-dark hair now sprinkled with gray. Her long silver-and-turquoise earrings matched the multiple rows of rings she wore on both hands. An attractive woman, Julianna decided, but she seemed unusually concerned about Abe.

"I can have him get in touch with you when he's feeling better."

The comment brought a hearty laugh. "My dear, you don't know, do you?"

"Know what?"

"Abe hasn't talked to me for twenty-five years. I didn't expect he would now."

Julianna frowned, even more confused. "And yet you're concerned about him? Enough to come over."

Stella gave a big sympathetic smile, as if to say she couldn't expect Julianna to understand. "Of course I'm concerned. I've known Abraham a long time. We were important to each other once and when I realized he wasn't feeling well, I knew…I knew I had to make an effort before…"

She looked away, as if to compose herself. Then she said, "We have to let the bad things go if we want some kind of peace in our lives."

As Julianna opened her mouth to speak, Stella turned to leave.

"Stella, wait."

The woman stopped.

"Do you know anything about a corporation wanting to buy property around here?" she blurted, remembering her conversation with Luke.

"Yes, I do. They've asked me to sell mine. I think they asked Abe, too. I tried to talk to him about it a couple of times, but you can imagine how that went."

"What did you tell these people?"

"I said no, of course."

"Does Abe know that?"

"I don't know. But I think he'd prefer it if I did move."

She gave a resigned smile, then continued. "But my friends and family are here. That means more to me than money."

Julianna wondered if she included Abe in the friends category. "Do you mind if I tell Abe what you said?" Julianna didn't know why she asked that, but she felt Abe should know.

"If you wish," she said. "And please tell Abraham I hope he feels better soon." Then she left.

The woman's words resonated in Julianna's head. *Peace.* Did people really ever achieve that state? She doubted she ever would.

Back inside, she was even more curious about Abe and Stella. Apparently they'd been *friends* at one time, but Abe had never spoken of it. "Stella wanted to know how you were, Pops. I saw her in town when we were there the other day and told her about your hand," she said crisply. "She said to tell you she hopes you feel better soon."

His expression switched from cranky to surprised. "My hand is fine. In fact I need to take this bandage off so I can get back to work."

"Oh, and she said she wasn't selling her property to that corporation. She's not leaving."

His eyes sparked with interest, but the look dissipated quickly. Okay, he wasn't going to talk about it. Fine. She wouldn't either. At least not to him. But she would find out somehow why Abe and Stella hadn't talked for twenty-five years. Journalists were skilled in ferreting out information. Not unlike detectives.

"You leave that bandage on until tomorrow like the doctor said. Now is it pancakes or French toast?"

"I'm not hungry, but I'll have that coffee."

She poured them both a cup and as she handed him his mug, she said, "You have to eat. Breakfast is the most important meal of the day. And I'm not taking no for an answer."

He grumbled something under his breath that sounded suspiciously like *"women"* before he said, "Pancakes."

LUKE WALKED from the barn toward the house just as a battered green pickup kicked up a trail of dust down the road away from the house. He didn't recognize the vehicle.

But then why would he? He hadn't been here for a year, and the last time had only been a quick stopover. The thought produced a wave of guilt. If he'd known his dad was doing so poorly…

Yeah, what? What would he have done? If nothing else he needed to be truthful with himself. Fact was, he probably wouldn't have come any sooner. He'd needed to get his own head on straight. Get his life back to some semblance of normal. Not act like the walking dead. He'd been that way for too long and wasn't going to backslide, no matter what.

Staying here with Julianna was definitely a challenge, but after last night, he knew he couldn't abandon her while she was in danger. If she would just listen to him…

He kicked the dirt off his boots before he went inside. "Something smells good," he said, apparently to himself because when he glanced around, the room was empty. He felt a twinge of disappointment. He liked having breakfast with other people for a change. With Jules.

"Pops? You here?" He'd expected him to come out to the barn to help, but he hadn't.

"He's not feeling well." Jules's voice came out of nowhere.

Looking up, he saw her standing in the kitchen archway wearing a pair of low-rise jeans and a white T-shirt that didn't quite meet the top of the pants. He didn't remember her wearing such sexy clothes before.

"He had breakfast and then decided to lie down again."

Luke frowned. "That's not like Abe."

She walked to the stove and held up the coffeepot.

Nodding, he pulled out a kitchen chair, turned it backward and then straddled it. After pouring the coffee, she stood across from him, her hands on the back of a chair. "I know. He says it's a flu bug, but if it was he'd have a fever or something. And he's finding it hard to breathe."

"Who was driving the pickup?"

"The neighbor. Stella Hancock. She came to see how your dad was doing." When he frowned again, she quickly added, "I ran into her and told her about his hand."

"He doesn't need her concern."

"Maybe not, but he does need yours. I think you should talk to him."

Luke scoffed. "I could talk to that stone wall outside

and get a better response. He doesn't want to hear anything I have to say."

Shoving the hair from her eyes, Julianna came around and sat next to him, elbows on the table. "Don't be so sure."

"Why? Nothing's changed. My being here is more of an aggravation to him than anything."

Jules's expression turned serious. "Luke, I've never meddled in your relationship with Abe, but I know he needs you now." Her eyes pleaded with him. "Even if he won't admit it."

He lifted the cup to his lips. The coffee tasted strong, as if it'd been heating all morning, and it was so hot, it scalded his throat as it went down. What did she know about it? After a moment, he said, "I'll talk to him, but I know anything I say will fall on deaf ears."

She grinned. "He's only deaf in one ear. He'll hear you."

"Funny."

"But true. Whether he does anything about it is another story." She cleared her throat. "When I told Stella that I'd give Abe the message that she was here—" her gaze came up to meet his "—she laughed. She said she hadn't talked to your father in twenty-five years."

Luke shrugged. "So?"

"I wondered why, if they hadn't spoken for so long, she was coming over now?"

"You didn't ask? That's not like you, Jules. The journalist in you asks questions even when you shouldn't."

Julianna laughed. He knew her too well. "Okay, so I did ask."

"And—"

"She said something about being friends once and letting things go in order to be at peace with herself." As she spoke, Julianna studied Luke's face for a reaction. The woman's words had touched Julianna more than she could've imagined. Maybe they would touch Luke, too.

"Fine," Luke said. "Let her be at peace at her own place. She doesn't need to come around here stirring up more trouble."

"More trouble?"

Luke ignored the question, pushed his cup away and stood. "I've got to shower before I go talk to Clyde Davis."

"Clyde Davis?"

"Someone who might be able to help out here after I leave."

After I leave. The words should've made her happy. Instead she felt oddly let down. "Good. Where'd you get his name?"

"I called around. Got a few referrals."

"Well, I hope they're good referrals. Considering the calf and…other things, it pays to be careful."

The second she saw Luke's wide grin, she wanted to retract the words.

"That's what I've been telling you, sweetheart," he said, drawing out the last syllable. "I'm glad you're finally admitting I'm right."

If she'd had something to throw at him, she would've.

"ABE, WAKE UP." Luke touched his dad on the shoulder. "You're going to sleep the day away." Hell, the day was almost gone.

Abe tried to sit up, but fell back. "I'm awake, dammit."

Luke pulled a chair up next to the bed, the scent of tobacco lingering in the air, in the fabric of the furniture. "How do you feel? Julianna said you might have a flu bug."

"I feel fine and I'd feel a lot better if I didn't have people poking me in the middle of the night."

"It's not nighttime, Dad. It's dinnertime. I can bring your meal in here if you'd rather not get up."

His old man grumbled something and took another stab at sitting up. This time he made it.

"So what do you say?" Luke didn't like the way Abe looked. His face seemed ashen and his voice weak— even through the bluster. And he seemed disoriented. His dad had always been sharp, quick with the words and even quicker with his comebacks.

"I—I say you go ahead. I'll be there in a little bit. I have to wash up first."

More likely he wanted to go outside and smoke another cigarette. But Luke left anyway. His father was a proud man, too proud sometimes. Too proud to give an inch. Ever.

"He'll be here in a few," Luke told Julianna as he entered the room, then went to the fridge for something, but closed the door again.

"There's wine if you'd like that," Julianna said.

"No thanks. I've sworn off the stuff."

"Really? You used to love wine with a good steak."

Luke had offered to barbecue some steaks for dinner and Julianna had snapped up the offer. Why she thought it was her job to make meals, he didn't know. But he hadn't refused a single one. It had been too long since he'd tasted real honest-to-goodness home cooking.

"Merlot? It's been in the fridge for about a half hour. It's better with a tiny chill."

He raised a brow. "You're a wine connoisseur now?"

"No way. But living in San Francisco it's hard not to learn simply by osmosis."

Luke got out the wine and poured one glass and handed it to her. He grabbed a Coke for himself then raised the can. "To a great future for us all."

Her eyes met his. "To us all."

Luke felt an urge to step forward, to taste the wine on her lips. Instead, he took a sip of his soda. "Are the steaks ready to grill?"

"Ready as they'll ever be," she said. "I made a salad and I'm baking some potatoes."

"I'm salivating already." As Luke turned from getting out the steaks, he saw his dad leaning against the archway. "There he is," Luke said. "Glad you could join us, Dad. We've got some mighty fine steaks ready to throw on the grill."

Abe wheezed. "I don't think I can eat anything. I'm going back to bed."

Julianna rushed over, put her hand to his forehead. "You don't feel as if you have a fever, but then maybe you're just working up to it." She smiled sympathetically.

The woman could cajole a stone, and Abe wasn't immune.

"I just need to lie down for a little while longer."

"Do you want us to take you to the E.R.?"

He jerked away, stumbled and bumped the wall with his shoulder. "What the hell for?"

Julianna stepped back, her expression shocked. Then she glanced to Luke as if asking for help. Abe had talked harshly to Luke for most of his life, but he'd never snapped at Jules.

"No reason, Dad," Luke said, walking over to him. "You know women…they're always concerned and want to help."

Abe nodded as if repentant. He looked at Julianna like he wanted to say he was sorry, but they both knew he'd never get out the words. "Like I said, I'm going to lie down for a little while longer."

"We'll put a steak on for you and you can eat it when you feel like it," Luke said as he watched his dad make his way down the hall.

As soon as he was gone, Luke picked up the phone. "What's the name of the doctor you took him to for his hand?"

"Dr. Terry. His number is right there on that pad." She pointed to the paper on the counter below the phone.

Julianna watched as Luke punched in the number. He waited, listening, then left a message.

"He's not there. And if he doesn't call back soon we're going to the hospital."

Nipping at a cuticle on one finger with her teeth, Julianna said, "I'll go along, too."

Luke's head came up. "I wouldn't let you stay here alone if you wanted to."

She should've bristled at the comment, but for some reason she felt good instead. It had been a while since anyone cared where she went or what she did.

The phone rang and Luke answered. He nodded at her that it was the doc. Thank heaven for small-town doctors who didn't wait days to respond.

After explaining his father's symptoms, Luke's end of the conversation was pretty much yes and no answers. When he hung up, he gave her a strange look. "Well?"

"He said to watch him tonight. If he develops any chest pain, pain down the arm, inability to put sentences together, we should give him an aspirin and bring him in right away."

"How will we know if Abe doesn't tell us?"

"I'll go check on him in a little while and see if I can get him to answer some questions. Other than that, the doc seems to think he's got a virus of some kind, and he's just not as resilient as he used to be. Illness is bound to affect him more at this age than it used to."

Julianna leaned against the fridge, relief seeping into her. She hadn't realized until now how worried she was about Abe.

As if he knew what she was feeling, Luke reached out and touched her arm. "He said there's no need to panic."

Something fluttered inside. She felt warm. No, she felt hot. "I'm glad," she said, her voice sounding low and froggy. "I—I don't know what I'd do if something happened to—"

Luke pulled her close, cradling her in his arms as if it were the most natural thing in the world to do. "He's okay. Don't worry." He lifted her chin with two fingers and stared directly into her eyes.

She thought his mouth moved closer, or maybe hers did. She felt he might kiss her and her heart raced as if she'd just run a marathon. He could probably feel it thudding against her chest. Suddenly she couldn't breathe, and pushed away.

"Thanks. I guess I do overreact a little."

His smile seemed guarded. Either he didn't like that she'd pushed him away or he didn't like that he'd held her in the first place. God, why was she second-guessing everything? What did it matter what he was thinking?

"I'll get those steaks on now," he said. "And why don't we eat on the patio. It's really a nice night."

She straightened. "Sure. I'd love to," she said. "I'll get the table settings."

Thankful to have something to do, she collected what they needed, a couple of straw place mats, plates, flatware and napkins. And the wine. Had to have the wine. She brought everything outside, to the area out back where the grill was located. It wasn't a fancy patio, but a big rectangle of adobe tiles, some chipped and worn, the outdoor fireplace in the corner, and the whole area covered by a crosshatched trellis with pink flowering vines growing over the top. The vines provided shade in the summertime and tonight, the twinkle lights left over from the previous Christmas made it utterly romantic.

A few potted cacti dotted the edges of the tile, plants Julianna had given Abe years ago because he couldn't kill them if he wanted. All were doing beautifully, as were the bright red bougainvillea that spilled over the adobe wall surrounding the patio. A hanging ristra and a rustic wooden table and chairs completed the decor. Her heart warmed just being here.

"What can I do to help?" she asked when she finished setting the table.

"Pour yourself some more wine and then sit down and talk to me. These will be done in a few minutes." He glanced over. "That's if you still like your steak medium-rare."

"I do," she said, feeling good that he remembered. She realized then that she'd hate it if they'd spent all those years together and he simply blotted everything from his mind. While she didn't dwell on the past, she did have some fond memories.

"Do you still hang out with Jordan and Rico and… who was that other guy? Oh, wait, don't tell me. I know. It's on the tip of my tongue."

Luke gave a hearty laugh. "You never could give anything up, could you."

"Tex. That's the guy. I only met him a couple of times."

"Yeah, they're all still there. Only the state of bachelorhood among them has been seriously challenged. Rico's married now and Jordan is about to take the plunge. Tex has been living with someone for a couple of years and I'll bet my paycheck that he's practicing marriage vows as we speak."

"Wow. That only leaves you, then, doesn't it?" She leaned a shoulder against the wall next to him and took a sip of wine. "Why did you never marry again?" She shouldn't have asked the question, but couldn't help herself.

His head came up. "You forget. I didn't do very well the first time, so—" He shrugged. "What's the point. I know what I need and what I don't."

His words stung, but she didn't know why.

"How about you?"

"I don't know. It just never happened."

"No steady or live-in friend?"

"Nope. Not now anyway. You?"

He shook his head. "Not for a long time."

"Wow, we're really a pair, aren't we?" she joked. But joking aside, she had to wonder. "Think there's something intrinsically wrong with us that we can't commit?"

Another hearty laugh. "Speak for yourself. My psyche is just fine. In fact it's taken years to hone my inner self to this state of perfection."

She pretended to choke. "Excuse me, I think I'm going to be sick."

"No hurling until after dinner," he said. "And right now I need plates."

She stood, handed him one plate and then the other. Leaning toward the grill, she inhaled the meaty scent. "Mmmm. The steaks smell wonderful."

His brows rose a tad, as if he'd just thought of something. "You do still eat steak, don't you?"

"Of course I do."

They sat down together. "Well, living in the same town as your mother, anything could've happened."

"True. She's always trying to get me to embrace the vegan life. With no luck, I might add. I'm still in search of the best hamburger in San Francisco. I haven't found anywhere as good as Bernie's." They'd spent a lot of time at Bernie's, with and without his buddies. Bernie's made the best hamburgers in L.A.

Luke raised his drink and she followed suit. The crisp ping of her glass touching his metal can seemed somehow symbolic. Glass was delicate, easy to break if you weren't careful. Metal was tough, resilient. And all the small talk wasn't going to stop the current of emotions that coursed between them.

As his eyes met hers, he leaned forward, his face close—close enough for her to feel the warmth of his breath against her face. Her heartbeat quickened. Her palms started to sweat. Lord help her, she wanted to kiss him. Worse yet, she knew he knew exactly what she was thinking.

"Uh…we better eat or the steaks will get cold," she whispered.

As the words left her lips, his mouth met hers.

CHAPTER SEVEN

KISSING JULIANNA FELT as natural as breathing and it was a struggle for Luke to pull himself away. Especially as she leaned into the kiss, her lips warm and soft and willing. With their faces only inches apart, he said, "Bad move, huh."

His hands still on her shoulders, he said, "I'd say I don't know why I did that, but it would be a lie. I've wanted to since the day I got here."

"But you didn't." Her tongue darted over her lips.

"I don't always do everything I want to do. If I did I'd be in big trouble."

"Well, now that you've got it over with, you don't have to think about it any longer." She moved from under his touch.

He laughed. "True. I'm sorry, though."

"It's okay. I wondered what it would be like, too."

The admissions seemed to make them both self-conscious. After another moment of silence, he said, "Let's call it a curiosity kiss and leave it at that."

"Deal," she said. "Now let's eat this steak."

By the time they finished the meal, they'd talked

about the past five years: his career, though he didn't tell her the worst of it, her career, their mutual friends... they'd talked about everything. Everything but...Michael. The heartbreak of their lives.

Like a two-ton elephant in the room, they chose to ignore that part of their life altogether. Because they both knew the reality of their loss. It wasn't something that could be fixed.

"So," he finally said. "I think I'll go do a quick check on Pops."

Pensive, she nodded.

He placed his hand over hers, but the words he wanted to say wouldn't come out.

"Go ahead," she said. "I'll clean up here. Then I've got some work to do."

With that, he stood and walked down the hall, want and need nipping at his heels, regret replacing the emptiness he felt inside.

Abe's room was dimly lit by a small night-light glowing in the bathroom. He wondered if Abe had put it there so he wouldn't stumble when he got up at night.

Not wanting to wake his father, he lightly touched Abe's forehead with his fingertips. He seemed hot. His breathing was shallow. If he had the flu, he would have a fever. Unsure what to do, Luke went back to the kitchen where Julianna was just finishing up. "He's hot," Luke said, "and his breathing is labored."

She handed him the phone and the paper with the doctor's number on it. "Thanks," he said and punched in the number. He got the answering service again and left another message.

"Do you think he's had a flu shot?" Julianna asked.

Luke shrugged. "I doubt it." And they both knew the ramifications of that. Many seniors died every year from the flu, even some who'd been immunized. "We don't know if he has the flu either. Maybe it's something else."

"Perhaps we should take him to the clinic, just to be sure?"

"Yeah. But let's wait to hear what the doc has to say first." They stood there for another awkward moment before Luke said, "Why don't you go do whatever you need to do. I'll wait here for the doctor to call back."

"Okay," she said reluctantly, as if she knew he was trying to get rid of her.

And he was. He needed to be alone. He hadn't thought about his father dying. Ever. Somehow it played into his own feelings of mortality. A subject he avoided like he avoided going to church. His job made denial necessary, because any second of any day could be his last.

The phone rang. It was Doctor Terry who asked a bunch of questions, then told Luke to bring Abe into his office in the morning. "What about now?" Luke asked. "I'd feel better bringing him to the clinic now."

"There's only a nurse on call tonight and I can't get there until tomorrow."

Luke tightened his grip on the phone. Something told him they couldn't wait until morning. "Is there someplace else I can take him?"

"Saint Vincent's Hospital in Santa Fe," the physician

said. "If you're going to do that, I'll call ahead so they'll be expecting you."

Luke thanked the man and hung up. He didn't know why this felt so urgent, but it just did. Getting Abe to agree to go along wasn't as difficult as Luke had expected. That's when he knew his father was really sick.

An hour and a half later Luke and Julianna sat in the sterile white hallway waiting for Dr. Martinez to tell them what was wrong with Abe. Luke was reminded of another sterile, white room. The memory made his heart ache. He studied Jules, who sat quietly next to him reading a magazine. This had to be affecting her as well. But she seemed to have nerves of steel. A total switch from the woman he'd known five years ago.

"Mr. Coltrane." Dr. Martinez came over to sit in the chair next to Luke. "Your father should have some more tests but it looks like pneumonia, and his emphysema exacerbates the problem, making treatment more difficult."

"Emphysema?" Luke looked at Julianna who shrugged. Apparently she wasn't aware of it either. But it made sense. Abe had been smoking since he was fifteen.

The physician gazed sympathetically at Luke, as if apologizing that Abe hadn't told his own son what was wrong with him.

"He didn't tell you."

"I—I don't get home much," Luke said.

"Well, he needs to be hospitalized to clear up the virus, and I also recommend that he stay a few days extra for observation and tests."

Luke shot from his chair, clenched and unclenched

his fists at his sides as he paced the confined area. "I can't believe he didn't tell me he had emphysema."

"I'm not surprised," Julianna said. "He's a proud man."

"Well, that won't help him one bit if he's a proud dead man."

The physician stood. The skin sagged beneath his eyes and Luke remembered the man had been ready to go home but had stayed to see his father.

"Emphysema gets worse, doesn't it?" said Luke.

"True, but slowly. Depending on the outcome of the tests, he may have to use oxygen at some point, but with treatment, I'm sure he'll be fine for a while. He's a strong man."

Luke felt relief seep through him. "That he is."

Dr. Martinez said, "I suggest you go home and call him tomorrow. I've already talked to him about the tests and further evaluation, and he's sleeping now. Don't plan on taking him home for a few days."

Before Luke and Julianna left the hospital, he peeked in on Abe and despite the oxygen tubes in his nose, he did seem to be sleeping peacefully.

"I'm so glad we took him in tonight," Julianna said on the ride home. "That was a good call on your part."

He looked at her. "I still can't believe he never said a word about being sick."

She arched one eyebrow. "Really. I think it's typical Abe."

"Yeah." He hit the steering wheel with the butt of his hand. "But this is serious. People die from emphysema."

After that they were silent, the only sound the hum

of the tires against the asphalt. The night was cool and the stars shone brightly above them. As he drove, Luke thought about Abe and how he'd been going through all this health stuff alone.

His father had told Jules Luke stayed away because when he was a kid, he couldn't accept authority and that somehow soured everything. Only that wasn't the half of it. And dammit, his father knew that.

The past few years had separated them even more because Luke had been too stuck in his own quagmire to pay attention to anyone else.

Yeah, they had issues all right. But if his father had died leaving things as they were, Luke would never have forgiven himself. He made a silent vow to change things when his dad came home.

"You missed the turnoff, Luke."

He screeched to a stop. It was late, there were no highway lights and theirs was the only vehicle on the lonely back road. If it weren't for the headlights, all they'd see was an inky blackness. "Yeah, I did." He turned the car around and sought out the road where he should've turned.

"I'm sorry about Abe," Julianna said, her voice choking a little. "I was really frightened."

Luke realized he'd been thoughtless. Jules loved his father and must be just as worried as he was. Probably more. He reached to place his hand over hers. "I know. I apologize for being so self-absorbed."

"He's your father, Luke. Your concern *should* be for him, not me."

Yeah, just like the concern he'd had for Michael. Only

he'd failed in his quest to find his son. Pain stabbed in his chest. Taking in some air, he forced his own torment away and squeezed her hand. He wanted to say thanks for being so understanding, but couldn't get out the words.

After another long silent stretch, he said, "I'm sorry...."

She looked over at him, questions in her eyes.

"I'm sorry for being such a...bad husband...for being gone all the time—"

"Don't, Luke. Don't say any more. Please."

Yeah. The time for apologies was years ago. He couldn't blame her for not wanting to listen to them now.

THE HOUSE SEEMED EMPTY without Abe, and though it was late, Julianna couldn't sleep. She got out of bed, threw on a baggy sweatshirt over her pajamas and went to the kitchen. The nearly full moon shining its buttery light through the high windows made it easy to navigate and, with the added light from the fridge, she poured herself a glass of wine left over from dinner. She headed for the back door, hoping the crisp fall air might help her think more clearly.

It was obvious she was going to have to make some decisions. Staying here with Luke had her doubting herself. She'd worked too long to learn how to trust her own instincts and she wasn't going to throw it all away because she had feelings for Luke. Yes, she admitted it. But those feelings didn't mean squat in the whole scheme of things.

Luke's personality was so strong, he could over- power a weaker person in ways he didn't even realize.

Like he'd overpowered her. During therapy, she'd realized that regardless of what had happened to Michael, their marriage had been doomed from the beginning. It's why she'd left. So what was the problem? Why did she keep thinking of him, wondering if—

Dammit. She was not going there again. Though Luke had said he wasn't staying, things had changed drastically and it was obvious he wasn't going to leave anytime soon. Certainly not by tomorrow.

Despite all that, she felt a sense of satisfaction in proving her point that she was safe here. With her hand on the knob, she saw a shadow of movement through the curtain on the door. She gasped and jerked back. Muscles taut, senses on high alert, she gulped some air and inched toward the window again. Probably an animal. God knew there were enough of them out here.

Taking it extra slow, she slid the curtain aside. A man's face appeared on the other side of the glass. She lurched back, stumbling over her feet before realizing it was only Luke. Oh, God, it was only Luke.

The door burst open. "What are you doing?"

She tried to breathe, but could only draw a few jagged breaths. She didn't know whether to be relieved or mad as hell. In short spurts, she said, "You...scared...the bejeebies out of me." Okay. Angry it was.

His expression went blank. "I didn't know you were here. You should've turned on some lights."

She closed her eyes in an effort to calm herself. "I couldn't sleep. I was going to have a glass of wine, hoping it would help."

He held up a glass of milk. "Great minds think alike."

"What were you doing outside?"

"Looking at the stars." He grinned. "Wondering how in the world things got so screwed up with my dad."

Yes, she wondered too, only she didn't mean with Abe.

"You need an ear?" she offered, though she knew he'd say no. Why would he want to talk to her now when he hadn't during most of their marriage?

"Sure," he said. "Let's sit outside." He opened the door and gestured for her to go first.

Surprised that he'd actually agreed, she hesitated, noticing he wore pajama bottoms and a navy sweatshirt.

He plucked a black leather jacket from the closet near the door and dumped it on her shoulders.

She went ahead, but something told her this wasn't a good idea.

"Steps or rockers," he asked.

"Rockers," she answered as she walked over to the two wooden chairs at the opposite end of the patio. Rockers were safer. There'd be some distance between them.

Sitting in the chairs, they rocked together, the curved runners making a rhythmic clacking sound against the adobe-tiled floor.

"Just like a couple of old people," Luke said.

"Speak for yourself, Methuselah."

"I remember when my dad made these chairs and how my mother loved them. They'd sit out here every night in good weather."

"That's a lovely memory."

"Yeah. One would think."

Frowning, Julianna stopped rocking and looked at him. "So, even though you said before that your mom and dad had problems, they were happy together."

He closed his eyes and kept rocking. "I guess there were good times and bad, like any marriage. Anyway, I was thirteen when she died and maybe what a kid thinks isn't always the way it is."

"I know what you mean. I always had this fantasy image of what my father was like, what my parents were like together. Then when I was about ten, I learned he'd deserted us without a thought and my fantasy took a nosedive. It took me the longest time to come to grips with that whole thing. Sometimes I wonder if I ever really did." She glanced at him. "But I've told you all this before, haven't I."

She'd bared her soul to the man she'd loved—and he'd returned next to nothing.

"You did. That whole thing sucks."

She moistened her lips.

He turned to gaze at her and his blue eyes looked like moonstones against the dark of the night.

"A child should be able to keep a few fantasies."

She sighed. "It would be nice, wouldn't it. But things never seem to work out that way." Before they'd married she'd had a fantasy or two about what their life would be like, but she'd learned a lot since then. "Fantasies are simply a way for people to delude themselves, to pretend life can be what they want it to be."

Luke felt the bite of her words. He'd promised her everlasting love, and dammit, he'd never wavered from that promise. She was the one who'd left…the one who'd torn their marriage apart. And he still didn't know why. Not the real reason. "Things work out one way or another, depending on the choices we make."

"And when there is no choice? What then?"

He didn't want to get into this. He really didn't. But he couldn't keep from saying, "People always have choices."

"Yes, I suppose. Even if they're bad ones."

"So, then we adjust."

She looked into his eyes. "Sometimes that's impossible."

"Well, I see things differently. If you want something you go for it."

"Sometimes what we want isn't what's best for us."

Now she was talking in riddles. He hated when she did that. He stood, walked to the edge of the patio and shoved his hands in his pocket. "Speaking of impossible," he said, "Dad will go ballistic if I tell him I hired someone. I'm not sure how to approach it."

"You hired someone?"

"Not yet. But I hope to tomorrow. I had to call the guy and tell him I couldn't make it today. I'm hoping he's still available when I see him."

"So what will you do if Abe refuses the help?"

Luke gave a futile shrug. "I'll cross that road when I get there."

"Maybe you could convince Abe that since you won't be here, he'll need a hand while he recovers. If he thinks it's temporary, then he might be more accepting."

"And then, after a while, he'll realize he really does need help and may ask the guy to stay on."

She nodded. "Exactly."

Luke had to laugh. "You learn those devious methods in San Francisco?"

She grinned. "I'm a journalist. You learn to be creative. I think this is one of those times."

"Maybe so." She'd been right about several things. But one thing still bothered him. The threats she'd received. He felt an ominous dread about it. Like the ominous dread he'd felt one horrible night five years ago.

CHAPTER EIGHT

THE NEXT MORNING on the way to Santa Fe to see Abe, Luke pulled into a Circle K gas station. While he filled the tank, he scoped out the area, his senses on alert since hearing the calls Jules had received. Two cars were parked in front of the store, one black, one silver-gray.

Just then Jules got out of the car and came around to his side. "I'm going inside to get a coffee. Would you like one?"

"A giant Coke with no ice would be good."

She stuck her hands in the pockets of her low-rider jeans and laughed, a light teasing laugh. "Same old, same old."

He shrugged. "Gotta have my fix. And it's not as expensive as a Starbucks."

She turned and walked toward the store. And he kept watching, not just to keep an eye on her, but because he couldn't tear his gaze away from the quick swing of her arms, the subtle movement of her hips. He felt a primal urge. Looking at Julianna had always been a turn-on. The passage of time hadn't changed a thing.

When she reached the entrance, he was about to look

away but just then a guy wearing a Stetson got out of the silver car and followed Jules inside.

Odd. Had the guy been sitting there…waiting? Luke dropped the nozzle and sprinted across the asphalt, his heart racing. Inside, he scanned the store for Jules. Where was she? And where was the guy in the cowboy hat?

He went down one aisle and the next until he reached the beverage section at the back of the store. He stopped. Jules stood with her back to him, talking to the man who'd followed her in. She turned when Luke walked up, surprise in her eyes.

"Luke? What's wrong?"

He grabbed her arm and herded her toward the door.

"What's going on?" she said, wrenching away. "Are you crazy?"

"Who was that guy and why were you talking to him?"

"He asked for directions, that's all. Sheesh! Stop acting like a cop all the time."

Luke gritted his teeth. "It's what I do," he said, throwing her earlier words back at her. But was she right? Was he overreacting? It was natural for him to be suspicious of everyone. If he wasn't it could cost a life—his or someone else's. "Just get your stuff. I'm ready to go."

As he returned to the pump, another vehicle chugged up into the next stall. A faded maroon Pontiac with steam rising from the hood. The driver got out and nodded at Luke.

"I think I'm overheating," the man said, pushing back his battered baseball cap.

"Looks that way," Luke answered as he watched the

door for Jules to come back out. "Or maybe you have a leak in your water hose."

"Well, whatever it is, it's not good. I've got business to take care of."

Still agitated, Luke didn't respond. The guy wanted to chit-chat because that's what people did here. They had nothing better to do. Well, he wasn't going to get sucked into a conversation he didn't want to have. He had more important concerns—like keeping an eye on Jules who thought chatting with anyone who asked her a question was no big deal.

Finishing, he closed the gas cap. Julianna returned. "Here you go," she said handing him his drink. "Cola with no ice."

"Perfect."

On the road again, Luke turned on the radio and found a country station. Jules gave him a skeptical gaze.

"What?" he asked. "You don't like country?"

"I've never tried. I didn't know you liked it either."

He shrugged. "I didn't until I won some free tickets to an Alan Jackson concert."

"Uh-huh. Did you stay for the whole thing?"

Zing. She was good at that. "I did. Not one call out," he said. "That only happened when I was with you."

"Well, I'm glad I was so special." She smiled. "What is it that you like about the music?"

"Honest lyrics straight from the heart. It's music that tells a story."

"You mean like 'My girlfriend dumped me when I crashed my pickup and now I'm so lonely I could cry'."

He laughed. "Hey, it happens."

"I did like that girl Carrie on American Idol. She sang country."

Now it was his turn to be skeptical. "You watch reality shows?"

She shrugged, grinning. "My dirty little secret."

"I listen to country and you watch reality shows. So much for thinking we're the same people we were five years ago."

"Thank God," she said.

He didn't know if she was referring to him or herself, but it was a can of worms he wasn't going to open. He drove on—silently—until he felt her watching him.

"What?"

"Well, now I'm wondering what else has changed."

He waggled his eyebrows and gave a lecherous grin. "Some things never change."

"Oh," she said dryly, "I figured that out already."

"Me, too." He kept his eyes pinned to the road. "But don't worry. I've learned self-control."

That brought another long silence.

Finally she said, "I'm curious. Do you think I've changed?"

He glanced at her. "Some."

"In what way?"

Luke tightened his grip on the wheel, unwilling to give voice to what he really felt. *Keep it light, Luke. Just keep it light.* "Well, some things are still the same. You're still in great shape."

She turned, touching the collar of her shirt. "You think so?"

"Uh-huh. And you still answer a question with a question."

She grinned.

"You still have a weird sense of humor and your laugh is the same."

All traits he admired. Traits that had drawn him to her from the first day they'd met. He scratched his chin. "As to what's different, you used to wear your hair pulled back most of the time." He fixed his eyes on the road, only glancing over once in a while. "And the lipstick. I don't remember you wearing any kind of makeup before."

He wondered if he should say more. Could be risky. But what the hell. "You seem more at ease, more self-assured." He smiled. "I like that. It's…sexy."

She tagged him on the arm. "Damn. It's always about sex with you."

He turned to glance at her. "I seem to remember I wasn't alone in that thinking. In fact—"

She averted her gaze. "That was a long time ago."

"True." He had to remember that. "Yeah, five years can make a big difference in a person's life."

"True. But *you* don't seem all that different."

If you didn't count the years he'd spent trying to forget how she'd ditched him when he needed her most. For him, it'd been four years of hell and another year of clawing his way out of the inferno. "Same old, same old. That's me. Same job…same friends."

"Well, I have noticed one thing that's different about you. You seem more concerned about your dad than before."

A skunk darted across the road in front of them. Luke pulled the wheel to the left, swerving out of the way. "For all the good it'll do me." He sighed. "I came here with an idea that maybe we could clear the slate and attempt a normal father-son relationship, but I know now that isn't going to happen. Whenever we're together— it doesn't matter what we're talking about—I feel this undercurrent of disapproval."

"But you're trying to change things. I think that's admirable."

"No, it's not. It's selfish, something I need to do for me."

He gave a wry laugh. "Well, I know now it doesn't matter. You can't change people and you can't change the past."

"Don't I know it," she said, her voice so low he barely heard her. The pretty smile had switched to a frown. She pinched the bridge of her nose with her thumb and forefinger, as if she might be getting a headache.

Damn. He'd probably stuck his foot in his mouth again.

Reaching the hospital, he cranked the steering wheel, swung into the parking lot and into a visitor's space. "Come on. This can't take too long because I've got to interview that guy at eleven."

"GET ME OUT of here," Abe demanded the instant Julianna and Luke entered the room. Nothing they hadn't expected.

Julianna saw Luke's jaws clench. She elbowed him in the ribs, urging him to say something. Something nice, she hoped.

"We've got to talk to your physician first. In fact, I'm going to see if I can track down Dr. Martinez right now." Luke turned and left the room.

Abe still had the oxygen tube in his nose, but seemed feistier than the day before. He also had an IV in his arm.

"What's that for," Julianna asked.

"They say I'm dehydrated, but I think they're pumping me with drugs."

She raised a brow, then sat in the chair next to Abe's bed. "But you're looking better, Pops."

He placed a hand over hers. "You and Luke getting along?"

"We're doing fine," she answered. "We're adults. We can be civilized for a little while."

"That's not what I meant."

"Oh." She realized Abe had some misguided notion that she and Luke should still be married. It had taken him a long time to accept their divorce, and when he finally did, he blamed Luke. She'd tried to explain it was no one's fault, but that wasn't Abe's mind-set. If something happened, someone had to take the rap for it.

Just then Luke came back in with Dr. Martinez.

"Good morning, Abraham," the doctor said.

"When do I get to go home?"

The silver-haired man walked over to the bed and picked up the chart. "Nothing's changed since last night.

As I said then, I want you to stay for a few days until we get the infection under control."

The physician took Abe's pulse. "You can go home when we're sure you're one hundred percent."

The older man grumbled something about the food being terrible, the beds being hard, and that there was nothing good on television. By the time Julianna and Luke left, they weren't sure he wouldn't bust out of the place.

"He's so...ornery," Julianna said on their way down the hall.

"So, what's new?" Luke opened the door for her to go out. "We've still got some time before I have to be back for the interview. Want to have coffee in the plaza?"

The plaza. It had been one of their favorite places when they came to visit Abe at the ranch. She didn't want to see it, but maybe she should. Her therapist had said she needed to face the past before she could go on. She'd disagreed and thought she'd done just fine. So what was holding her back? "Sure. I haven't been there for years," she said.

It wasn't far from the hospital to the old plaza square in downtown Santa Fe. The air was crisp and the sun was shining, a perfect fall day. They parked on a side street and walked into the courtyard lined on three sides with tiny boutiques and upscale art galleries. More galleries and trendy restaurants filled the narrow streets that jutted from the plaza, the heart of Sante Fe.

Local artisans were setting up shop on their blankets and tables under the Palace of the Governors' portico, a building that dated back to missionary days. Displays of turquoise-and-silver jewelry, Navajo pottery and handwoven blankets and baskets were laid out on sidewalks on both sides of the portal, leaving space for customers to walk down the middle.

Some people said the displays of jewelry weren't really the Native American handcrafts they purported to be, that most were just knockoffs imported from China or Malaysia. Having grown up in the area, Luke was pretty astute when it came to knowing the difference.

As they strolled past, a bracelet caught Julianna's eye, and even she was pretty sure it was the real thing. She stopped to look at it, but Luke kept walking. As she gazed through the crowd to see how far ahead Luke was, she had the eeriest feeling that someone was watching her.

She gave a furtive glance around. No one was even looking at her, except for one woman urging her to examine her crafts.

Luke was ten feet in front, obviously more interested in getting coffee than checking out the displays. She turned back to the bracelet again, then saw a man standing near another vendor quickly avert his gaze. It struck her that she recognized him. But that was silly. She'd been to Santa Fe only a half dozen times and all of them more than five years ago. She didn't know anyone in the city.

Still, the edgy feeling persisted. She hurried to catch up with Luke then touched his arm to get his attention. He slowed his pace. "Don't look now, but there's a man back there who I think is watching me." Luke stopped at a blanket at the end of the walkway, bent down to look at some belt buckles. She bent down, too, and whispered, "Black hat, black outfit, silver belt."

He cast a surreptitious glance back.

When she looked herself, the man was gone.

"You sure," Luke said.

Feeling stupid and a little paranoid, she shrugged it off. "Must've been my imagination. My brain has been working overtime lately."

His eyes widened…as if he'd never expected her to admit she'd had any misgivings about her situation.

"Any other defining features?" Luke scanned the area, his gaze like a camera on motordrive, clicking off images to file away.

"He was tall. Six feet, maybe. His face was shadowed by his hat, but something about him seemed familiar." She shrugged. "I don't know anyone in New Mexico except Abe, so…so, it's probably nothing."

He took her arm and led her down the street toward Zele's coffee shop. "Basic instincts are usually right. When your gut tells you something, you need to listen. Especially now."

Maybe. But she felt a little foolish, and she'd flat-out admitted she wasn't as blasé about her would-be stalker as she'd like to think. "Right now my gut is growling from hunger. Do we have time for breakfast with that coffee?"

The restaurant was less than half full, a hangout for locals, apparently. Julianna could always tell the locals from the tourists by the way they dressed. Tourists favored Native American knock-offs.

"Table for two," Luke said. "Preferably by the window."

When they were seated, Luke sat facing the door where he could see everything, a habit she'd gotten used to long ago. The fragrant scent of sopaipillas filled the air. Her salivary glands kicked into action just thinking about filling one of the fried pastries with warm honey and gobbling it down, but her sensible side won out. Too many calories.

After they ordered, huevos rancheros for him and a chili pepper omelet for her, Julianna said, "It really isn't necessary for you to stay, you know." She peered at him over the rim of her cup. "I mean, I know you need to get back to L.A. and I can do whatever is necessary for Abe."

He kept looking around. "Stop trying to get rid of me. I'm staying until Abe is out of the hospital. After that, we'll see."

Good Lord, that could be days, a week even. Could she handle that much time with Luke?

After that, she had nothing more to say and after breakfast they were soon back on the road, arriving home ten minutes before Luke had to leave for the interview. As they drove up to the house, she saw Stella Hancock's truck parked in front.

Luke cursed. What did she want now? And why was she so damned persistent? As far as Luke knew, Abe had made it clear he didn't want anything to do with her, and considering how she'd torn their lives apart before his mother died, he didn't want anything to do with her either.

Luke and Julianna climbed from his car. He opened the rustic wood doors to the front entry and found the woman sitting in the shade of the ruby-colored bougain-villeas that tumbled over the adobe wall. "Can I help you with something," Luke asked, striding toward the front door.

She stood and Luke noticed her eyes were a bit red, as if she might've been crying.

"I had this…feeling that something awful had happened to Abraham and I couldn't get it out of my head. Is he okay?"

Her pewter-gray hair was pulled back at the nape and she wore flared pants, boots and lots of turquoise and silver on her hands. For a second he wondered if all the rumors were true, that she had some kind of sixth sense. She was part-Navajo, an *alni* he'd heard, one who walked the line between traditionalist and modern culture. There were rumors that she came from a long line of healers.

Luke had his own views on the tradition of Native Americans on the res using their own healers to treat their tribes' illnesses. To him it was like practicing medicine without a license, and the result could be fatal for someone who needed immediate care. Like his mother. His father knew the dangers and yet he'd done it anyway. This woman was as much to blame as Abe.

Jules spoke up. "Abe is in the hospital. He has pneumonia and will be there for a few days. But the doctor says he'll be fine."

The lines in the woman's face softened. "Oh, that's why he was having trouble breathing."

Luke exchanged glances with Julianna. How did *she* know that?

"I thought it might be due to his smoking."

This was getting more weird all the time. The most logical explanation was that Mrs. Hancock had called the hospital to find out about Abe. Even though they weren't supposed to give information to nonrelatives, she might've sweet-talked one of the nurses into telling her. But how would she have known he was even there?

Hell, he didn't have time to stand out here jawing. He had only a few minutes to get to Pecos to meet the guy he was going to interview for the job.

Having his father hospitalized had made Luke more aware that it was important to find someone good, someone who could do more than just help with ranch chores. If Abe was alone and got sick, or injured himself in some way…it could be disastrous. The solution was obvious. Abe's hired hand would need to live at the ranch.

"I've got to go," Luke said to Julianna.

"Sure. Good luck."

STELLA HANCOCK STUDIED Julianna, hoping to get some positive feelings from her. She'd had a disturbing vision about the young lady, but she'd learned long ago that disclosing her special gift to non-natives usually made them think she was a witch who practiced voodoo or something.

She'd had a similar vision about Abe and had felt such an urgency, she'd been compelled to come over.

"Would you like some tea?" Julianna asked.

Stella smiled. "I'd love some. Thank you."

"Come with me," Julianna said. "Since it's so nice out, we can sit on the patio if you like."

They went inside, and walking through the darkened rooms with their thick walls and small windows, Stella felt a lump form in her throat. Everything seemed just as it had been so many years ago when she and Lizzie had been close—as close as sisters.

When they reached the kitchen, Julianna said, "Go on out to the patio. I'll bring the tea."

Stella went outside, forcing herself to stay focused. She was here to find out about Abe. Not to visit old memories that should have faded long ago—like the dried bouquet of flowers her lover had once given her.

She found a chair with cushions that were of the same Kokopelli design that seemed to adorn so many New Mexico homes. A few seconds later, Julianna appeared with a tray holding a teapot and two cups.

"Is it warm enough out here?" Julianna asked as she set down the tray. "I can start a fire."

"It's lovely. And I'm quite used to the outdoors."

"I can see why. I live where it's damp all the time and I love the arid climate here."

"Where do you live?" Stella asked, hoping the answer might give her some insight about the disturbing image she'd had about the young woman sitting next to her.

Julianna hesitated. "Uh…California."

"So," Julianna said. "How did you know Abe wasn't well?"

She poured two cups of tea and handed one to Stella. "It was a feeling I had. A strong feeling." She reached for the cup offered her.

Julianna nodded, as if she might understand.

"I learned a long time ago not to ignore my strong feelings, even if they turned out to be wrong."

"Uh-huh," Julianna said, pensive, as if deciding whether she should buy into what Stella was saying or not.

After all these years, Stella was used to that kind of response and paid no mind to it. "I'm happy to hear Abraham is going to be okay."

After another thoughtful moment, the younger woman looked directly at Stella and asked, "Why haven't you and Abe talked for twenty-five years?"

Stella suppressed a smile. She liked the girl's forthrightness. "Our families had a falling out," she answered. It wasn't a total lie, but she saw no reason to tell a stranger the whole story.

"So you were friends once?"

"A long time ago."

"You and your husband?"

Surprised that Julianna continued asking questions, she said, "Abraham and I went to school together. We were…good friends at one time. Lizzie and I were, too."

Julianna's eyes widened. "Really. You knew Luke's mother? I'd love to know more about your friendship with her."

She hesitated. "I'd rather not talk about it, if you don't mind."

The look on Julianna's face was priceless. She obviously hadn't expected a refusal. Few people could resist talking about themselves, but she wasn't one of them.

"Oh, I'm sorry if I seemed to be prying. I'm a journalist and asking questions is what I do. And in this case, whenever I ask Luke or Abe about…Elizabeth, I get nothing. It's as if talking about her would hurt too much."

Stella took another sip of tea. "I can understand that. I don't think either one has ever been able to deal with the fact that Lizzie's death was inevitable—that it was her time, and they couldn't do anything to help her."

As she said the words, Stella noticed the younger woman's face pale. She reached for her hand. "We can't always help those we love, no matter how much we want to. Some things are out of our hands."

When Julianna didn't reply, Stella said, "I suppose I better leave now. I'm sorry if I said anything to upset you."

Julianna squared her shoulders. "Uh—no. You didn't. I appreciate you coming by to check on Abe. Even if—"

"It's okay," Stella said quickly. "I know how they feel, and it's okay." She cleared her throat and stood to go. But before she left, she said, "Please be careful while you're here."

THE GUY WAS LATE. Luke ordered a cola and decided to give him ten more minutes, hoping he had a legitimate excuse. He had no other leads on a hired hand for his dad, but he wasn't going to hire a slacker either.

When the guy didn't show, Luke paid the waitress and got up to leave. As he walked to his car, his cell rang. He fished it from the pocket of his leather jacket and glanced at the number. Not one he recognized. "Coltrane," he said.

Nothing. "This is Luke." Then a crackling sound and the dial tone. Dammit. He hit a couple of buttons. No call back number, but his phone was working fine. Maybe the call was cut off on the other end. Maybe it was the guy saying he'd be late. Or maybe it was Jules. He punched in his dad's number.

No answer. An awful awareness came over him. He'd left when the Hancock woman was there, not thinking that Jules would be on her own when she went home. Fear sent a spurt of adrenaline into his veins. Someone could've drawn him away under the guise of an interview to get at Jules.

He got into the car, caught his jacket on the corner of the door as he sat, then yanked it off and heard a rip. He slammed the accelerator to the floor and hauled ass down the highway, his heart hammering triple time. If something happened to Jules—dammit! How could he be so stupid as to leave her alone.

All he'd wanted to do was get away from Stella Hancock. He'd reacted on emotion. He never did that. For once in his life, he hoped the neighbor hadn't left and they were simply talking and hadn't heard the phone. Or maybe Jules was in the bathroom.

But whatever scenario he came up with didn't ease his mind and when he barreled up the road to the house, dust and dirt spiraling behind him, his heart felt as if it would burst from his chest.

He'd barely set foot from his vehicle before Jules met him outside. "Back so soon?" she asked. "Did you hire him?"

His stomach did a belly flop, but he sucked in some air and tried for nonchalant. "No. He didn't show." His words came out sharper than he wanted.

"Really? You think something happened?"

She hurried alongside as he stormed toward the house.

"It doesn't matter if something happened. He showed his character by not bothering to call." Irresponsible people annoyed the hell out of him.

"Is something else wrong?"

"No—" he tried to soften his voice "—nothing else is wrong." Except that he'd been rookie stupid and if something had happened to her… He slammed open the door.

"Do you have some other leads on someone to hire?"

"I put the word out with some local people, and I hung a notice at the Circle K. And there's the ad in the paper. We'll see what comes up."

As they walked inside together, Luke half expected Abe to greet them, then realized he wasn't there. They were alone. "I need something cold to drink. How about you?"

"I made some lemonade."

"Fine."

Luke watched Julianna as she went to the fridge and then poured two glasses of lemonade. He liked to watch her. She moved with an easy grace that he found sexy as hell.

But what he thought one way or the other didn't matter. How he felt about her didn't matter. He couldn't let any of it matter. "I'd like to see those e-mail messages again."

"Why? You know what they say."

"Yeah, but I had some ideas. I thought of a way to find out where they came from."

"I tried that already. The messages are scrambled somehow. I even asked a friend who's a computer geek and he said to forget it."

"I know an expert."

"Someone here?"

He shook his head. "No, Rico. Remember?"

"But he's in Los Angeles."

"Go ahead. Pull them up. Then I'll call him and see if he can help us do a search."

Luke followed Jules into her bedroom. The laptop was on the unmade bed, and as she sat and turned on the machine to pull up her e-mail, he stood opposite her, staying his distance. He couldn't guarantee what might happen if he didn't. Just being close to her made him aware of how good they'd once been together.

He watched as she clicked on the keys, then used the mouse. The soft light from the screen illuminated her pale, beautiful face, but hid the intensity she carried inside. He knew what she was thinking, her brain ticking off the moments until he left. And that only made her more desirable. Why the hell did he always want what he couldn't have?

He sat on the end of the mattress, still keeping his distance. Her unique scent rose from the bedding like an aphrodisiac, like opium, sucking him in. He wanted to pull her down between the sheets with him, bury his head in her silky hair…bury himself inside…

"Oh, God," she whispered. Her face went white.

He jumped up and came around behind her. "What?"

She didn't speak and simply waved at the computer.

He looked down to see a new message on the screen.

"I know where you are."

CHAPTER NINE

"YEAH," a sleepy voice answered when Luke made the call to Rico.

"Sorry to wake you, buddy, but I need your help."

"Luke? Where are you?"

"I'm still in New Mexico. I've got a favor to ask. A couple favors as a matter of fact."

"Shoot."

Luke could always count on Rico and Jordan, LAPD's finest detectives and the best friends anyone could have. No matter where, when or how difficult the task might be, they were there. "I need your computer expertise. I have some e-mail messages and I need to find out where they came from."

"You have a computer with you?"

He cleared his throat. "It's not mine. But I need to track the messages to find out who sent them."

"Did you click on Reply?"

"Click on Reply," Luke directed Julianna.

"I did. The reply address is garbage."

"Doesn't work. What else?"

"Nothing that I can do from here. If I had the computer I might be able to figure it out. There's always a way."

Luke thought for a minute. "That's not possible. At least not right this minute." He shoved a hand through his hair, his frustration rising. "There has to be a way to do this."

"Sounds important," Rico said.

"Yeah. It is." Luke quickly explained the threatening e-mails, and that Jules's life might be in danger.

There was a long pause on the line before Rico asked, "Can you express mail it to me?"

"That's a thought. I can do it tomorrow morning."

"You said two things."

"Yeah."

"What's going on?" Rico sounded more awake now.

"Renata Willis. Seven years old. Abducted and murdered fifteen years ago."

"That's an old case. Really old."

Before either Luke or Rico worked in the RHD. "I understand there were no viable leads and the case went cold."

"You got a lead on it now?"

"Not exactly. I asked Jordan to pull the old file."

"You think the e-mail is connected to the case?"

"Maybe. Keep that in mind when you're working on it."

As Luke hung up, he contemplated what to do. "Rico thinks he can find out where the messages came from but he needs the computer."

Her eyes widened. "*I* need my computer. I can't finish my work without it."

"Would that be the worst thing in the world?"

When she didn't say anything, he knew the answer. "If you want to track down this guy, you'll have to do without your computer for a while."

"I have a deadline to meet."

"What's more important, a deadline or your life?"

"It's just an e-mail. It doesn't mean he really wants to hurt me and it doesn't mean he really knows where I am. He probably thinks I'm still in San Francisco. For all we know he's just a crank who gets his kicks scaring people."

"But we don't know any of that and we won't know until we find out who this creep is. We have to assume he means what he says. So, save your stuff on a CD and we'll get you another laptop."

Lines formed around her mouth, the way they always did when she dug in her feet over something. She closed the lid on the laptop.

Scrubbing a hand over his chin, Luke stood, paced, then stopped in front of her. "I have a better idea. Pack your things."

"What—"

"We're going to L.A."

"L.A.? But…what about your father?"

"I'll call the doc and find out how long he's going to be there. If we leave early in the morning, we'll be there in a couple hours and on a plane back by evening."

"I—I don't know."

"What don't you know? You do want to know who this sicko is, don't you?"

She nodded. "But if the police already refused to do anything, what good will going to L.A. do?"

"We'll take the laptop to Rico. Then I can check the Willis file myself."

"So, you go then. I'll stay here in case anything comes up with your father."

"I'm not leaving you here alone. Your only other options are to get another computer or to quit writing the story."

She gave him a look that could've wilted steel.

"That's what I thought. So, we'll leave first thing in the morning. You won't lose a minute of writing time."

She realized Luke fully believed whoever was threatening her meant business. Otherwise he'd leave her here and go to L.A. alone.

Feeling a chill, she rubbed her arms. She'd wondered more than once how serious the guy really was, but she always thought she was overreacting because of the past.

After losing Mikey, every noise, every look from a stranger had seemed threatening, every person she passed seemed sinister in some way, and she'd spent her days in a perpetual state of suspicion and fear.

She'd finally had to seek more grief counseling to help her crawl from the abyss of sorrow that almost destroyed her.

Now, a feeling of dread came over her. Was the threat as real as Luke thought it was? Or was she relapsing?

"You okay?"

She nodded. Rubbed her arms again.

"It's okay to be scared, you know. I'm scared every day when I go out on the streets."

Her head came up. His admission surprised her. "I—

I didn't think it bothered me, but tonight it feels…eerie. We're so far away from everything."

He reached out, lifted the laptop off the bed and set it on the night table. Then he sat next to her and slipped an arm around her. "I'll stay here with you tonight."

It was a bad idea, but an offer she couldn't refuse. It wasn't like she'd never slept with him before, and tonight, she needed to feel the physical warmth of another human being. She needed to draw on his strength. To be close to someone who cared about her.

Despite their divorce, she believed he did care, if for no other reason than their history together. The fact that they'd had a child. She leaned into him, resting her head on his shoulder.

Still holding her, he leaned against the pillow, his face nestled in her hair. She felt him draw in a long, deep breath, then he stroked her head. "Go to sleep now," he whispered. "We've got a busy day tomorrow."

MORNING CAME too soon, and after a drive to Albuquerque and the short flight to Los Angeles, they were in a rental car speeding down the freeway to Rico Santini's house in Anaheim.

A wave of apprehension swept through Julianna. She'd last seen Rico not long before she and Luke had separated and it hadn't been pleasant. She felt embarrassed just thinking about it. She'd found Luke and his friends at Bernie's and she'd gone inside and stood there shrieking at them like a banshee, telling them that sitting around watching football wasn't going to help find her son. She'd said some horrible things, including that they were to blame for not finding Michael. She'd totally lost it.

Apparently Luke sensed her nervousness and took her hand. "It'll be fine," he said.

"The last time I saw Rico, I was so horrible to him… to all of you."

"Don't worry, guys get over things like that. They know you were emotionally stressed. I was, too."

She inhaled. "I don't know how you can handle what you do all the time. I'd be a wreck."

"That's why you're not a cop," he said, trying to diffuse her nervousness. "Hey, come to think of it, I used to know a good remedy for stress."

Julianna couldn't help smiling. Whenever things got too bad, they'd wind up in bed. And he was right. It was the best stress-buster around.

But even good sex hadn't been able to save their marriage—or mend their broken hearts.

"Here we are," Luke said, pulling into the driveway of a small cottage that sat back from the tree-lined street. She'd been to Rico's home many times before and felt a twinge of nostalgia. Rico had always liked big barbecues and coming from a large Italian family, he knew how to cook and did it well. They'd had many memorable times at Rico's.

"I can't believe Rico, the quintessential playboy, is married now. It's so…unlikely."

"Yeah, I couldn't believe it either. They adopted a little boy that Macy had in her charge as a ward of the court and voilà, instant family. Billy's great, too."

She couldn't help but wonder if Billy reminded Luke of Mikey. If every time he saw a child that age, the pain swept back, again and again.

Luke smiled, then reached across her lap to open the car door on her side. "Life is full of surprises."

Julianna climbed out and hoisted the strap of her laptop case over her shoulder. "Do you think Rico can do it?"

"Rico's brain is a computer, so if anyone can do it, he can."

"Do you think it'll take very long?"

"No clue. But you know me and computers. Two left hands."

Rico opened the door almost as they reached it. "Yo, buddy," Rico said, doing one of those handshake hug things that guys do. "Hi, Julianna," he acknowledged and gave her a quick hug too. "Really great to see you again. Come in."

As they went inside, Julianna noticed the house seemed brighter, more homey than before.

"Macy's made a few decorating changes around here."

"It looks wonderful. She has a designer's touch."

"Where's Macy now?" Luke asked.

"She's at work and Billy's at school. I've got to leave shortly, too. Just had a call from the boss."

Julianna looked at Rico. "Do you have any idea how long this will take?"

Rico shrugged. "Could take an hour or a couple days. I won't know until I get into it."

"She's worried about a deadline on a story."

"No problem. Follow me." Rico led them down the

hall to one of the bedrooms that he used as his office. Three computers were lined up across the oak desk that took up most of the room. "Here," Rico said, picking up a laptop from one of the bookshelves. "You can borrow this. I never use it."

"Oh, I couldn't—"

"Yes, you can. Take it with you. Really."

"Geez, Rico. What do you do with all these computers?" Luke looked befuddled, which wasn't a surprise. He had no clue why anyone needed a computer at all except at work to catch bad guys.

Rico shrugged. "One belongs to Macy."

"So, when will you be able to work on mine?" Julianna asked.

"Later tonight. I'll give you a call when I get back and let you know if I need any information."

"I'll be down later to take a look at the Willis case," Luke said.

"Where are you headed now?"

Luke avoided looking at Julianna when he said, "My place. You can get me there or on my cell."

When in the car and on the 405 toward Venice, Julianna was as silent as a stone, the tension in the air palpable. He knew she might be worried about going to the home they'd shared, a place where memories were embedded in every room, in every knickknack and piece of furniture. "We have to go somewhere," he said. "We might as well be comfortable."

After that, he couldn't think of anything to say that might assuage her fears. He'd had his own misgivings about staying in the house after the divorce. It had been the place where they'd shared their dreams and fantasies— and the place where they'd lost Michael.

But for Luke, the house was comforting. They'd lived there as a family, and every day since then he felt Julianna and Michael's presence there. For him, that was a good thing. But if she hadn't felt the same, there was no point trying to explain. She'd been intent on leaving. Intent on putting him and their life together behind her.

"It's apparent we're not going to get out of here until tomorrow, and it's the safest place I know. If someone is trying to find you, he's not going to look for you at your ex-husband's house. But…if you are uncomfortable with going there, we can check into a hotel."

When she looked at him, her eyes were dark and unreadable. "No, it's okay."

He wasn't convinced. But he didn't push it. They rode the rest of the way in silence, but then on the way past the beach, Julianna said, "Can we stop at the pier?"

Surprised, he said, "Sure." He made a sharp turn and pulled into the public lot. Even though it was fall, the tourists still loved coming here, many of them to gawk at the unusual, visit the funky shops and be entertained by the jugglers, dancers and musicians. It took a couple circles around to find a parking spot.

For Luke, the uniqueness of Venice Beach was what made it appealing. Jules used to feel the same way, and he hoped that was why she wanted to stop. When they got out of the car, she didn't say a word, but simply stood with her eyes closed, inhaling the salty sea air.

A cool breeze ruffled her hair, blowing it back from her face. "It's…revitalizing," she said, then started walking toward the sand.

Luke followed. "Do you want my jacket?"

"No, thanks. I need a jolt of fresh air."

They walked leisurely over the hard-packed sand, then she stopped at the water's edge and kneeled down to pick up something embedded there. "A sand dollar," she said, then looked up at him, wistfulness in her eyes. "I—I came here a lot with Michael so he could play on the beach."

"He loved the water." Luke had been teaching Mikey to use a boogie board and Jules had had a fit, thinking her little boy was going to get hurt or washed away.

"On the way here I didn't think I could do this. I thought all the reminders would make me fall apart."

"And now?"

She turned away, but not before he saw, her eyes well with tears. "I—I don't know. It's…almost like I can feel him here. Like the wind is Mikey, wrapping his arms around me."

Luke swallowed hard, put his arm around her and they slowly walked back to the car. No words were necessary. They both knew what they'd lost.

JULIANNA HAD BEEN nervous about going into the house, but her fears were quickly quelled when she stepped into the kitchen. Luke still had her photos, yellowed and curled as they were, pinned on the cork board.

She asked him to wait in the kitchen while she

walked through the rest of the house. It was something she had to do. Alone. She had to dispel her demons right away, or she'd regret it. She knew that about herself as well as she knew her own heartbreak.

As she moved slowly from room to room, like ghosts the memories whispered from every corner. Upstairs, she stopped in front of their bedroom. Luke's room now.

The family photo was still on the dresser, the furniture arrangement was still the same, even the lace coverlet that she'd so desperately had to have was on the bed. And the horribly distorted afghan she'd made when she first learned to knit lay over the top of the rocker in the corner. She brought her hand to her mouth, her fragile emotions threatening to spill over.

Luke had kept everything as it was before she left.

Except for Mikey's room. Only that had been her doing. During one particular despairing rage, she'd gone on a rampage and cleared everything out of Mikey's room, giving away her only son's clothing and toys to the children at the shelter. It had seemed a good idea at the time, a way to purge the reminders.

But afterward, when it was too late, she'd regretted it like nothing she'd regretted since.

The only things she'd saved were some pictures, some shells Mikey had collected on the beach, and a jar full of colorful stones worn smooth by the water. Odd stuff, she realized now. Later, after her cleansing streak, looking at his empty room had been devastating. She couldn't believe what she'd done. By getting rid of everything, it felt as if Mikey had never existed. She wanted to take it all back. But she couldn't, and her despair grew even darker.

Luke had never said a word to her about what she'd done. She guessed he was battling his own demons. The irony was that she'd always heard families drew together to get through the bad times, that sometimes a crisis made them stronger.

But they'd failed the test. Neither of them had been able to help the other.

"So," Luke said when she came back into the kitchen. "You okay?"

Apparently he knew he had to let her work this out on her own. "I'm fine. The place feels more like you than before."

"You mean it's messier."

She managed a tiny laugh. "Something like that."

"Are you hungry?"

They'd left so early this morning it felt as if it should be bedtime already, but it was only early afternoon and they hadn't had lunch and she was starving. "I'm famished."

He peered into the fridge. "Well, I didn't buy any groceries before I left for New Mexico, so maybe we better go out and get some fast food or something."

"Okay. Or I can look and see what you have that I can whomp up."

He looked surprised, then gestured toward the cabinets. "Be my guest. But I think all you'll find is that stuff to mix with hamburger."

She stuck a finger in her mouth in a gagging gesture.

"Maybe you're right. But instead of going out, why don't we order takeout?" She pulled open the drawer where they'd always kept the restaurant menus, took a couple out and started to look them over. "What's on the agenda after we eat?" she asked absently.

"I need to go to the station to look at the Willis file."

She stopped reading. "You're really going to look into it?"

"As much as I can. But no guarantees. The case went cold for a reason."

"But it's important. Why don't you go ahead right now and grab a bite to eat along the way. I'll find something here and that way we'll save time and I can get some work done, too."

He shook his head, his expression puzzled. "Work doesn't always come first, you know."

She stood straighter. Taller. "Well, it always did before."

He winced, almost imperceptibly, but she saw it.

She felt as if they were fencing, parrying and lunging, repeating the same moves over and over until one of them stabbed too hard. She was as much to blame as he was. But she couldn't seem to help herself. "And in case you've forgotten, *I* didn't always work so much."

"Touché," he said, looking directly at her. Then he turned and walked toward the door. On his way out he said, "I'll be back later. Put the security alarm on and lock the door after me."

ARRIVING AT HEADQUARTERS and feeling a need to release his pent-up energy, Luke took the stairs two at a time. At the top, he unzipped his leather jacket, then palmed open the door into the RHD.

About half the detectives in the unit were at their stations in the open room. Rico's desk was across from his and Jordan's was butted up against Luke's in the back of the room. Walking toward his desk, Luke saw the captain glance up. Carlyle waved him in. "I'll be back," Luke said and gave Rico a pat on the shoulder as he passed by.

Inside the captain's office, Luke held up a hand. "I'm not here to work on the Renfield case."

"Then what are you doing here?"

Luke sat in one of the oak chairs. Since Julianna's problem involved an old LAPD case, he told the captain everything Jules had told him. "If we can find the guy who's threatening her, we may solve the other crime as well."

"You mean if he's not some idiot wanting attention. You know how often that happens."

Too often. Every homicide case generated dozens of calls from people who thought they knew something. Some were legit, many weren't. But they had to treat each one as if it were the real thing.

"How's your father?" Jeff asked.

Luke wasn't aware the captain knew anything about Abe's illness.

"Jordan told me."

"Oh." Luke nodded. "He's in the hospital with pneumonia. I talked to his physician this morning and it looks like he'll be there a few more days. I'm going back tomorrow morning. I have to make sure he gets some help on the ranch."

The captain steepled his fingers.

"So, what do you think about the Willis case," Luke asked.

"It was before I came to the RHD, but I do remember the media coverage. The FBI was involved."

"Initially they were, but it was so long ago, I don't know what procedure they followed."

Luke thought for a second. "You could contact the suits." He gave his boss one of his best smiles.

"You mean if I agree that we move forward on this. And I'm not sure we have the jurisdiction to do that. You said the threats happened in San Francisco and New Mexico." Carlyle gave him a hard look.

"The Willis case was ours and it still is. We can open a cold case anytime we want, especially if we have a new lead. It's a long shot, but the threats are about the Willis story, and I call that a new lead."

The big black man rubbed his chin. "A lot has changed in fifteen years."

"A lot that may finally help solve this case."

"You still have a week left of your vacation."

"I know. If you give me the go-ahead on this, I'll keep track and switch out the time."

Carlyle grinned. "You're like a dog with a bone. You never leave anything alone." He tapped his pen on a stack of papers on his desk. "Yeah, go ahead."

Luke's blood pumped. "Thanks, boss." On his way out, Luke said, "I'll let you know what I find."

Between Rico tracking down the person making the e-mail threats, and researching the old file and the old evidence, to see if any was still viable, they just might get lucky.

As he passed Jordan on his way back to his desk, his buddy stopped him. "I hear you brought Jules back and she's staying at your place."

Luke frowned. "Who said?"

Jordan nodded at Rico.

"Uh-huh." Luke gave Rico the evil eye and in turn, Rico shrugged, palms up. "Then I assume he also told you she's there under my protection until I can find out who's making the threats on her life."

His partner smiled. "I pulled the Willis case." He indicated the three boxes on the floor next to Luke's desk.

"Oh, man," Luke groaned.

"So you're back?"

"I'm not on the clock. But I want to get things moving because we've got to go back to New Mexico in the morning."

"Okay. I'm in. Let's get started."

Luke and Jordan culled the files, reading notes and searching for anything that might signal a connection with Julianna's caller. The only thing Luke found was that little Renata's mother and stepfather had split about a year after the discovery of the child's body. It happened frequently in cases like this. Some traumas were too big to be overcome.

He knew that only too well.

Another entry said the mother's brother had visited

earlier in the month, but he'd been questioned only briefly since he'd gone back home before the child's disappearance.

Luke noted that the stepfather had been the most likely suspect, which was usually the case. Family members were always the first to be scrutinized when someone was the victim of a violent crime. He made a note to interview the main parties again, and also the neighbor's boy, who'd said he saw a man around the house a few days before.

It was after six when Luke realized everyone else had gone home and the next shift was straggling in. Jordan and Rico had been long gone on a call-out. Quickly he wrote down the numbers he needed and stuffed the notepad into his pocket.

On the way home, he called Jules to see if he should pick up anything. It felt strange, almost like they were married again. After five rings, he clicked off and searched his pockets for her cell phone number. When he found it, the waning light made the number difficult to see. Finally deciphering his scribbles, he punched in the number.

No answer there either, so he left a message. But why wouldn't she answer her cell phone? He hit the redial to call again, just in case he'd gotten it wrong. One ring. Two rings. Three—he stomped on the accelerator.

"Hello."

Relief swept through Luke. "It's me. Everything okay?"

It took a moment for her to answer. "Yes, everything is fine. Why?"

His heart still thumped like a drum. "No reason. Just checking in."

He heard her breathing heavily.

She didn't sound right. Maybe she was more bothered about being there than she wanted to admit. "Do you want me to pick up anything at the store?"

A long silence. "Yes. Can you get some coffee? I...I couldn't find any."

CHAPTER TEN

SOMETHING WASN'T RIGHT, Luke decided, as he sped home through the lines of traffic, darting in and out of clogged lanes to capture a few extra seconds. He was probably overreacting to the hesitancy in her voice, but that he'd heard it at all put him on edge. Despite his NASCAR driving skills, it took another half hour to reach the house.

He didn't bother pulling into the garage and bounded up the front steps. Before he reached the door, he could see there were no lights on inside. Jules wouldn't be sitting in the dark. Unless maybe she was working in the bedroom. Logical reasons flitted through his brain as he searched each room, calling out for her as he went. "Jules? Dammit, answer me will you!"

The moment he realized she wasn't there, panic tightened in his chest. He hadn't imagined she'd leave the house or even where she might go without a car. His gaze darted. An empty cup on the kitchen counter next to her purse, the coffeepot with the cover off. Had she decided to get the coffee herself? He rejected the idea. She wouldn't go to the store without her purse. And she knew the closest one was near the beach. *The beach.*

He launched himself down the front stairs.

The multicolored lights and signs along Venice Boulevard gave an eerie circus quality to the night, and the people in various states of dress or undress only added to the surreal image.

His heart in his throat, he pushed past the tourists and the regulars, inadvertently knocking the balls out of a juggler's hands. "Sorry, bud," he said, shouldering forward through the crowd. He circled around a couple of guys twisting their bodies into contortions for whatever money onlookers tossed in a box.

Despite the crispness of the evening, sweat beaded on his forehead and he felt the dampness under his arms as he barreled ahead, eyes scanning the crowd, searching faces. He saw a woman with long dark hair, but when she turned, it wasn't Jules. He tapped another on the shoulder, not her either.

Then he realized that if she was here, she would be down by the water. She hated crowds.

As he headed toward the beach, he noticed a bench ahead with a lone person on it. A woman, he could tell by the silhouette. But he couldn't tell if it was her. "Jules," he called out. The woman's head came up. Yes! His blood rushed. Thank God.

He walked over and dropped onto the bench beside her, relief filling his chest. "You scared the hell out of me, Jules. What were you thinking coming out here alone?"

She stared at him, a frown forming. "I thought you said this was the safest place for me. Either I'm safe or I'm not."

His muscles tensed, his annoyance spiraling. "I said my place was safe. I didn't expect you'd be wandering around out here alone. That in itself is dangerous, even without the other stuff. Why didn't you call and tell me?"

She pulled back. "I just stepped out front for some air. I wasn't planning to come down to the beach, but suddenly, here I was. You didn't tell me not to leave, so I never thought twice about it. I'm sorry if I worried you."

Worried? How about frantic? He leaned against the wood slats and draped an arm over the back of the bench. "It's just that…I brought you here under my protection. It's my job to worry. It's what I do." And if anything had happened to her… He felt his chest constrict.

"Would you like to walk a little?"

Standing, he shrugged to ease the tightness in his shoulders and neck. "Sure," he said, stuffing his anger. It was true, he hadn't told her not to leave. He should be mad at himself for neglecting what should come naturally. The woman was driving him insane. Or at least causing him not to think sanely. That happened when a cop was emotionally involved. It was the reason cops didn't work a case when it concerned their family. But he'd always thought he was immune. That he could always keep a clear head. No matter what. Yeah, so much for that theory.

As they started toward the pier, he asked, "Did you eat?"

"I found some peanut butter and crackers."

"That's it?"

She nodded.

His gaze circled. "I didn't have time to eat either, so let's go find something."

JULIANNA REMEMBERED a café near the pier, but restaurants in the area changed like the shifting sand. "The Venice Whaler. Is it still there?"

"Yeah, good thought. I'm up for that."

He placed his hand at the small of Julianna's back, directing her toward Washington Square. The warmth of his hand against her felt comfortable and natural… and it stirred deep longings. Longings that conjured memories of sweaty passion-filled nights and fun-filled days. When had all that ended? Long before they lost Michael, she realized. But what good did it do to think about all that now?

As if he knew what she was thinking, Luke stuffed both hands in his jacket pockets and glanced at the horizon between sky and sea. A fat yellow moon seemed suspended just above the water, lighting their way.

"Do you go to the Whaler often?"

"Nope. Not since—"

"Oh," she interrupted. "Sorry. It's a bad idea."

"No, it's an excellent idea." He put a hand on her shoulder and they kept walking. "I'd probably have gone before this if I'd thought about it, but…you know me…always busy someplace else."

Yes, she knew. Only too well. And while she understood what his job entailed when they'd gotten married, she'd been so young, so blinded by love, that she never imagined the LAPD would disrupt their lives so much. That was her fault, not his.

There was a line in front of the restaurant. Nothing unusual; the place was as popular with locals as it was with tourists. She glanced at the people waiting, mostly young couples, but there were a few older people sitting apart on a bench, some in their thirties talking and touching, and some gen-Xers ready to party and who had no qualms about a little PDA. She smiled. Luke never had a problem with public displays of affection either—and way back when, neither had she. God, that seemed so long ago.

The thought made her feel old and staid. She'd give anything to have that carefree feeling back again.

"It'll be ten minutes," Luke said after putting their names on the wait list. "Can you make it that long?"

"I think so." If she could forget about the past. Turning, she walked to the balcony overlooking the water, stood at the rail and Luke came up beside her. The sound of the waves slapping against the pylons underneath them seemed to echo the rhythmic salsa music vibrating from the restaurant. The music underscored the nature of Venice Beach. Party city. And while she didn't feel like partying, the music energized her and she was glad they'd come.

They were seated near a window that overlooked the

ocean. If the weather had been warmer, she knew Luke would've preferred sitting outside on the deck. After returning with their drinks, a Bud Light for her and a non-alcoholic beer for Luke, the waiter took their dinner orders. Luke chose his usual. The surf, steak and jumbo shrimp. Rather than thinking about the menu, she requested the seafood platter, an assortment of fish, crab, shrimp and scallops. Too much food, she knew, but Luke would eat what she didn't.

"I can't believe everything is exactly as it was," she said. "Right down to the fish net on the wall."

Luke lifted his drink. "Why mess with a good thing?"

"Hear, hear." She lifted her beer in a salute.

"To friendship," he added.

"Yes," she said, then took a big swig. But they weren't friends anymore. Friends had contact, they kept in touch. Friends shared the ups and downs of life and supported each other no matter what. They'd been best friends once, and it made her sad to think that the most wonderful part of her life had ended so badly. In that one moment she wanted it back again…wondered if they could ever… The thought faded as quickly as it came. Nothing had changed. Nothing would be any different now.

"So, what's next? Did you have any success today at the department?"

"Yes, I did. Jeff supports taking another look at the Willis case." He kept his voice low so she could barely hear him over the music. She switched chairs to sit beside him instead of across the table.

Smiling, she said, so he didn't get any crazy ideas, "Hard to hear over there."

His shoulder touched hers as he leaned in to talk. "I'm going to try to interview a couple of people in the morning before we head back to the ranch."

The ranch. She realized she was anxious to get back. To see Abe. "Have you talked to your father or the doctor?"

Luke pressed closer, close enough for her to smell his aftershave, a light, woodsy scent.

"I spoke to Pops a little while ago and told him the doc said he had to stay a couple more days. Barring any new problems, he'll probably be able to come home on Friday."

"Oh, boy. I can imagine his response."

Laughing, Luke said, "Right. I'm glad I wasn't there to tell him in person. And since we're out here, he can't insist I take him home."

The waiter brought them big plates of steaming seafood, bowls for the crab shells, extra napkins and some wet wipes.

When he was gone, she said, "I feel bad that Abe has no one to visit him."

"Nothing he hasn't brought upon himself."

"Maybe Mrs. Hancock will visit? She's really concerned about him."

Luke grunted, then picked up one of her crab legs and snapped it in half.

When he didn't respond to her question, she asked, "Why do you hate her so much?"

His head came up, a surprised look in his eyes. "I think *hate* is a little strong."

"So, you don't hate her. You could've fooled me."

"I don't *like* her. There's a difference."

"Which means she's done something you don't approve of, otherwise it wouldn't be important enough for you to dislike her."

"It's not important." He leaned back in his chair and took a gulp of his O'Doul's. "Leave it alone. Okay? We've got more significant things to worry about."

She bristled. She felt as if she were five years old again, chastised like a child. Going back to her meal, she said, "Sure. You never told me about it in five years of marriage, I don't know why I was dumb enough to think you'd tell me now."

LUKE WISHED he could snatch back the words, but as usual, it was too late. And he wasn't going to apologize. His feelings about his father and that woman had nothing to do with Jules.

After a long silence, she finally said, "I'm sorry. It's none of my business and I should know better. I'd blame it on my journalist training, but I'd be lying. I really wanted to know more about you."

He stopped eating midbite. "Jules, if anyone knows about me, it's you. You know me better than anyone."

"Better than Jordan?"

"Yes," he said without hesitation. "Better than Jordan. And better than Rico."

Stabbing a piece of crab with the tip of her fork, she looked over. "Things change." She dipped the meat in melted butter and lifted it to her mouth.

As he watched her slowly nip the succulent morsel between her perfect white teeth, his groin tightened. "Some things never change, no matter how much we want them to." Like his pure animal lust for her. Like his love. His need. Which suddenly seemed overwhelming.

She glanced away. "Do you want me to check on a flight out tomorrow?"

"Yes, but we can't go until after I talk to a couple people."

Between Rico getting the computer information and making arrangements to set up a wiretap on Jules's home phone in San Francisco, he figured he had all bases covered. If the guy threatening Jules was truly serious, they'd soon find out.

After dinner, they decided against coffee and opted to walk off their meal by going the long way home down the boardwalk. As they strolled, Jules popped into one tiny store after another, marveling at all the funky items for sale. They stopped to watch an artist named Tony who'd been selling his work on the beach ever since Luke moved there.

Tony's hands glided over the paper as he created pastel sketches of tourists who wanted a memory of their visit to Venice Beach. When the last person got up, Tony urged Julianna to sit for him.

She balked at first, but then she said, "What the hell," and plonked down in the director's chair.

Luke watched as the artist sketched her fine cheekbones, her wide-set brandy-colored eyes and long sooty lashes. The artist captured her perfectly and when he finished, he held the sketch up for Julianna to see.

"Oh," she said, blinking at the sketch.

"You don't like it?" Tony asked.

She reached out for the picture. "Oh, no. I love it. It's just that…"

Luke paid the man and said, "Just nothing. It's beautiful."

They walked home without saying much. The night was crisp and the air snapped with potential. He hadn't been so relaxed…hadn't felt so alive, since…since before Jules left.

Getting out his keys, he stopped at the front steps. "What is it about the picture you don't like?"

She climbed to the top step, gave him a quizzical look and unrolled the picture. "I do like it…only it doesn't look very much like me." She tipped her head for another glance. "The woman in this picture is beautiful."

He remembered she'd always thought she wasn't as pretty or as smart as her sister, but he'd never taken it seriously. How could she not know what she looked like? He stepped up next to her, took her by the arms and looked directly into her eyes. "It looks exactly like you, Jules. You are beautiful."

She'd been pretty before, but now she *was* beautiful, and he wanted to kiss her in the worst way, wanted to hold her in his arms again, and just as he was thinking it, her lips met his. Warm and soft and inviting.

It was all the encouragement he needed. He deepened the kiss, breathing in the scent of the woman he'd never been able to forget. When she melted into him, he couldn't help the moan that escaped, couldn't help thinking she wanted this as much as he did, and even if this was going to be the most stupid thing he'd ever done, he couldn't stop. The only way that would happen was if she objected.

She didn't.

Still kissing her, he fumbled to get the key into the door with his left hand and the second it was open, they moved inside as one. He felt her heart beating like a drum against his chest, her breathing came in short passionate spurts, and he crushed her against him, unable to get enough of her. When she reciprocated, he scooped her into his arms and headed for the bedroom. She felt hot, he *was* hot.

His need was so intense, they didn't make the bedroom. He dropped onto the couch in the living room with her still in his arms. She unbuttoned his shirt, her hands like an inferno on his chest. He kissed her mouth, her ears, her eyes, her neck and her fingertips. So long. It had been so long. He wanted to devour her, to get inside her and never leave.

Dammit. He'd told himself he wasn't going to let this happen, that he wouldn't fall back on old feelings. But he hadn't anticipated that she'd be so willing. And that she would fuel the fire that burned inside him. The emotional fire. It wasn't all about sex. It was about sex with *her.*

Her small moans of pleasure spurred him on. He wanted to feel her, taste her, plunge inside her. Some part of his rational mind said he should stop. Get up and walk away. But when her legs wrapped around him, he kissed her long and hard, condensing the passion, desire and frustration of all the lost years into this one moment.

"Take off your clothes," Julianna whispered. And as he stood to undress, she began removing her clothes, too. He was stunned at her beauty and for a moment, simply stood there watching her.

"Do it," she reminded him.

As Julianna watched him remove his pants, some basic instinct took hold. She loved looking at him, always had. His body was perfect, except for two scars he'd gotten from a bust gone bad. His hard muscles were evidence that he took great care to keep them that way. Workouts. He'd always been vigilant in his workouts.

Watching him, she knew this was insane. One kiss and she was disrobing him. She felt wanton and wild and wet, and she ached to have him inside her. She might as well admit it. She'd wanted to make love with Luke from the moment she'd seen him again. She'd been convinced she had enough self-control to keep her wits about her when he was around. And she had. She'd maintained her distance, both physically and emotionally. Or thought she had.

What made tonight different? As she thought it, she knew. Luke had shown a side of himself she hadn't seen before. It wasn't the fact that he'd said she was beautiful, but more that he'd cared enough to say it to make her feel better. And at this moment, all the self-convincing in the world couldn't make her feelings for Luke disappear.

Without a word, he dropped down next to her, his eyes hungry and filled with something primal, as if he wanted to consume her. And, oh, man…she was more than willing to let him do it.

Still gazing into her eyes, he touched her breasts with his fingertips, gently, almost reverently. He hadn't forgotten that she liked their lovemaking slow. Slow and seductive. Tantalizing. But tonight, she didn't think she could stand the waiting.

As they lay side by side on the couch, she reached to touch him and almost fell onto the floor. "Bedroom," she said quickly, then got up and pulled him to his feet along with her.

The next thing she knew they were on the bed, their bodies entwined. He kissed her mouth, her earlobes, her neck, her breasts, taking time to tease the tip of one nipple with his tongue, then he kissed her belly and her thighs, all the way to her toes. On the way back up, he stopped midway, right there, pressing his lips and his tongue against her in a way she remembered oh, so well.

Her muscles contracted, her body thrummed with anticipation until she thought she might explode. He continued to tease her, bringing her just to the edge… and then he stopped and she felt his fingers, alternately stroking, then slipping inside.

A small moan of desperation escaped her throat. The combination of emotion and physical pleasure took her to another plane where the frenzied sensations brought her to the brink of ecstasy. Within seconds, her body convulsed with pleasure and she closed her eyes, giving in to the insatiable need inside her. A primitive need. A need for *him*. And only him.

He'd been watching her, she realized, but there was no embarrassment on her part. No repentance. She reached for him, wanting to make him desire her as much as she desired him, to need her as much as she needed him. She had to have him inside her. Now.

As her hand curved around him, she knew her memory hadn't played tricks. He was exactly as she remembered. When he moaned, she smiled.

In the next instant, he was on top of her, spreading her legs. He reached to get something from the nightstand. "I hope those aren't from five years ago," she teased.

"Nope. But they're not new either. I've been saving myself."

"Me, too," she said, her voice low and husky. She hoped they were both talking about the same thing, but right now, it didn't matter. All that mattered was this moment. Everything else faded into the background.

Finished sheathing himself, he kissed her again, his tongue exploring her mouth, and she kissed him back in exactly the same way and at once she was lost in the passions she remembered so well.

She'd never imagined their lovemaking could improve, but she'd been wrong. So very wrong.

His mouth raged over hers and she felt him against her, hard and ready as he entered her. It took two seconds to find the familiar rhythm they knew so well and not much longer for her to reach the point of climax again. Her body stiffened under him, muscles taut, desire rising and rising to that pinnacle when she shuddered and a thousand searing sensations ripped through her.

He moved slowly inside her, and her muscles again tightened around him as he brought her amazingly quickly to another point of no return and simultaneously gave a guttural moan, stiffened and erupted in a tempest of liquid heat.

Her heart pounded wildly, his eyes raked over her with blistering intensity. Then he lowered himself next to her, resting at her side, their breathing heavy. Making love didn't get any better than this.

LUKE LAY AWAKE watching Julianna sleep, her dark hair splayed across the pillow, her lips parted. Moonlight streamed through the dormer windows, highlighting her flawless skin. He reached to touch her, wanting to feel that smooth flesh under his fingers once again, then resisted and pulled his hand back.

He'd thought that quenching his desire for her would be the end of it. But it wasn't. He wanted her again. And again. Nothing had changed in that respect.

It was stupid, but where Jules was concerned his hormones had never listened to reason. Why should they now?

They'd both succumbed to desire, to the need of the moment. It wasn't the first time that had happened and it was stupid to make any more of it. Once after they'd separated, they'd bumped into each other at a friend's party and at her coaxing, ended up in a hotel room together. The sex had been great and he'd thought it was her attempt to mend their relationship.

Two days later he'd been served with divorce papers.

He wasn't going to make the emotional assumption that one night together had some deeper significance. Not again. Whatever need had driven her to make love with him five years ago was probably the same as last night. He'd be kidding himself to think of it as anything more. But he'd damn sure enjoyed it.

While he hadn't been celibate for the past five years, he'd stopped trying to find solace through sex a long time ago, and it'd been over a year since he'd slept with a woman. He had needs and so did she. Last night they'd *needed* each other.

Still asleep, she snuggled closer. On his side, he spooned himself against her and rested his arm across her waist. Her hair smelled good and he wanted to bury his face in it. God, he missed this.

Luke's chest constricted in pain, as if a giant vise wrapped around him and was squeezing the life away. He missed being with her, missed the way she touched him, the way she used to look at him. He missed being a family…and the closeness they shared. He missed the feeling he got knowing that someone knew everything about him…and loved him anyway.

The longing filled him with sadness.

But she was here now. They were together now. It didn't matter what happened in a few hours when they returned to business as usual. Right now he just wanted to feel. To feel her next to him…to ease the ache in his soul.

JULIANNA ROLLED OVER, stretched her arms out on the other side of the bed. Empty. She touched his pillow. Cold. Apparently Luke had been gone a while, though his scent still lingered in the sheets. She'd slept so soundly, hadn't awakened even once as she usually did, and she hadn't even heard Luke get up.

She glanced at the clock on the nightstand. 7:00 a.m. Because she worked mostly at night, she usually slept until about nine, but since Luke was already up, she figured she should do the same, see what his plans were.

His plans. The thought made her tense up. He was making all the plans, and while it felt good not to be in this alone, she'd gotten accustomed to doing things for herself, making her own decisions. It was part of the personal transformation she'd desperately needed to make in order to go on.

Her blood rushed as another thought hit her. What was she going to say to Luke about last night? Maybe it was best not to say anything. Their lovemaking had filled a need, she wasn't going to make it into any more than that. And she hoped he wouldn't either. Still…

Rolling over, she snuggled in for few more minutes and couldn't help smiling. Her libido had been dormant for so long, she'd felt as if his every touch, every kiss, was more intense than the one before—as if each one might be the last and it had to be memorable. The irony in that didn't escape her.

Being with Luke had felt wonderful, like being with an old friend…and yet everything about last night seemed new and exciting.

She could see why some people got back together after a divorce. The familiarity made it easy. She didn't need to worry about being on her best behavior or engage in all the game playing that single people did when getting to know one another. There was no pretending. They had history.

But just because they'd found comfort in each others' arms for one night didn't mean anything else had changed. They were the same two people with the same baggage as before.

Soft light filtered through the gauzy curtains covering the narrow windows, reminding her of other mornings in this room. The morning when she told Luke she was pregnant. The morning of their first anniversary when he brought her breakfast in bed. Mornings after Michael was born when he slept in a bassinet at their side.

Good memories, she realized, as she glanced around the room. It was a small room, with the big king-sized bed taking up most of the space. The old rocker that belonged to Luke's grandmother, the dressing table where Julianna used to sit and comb her hair and…she glanced to the wall beside the door…the matching chest of drawers with the silver-framed photo on top. Her mouth went dry.

She tore her gaze away. She had many old photos herself, but in an effort to get on with her life, she'd packed them away. Except one of Michael that she kept in her wallet.

She stared at the photo, until drawn like the proverbial steel to a magnet, she slipped out of bed and walked to the dresser. Her hand shook as she picked up the picture.

In the photo, Luke had one arm around her and was holding Michael in the other. It was a simple snap, taken in the back yard by one of Luke's friends during a party. Michael's toys were strewn in the grass around them.

With the pad of her little finger, she lightly touched Michael's face. Her heart wrenched. Tears filled her eyes.

Mourn him, and then let him go. Her therapist's words intruded. With a jerky motion, she put the photo back, then walked across the hall to the shower.

Love him. Then let him go.

CHAPTER ELEVEN

"Dr. Martinez says Pops will be ready to go home Friday by noon," Luke said, hanging up the wall phone. He came over and sat next to her at the kitchen table again. "If we get a flight to Albuquerque early Friday morning, we can get the car and then pick up Abe on the way back to the ranch."

Friday morning? Julianna bit off another piece of toast. A hot shower had helped her shake off the heartache she'd felt after looking at the photo in Luke's room, but it hadn't diminished her need to get away from here. The place was a reminder of everything she'd once had—and of everything she'd lost.

Luke had showered already and was dressed in black pants and a tan mock turtleneck. Work clothes. His black sport jacket and holster hung on the back of the chair. A familiar scene that flung her back to the past. For one fraction of a second, she felt as if the last five years hadn't happened. Even his familiar scent had the same effect on her. Desire spasmed between her legs. "Are you saying you want to stay here another day?"

Luke looked at her nonchalantly. "Is that a problem?"

Julianna shifted. She shook her head. "I'm thinking of Abe. He probably hasn't had a visitor since we left."

Luke picked up his plate and took it to the sink.

"And didn't you want to find someone to help him?"

"I do. But I could use an extra day here for more research on the Willis case." Studying her, he frowned. "What's wrong?"

"Nothing," she lied.

He didn't believe her. She could see it in his expression. "I hope you don't want me to say I'm sorry about last night because I'm not."

She shrugged. "No more than you want me to say I'm sorry. Let's leave it at that."

He looked at her. "Y'know you enjoyed it as much as me."

She cleared her throat. "Yes, I enjoyed it—for what it was."

He frowned. "And what, exactly, was it?"

Julianna stood. She'd wanted to forget about last night, pretend it hadn't happened. "I don't know. Two needy people. A one-night stand. Whatever it was, it won't happen again."

He arched a brow. "Uh-huh. Well, if you say so." He grinned lasciviously as he put a cup into the dishwasher.

A *Number 1 Daddy* cup Mikey had bought with his piggy-bank money so he could give Luke a present on Father's Day.

She closed her eyes. Everything here reminded her

of Mikey. Her head started to throb. She rubbed her temples with two fingers.

"What's wrong?"

"Nothing. I—I'm just better away from here." She looked away. "Too many bad memories."

Luke's shoulders stiffened, eyes darkening as he studied her. "Good ones, too. You can't forget all the good things."

His words hit her like a blow to the solar plexus. She tried to catch her breath, but suddenly it seemed as if all the oxygen had been sucked from the room. Finally she managed, "No…but good or bad, I can't live in the past." Just being here brought it all back in spades. Her voice felt hoarse when she said, "I don't know how you can do it."

He leaned against the counter. "Do what?"

"Continue to stay here. Doesn't everything remind you of…what happened?"

He crossed his arms, sadness reaching his eyes. "Yes. Sometimes. But mostly I'm reminded that Michael was a beautiful little boy and one of the best parts of my life. Our life. I don't ever want to forget that."

She didn't want to forget Michael, either, but through therapy, she'd finally been able to accept that he was gone forever. That she had to let him go. In order to do that, she had to relinquish their life together.

"Walking on the beach yesterday reminded me of all the times I'd taken Michael there. It reminded me of how he'd collected shells and put them in a jar and gave them to me on my birthday. But I can't build a life on memories." Remembering meant sadness and pain. She couldn't deal with any more pain.

Luke turned, his lips moved as if he were going to say something, but nothing came out.

"I'll make flight reservations if you want me to," she said softly.

He straightened, shrugged. "Sure. Try to get one early tomorrow morning. Six o'clock if you can." He was trying to be nonchalant, but the sharp edge in his voice gave him away. He grabbed the holster hanging on the back of the chair and slipped it on. Then the sport coat. "I'll call in a little while."

As Julianna watched him go out the door, he turned and said, "Stay inside until I get back. And lock the doors."

She stared at the closed door, emotions warring inside her. She hugged herself, as if that might ward off the bone-deep loneliness she knew would come. She felt it now more than ever.

Luke didn't understand the decisions she'd made. He never had. When she'd left him, he'd accused her of running away. He'd told her a change of scenery wasn't going to solve anything. But he'd been wrong. She'd made another life for herself and was getting along just fine…until she saw him again.

Staying with Luke would've destroyed her. And in turn, destroyed him. Last night she'd allowed herself to enjoy the warmth and comfort of Luke's strong arms, had told herself that's all it was.

But in the bright light of morning, she realized she couldn't escape the truth.

She wanted to feel again, passion, love…even anger. She wanted to feel something—anything. And she wanted to feel it with Luke.

LUKE HEADED FOR the RHD, his shoulders tight and his mind reeling. He couldn't get Julianna out of his head. Couldn't stop wanting to shake some sense into her. Tell her the divorce was a mistake. But regardless of what they'd once been to each other, he knew now he was just another ugly reminder of her past.

He remembered vividly one of their last conversations as a married couple—the night before she'd left him. The scene was embedded in his brain like a faulty microchip that kept playing the same program over and over.

They'd come home from a group session for parents who'd experienced the death of a child. He'd wanted to make love with her because the one thing that made him feel whole again was being as close to Jules as he could possibly be. Loving her salved his ragged soul and gave him a reason to go on, and he'd thought it was the same for her. But that night when he'd reached for her, she'd batted his hand away.

"None of them know what we've been through," she'd spat out. "Our situation is unique. How can anyone say they understand?"

"They may not have had the exact same experience, Jules," he'd said. "But they've all lost a child. They know what that's like."

"But none of them had the opportunity to save their

child. We did. We didn't try hard enough. That's on us."
Her face had twisted in anguish. "No one knows what
that's like."

Luke knew when she said *we,* she meant *he.* He was
an officer of the law. He had the whole police force at
his fingertips. She believed he'd had the ability to find
their son. And he hadn't.

She blamed him. She would always blame him.
Because it was true. He hadn't found their son. And that
was a truth that would haunt him every day of his life.

Realistically, logically, he knew what happened to
Michael wasn't because he hadn't tried hard enough. He
couldn't have done any more. But logic wasn't going to
change Julianna's belief that he could've. It wouldn't
change the guilt he felt.

Entering the RHD, Luke heard his buddy Jordan's
voice.

"Hey, Coltrane. I thought you'd gone back to New
Mexico."

Luke walked over to Jordan's desk and lowering his
voice, he said, "Tomorrow morning. I've got some stuff
to do on the Willis case." Luke had told both Rico and
Jordan about Julianna's *situation.* "I don't want it to get
out that I'm working on the case. Not yet anyway.
Someone could easily make the connection between
me and Jules."

"You saying the stalker and the Willis kid's killer are
one and the same."

"It's a possibility."

"What's the plan?"

Luke pulled the numbers from his pocket for the child's mother, stepfather and the brother. "We need some stats run on all of these people. Current addresses, phone numbers, et cetra. Then interviews."

"Under what premise?"

"Let's say we're going through all the cold cases for DNA evidence. We have more high-tech testing methods now, tests that weren't available fifteen years ago. See what reaction we get."

"I'm on it," Jordan said.

"I'm going to pull the physical evidence file."

Jordan picked up his phone and Luke went to the evidence room, brought a box back to the desk and started sifting through the plastic bags of blood-stained clothing and envelopes with who knows what inside. Apparently the preservation of evidence wasn't a top priority fifteen years ago. Bags weren't sealed properly and several items had been taken out and never put back in their containers, contaminating evidence they might've provided.

An hour later, Luke had culled a few things he thought might be possibilities for further research. In particular, two pieces of fabric with spots that could be blood. Evidence in hand, he headed for the Scientific Investigation Division downstairs. The techs were always busy and with the number of cases that went through the department, most results took several weeks. Unless it was a high-profile case or threatened the public at large. A fifteen-year-old cold case wasn't going to the top of the list. But he had to start somewhere.

At the SDI desk, he saw Tex with Cecilia Deleone, one of RHD's newer detectives, chatting and looking more friendly than two detectives in the same unit ought to look. So caught up in conversation, they didn't even notice him. Luke cleared his throat.

Tex turned, his expression guilty as a thief. "Luke. Hey."

"What's up?" Luke asked, trying not to smile.

"Uh, I'm doing some research on the Studio Killer's first victim. Deleone has a theory…" Tex glanced at the young detective. "We're going to see if it holds water."

The detective pulled herself up, shoulders back, head high. She was an attractive woman. Dark hair and almond-skinned, she'd gotten a lot of flack her first few weeks in the department, but she'd handled it well.

She reminded Luke of Julianna. Smart, determined and just a bit unpredictable.

"Thought you were on vacation," Tex said.

"I am. But I have to clear something up first." Luke and Tex, aka Will Houston, who just happened to be from Texas, were good friends, but Luke wasn't as close to the Texan as he was with Rico and Jordan. Tex waited for Luke to explain, but he didn't. The fewer people who knew about Julianna, the better. No one knew she was at his place except Rico, Jordan and the captain.

"It's a cold case. Nothing urgent." He leaned closer to Tex. "Vanessa know about this?"

"I'm going back," Deleone said. "Let me know what you find out." With that she left.

Watching her walk away, Luke said, "Bad idea, buddy."

Tex shrugged. "Maybe. But nothing ventured, nothing gained."

"What about Vanessa?" If there was one thing Luke couldn't tolerate, it was infidelity. If a guy did that, how trustworty was he?

"It's not working with Van," Tex said, "everything's off." Then he leaned against the counter, and in his lazy Texas drawl, said, "I learned early on when opportunity knocks, you gotta answer. You may not have another chance."

His buddy had a point. How many chances had he thrown away with Jules? "Still, it's a bad idea. You work together."

Tex lifted his hands, palms up, and walked away. Luke took his evidence into the lab. The tech filed Luke's request in a slot next to a dozen others, which meant he wasn't going to be getting a response back anytime soon. On the way out, Tex's homespun philosophy played in his head. *You gotta answer when opportunity knocks.*

Yeah. He'd done that last night. For all the good it did him.

JULIANNA CLOSED her laptop, got up and went into the kitchen. Though late evening was her preferred time to write, she'd spent the day working on her story. Getting up so early, she knew she'd better take advantage of the time since her deadline for the last article was looming and she didn't know what Luke had planned.

Having been cooped up all day, she opened the back door and stepped out onto the redwood deck, a new addition since she'd lived there. Five years ago, there had been only a small porch out here with screens all around. Now the weathered redwood sprawled across the entire back of the house. A barbecue, table and chairs took up one corner and assorted pots and flowering plants made the area seem garden-like. Odd. Luke had never been one to putter around the house when they'd been married. When had he developed a green thumb?

Or maybe the plants were someone else's idea. A friend maybe. A woman. She hadn't thought about him having a girlfriend, and as she wondered about it, a strange possessiveness coursed through her. Because he'd never married again and never mentioned dating anyone, she'd assumed he had no one special. What if she was wrong?

Last night she'd felt connected to Luke in a way she hadn't before. If he had someone else, he wouldn't have been with her. She knew Luke wouldn't cheat.

Not that it mattered. They'd spent one night together. No commitments had been made, no words of love murmured in the throws of passion. They'd had sex. Hot and sweet. That's what she'd wanted. Nothing more. Apparently, he felt the same.

Forcing the thoughts away, she crossed to the railing. The sun had just barely dipped below the horizon, the palm trees and rooftops were silhouetted by the gray of twilight, a familiar image that sent a wave of nostalgia through her. She felt for a moment as if she were caught between the past and the present…and then a brisk gust of wind blew her hair back, and she breathed in the crisp Pacific air. It was so quiet, she could hear the breeze rustling through the palm fronds.

There was one last installment to the Willis story; then maybe the crackpot who'd been the bane of her existence these past weeks would quit bothering her. And her life might just go back to normal.

Another sharp gust made her suck in her breath. In her peripheral vision, she caught a shadow…something moving. Her heart skipped a beat. She jerked around, scanning the pink flowering oleanders that stood over six feet tall and served as a barrier between Luke's property and the Baxters' next door. Suddenly a cat screeched and darted from the bushes. Jules let out a choked cry and jumped back, her heart beating triple time.

God. It was just a cat. But suddenly she felt chilled, and pulling her sweater closed in the front, she opened the sliding glass door and stepped inside, nearly colliding with Luke.

He caught her with both hands. "Hey, nice to see you, too."

She pulled away, her pulses racing. "You could make a little noise or knock or something rather than scaring a person to death," she said breathlessly, then shoved a hand through her windblown hair.

"Sorry. It wasn't intentional."

"Those bushes are too tall and need cutting."

He frowned, as if he hadn't a clue what she was talking about. But that wasn't unusual, either. He held up both hands. "Whatever I did, forgive me." He lowered his head to look into her eyes. "Something wrong?"

Moving past him to go inside, she said, "No. You surprised me, that's all."

"Okay." He went to the fridge and pulled out an O'Doul's and a Bud Light. Handing her the Bud, he said, "I seem to be doing that a lot lately."

"I—I think my nerves are on edge with all this crap going on. I'm so sick of it. I just want to write my stories and hope that they do some good."

Luke motioned her to the door to the deck. Once outside, they sat at the table together. Silent. After a moment, he said, "What kind of good do you expect your stories to do exactly?"

She shrugged. "I'm hoping that they'll provide some kind of solace to the victims' families. That they'll know their loved ones haven't been forgotten. I'm also hoping that by keeping these stories in the public eye, the police will continue investigating instead of dumping them in a cold case warehouse somewhere." She lowered her chin. "Michael's case included."

"But you didn't write a story about him?"

She looked away, ran a hand through her hair.

"You didn't." Standing, Luke stared at her, his face visibly hardening. "You didn't write one on Michael, did you?"

Suddenly it was hard to breathe. She gave a reluctant nod. "My first."

He sprang to his feet and slammed a hand on the table. "Why? Why in God's name…"

Oh, God. She'd expected anger, but not this. Not the pain she saw in his eyes. "I—I used fictitious names. I thought it would…help. That it would be cathartic." She squeezed her eyes shut, unable to look at him. "I thought that by detailing everything that happened, I could somehow purge myself. It didn't work that way, though. I just became more—"

"Obsessed."

"I guess."

The tension was palpable. Luke's jaws clamped tight, the veins in his neck popped out, his body tensed. He tipped his head to one side and then the other, as if trying to release the stress.

"Well," he said, "you've achieved one of your goals in the Willis case." He clicked his fingernails against the side of the beer bottle. "And…you've achieved some other things that I doubt you wanted."

She'd thought he was going to lambaste her for writing about Michael and when he didn't, she released a silent sigh of relief. "You're right there. I never in a million years expected someone to start threatening me over one of my stories. And not knowing whether it's just some crank or if the guy's serious, makes me really nervous. I seem to be jumping at every little thing."

LUKE STUDIED HER as she spoke, squelching the anger that mushroomed inside him. *Clear head.* Keep a clear head. He sat at the table again.

"And what if this guy *is* Renata Willis's murderer?" she asked.

"If it is, we'll catch him." He didn't know exactly how, but he was certain they would.

"You'll catch him?" she said, her tone doubtful. "Just like that?"

Yeah, he knew what she was thinking. If they hadn't caught the guy in fifteen years, what made him think they'd get him now. He cleared his throat. "If he's the one, we've got a lead, something to go on now. We didn't have that before. And we didn't have the testing methods we do now."

He saw a flicker of hope in her eyes.

"You think it's actually possible? Because if it is, that would really be something."

And along with that hope came the inevitable question.

"Do you think—"

He placed a hand on her knee. "No, I don't think. I take it one step at a time. We've got to finish what we started here, so don't get ahead of yourself. Right now the most important thing in the equation is keeping you safe."

She glanced at his hand on her leg. "Most important to who?"

He retracted his hand. It wasn't a question he was going to answer. "Rico and Jordan are working on some things behind the scenes. We'll see what comes up."

Scraping her long hair back, she forced a wobbly smile. "Thanks."

"For what?" he said as he raised one foot to the rung of the chair she sat on. "I haven't done anything."

"Right. Except keeping me out of trouble and making an effort to track down whoever is threatening me. I think that's something."

He shrugged. He didn't like taking credit for doing what came naturally. Protecting people, seeking justice, was what he did. It had nothing to do with any feelings he might still have. Right. Who the hell was he kidding?

He took a swig of beer. "Have you had any more messages on your home phone?"

"No. Nothing."

"Hmm. Not sure that's a good thing."

"Why on earth not? I was hoping that since he wasn't getting the response he wanted, he gave up?"

"I'd like to think that, but my experience tells me different. When is the next installment coming out?"

"Soon. A week maybe."

He nodded. "So it's logical that he'd wait until after that to call again."

"There's one more in this series, next month."

"What then?"

"I write another, of course."

"Same subject?"

She picked at the label on her beer bottle. "Yes, same subject. I have it started already. And I'll continue until I'm asked not to."

Luke felt his muscles bunch. "What if we don't get this guy, and…and this continues to happen?"

"This? You mean if the caller keeps calling?"

"Uh-huh."

She raised her head, pushed her hair back from her face. "I don't know. I don't have a plan. I guess I'll just keep playing it by ear."

And if she did, she could end up dead. "Well, you know what I think of that."

"Yes, I do," she said, giving him a big smile. Her quick smiles used to make him feel ten feet tall. Now he felt as if she did it to placate him.

"So…" he glanced at his watch. "I have to go out again. I have one more thing to do before tomorrow. Did you get the flight reservations?"

"I did. Six a.m."

"Great. And—" The jangle of his cell phone interrupted them. "Coltrane."

"I'm near your place," Jordan said. "I've got the stats you wanted."

Luke pushed to his feet, then glanced at the time again. "Great. I've got an address, too. Mrs. Jenner. I'm going out to do the interview. Want to come?"

"Man, I'd really like to, but Laura and Cait are with me." He paused. "Hey, would Julianna mind if they hung out with her for a little while?"

He glanced at Julianna. "She's not going anywhere."

When he hung up, he said, "Jordan's going to stop by with his fiancée and her daughter. Do you mind if they stay here until we get back?"

Her eyebrows arched. "And if I did?"

"Do you have any kids?" Caitlin asked.

The question caught Julianna off guard. It wasn't the

first time since Michael died that she'd been asked the question, but the years hadn't made it any easier to answer. "I did once, Caitlin. But he's in heaven now."

The child looked amazingly like her mother with strawberry-blond hair and big eyes, though brown not green like her mom's. Laura Gianni hardly looked old enough to be anyone's mother.

"My daddy's in heaven, too," the child said, matter-of-fact.

Cait was sitting next to Julianna on the couch. "I'm sorry to hear that," Julianna said, but after those few words, she couldn't think of another thing to say. She hadn't been around children much since moving to San Francisco and when she was, she was always at a loss.

"Would you like to watch television?" Julianna looked to Laura for a response. "I don't know if Luke has anything else here for kids to do."

"She'd love to, I'm sure," Laura said, motioning to the child who had already picked up the remote. She clicked on the TV and went right to the cartoon channel.

"Would you like something to drink?"

"Sure," Laura said.

"Iced tea? Coffee? Soda? Something stronger?"

"Iced tea is great."

Julianna got up and went to the kitchen. As she took the pitcher of tea from the fridge, Laura followed her.

"I apologize for Cait. I should've told her but didn't think."

"It's okay. Can you get a couple glasses from over there?" She gestured to the cabinets with the glass doors. "So," said Julianna, changing the subject, "I hear a wedding is on the horizon."

Laura nodded, a big smile forming. "Yes. And I have to say I'm getting more than a little nervous."

After filling the glasses with ice and pouring the tea, Julianna handed one to Laura. "Would Cait like something?"

"She's okay for now. I'm sure she's happy." Laura sat at the table instead of going back into the living room.

Leaning against the counter, Julianna took a sip of her drink. "Will it be a small wedding?"

Laura rolled her eyes at the ceiling. "I wish. I wanted it small, but somehow it got out of hand. Jordan's family… well, they have lots of people to invite. The wedding party is fairly small, though. Just three bridesmaids and three groomsmen, Luke and Rico and Jordan's brother Harry."

Sitting across from Laura, Julianna smiled. "That's big to me. Mine was half that size."

"Oh," Laura said, looking surprised. "You're married now?"

Julianna felt a sudden heat in her cheeks. "Oh, no. I meant when Luke and I were married." She shook her head. Why the hell had she even mentioned that? "It was a small wedding. Just family. My sister was the maid of honor."

Laura tipped her head, questions in her eyes. "I guess Luke told you I was married before."

Jules nodded, not sure what to say to that. Before Laura and Cait had arrived, Luke had mentioned that

Laura had withheld information about her ex-husband's death from the police to protect her daughter, but finally she testified against her ex's uncle, a Mob boss. But Julianna wasn't going to bring that up.

"And did he tell you the other stuff…about Cait's father's death? That I had to testify?"

"A little," Julianna answered. "He told me how you'd met Jordan." Lord, it felt awkward talking about such personal things with someone she barely knew, and yet it made her feel closer to Laura. She hadn't been close to anyone in such a long time.

"Regardless of the circumstances, I was so lucky to meet Jordan," Laura said. "He literally saved my life. And he's wonderful with Caitlin. She adores him."

Laura beamed when talking about Jordan, and Julianna couldn't help but be happy for her, though a little envious. Would there ever be a time when she'd feel like Laura did?

"Luke's great with Cait, too. I was hesitant to bring her here when I found out—" She stopped, as if aware she'd said the wrong thing.

"It's okay. You can say it. My son is gone. I've learned to live with it." It wasn't totally true, but it was easier than admitting there wasn't a day that went by when she didn't think of Michael. Few people knew what to say to someone who'd lost a child. Herself included.

Laura smiled at Julianna. "I can't imagine," she said. "You're a stronger person than I'd be under the circumstances."

Laura's compassion touched her. Here was a woman

who'd gone to hell and back to protect her daughter and she thought she wasn't as strong as Julianna. What a laugh! Julianna was only as strong as she could act, and that varied from moment to moment. Sometimes she felt as if she had to push herself just to make it through a day.

Luke had once said running away wouldn't solve anything. And there'd been many times in the past week with him that she'd wondered if he wasn't right. Had she only kidded herself that she had to leave to start a new life?

"What I was going to say," Laura went on, "was that I was hesitant because I'd made such a big blunder with Luke. Did he tell you about that?"

"No, he didn't. What happened?"

"There was a point during the investigation when both Luke and Jordan seemed to be questioning what I'd done to protect my daughter. I got angry. I lashed out and said they didn't have kids and couldn't possibly know what it was like to want to protect their child. I had no idea."

Julianna felt a wave of empathy for Laura. "Luke's got a thick skin. I'm sure he didn't think anything of it."

"No, he was deeply hurt. I saw the pain in his eyes. He left the room, wouldn't even tell me what was wrong. I heard later from Jordan that Luke had had a few bad years after the divorce. That he'd almost lost his job."

"I—I didn't know that." She knew Luke had been drinking too much. He'd told her that himself. But she couldn't imagine he'd do anything to jeopardize his job. He was a dedicated officer. He lived for his badge.

"I apologized, and since then, we've become good friends."

Julianna smiled. "That's great. If Luke's your friend, you've got a buddy for life." As she said the words, she felt a far-reaching sense of loss. She and Luke had once been best friends.

Tears suddenly welled behind her eyes. She blinked them back, and then asked Laura about her job and the shelter she ran. After Laura explained how she helped runaway girls get off the streets, Julianna felt an even greater connection with the woman. They were much alike in their desire to help others. Soon they were talking about all kinds of things and found they had many common interests. The rapport was so easy, Julianna felt as if they'd been friends forever. She regretted that, after today, she'd probably never see Laura and Cait again.

CHAPTER TWELVE

LUKE KNOCKED on the door of the upscale home in Pasadena, and within seconds a woman answered. Mid-fifties, short and plump.

"Mrs. Jenner?"

"Yes."

Luke flashed his shield. "I'm Detective Coltrane and this is my partner Detective St. James. We'd like to talk to you for a few minutes. Can we come inside?"

The woman stared. "Uh…what's this about?"

"It's about your daughter's case."

"But…that was fifteen years ago." She finger combed her graying hair but she stood back to let them in.

Glancing around, Luke noticed Mrs. Jenner's standard of living had greatly improved in the past fifteen years. At least compared to what he'd read in the file.

"We're taking another look at the case and we'd like to go over some facts with you."

"Okay. If I can remember."

How could she not remember! Luke recalled every minute following his son's abduction, the searching, the calling, the seesaw of emotion, one moment hope—

and then the soul-wrenching devastation when they didn't find him. The unbearable heartbreak when they did. "I know this is difficult to talk about, but it's important."

She indicated the couch, but Luke took the chair. Jordan preferred to stand. The woman sat on the couch. "You remarried a short time after Renata's disappearance—is that right?"

"Yes. Rennie's stepfather and I weren't doing all that well before…what happened, and it got worse afterward."

"How did Renata get along with her stepfather?"

"I told the police before that they had problems, but Fred would have never done anything to hurt her."

"We're only asking questions, Mrs. Jenner. Not accusing anyone."

She wrung her hands together, her lips thinned. "Well, the police did before! They wouldn't leave us alone, kept asking us questions and more questions. They even hunted down my brother who only stayed with us for a little while."

"I understand." More than she could know. Even though he'd gotten a bit of a break when Michael went missing because he was a police officer, he and Jules were still questioned ad nauseam. Jules had nearly had a breakdown because of it. "It's standard procedure to start an investigation of this type with the family. Most crimes against children are committed by family members—or someone close."

"While the real murderer gets time to escape."

Jordan glanced at Luke. "Can you tell us where your brother is now?" Jordan asked.

Luke studied the woman. The mention of her brother made her sit up straighter. They'd been able to get an address for the ex-husband and for the girl's biological father, Terrence Willis, but they hadn't been able to locate Mrs. Jenner's brother.

"He's a good man."

"Do you have his address? We'd like to get in touch with him."

She shook her head. "He's a restless sort. Moves around a lot."

"So how do you contact him? Do you have his number?"

"No. He calls collect."

"How often?"

"Once a month maybe. He's called more lately though since I told him about that magazine that's doing stories about Renata. He worries about me."

Luke felt the hairs on the back of his neck prickle. "So, have you talked to the person writing the stories?"

"A few times, then I decided not to anymore. It was too upsetting."

"When did your brother last call?"

"A week ago."

"Do you know if the writer talked to him?"

"I don't think so. I told him she wanted to, but he didn't want to speak to her. It made him mad that she was digging up all this after so long."

"Do you keep records of your phone bills and

payments? You could easily tell where his phone calls came from."

Her eyes narrowed.

"Can I see your last couple of bills."

Without answering, she got up and went into another room. The woman was gone so long, Luke was about to go see what she was doing, but just as he stood, she came back.

"No, I don't have them. I'm sorry."

Jordan gave Luke a disbelieving glance. Finally, after another half hour of questioning about her ex-husband and other people who were in their lives at the time Renata was murdered, they had little more information than when they came. "One last question," Luke said. "Your brother wasn't married when Renata disappeared. Is he married now?"

"Not anymore."

"Do you know where his ex-wife lives?"

"Of course. Marion was my sister-in-law."

"Did they have children?"

"A boy and a girl."

"Why did they divorce?"

Mrs. Jenner pulled back. "I'm sorry, Detective, but I don't see the point."

Luke wasn't sure there was one. Except that his ex might know more about Beau Thatcher than anyone else. Before they left, Luke made a point of getting the sister-in-law's name, address and phone number, gave Mrs. Jenner his card and told her to call if she remembered anything else.

Backing out of the driveway, Luke said, "It's suspicious that her brother refused to be interviewed for Jules's story."

Jordan shrugged. "It's natural for a brother to be protective and not want to see his family hurt again. What I don't get is the no address thing. The brother calls her, but she doesn't know where he lives. How bogus is that?"

"My take, too."

"On the other hand, maybe he's avoiding support payments. People do odd things, but it doesn't mean they're serial killers."

Luke glanced at Jordan. His buddy always gave people the benefit of the doubt. A great quality, but sometimes Jordan's analyzing slowed the process. Luke's mode was action—as quick as possible. "Right. Now let's see if we can get Mrs. Jenner's phone records."

"What about the mother's ex-husband. I've got an address for him."

Luke stopped at a traffic light. "Right now, I'm more interested in the brother's ex-wife."

"Because?"

"Because he called his sister more often after hearing about Jules's story. Because they have kids together. He may have visitation rights or send support payments. She might know where he is. Because this guy was barely looked at in the previous investigation."

"It's late. Let's do it tomorrow," Jordan said.

"I have a flight out in the morning."

"So, I'll do it then."

Luke tightened his grip on the wheel. Damn, he hated when his personal life interfered with his job.

But his father wasn't in any shape to go home on his own. And there was no way he'd send Jules back alone.

CAIT WAS SLEEPING on the couch and Julianna and Laura were in the kitchen when Luke and Jordan returned.

"Sorry we were gone so long," Jordan said, greeting Laura with a kiss.

Julianna looked away. The adoring glances between the two only magnified the gaping void in Julianna's life—a void she hadn't realized was there until she'd seen Luke again. Until she'd witnessed a normal loving relationship.

For the past five years, her career and her friends at work had filled her days and many nights. She'd gone out on assorted dates, most of which were pleasant, and she'd even dated one guy for a couple months. But mostly it was just something to do.

But whenever a guy wanted to get serious, she immediately stopped seeing him. She wasn't ready for that. She doubted she'd ever be. But why not?

Maybe Luke had been right. Maybe she had run away. Maybe she was still running. At least in the romance department.

Loving someone meant opening yourself up for more heartbreak. She couldn't put herself through that again. Couldn't even chance it. She felt anxious just thinking about it.

"I'll carry Cait to the car for you," Luke offered.

Laura gathered Cait's things, Jordan wrote something on a piece of paper and left it for Luke on the desk, and Luke gently picked up the sleeping child. The wistful look in Luke's eyes as he cradled Cait in his arms tugged at Julianna's heart.

He'd so wanted another child. But she'd been adamantly against it. She'd told him they couldn't simply replace their son. Told him no one could take Michael's place in her heart. After that, the crevice in their relationship kept widening and widening until it was a canyon neither could cross.

They said their goodbyes to Jordan and Laura and when Luke came back inside, he went to the fridge and grabbed a Coke. "You want one? Or something else?"

She and Laura had already had tea and later some wine. Enough so that she was a little sleepy. "No thanks."

Luke shifted the bottle of soda from one hand to another, bounced around the kitchen as if looking for something to do, then went to the back door and peered out. He was wired, a familiar pattern when he'd just come off the job. Sometimes it took hours for him to wind down.

"I'm going outside," he said, opening the door.

He didn't ask her to join him, he wanted to be alone. In the past, she'd allowed him his time—but not tonight. She wanted to know what had happened with the people he'd talked to.

Luke stood at the rail, his gaze straight ahead.

"Did you and Jordan get what you wanted tonight?"

Slowly, he turned to face her. "Some things. Not all. I have to go out again."

"But it's nine o'clock."

"I know."

Luke's cell phone rang, cutting off her protest.

He pulled the phone from inside his jacket, looked at the number then answered. "Yo, Rico. You got something good, I hope."

Luke listened. "Which means?" Then he nodded and looked off into the distance. "Okay. Enough." Chuckling, he said, "Too much information, dude."

She wished she knew what he was talking about. Had Rico uncovered who sent the e-mail messages?

Looking at her, Luke said into the phone, "Bottom line, we've got squat, right?"

After he hung up, Julianna waited for him to explain. But he didn't. Instead, he paced, his thoughts elsewhere.

"You're going to wear out the wood if you don't stop. What did Rico want?"

He banged the back of a chair with the palm of his hand. "The guy uses Anonymizer sites for his e-mail messages."

"What?"

"Web sites that are located in other countries. They receive the e-mail message, strip its ID, then send it to another site in another country that does the same thing. The message goes through the process up to a couple dozen times. Most Anonymizer sites don't keep records.

That's why the messages are almost impossible to trace unless someone makes a mistake."

"That's it, then?" she couldn't hide her disappointment.

"Yeah. Rico said it's how some computer viruses are sent and that's why it's so hard to track them down."

"For someone who never gave a rat about that kind of thing, you sound quite knowledgeable."

"I've learned a couple things over the years. Mostly through necessity." He gave her a tired smile. "But I still rebel at the intrusion. How did the world ever get along before computers?" he said sarcastically.

"So, we're back at square one?"

"Not completely. The fact that he uses the sites says he's experienced. That he doesn't want to get caught. That he's playing a game with us. With you."

Luke was still holding his cell when her own rang. Fear sent a quick chill down her spine. Dammit, she should've turned off her phone. But it was too late now. Most likely it was nothing. Could be her mother or her sister. Her editor, Mark. None of them knew where she was, but all had her cell number. She pushed the On button and raised the phone to her ear. "Hello."

"I know where you are."

Her heart raced. She closed her eyes, digging deep for strenghth she doubted was there. It was just a voice. *Just a voice*. Suddenly a strange calm enveloped her. If he really knew where she was, wouldn't he have done something by now? He wouldn't just keep calling, would he? How could he know anything, anyway? He was bluffing.

She tightened her grip on the phone. "I don't believe you," she spat out. "If you know where I am, then prove it."

A second later, she couldn't believe what she'd done. but dammit, she was sick of the games this weirdo was playing—and they had to stop.

She waited for a response and when none was forthcoming, she handed the phone to Luke. "It's him," she mouthed.

Luke took the phone, listened, then shook his head. "He's gone." His eyes met hers. "And that was a pretty stupid thing to do."

A HALF HOUR LATER, Luke exited Highway Five on Jeffrey Road on his way to Marion Thatcher's house in Irvine. "It won't take long," he said, glancing at Jules in the passenger seat.

The last thing Luke ever wanted to do was take a civilian along on a job. But he needed to interview the woman and he needed to do it tonight. After that phone call, leaving Jules at home wasn't an option. The guy knew her cell number. He had to know what he was doing to get it. He had to have the means. The thought made Luke's mind go nuts.

But, stubborn as she was, Jules wasn't happy about going along either, and she sat like a statue in the seat next to him, arms crossed, lips compressed.

"So, what am I going to do while you're interviewing this woman," she asked finally. "Sit in the car?"

He gritted his teeth. "No, you're coming in."

She glanced over, her mouth half open. "Won't you get into trouble?"

Yeah, he might. But it didn't matter. Jules's life was worth more than any reprimand. Worth more than his job. "Not if I play it right."

"Who is this person again?"

"Renata Willis's uncle's ex-wife."

"Oh, that explains it," she said facetiously.

"The ex-wife of one of the suspects in the Willis case."

"Ah, the guy I couldn't find."

When Luke looked at her, he didn't even try to hide his feelings. Exasperation or irritation, she wasn't sure which. Probably both.

"What? I tried and I couldn't find him," she said indignantly. "You think the ex-wife knows something?"

Luke grinned. "I don't think anything. I keep an open mind and put the pieces together later."

"And what are the other pieces?"

Glancing at the signs, he turned on Alton Parkway toward Lake Forest. "I can't say. It's a case. It's confidential."

"So, I can go along on the interview and listen to whatever happens, but you won't tell me anything more."

"Actually, I was hoping you'd make yourself scarce while I do the interview. Go to the bathroom or something."

"You're joking."

"No. I'm very serious. I'd like to keep my job." And he wanted to keep her safe. He hadn't realized just how much until that phone call when he'd seen the fear in her eyes. He'd noticed her hands trembling. For all her bravado, she was scared to death. The thought pissed him off. Made him want to punch something. Preferably the son-of-a-bitch causing it all. In fact he'd like to do more than that.

"He said he knows where I am, but I don't believe him. If he did, wouldn't he have done something to prove it?"

Luke tried to calm himself. "Not until he's ready."

"What do you mean?"

"He's playing with you. Sociopaths have huge egos. They don't want anyone forcing them to do something before they're ready. If they think they're going to be caught, they want it to be on their terms."

"That's sick."

"Yeah."

"So, why are we going to see this woman?"

He grinned. "Nice try, sweetheart, but my lips are sealed."

Luke drove up and down three streets before he finally found the right one. All the lights were out but, too bad, it couldn't wait.

When they reached the door, he said, "Just follow my lead, okay?" He rang the bell, then knocked for good measure.

Jules nodded her agreement, though he could tell she wasn't happy. It felt really weird having her there while he was working. He'd always made a point of keeping his personal and his work lives separate.

"No one's going to answer," Jules said.

He rang the bell again, and as he did, a light flicked on inside.

"Who's there?" a female voice came from behind the door.

"Police, Mrs. Thatcher. We need to talk to you." He held his shield up to the peephole.

The door slowly creaked open. A woman peered out. "What do you want?"

"I'm Detective Coltrane and…this is my partner. We'd like to come in and talk to you about your ex-husband, Beau."

"My children are sleeping. Can't this wait until tomorrow when they're in school?"

"No, I'm sorry, it can't."

Reluctantly the woman opened the door and let them in. Standing in the entry, Luke saw the house was sparsely furnished and the woman was so thin he wondered when she'd last had a meal. "We're really sorry to barge in like this, but we'll make it quick."

"Do you want to sit down?"

"Can I use your restroom?" Jules asked.

Good going, Jules.

The woman pointed down the narrow hallway. "First on the right," she said, then led Luke into the living room.

Luke sat on the lumpy couch. The only other piece of furniture was a small television set that looked as if it had been around since the Stone Ages. "When was the last time you saw your ex-husband, Mrs. Thatcher?"

"It's been a while. He doesn't see the kids, so there's no reason for him to come around here."

"Why doesn't he see the kids?"

Thatcher raised a hand to her mouth. Her dark eyes were large in a painfully gaunt face. "I had a restraining order during the divorce and for a while afterward."

"Was he abusive?"

"Not with the children. But I didn't want to take the chance that he might be."

"How long ago did you see him?"

"A year maybe."

"And do you know where he lives?"

She shifted in her seat. "Has he done something wrong?"

"No, we're just looking into an old case, his niece's abduction several years ago. I'm sure you know about that."

"Oh, yes. That was so terrible. We weren't married then, but he told me about it."

"What did he tell you?"

"He was worried that someone would think he had something to do with it."

Luke's interest piqued. "Did he say why?"

Rubbing her hands over her bare arms, Thatcher said, "Because he spent a lot of time with her and he'd been there visiting right before it happened. Funny they never found who did it."

Yeah. Funny. "Where does he live?" Luke repeated.

"I don't know. Last I heard he lived somewhere near San Francisco."

Luke looked up to see Jules standing behind Mrs. Thatcher, her eyes wide.

"Do you have a phone number to reach him if there's an emergency with the children?"

"Yes, but I don't know if it's any good anymore." She got up and went down the hall, returning a few moments later with a piece of paper. "This is it. Are we done now?"

"Sure, just one more thing. Do you have a photo of your ex-husband?"

"I do, but it's an old one."

"That's fine. Can I see it please?"

Luke couldn't believe his luck. An old phone number was better than no number. A photo was even better. At least they had a starting place, and the fact that the guy was near San Francisco was very interesting.

"Is this good?" Jules asked on their way to the car. "It's creepy that he lives near San Francisco."

"I don't know if it's good or not, but it's something." Luke slid inside, started the engine, then waited for Jules to get in before he pulled the photo from his jacket pocket and showed it to her. "Does he look familiar at all?"

She shook her head, frowning. "No. But he looks scary."

"Yeah, but the last I heard, looking scary isn't a crime." He'd been amazed that the woman had given him the photo. He'd fax it to Jordan and let him check it out. If the guy was in the system at all, it could help in locating him.

"So, what now?"

"We go home, sleep a little and then head for New Mexico in the morning." He gunned the motor and headed for home. Turning onto the freeway, he took out his cell and called Jordan. "Sorry to call so late, but I've got some information for you."

"Shoot."

Luke gave his partner the lowdown on Thatcher and asked him to follow up once he sent the photo. That's all he could do for now. He pocketed the phone.

After a few more minutes humming along the highway, Jules said out of the blue, "What if he really does know where I am?"

He turned to look at her. In the pale yellow glow of freeway lights, she looked drawn, tired. For the first time he noticed the dark smudges under her eyes. The tense set of her jaw. Though she wouldn't admit to being scared, nothing could hide the physical evidence.

"Don't worry. No one will get past me."

The doubt in her eyes made him feel like crap.

THE PLANE HIT the runway at seven-thirty the next morning, and they were on the road to the hospital in Santa Fe within a half hour. Julianna glanced out the window at the dark foreboding sky. The weather gurus had predicted rain and Luke had said he wanted to get his father and head back to the ranch before the highways got slick.

The narrow roads between Santa Fe and the ranch could be treacherous when wet, she knew and even now, Luke seemed to be concentrating heavily on his driving. Or was he figuring out another strategy?

"I've been thinking," Julianna said.

"Uh-oh. That means trouble." Luke kept his eyes riveted on the road.

He seemed in a good mood despite the fact that he'd spent the night sitting in a chair at the foot of her bed, his weapon at his side. Every time she'd awakened and looked at him, he'd been alert. Poor guy probably hadn't slept but a few minutes. But then, she hadn't either. It was amazing they hadn't snapped at each other more often when hurrying for the flight.

Always in the back of her mind was the knowledge that Luke was only there to make sure nothing happened to her. He'd given his word and she knew he'd try to keep it no matter what. If his father hadn't needed him, Luke would've split the same night he'd arrived at the ranch. A night that seemed so very long ago and yet was little more than a week.

"I have an idea. I've thought this over for most of the night and this morning. I want to run it by you." The lightness in her voice belied what she was about to say.

"O-kay. I'm listening."

Hesitant, she nipped at the soft skin on the inside of her lower lip. He was going to think she was crazy, but then that wouldn't be the worst thing he'd ever thought about her. "I have a plan to entrap the stalker."

Luke jerked so fast to look at her, he swerved over the center line. Fortunately, there were no other cars on the road and he quickly corrected the maneuver. "Excuse me?" he said incredulously.

"I have a plan that I think will work to catch this creep."

The sound that came from Luke was half laugh and

half hysterical gurgle. "The LAPD is trying to find him. I have the best guys in the field working on it as we speak. *We* have a plan."

"Mine is better."

She saw his grip tighten on the wheel. Then he cleared his throat and said, "What's better than the LAPD?"

"Using me as bait."

He stomped the brake and skidded to a screeching halt and at the same time, his arm flew out and whapped her across the chest to keep her from smashing into the windshield. Gravel crunched under the tires as he pulled off onto the shoulder and then killed the engine.

Before Luke had a chance to get a word out, and she knew what those words would be—nutcase, insane— she said, "Please listen to me. Don't shoot me down before you even hear what I have to say. I'm not some quack with a flaky idea. Someone is threatening me. It's my life. I'm involved, just about as involved as anyone can be. And I think I know a way to get this guy."

Luke shook his head. "It's a complicated case."

"That's the problem. I'm not talking about the Willis case. I'm talking about this psycho, this sicko who's driving me crazy. *You're* making it more complicated than necessary."

"What? By following procedure?"

"Yes. We both know how that can screw things up." She'd had no intention to throw their past into it, but if it made him understand… "I think I know how to lure him out. If he intends to hurt me as he's threatened to do, why shouldn't we be prepared? Why shouldn't we be proactive and get him on our terms, not his?"

Luke clamped his lips together, turned the key in the ignition and started the car again. Looking both ways, he pulled back onto the highway.

"At least listen to me."

"That's the most ridiculous thing you've ever come up with. For crying out loud, Jules. He could be a serial killer."

"He probably is. All the more reason to entrap him."

"I don't want to hear any more about this. You're naive if you think this is some kind of game. And I'd lose my job if I agreed to do anything like that."

His job. Always his job. Years of suppressed anger threatened to erupt. Only she couldn't let it. "Naive or not, I can't sleep at night wondering when he's going to pop out of the woodwork. I can't sleep knowing that if he is the one who killed Renata Willis, he's probably killed again since then. He might even be the one who—" The rest of the sentence strangled in her throat.

She closed her eyes for a moment to pull herself together. "You can't tell me you haven't noticed the similarities."

His hands clenched so tight on the wheel, his knuckles went white. She saw a muscle working in his jaw, the way it always did when he tried to suppress his anger.

"That's just it," he finally spat out. "The similarity isn't just in these two cases. There are other crimes as well. This could be big. Really big. And if we get any evidence and don't follow procedure, none of it will be admissible."

"It will be if you listen to my plan."

Luke's face went red, and he started to say something, but a hospital sign appeared on the left side of the road and he swerved to make the turn. A few minutes later, he pulled into the visitor's parking lot. "I'm going to get my father discharged. You'll have to come with me."

She crossed her arms. "I don't *have* to do anything."

If looks could kill, she'd be dead. But she had the edge. He wouldn't leave her in the car alone and unprotected. His training wouldn't allow it. "I'll come with you if you promise to listen to my plan later." She smiled, a gesture she knew would make him even more furious with her. But sometimes pushing him to the limit was what it took to make him see that his way wasn't the only way.

He continued to glare at her. Then finally managed to say, "Okay. Now get out of the damned car."

CHAPTER THIRTEEN

"IT'S ABOUT TIME." Abe was sitting on the edge of his hospital bed, fully dressed and looking meaner than a snake.

Luke sauntered over, his nerves still taut from his conversation with Jules. Now he had to deal with his father, too. "You look great, Pops."

At that moment, Dr. Martinez came into the room. "I haven't discharged you yet, Abraham."

"Well, do it, then. I've been ready to go for hours."

The doc walked over with his stethoscope, placed it on Abe's chest, then on his back. "Take a big breath and let it out.

"Good," the physician said. "I'm going to give you a couple of prescriptions and I want you to take all the drugs as prescribed. Don't stop just because you're feeling better." He glanced at Luke as he talked, apparently thinking Luke could monitor his father. Man, was he wrong.

Jules, who'd gone to the ladies' room, walked in and went over to the bed. "You look fantastic, Abe. How do you feel?"

His old man harumphed loudly. "I feel the same as I did when I came here."

"Maybe. But you didn't look as good when we brought you in," Jules cajoled.

"Does he have restrictions of any kind?" Luke went to help his father off the bed, but Abe shrugged him off.

"No restrictions. He just needs to quit smoking and take the medication."

"Hear that," Luke said to his father, for all the good it would do. Abe did what he wanted when he wanted. Luke was surprised he'd actually stayed in the hospital.

"Okay. You're ready," the physician said. "You take care of yourself, Abraham."

As the doctor walked out, Abe slipped off the bed and carefully put his weight on first one leg and then the other.

"Who are the flowers from, Pops?" Julianna walked over to the table by the bed and smelled the purple-and-yellow bouquet. "They're beautiful."

Abe waved a hand in dismissal. "I don't know. I don't like flowers. The smell gives me a headache."

"So why'd you leave them in the room?" Luke asked. He picked up the tiny card stuck in the middle of the ar- rangement. The card read, Get better. S.H. He tensed then tossed the card onto the tabletop.

"Let's go," Abe insisted. "I've had enough of this place. The food is bad and the room is always cold."

"What about the flowers? Let's take them along." Jules picked up the vase.

"He doesn't want them. Leave them here," Luke snapped as he followed his father out the door. When

Jules caught up, she was carrying the flowers. Her expression dared him to say anything.

Silence filled the car on the ride from the hospital to the ranch. Luke's mind spun trying to sort out everything that had happened. He'd gotten a lead on the Willis case that could be big. Or it could be nothing. One thing was certain, it was more than they'd had before.

He had no clue if this guy was in any way connected to the threats Jules had received. But if he was their serial killer and they screwed up…everything could go down the tubes.

And Jules had a plan. He almost laughed. The woman was mad.

As if she knew what he was thinking, Jules reached out and turned on the radio to a soft jazz station. Her favorite kind of music. He remembered how she'd liked to soak in a tub of bubbles with a good book and listen to jazz playing in the background.

The thought made his groin tighten. He'd never been able to resist a naked woman in a tub of bubbles. But he wasn't going to let memories cloud his judgment.

What Jules had said about the similarities between the Willis case and Michael's triggered every bitter, vengeful emotion he'd felt five years ago. Fellings a cop couldn't afford to have. But if this guy was one and the same, and they could somehow get him… Adrenaline shot through his blood like an injection of speed.

But as he turned onto the road to the ranch, his sanity returned. He couldn't allow Julianna to act as bait to lure the guy in. He absolutely couldn't. Even if it meant catching Michael's killer. He'd already lost the two people he'd loved most in life. But at least one was still alive. There was nothing Jules could possibly say that would convince him to do anything that would put her life in danger. Nothing.

"THE FLOWERS CAME from Stella," Julianna said after Abe had gone to bed for the night. "Her initials are on the card."

Luke shrugged, then picked up the remote and clicked on the television, surfing channels until he landed on CNN.

It was 9:00 p.m., time for her to start working, but she had to talk to Luke first. They'd had no time before now because Luke had been on the phone most of the morning.

First he'd talked with Jordan and Rico, and then with some people who'd called about the job at the ranch. He'd had one guy come out to see him, but Abe had made such a big stink, the man had all but left a streak on the road in his hurry to escape.

Luke and Abe had argued and finally Luke stalked out. He was gone for the rest of the day and had come back only a few minutes ago.

Julianna went over and sat next to him on the couch. "So, if you don't want to talk about Stella and your father, let's talk about my plan."

He pressed the Up arrow for the volume on the remote and the newscaster's voice blared. She snatched the remote from his hand and hit the power button. Luke's eyes widened in surprise.

"I said I want to talk. You agreed."

He turned back to the blank television screen. "There's nothing to talk about."

She folded her arms across her chest. "I think there is and for once in your life I want you to listen to me."

His head practically spun around to look at her. "For once in my life?"

"Yes. I think my idea is a good one. I wrote something in the article that might force the issue."

Leaning forward, elbows on his knees, he rubbed his hands together. "What did you write?"

"This guy thinks he's smart and can outwit the police, so I insulted his intelligence. I intimated that he'd already slipped up and that it was only a matter of time before he was caught." She cleared her throat. He wasn't going to like the next part, so she had to hurry through it to finish. "So, the next time he calls, I'll egg him on some more, tell him I think he's a crank caller, all talk and no action. I'll play on his vanity. I already told him I didn't believe he knew where I was and it seemed to tick him off. If he really does know, that's where my plan comes in. We give him the opportunity to prove it."

Luke's eyes lit up. "How so?"

His question wasn't much, but at least he hadn't gotten up and left the room. "I do something predictable on a regular basis, like feeding the chickens or going out alone to the stable to tend the horses every day at a certain time. If he is watching as he says he is, he may do something."

"Like kill you."

"No. I'll be protected. I'll wear a wire every time I go to the stable. You'll be nearby and hear everything that goes on. And I'll carry a gun."

"You hate guns."

"I know. But this is different. I'll use it if I need to."

"The last I heard you didn't have a clue how to handle a weapon of any kind. Except to hit a guy over the head for no reason."

She ignored the barb. "You can teach me."

Almost before she got out the words, Luke pitched back on the couch laughing. "A gun-toting pacifist. That's a picture."

She had to admit, it was the last thing she'd ever have imagined doing. But some things called for change. She waited until he calmed down, then said, "I'm serious. Dead serious. And if you don't want to help me, I'll find someone else who can."

Luke sucked in some air. "Who? My father?" His frown deepened. "Which brings up another issue. How does he fit into your *plan?* Endangering other people's lives because you have a mission is ridiculous."

"Hearing you talk about me like I don't have a mind of my own is ridiculous." Abe's voice came from the doorway. "If I can do something to help, I will."

"And how long have you been standing there?" Luke snorted. "Do you always listen to other people's conversations?"

"Only when I hear my name mentioned." He came in and sat in his old leather lounger. He seemed to be moving around a little easier.

"Well, I'm not putting either of your lives in danger and that's that."

Julianna looked from Luke to Abe. "I don't know about you, Abe, but I don't need anyone's permission to do anything."

Abe laughed. "Ain't needed permission for more years than you've been alive, sweetheart."

Luke's face reddened. "You're both crazy."

"Crazy enough to want to see a killer go to jail," Julianna said. "And I can't believe you don't feel the same way."

Luke stood, anger bubbling like a cauldron inside. Yeah, he felt that way. With every fiber in his being he felt that way. But it wasn't enough to make him want to put Jules and his father within a killer's reach.

"If he's going to come anyway, why not be prepared," Jules said.

"Because we don't know he's going to do anything. Neither one of you have my experience and you need to listen to me. This isn't some action movie where you can take things into your own hands and the bad guys always lose. You'd be risking your lives. Someone could get dead. And even if you two don't care about that, I do." And then he stalked from the room.

As Luke walked toward his bedroom, rage made his stomach knot. How could Jules be so unrealistic? So stupid. And his father. He was a sick old man who couldn't even take care of his ranch. What could he do to help?

Three hours later he was still awake, his mind

whirling like a blender on high speed. But the more he thought, the more Jules's stupid idea seemed to make sense.

And he was an idiot. A delusional, sleep-deprived idiot. He rolled from the bed and headed down the hall. Seeing a soft glow of light radiating from under the door in the den, he realized Jules was still up…probably writing. Getting herself into more trouble.

Feeling an overwhelming urge to talk some sense into her, he paused by the door, then remembered that talking to Jules when she had her mind set was like talking to a statue. He went to the kitchen and on his way back with a Coke, he turned and headed for the living room.

He dropped into his father's chair and flicked on the floor lamp next to it. He glanced at the magazines in the basket. Several copies of *The Achilles' Heel* were on top. He reached, then drew his hand back. He didn't want to do this. He didn't want to read about abducted children. He didn't want to read about Michael.

He didn't want to…but he had to.

He picked up the stack and went through each magazine, searching for the first article Jules had written. The one about their son.

As he flipped through the magazines, he noted that "Missing" was the name for the whole series. Each story had another title of its own. Usually it included the name of the child. When he came across one that was called "Michael's Story: with love, from his mother." Luke's heart lurched. She'd used a fictitious last name, but not the first. He started reading and noticed imme-

diately that the story was told in a different way from
the others he'd glanced at. It was in the first person.

By the time he'd finished reading three pages, his
heart felt as if it were going to crack. Jules told of Michael's abduction from the first moment she'd noticed
him gone, describing her panic, disbelief and fear in mo-
ment-by-moment detail.

*I couldn't believe he was gone. I wouldn't believe it. I
kept telling myself he had to be hiding, or playing a game.*

As one realization after another hit him, Luke's heart
ached for Jules. She'd been alone. He hadn't been there
for her. When she'd told him how she felt, he'd said he
understood, but had he really? She'd said he couldn't
possibly know how it felt to be responsible for losing
their son. How many times had she told him that? How
many times had he told her it wasn't her fault, that it
could happen to anyone. He'd seen it in his job more
than once.

With every second that passed, with every negative
reply from the department-store manager, panic
clawed at my insides. But I had to stay in control.
I had to find my son. Shivering with fear I called
out. "Mikey, Mikey." I kept calling and calling.
The security guards came. Someone phoned the
police. When I finally realized that Michael, my
four-year-old son, my only child, wasn't in the
store at all, I felt a bone-chilling fear. A kind I
could never before have imagined.

I ran out the door to search every inch of the

mall, but the corridors seemed like tentacles reaching out in all directions. Oh, God. What should I do? If I left and Mikey came back, I could miss him. But I had to look. I ran…searching, calling out his name in every shop, asking everyone if they'd seen him, store clerks and people doing their shopping, people sitting on benches, eating at the food court. "Have you seen a little boy in a red shirt and blue shorts? Did a boy wearing a Dodgers' baseball cap come by here? Please won't someone help me look for him?" Somewhere in my purse I found a photo and went back again, tears streaming, covering the same walkways, the same shops, asking the same questions of the same people and showing the photo.

A tear fell onto the page and then another. Luke felt Jules's panic as if it were his own, her pain, her guilt, he felt it all. And by the time he read the last paragraph, tears flowed like rivers down his cheeks.

I see Michael every day in my fantasies—and at night in my dreams—and in the eyes of all the children I meet. I still search for the person who took my little boy away. I will always search. I have nightmares about what he did to my child, and I won't give up until he's behind bars. Not a day goes by that I don't blame myself. Not a day goes by that I don't think of my little Michael and wish it had been me instead.

Luke's chest spasmed in despair, his grief so great he couldn't stop the unconsolable sobs that wrenched from within.

THE NEXT MORNING, Julianna heard Luke long before she saw him coming from the bathroom. He'd showered, but he looked drawn, his eyes were bloodshot as if he hadn't slept.

Because he wouldn't listen to her, she was at a loss as to what to say or do, so she just kept on heading to the kitchen. Abe had volunteered to help with her plan, but realistically, she couldn't endanger Abe. She had to think of something, maybe someplace he could go until all this was over. Abe leaving the ranch was about as likely as him winning the Boston Marathon.

Abe was already in the kitchen when she got there. The aroma of coffee tantalized her. Abe liked his coffee strong enough to grow hair on your knuckles, and she'd gotten to enjoy it that way, too.

"Coffee's ready," he said. "Been up for a couple of hours and had breakfast, too. But I can whomp up a batch of eggs if you want."

"I'm not very hungry, Pops, but thanks anyway." She poured herself some coffee and popped in a couple pieces of toast. "This will be just fine."

As she set the plate of toast on the table, Abe said, "I hate to say I agree with Luke, but you could get hurt if you go through with this idea of yours."

"I know that, Abe." She placed her hand on his. "But

I need to try. This…perverted lowlife could be Michael's murderer. It would be worth my life to take him down."

Abe's rheumy eyes sparked. "Michael's—you sure?"

"No, I'm not sure. But there are too many similarities for me not to entertain the possibility. Regardless, the man is going to continue to threaten me unless something is done. But in all good conscience, I can't put you at risk."

"You let me worry about that," he said. "If you're going to insist on doing this, then I'm going to help. Just tell me what I can do?"

Could she? Could she even consider including Abe in the plan? It wasn't his mission, it was hers. If something happened to her, so be it. But not Abe. "The one thing you can do to help is let me find a place for you to stay for a little while. A vacation spot. Maybe someplace beachy and warm."

Abe frowned, then pushed to his feet, his chair scraping on the adobe-tiled floor. "I may be an old man, Julianna, but I'm not dead. I don't have a lot of years left and dammit, if there's something I can do, by God, I'm going to do it. And that doesn't mean going somewhere to rot on a beach."

Luke was right. The whole thing was ridiculous. A bad plan. Not a bad idea, but a bad plan since it would inevitably involve other people. She couldn't justify that. Especially not Abe. Luke, yes. He had law enforcement experience. He had a stake in the outcome. In more ways than one.

"I heard you say you wanted to learn to shoot a gun. I can teach you."

Julianna's spirits perked. "Really?"

"Best teacher around. Taught Luke when he was a boy. He's won some shooting contests, you know."

She smiled. "I heard about his shooting skills, but not the contests." Luke had never told her. Funny how little she actually knew about the man she'd been married to for five years.

"I was a crack shot with a rifle in Vietnam, and I still am."

"I don't know, Abe. I'm thinking Luke might be right. It's too dangerous."

Luke stood in the archway listening. Since last night he'd done a lot of thinking about Julianna's plan and also about his contribution to the end of their marriage.

Instead of being supportive, he'd turned to a bottle. Instead of understanding, he'd said they needed to go on with their lives, start a new family. Truth was, he couldn't imagine anything worse than bringing a child into an unhappy home. And Jules had been right about another thing. They couldn't replace Michael. They could only begin again once they learned to live with their grief.

Neither of them had handled that part very well. But by writing her stories, Jules was doing *something*. He felt a pang of remorse. All these years she'd been focused on finding Michael's killer and doing it the only way she knew how. Instead of using his skills, he'd drowned himself in alcohol and self-pity. He was appalled at his own weakness.

The way Jules handled the loss was a testament to her

incredible strength. And she wasn't going to quit until she found the bastard who killed their son. He hauled in a deep breath. Perhaps working together would bring some kind of closure for both of them.

"Maybe dangerous. Maybe not," Luke said, walking into the room. He strode over, poured a cup of coffee and set it on the table, pausing before he explained. He didn't want either of them thinking he was condoning Jules's idea of taking matters into her own hands. He needed to make it a police operation. He ran a hand through his still-wet hair. "I've been thinking."

Julianna and Abe looked at Luke. "What about?" they said in unison.

Luke pulled out a chair and sat. "I've been thinking that if this plan was done in the right way, it might just work."

Jules's mouth dropped open. His dad frowned. Luke sipped his coffee. "We'd have to have backup. Sheriff Yuma, if he's around. Jordan and Rico in L.A. Rico has already set up a monitoring system on your laptop that makes all incoming messages traceable in some way. It's complicated and takes a while to follow up, but it's not impossible. If we get a location on the guy and he's in their area, they'll handle it from there."

When Jules and his dad simply sat there staring at him, he went on. "First thing for us to do here is get a tap on this phone. If the guy's using disposable phone cards, it won't do much good, but if he gets sloppy and uses a private phone somewhere, we might get lucky and locate the source. Jules, you'll keep your cell off, so if he calls it has to be the land line. Jordan is sending me wires, so we can be hooked up and transmitting all the time. No one will do anything without the rest of us knowing what that is. Even at night. And Jules, I'll train you to shoot a handgun."

"I can do that," Abe said.

"A handgun, Pops. Not your expertise."

"I taught you."

Luke rubbed his chin. "And a good job you did. But I learned even more at the police academy and by practicing at the gun range."

"I'm a good shot."

Luke felt as if he were battling a five-year-old who wouldn't give in. "Dad. I need control of the situation or we're not going to do anything. Lives are at stake. It's critical that we have one person in charge and that's me since I have the experience and the connections." He looked from one to the other. "Can you two agree to that? If not, that's it. We're not doing anything."

"Sure," Jules answered without hesitation. "You're the expert."

Finally, Abe reluctantly said, "Okay."

"You're the sharpshooter, Pops. I want you to find a place from where you can give the most cover to Jules when she goes to the stable each day. The second she goes out the door, you're going to be in position. I'll have the stable and other outbuildings rigged with cameras so we can see the entire place."

"If he's watching, won't he see us setting all this up?"

"If he's watching, all he'll see is us working. We'll have to be discreet."

Just then, Luke's cell phone rang. He answered, "Coltrane." It could only be one of three people. Jordan, Rico or the captain.

"Yo," Rico said. "We've got another e-mail message."

"What's it say?"

"It's weird. It's like a poem, but it's not. You want me to read it?"

"Sure. Let me get a pencil and paper."

As Luke finished writing, Rico said, "We've also got a phone number for Beau Thatcher from Mrs. Jenner's phone bill. There were several calls but only one we can track."

"Go for it," Luke said. "What about the stepfather?"

"Jordan's on it as we speak. The guy's moved around a lot."

Luke took a deep breath. He had to tell Rico about their plan, and he knew exactly what his by-the-book buddy would say. Better to wait until later when his dad and Jules weren't there. "I'll get back to you after I talk with Jules about the message. If we can decipher what it means, then we can send a response."

This was the perfect time to set the bastard up. Jules thought he'd likely respond after the article ran, so they had a week to put their plan together. But the sooner they got everything in place, the better.

After he hung up, Luke said, "Okay, are we all on the same page?"

Abe nodded. "What if this guy doesn't make a move?"

"Don't know. He's been pretty predictable calling after each installment and he's just sent another e-mail message." He picked up the paper. "It's some kind of rhyme. Jules, does this mean anything to you?"

"This is weird," Julianna said. She read the message out loud.

"In the cicada's cry
No sign can foretell
How soon it must die."

"It's like haiku, but I don't know for sure."

"What the heck's haiku?" Luke asked.

"It's a kind of Japanese poetry. I think there has to be a certain number of syllables to each line. I can look it up on the Internet." She got up and left the room.

"It's gibberish," Abe piped up. "And if that's all it says how do you know who it's from?"

"He sent it to Jules's attention, and signed it with a star, the same as the others."

Jules came back with her borrowed laptop, set it on the table and turned it on. "I'll Google it and see what happens."

Luke watched as she typed in the word *haiku* and instantly several references came up. One site explained the original construction of Japanese haiku poetry, that there needed to be seventeen syllables divided into lines of five, seven and five. After reading the explanation, Jules hit another link that showed popular haiku writers.

Luke shoved a hand through his hair. "This isn't doing us any good unless we know what he means."

"Since this has been translated, it doesn't seem to follow the exact description for Haiku structure, does it?"

Luke and Abe both shrugged.

"But I think he's telling me I won't know when he's going to strike. And by the way, it says here that particular poem was written by Basho, a seventeenth century samurai."

"So this psycho thinks of himself as a samurai? A warrior of some kind?"

Jules slumped back in her chair. "I don't give a rat what he thinks. It just creeps me out knowing he's probably not some Neanderthal idiot. Idiots aren't into poetry."

"Serial killers believe they're above the law, too smart to get caught. They'll even taunt the police like the BTK killer. They're narcissistic bastards."

"Another good reason for you to get out of that job, son."

Luke did a double take. He couldn't remember the last time his dad called him "son." He couldn't remember his father ever giving a damn about what he did with his life. Once he'd left the ranch, that was it. "I didn't know you cared," he answered, then wished he hadn't sounded so sarcastic.

Abe crossed his arms over his chest. "I don't. But other people do." He glanced at Julianna. "Maybe they shouldn't."

Julianna looked away. Started typing again. "This Basho guy wrote some two hundred haikus before he died. Weird, huh?"

"Do *you* know anyone who writes haikus?"

She smiled. "I know a macho guy who wrote a poem once. But he's no threat."

Luke blanched. One freaking time he'd tried to do something romantic and it comes back to bite him. He stood, pulled a gun from the back of his pants.

Jules gasped.

"You wanted to learn to shoot a gun. I'm ready to start now."

CHAPTER FOURTEEN

"ARE YOU SURE we won't be seen doing this?" Julianna eyed the tree in the distance where Luke had tacked up a homemade target.

"I'm sure. We're two miles out with nothing around but pasture and an occasional tree. How could anyone see us? Now stand still and get in position."

"Someone could've followed us."

He came up behind her. "Not the way we came. It was totally open. I would've spotted them. We've got a clear view all the way around. Both hands now."

She felt his body against her back. Warm and big and she fit perfectly against him. He placed his left hand on her arm, his face against the side of hers. Her heartbeat quickened.

"That's better," he said, his hot breath fanning her cheek.

There was no way in hell she could concentrate enough to hit anything with him so close. Her mind flashed to the night they'd made love in Venice Beach and her blood rushed.

"You're not concentrating." He stepped away. "Your

hand is wavering all over the place. You'll never hit anything like that."

"I will if you move away."

He smiled wickedly. "Distracting, am I?"

"Mildly."

"Well, get used to it. There will always be distractions, so you have to learn to focus. Keep the gun raised, with both hands on it and your eye on the target. Feet shoulder-width apart. Once you're ready, squeeze off a round to see how it feels."

"Don't I have to do something to prepare?"

"You are prepared. Now just do it. Think of this as a trial run to see if you want to continue."

She moistened her lips, took aim and squeezed the trigger. Blam! She jerked back and almost dropped the gun. Her hand felt as if a live grenade had gone off in it. "That's a mean kick."

"Only when you've never done it before. You'll get used to it now that you know what to expect."

She squinted at the target. "Did I hit anything?"

He grinned. "See that tuft of dirt sticking up? That's what you shot."

"I shot the ground. That's great."

"Do you want to go on?"

"Until I hit the bull's-eye."

He gave more instructions and she kept at it until her hand was red and swollen and by the time they rode back, it was late afternoon. But finally, she'd hit the target. Not dead center, but close enough. Taking the horses into the barn, Julianna looked at Luke. "Well, you haven't said how I did."

He smiled. "You did just as I expected you would."

"You mean I sucked." And maybe she did, but each shot had been better than the last.

"No, I meant that I knew you'd keep at it until you got it right. Now you'll have to practice or what you learned today won't mean a thing."

"I will. But isn't there a closer place to do it? I don't want to have to drag you with me every time."

Luke unbuckled Balboa's saddle and pulled it off. "Now how would you know if you were doing something wrong if I wasn't there to tell you?"

She laughed. "Believe me, I know when I'm doing something wrong. Don't you?"

He shook his head. "Nope. I leave that up to other people."

She wasn't sure if he was kidding or deadly serious. Didn't matter. There were more important things at stake than her relationship with Luke. *Relationship.* How ridiculous. She had no relationship with Luke. He was her ex-husband for God's sake.

"Besides, you're not going anywhere alone unless it's part of the plan."

That's what *he* thought.

But every day after that, Luke shadowed her. Whether she went outside to the patio or to the store, he went with her. When she practiced her shooting, Luke stood at her side. Or behind her. Or he lay on the grass a few feet away, studying her, critiquing when he felt the need. And the more he watched, the more acutely aware of him she became; his strong hands and long fingers, the way he tipped his head when he was thoughtful, the little dip between his bottom lip and his chin. His sensuous mouth. Luke was a hard man to ignore. Her heart raced just thinking about him.

On the third day, Julianna hit the outer edge of the bull's-eye. "Yes!" she called out and raised a hand in the air. She turned to Luke. "Hey, I think I'm getting the hang of this."

A rhythmic pounding sounded behind Julianna. She turned to see Stella Hancock galloping toward them on a brown-and-white pinto, slowing as she got closer. The older woman's hair blew free in the wind and for a moment, Julianna thought she looked much younger than her years.

Tugging the reins, the neighbor pulled the steed to a halt near Julianna. She smiled. "I was out riding and heard the shooting. I couldn't figure out why anyone would be firing a gun out here, so I came to see."

Luke scowled.

"Luke was just teaching me how to shoot," Julianna said. "Now, we're seeing who's the best shot."

Stella slid from the mare, stood next to Julianna and squinted at the target. "Not bad. I used to be a fair shot myself."

"Really." Julianna glanced at Luke who was now ignoring the woman. Being rude. "Want to try it?" Julianna held out the gun.

Rising from his spot on the grass, Luke all but growled, "We better go."

Stella shook her head at Julianna's offer of the gun and reached for her own weapon hanging on a holster from the saddlehorn. She released the safety, took aim and nailed the target dead-on.

"Wow. You're better than Luke," Julianna said, smiling. "You've obviously done a lot of shooting."

"Since high school."

"You must've had a good teacher."

"The best. Abraham taught me." Stella took aim and squeezed off another shot. Another bull's-eye.

Julianna's mouth fell open in surprise but not because of Stella's superb shooting. "Really. You've known Abe since high school?"

Luke couldn't not look. But he didn't say a word.

Stella looked at Luke, then back to Julianna. "As I mentioned before, Abraham and I have known each other a very long time."

She knew Luke was probably smoldering because she was talking to Stella, but she didn't care. She wondered if Luke knew that Stella and his father had known each other for so long. He must've. But looking at him, he seemed as surprised as she was.

"Here, I'll show you a trick," the older woman said.

Luke launched to his feet. "We don't have time for tricks. We have to go, Jules."

Stella didn't say a word, but after a few seconds, gave a resigned shrug. "It was nice talking with you,

Julianna." She turned, hitched herself up into the saddle and looking at Luke said, "You, too, Luke."

As Julianna watched the woman ride away, her mind spun. What a bizarre exchange. She swung around to face Luke. "That was rude."

"She wasn't invited."

She stomped over to him. "I was talking to her and whether you like it or not, I can talk to whomever I please."

He snatched the gun from her hand and holstered it.

"Whatever is with you, Luke, it's been going on for a long time. Get over it."

For the first time in years, Luke seemed speechless.

"Did you know that she and your father have known each other since high school?"

Luke kicked at a clump of grass, his expression odd.

He knew something. Enough to make him hate the woman.

"Did you know that Abe taught her to shoot?" she pressed for an answer.

"No," Luke snapped. "And I don't care."

They walked in silence to get the horses they'd tethered at the tree a few yards away.

Maybe he didn't care, but she did. Something had happened a long time ago that profoundly affected Luke's relationship with his father, and it had something to do with Stella Hancock. She was sure of it.

FOR THE REST OF THE WEEK, Luke barely spoke to Jules, but he dogged her wherever she went. The only time he allowed her to be alone was when she was in her room, when she went to the bathroom, or out to the barn at dinnertime to feed the horses. He knew she hated having him around all the time, that was obvious.

But it was part of the plan. And for the most part, it was *her* plan, so he knew she'd stick with it no matter how uncomfortable he made her feel.

Abe had taken on the job of feeding the horses in the mornings because he thought it might look suspicious if Jules did it all the time. Luke had to agree. And with something to do his father seemed more energetic and more eager to help around the ranch.

Normally his dad was a loner, but lately he seemed to thrive on conversation with Jules. But never with Luke, and that fact stuck in Luke's craw like a fish bone.

Waiting inside the back door for Jules to return from the barn, his mike on and his gun at ready, Luke scanned the area with binoculars. Nothing. Which was as he'd expected. The stalker had been quiet. No phone calls. No e-mail messages. Which could be a good sign or a really bad one.

Luke's natural instinct as a cop was to expect the worst, and he was even more vigilant where Jules was concerned. He wasn't going to let anything happen to her.

The surveillance cameras had arrived by special delivery at the beginning of the week and he'd set them up within a couple of hours. He'd also received more information from his partner. Rico and Jordan were putting together a location grid for all the abduction cases that had a similar M.O. A grid had been done in one of the previous investigations, but some cases were so old, they hadn't been included. The Willis case was one of them.

The plan was for Rico to e-mail the grid to Luke tonight. Now he just had to get Jules to pull it up on her laptop and then leave the room so he could discuss it with Rico and Jordan on the phone. Jules had always been piqued when he withheld information about his job, even though she'd known from the get-go that was how it had to be.

Watching from the back door, Luke fidgeted as he waited for Jules to come out of the barn. She was taking longer than normal. He checked his watch. His muscles tensed. Unnecessarily so. Both he and Abe were plugged in and would hear her if she breathed a word.

She did have her mike turned on, didn't she? He'd told her to make sure before she left. Dammit.

He flung open the door, heard it bang against the house as he loped across the yard. Halfway there, Jules appeared in the doorway. Feeling stupid, he slowed his pace.

Her expression switched from surprised to puzzled as he neared. "What's going on?"

He peered inside the barn. "Everything okay?"

She placed her hands on her hips. "Of course. You'd know if it wasn't." She zeroed in on his face. "Were you worried?"

"I—-uh…wanted to see if the horses had enough hay or if I need to go to town in the morning." He stepped into the barn. Yeah, like she believed that.

A tiny smile formed as she followed him inside. "There's enough for a couple days. But no oats. Doesn't Abe ever work the horses?"

Luke leaned against a bale of hay. "He used to. I think it's too much work for him now."

"Then he should let them pasture more to get some exercise."

Jules sat on a bale across from him, legs dangling. "Have you had any luck with hiring someone?"

"I've got another guy coming out in the morning. He sounds perfect. But you know how that goes."

"What about Abe?"

"I talked to him, told him if he screws it up again, I'm washing my hands of it."

"But isn't that what he wants?"

He shrugged. "I can only do so much."

She didn't seem interested in his response; she seemed to be studying him. "Do I have food on my face or something?"

"No." She laughed, almost self-consciously, looked away, then picked at the bale of hay where she sat. He liked it when she laughed. Especially when he made her laugh. It had always felt good knowing he could affect her in that way. He wondered if she ever remembered things like that about him. Not that it made any difference now.

Once, they'd promised to be there for each other no matter what. But when it came to crunch time, she'd bailed. That bitter truth tasted like bile in his throat every time he thought about it. The solution was not to think. But it was very hard to do when she was right next to him. When he could smell the sweet scent of her.

She looked up again. "I was just thinking that the next installment of the story comes out in the next day or so. It could be out already in some areas."

He couldn't blame her for being anxious. He went over and placed an arm around her shoulders. "We can call everything off the second you say so."

She leaned against him. "Thanks. But I have to see this through."

Their microphones suddenly crackled and whined. Jules winced at the screeching sound and fumbled with the switch. "What the devil?"

"Abe," Luke said as he bolted out the door, pulling Julianna along. They ran to the house and inside met Abe in the kitchen, sitting in a chair, his wire on the table.

"What's going on, Pops?" Luke panted, his heart hammering. For one brief moment, he'd thought something had happened to his dad.

"This thing don't work right. Can't hear a thing."

Luke looked at him. "Where did you have it?"

Abe pointed to his right ear. His deaf one.

Luke exchanged glances with Jules, then squelched a smile. "How about trying the other side?"

"I took it out to answer the phone, and couldn't hear a thing there either."

Jules sat next to Abe and rested her elbow on the table. Her eyes suddenly dark. "Who was it?"

"I couldn't hear very well, but it was a man, I know that much."

"What did he say?" Luke leaned forward, both hands on the table.

"He said he'd be here soon."

"Did he give a name? Or say anything about why he was coming?"

"No. That was it."

Luke's nerves crackled. The caller was either the guy he was going to meet with tomorrow…or the sicko bastard who was threatening Jules.

Jules shoved her chair back and stood. Her hands were trembling. "I'm going to bed."

"What about dinner?" Abe said.

"I'm not hungry."

Luke watched her walk from the room, her body stiff, her movements jerky. She was terrified. But if she wanted to continue what she started, she had to stay alert. Be on guard.

Later, he took her a sandwich and a Coke. Knocking on the door, he said, "Jules, are you awake?" When she didn't answer, he opened the door.

She lay on the bed staring at the ceiling.

"I brought you something to eat."

She kept staring at the ceiling.

"It could've been the guy I'm expecting tomorrow," Luke said as he set the tray on the night table.

"And it could've been someone else."

"Maybe. I was serious about calling everything off if you want to. I think we can get the guy without using you as bait. I never wanted to do this from the beginning."

She sat up, took half a sandwich. "Thanks for the snack."

He sat on the edge of the bed next to her. "I mean it, Jules. Don't ignore me."

After she finished chewing, she set the rest of the sandwich back on the plate, took a sip of Coke and blotted her lips with the napkin. She looked into his eyes. "I can't give it up, Luke. I have to go through with this."

He took her hand intending to comfort her, but at the same time, his frustration reached boiling point. "Why?" She was so damned stubborn it made him crazy. "Why, if we can do the same thing without putting you in danger? I don't understand."

She pulled her hand away and rested her head against the headboard. Sighing, she said, "I know you don't. You can't."

Luke launched to his feet. "What the hell is that supposed to mean? I'm looking out for you. I don't want anything to happen to you. How the hell does that translate into not understanding." Dammit. She was the one who didn't understand. She had no real clue what she was getting into and he wanted to shake some sense in her.

Instead, he stood there clenching his hands into fists. "Don't make this about us, Jules. It's about taking a killer off the streets. If you pull out, the result will still be the same. I'll still be doing my job and we'll get this guy."

She looked down, rubbed her arms as if suddenly cold. "I know what it's about. It's about making some psycho pay for the pain he's inflicted on his victims and their families." She moistened her lips. "Us included."

"You don't know that he's—"

"No," she interrupted. "And you don't know that he

isn't. With all the similarities, my instincts say he is, and that's good enough for me. I'll give up my life to get this guy if that's what it comes to. And you're not going to convince me otherwise."

Anger and empathy warred inside Luke. God knew he'd give his own life to get Michael's killer. But he wasn't going to sacrifice Jules. No way.

She turned to sit on the edge of the bed, her feet dangling, her hands clutching the quilt at her sides. "I want your word, Luke, that if anything happens to me, if the plan backfires somehow, that you'll get him."

If anything happens to me. Luke just stood there. If anything happened to her there'd be nothing to live for. The realization hit him like he'd been slammed in the chest.

"Please promise me that."

"Nothing is going to happen to you. That's the only thing I'll promise."

"But if it does, please swear that you'll do whatever you can to continue this investigation. Not for me, for Michael."

Luke suddenly felt as if all the blood had drained from his body. He dropped onto the bed next to her again. "You know I'd do anything for Michael."

"And if anything happens to me, promise you won't blame yourself."

He grasped her hand. "How could I not? I'm here to protect you. If I can't do that then I'm even more of a failure than I thought." His voice cracked as he tried to finish. "I failed before. If that happened again—"

Her hand came up to press against his mouth. "You weren't allowed to be on the case. You did all you could. You had rules to follow." She turned away again, thrust a hand through her hair, brushed it back. "I'm the one to blame. If it weren't for me…not watching…not paying attention—" She leaned forward, her face in her hands. Her shoulders started to shake. "Please forgive me, Luke."

The words were muffled, but he heard the pain. He leaned over her, his body like a protective cover. "There's nothing to forgive, Jules."

Rising up, she waved him away, silent tears rolling down her cheeks. "It *was* my fault. I lost Michael. I lost our son. It will always be my fault and there's nothing you or I or anyone in the world or even God can do to change that. I will live with that knowledge every day for the rest of my life."

She curled over again, rocking back and forth.

He kept soothing her, rubbing her back, saying, "It's not, Jules. It's not your fault. Believe me, I know. I've seen it happen before Michael and after. It's not you."

A few moments later, he felt her go still. Then she abruptly stood, eyes red and puffy, her face drawn. "I'm tired, Luke," she choked out. "I need to be alone."

LUKE HEADED FOR THE DEN feeling as if his heart were in shreds. No matter what he said, he couldn't get through to her.

His mind tracked back to other cases he'd worked on. In almost every abduction, the mothers blamed themselves. If only they'd kept better watch, if only they'd not done this or if they'd done that. And he'd always assured them it wasn't their fault. Just like he'd told Jules.

He realized now his words had been like wisps in the wind. Words weren't enough. They could never be enough. Jules had never believed him. And how could anyone in that situation?

God knew, he recognized his own failures where Michael's investigation was concerned. And it hadn't even been his case. Jules may not have been paying attention when Michael went missing, but that didn't mean it was her fault. If he'd been more understanding, more supportive, maybe he could've made her see that. Instead he'd drowned his sorrows in a bottle.

Either way, Michael was gone. He was never going to come back. Instead of realizing that and being there for each other, they'd let the tragedy tear them apart.

In the den, he closed the door and sagged against it. He couldn't change the past, but the least he could do was honor her wishes. Though he knew whatever happened to her, happened to him as well.

He went over to Jules's laptop on the table next to his father's chair. Normally he wouldn't use her computer without permission, but now was not the time to have her looking at anything concerning Michael's abduction. Sitting, he opened the PC and pressed the On button. He clicked on e-mail and five messages popped up. He was torn between respecting Jules's privacy and seeing if the stalker had contacted her again.

Seeing Rico's name on one message, he opened it. Rico had attached a chart and the message read, "I think we're onto something here. Let me know what you think."

Luke quickly opened the attached file and an L.A. city map popped onto the screen. *Holy moly.* His eyes darted from one pinpoint to another. The lines connecting them made the shape of a five-pointed star. And Southern Cal University was dead center.

All the profiles he'd read of serial killers indicated most committed their crimes either in or near their own neighborhoods. Most took souvenirs, and many left clues of some kind to show how smart they were. The star had been the creep's e-mail signature. Yes, they were definitely onto something. Now he had to find out what.

He punched in Rico's number.

"Yo."

"It's Luke. I got your message. Any ideas?"

"No, but I'm doing another comparison of the evidence, the suspects and persons of interest in all the cases to see if there's anything that could possibly connect them with the chart. Did you show it to Julianna?"

"No. Why?"

"Since she's the one getting the messages, she might see something we don't. Something specific to her."

"Okay. I'll ask her in the morning. She's…asleep."

Luke was glad Rico didn't pursue it. "You get any other messages?"

"She has a couple right now on the new e-mail address."

"Better check them out."

Luke knew if he did, Jules would be furious. She protected her privacy like the CIA protected the President. "They don't look like anything. Spam maybe."

"Okay. Let me know if you get any information from Jules. Tomorrow, Jordan and I are going to the university."

"You got a lead there?"

"No, but since it's the center of the star, maybe it's symbolic in some way."

After he hung up, Luke glanced at the list of Jules's messages again. He shouldn't read them. But what if one was from the stalker? Jules wouldn't read it until morning and time was of the essence in any investigation.

He clicked on the first message. Spam. Someone selling Viagra. Another had a similar title. He clicked on the third message that was blank in the subject line. The message opened and he read, "I miss you. When are you coming back? Love, M."

Luke's heart felt as if it had dropped to his toes. *I miss you.* She'd lied when she said she wasn't involved. She had someone. Someone who missed her. For five years he'd wondered whether she'd found a new love. But it had always been in the abstract because they hadn't seen each other.

But this was here and now. He'd spent almost two weeks with her and he'd been encouraged because he… His heart skipped a beat. *Because he loved her.* He'd never stopped.

"What's going on in here?" Abe's gravelly voice came from behind Luke.

He turned to see his dad standing in the doorway.

"You need my help?" Abe said.

Luke smiled. He needed more help than anyone could give him. "Thanks, Pops. Not right now. In fact, the best help you can give is getting enough rest so you're alert in the morning."

"How long do you think this is going to go on?"

He shook his head. "I wish I knew. If this creep follows his pattern, I think we can expect to hear something within a few days."

Abe sat in the chair across from Luke. "I wasn't talking about that. I was talking about you and Julianna."

Luke frowned and scratched his head. "What about me and Julianna?"

"I always hoped I hadn't raised a stupid son, but lately I'm beginning to wonder."

"Lately?"

"Lately since you've been here with Julianna. She loves you, you know."

Luke stared. Finally he said, "No, she doesn't. We have a history together. She cares about me like I care about her. I want the best for her and I hope she wants the same for me. But that's it. There's no more."

His dad rubbed his chin in an exaggerated gesture. "That's the trouble with kids these days. Always looking for the logical thing. Always being realistic. Wouldn't know the truth if it gob-smacked you in the face."

"I'm no kid, Dad. And being realistic is important in my job. People could die if I looked at the world through fantasy glasses. I know what Jules and I are to each other and I know what we aren't. No matter what you've imagined in your old age."

Abe simply smiled. "Love is there for the taking. You throw it away and you might never have it again."

Luke exhaled loudly. He heard the pain in his father's voice. The regret. "I know you loved Mom, even though—"

"Even though what?" Abe injected, indignance resonating in his words. "I loved her no matter what. That doesn't mean I never loved anyone else. It doesn't mean I always did the right thing. Mark my words, son, you may fall in love with someone else, but it'll never be the same. That first love will always be the love of your life."

Luke closed his eyes. He'd never heard his father talk like this before. Not about love. Not from the heart. Maybe now was the time for honesty. "So, why did you screw it up by seeing another woman?"

Abe's eyes clouded over. "Because I was an idiot. Because I loved her first. And I never stopped."

Luke lifted his head. "What?"

"We were high school sweethearts. We were going to be married when I came back from Vietnam. But she stopped writing and was gone when I returned. I was angry and instead of finding out what happened, I went on a binge. I let my stupid pride get in the way. Your mother and Stella were best friends back then, so finally Lizzie told me why Stella moved away…which is her secret to keep. But by that time Stella had married. I ended up marrying your mother and when the Hancocks moved back here, we all became friends. Living so close, being together so much, especially when your mother was sick…we…leaned on each other." He closed his eyes. "We made a mistake. But that doesn't mean I didn't love your mother."

Luke bolted to his feet. "I—I don't want to hear this." He didn't want to hear about his dad cheating on his mother. He'd seen his dad with that woman when he was thirteen…when his mother was dying. The vision was like a monster emerging from a dark closet. The closet he'd locked decades ago.

"Maybe you don't want to hear it," Abe said. "But it's time you did."

To Luke, talking about his father's affair seemed almost a sacrilege to his mother. "I don't. What you have to say doesn't matter. It doesn't matter because no matter how many reasons you had, mom died knowing you betrayed her—and nothing can change that."

Grim, Abe nodded. He started to get up, but then sank back in the chair. "Okay. But for what it's worth, what you think matters to me."

Luke scoffed. "Since when?"

"I don't know. Maybe it always mattered and I was too stubborn to let you know. But what's done is done and we can't change it. Right now I care more about what *you* think of yourself."

Luke looked at his dad. "What's that supposed to mean?"

Abe shifted in the chair, obviously uncomfortable. Hell, Luke felt antsy, too.

"I know it's hard for people to get over some

things," Abe said. "But believe me, if the love is there, it can be done."

Luke clenched his teeth. He couldn't do this. Not if he was going to stay alert and protect Jules.

"Your mother forgave me, you know." Abe's voice cracked. "She wrote me a letter. But I never forgave myself. Because of that, I never forgave Stella. I've ruined what little happiness we might've had, and when I see you and Julianna making the same mistakes, it makes me mad as hell."

"Mom wrote a letter?" Luke's throat constricted.

He nodded. "I still have it if you want to read it."

Luke cleared his throat. "Not now, Pops. I've got other things to do."

CHAPTER FIFTEEN

JULIANNA COULDN'T FIGURE out why everyone was so quiet at breakfast. Neither Luke nor Abe said a word. In fact they hardly looked at each other.

Luke got up to put his plate in the dishwasher.

Still sitting at the table, she asked, "Everyone sleep well?"

She hadn't. She'd barely slept a wink after Luke left her room. She couldn't stop thinking about what he'd said. But now she had to put it out of her mind. She had a job to do and that was that.

"Not very well," Abe finally answered. "But then that's nothing new when your body's old and everything aches."

"You could take some medication for that. The doctor gave you a prescription."

"Makes no difference."

"Well, if it helps you move faster, that's kind of important considering what we're doing here," Luke said.

Abe frowned. "Okay, okay. You made your point. I'll get the damned pills."

"Jules, I need you to look at something on the laptop. Rico sent it to me last night."

"And you're just telling me now?"

"That's right." The hard set of his jaw meant he wasn't going to discuss why he'd waited. She'd seen that look before.

"Okay. Let's go." They went into the den and Abe followed.

"Turn it on and go to the attachment Rico sent."

She did as he asked, then noticed there was more than one message and all had been opened. "Did you read my e-mail?"

"Yes. You went to bed and I didn't want to wait until morning to see if our psycho had sent another message."

She clenched her teeth. "You couldn't tell by the subject line or the names on the messages?" Her words came out sharp.

"No," he answered, seemingly unaffected by her irritation. As usual.

As angry as she was, she had to admit if she were in his position, she'd probably have done the same. She clicked on Rico's message then opened the attachment. A chart came up and she could see instantly what it was. "Wow. That's amazing. It's a star pattern." She looked at Luke. "What does it mean?"

"Don't know. I thought maybe you'd have some idea since you've researched some of the cases."

She sat in the chair and studied the screen. "Southern Cal is dead center. That's where Mark went to school."

"Mark?"

"Yes. My editor."

Luke gave her a strange look.

"He's a pussycat. Don't even think about it."

"Okay, but I guess he's the *M* in the other message."

She glanced at the e-mail. "Uh-huh. That's him."

She leaned back in the chair. "Does the star have to mean something?"

Luke rubbed the bridge of his nose. "Not necessarily, but in this case I can't believe it's just a coincidence. It's too perfect. What are all the things a star could indicate?"

"A Hollywood star. A celebrity," Julianna ventured.

"A constellation," Abe added. "Or a star on the Hollywood Walk of Fame."

"Maybe it's not the star that's important," Julianna said. "But the university in the middle. Maybe his next victim will be someone from there?"

"This guy likes children, not adults," Luke said.

"Maybe there's a day-care center at the university?"

Luke pondered the idea. Finally, he said, "Rico and Jordan are going to the university this morning. I'll call and tell them to check it out."

Abe pushed through to look closer at the screen. "Maybe you should check to see if any of the other victims or their families are connected to the university in some way?"

Luke turned to Abe and smiled. "Good thinking, Pops."

Abe beamed like he'd just won an award. Then, noticing that both Luke and Jules were looking at him, he sobered, apparently embarrassed. "I better go feed the horses," he said.

"And I better make a phone call." Luke pulled his cell from his pocket and he left the room.

Julianna glanced at the screen again, her mind searching for possible meanings. She and Luke had no connection to the university that she could think of. So that theory didn't hold up. The only luck she had was Mark. He'd gone to school there. But she hadn't known him when Michael…

Dammit. She couldn't go there. Taking Luke's cue, she told herself this was an intellectual problem, one where emotions only got in the way. She had to distance herself as Luke did. Think logically, not with her heart.

As her thoughts settled, she realized Luke's way of dealing with what he had to every day was pure self-protection. He had to be dispassionate or he couldn't do his job. How many times had he told her that? And how many times had she accused him of being cold? Uncaring?

Staring at the screen, a message popped up. You've got mail. Her heart skipped a beat. She closed Rico's attachment and clicked to retrieve her e-mail. As it popped up, a chill of fear jagged down her spine.

In the cicada's cry
No sign can foretell
How soon it must die.

No one travels
Along this way but I,
This winter evening.

In all the rains of day
there is one thing not hidden—
the ranch at Santa Fe.

"LET ME KNOW what you hear," Luke said, then hung up. He glanced at his watch. Just as he was thinking the guy who was coming to interview for the job should be here by now, there was a knock at the front door.

He strode to the entry, wondering where Jules had gone. She wasn't supposed to leave his sight except to go to the bathroom. "Hold on," he called out, casting about for a sign of Jules. Then he saw the door to the den was closed. She was writing again…or reading an e-mail from the guy who missed her and wanted her to come back. Probably some *GQ* executive type. The kind of guy she'd always wanted him to be.

He checked his thoughts, went to the door and pulled it open. A tall man dressed in a black hat and dark jeans stood there.

"I take it you're Mike Ryan," Luke said.

"And you'd be right," the man said and stuck out his hand.

He looked familiar, and then Luke realized it was the guy who'd asked Jules for directions at the gas station. "I think we've met before," he said, shaking hands.

Ryan frowned. "Have we? I haven't been in New Mexico for too long and don't know many people."

Luke craned his neck to see the man's car. Same car. "At the gas station outside Santa Fe about a week ago."

The man smiled, his expression searching, as if he might remember but wasn't sure. "Oh, yeah."

"C'mon in."

As the man walked inside, Luke took note that he was older than Luke, but not as old as Abe. He looked to be in okay physical condition. But something struck Luke as odd. He couldn't put his finger on it. Maybe it was the eyes. Flat gray eyes that scanned the room, examining, studying. Not unlike himself, Luke realized. But he was never as obvious. Maybe the guy had been in law enforcement in another life.

Ryan took off his hat revealing a full head of dark hair. Hair almost too dark to be natural, unless he was a Native American. But he'd said he wasn't from here and his name was definitely not native.

"Please sit down," Luke said, indicating the couch. He took the leather chair across from the man.

"What is it about this job that interests you?" Luke asked.

"To be honest—" the man scratched his chin "—I liked that the job included room and board. Since I'm new here, it would save me from renting an apartment."

Not exactly what Luke wanted to hear. Minus one.

"I also like working on a ranch. It's what I've done all my life."

Luke gave him a mental point for a good answer, glancing at the man's hands. Rough, callused. Ranch hands. "And if you find the people you work for are sometimes hard to get along with? How would you handle that?"

"I've worked with a lot of bosses and ranch hands in my time, and found the best thing is to let them simmer. I never take it personal and I let most problems work out on their own."

Not proactive, but not reactive either. Luke neither

added or subtracted points. "Did you bring a list of past employers?"

"Right here. It's my résumé."

Plus two. Luke felt a spurt of hope. He hadn't had much of that when he set out to find someone to help Abe because many ranch hands were drifters. Maybe he'd lucked out this time.

After more questions, Luke asked Ryan if he wanted to ask anything.

"I think you explained it all pretty well," he said. "But I thought you said there were no women here."

Luke's attention piqued. "I did. Why do you ask?"

The man pointed behind Luke. Jules's purse was on the counter top. "Oh, she's just visiting."

He nodded.

When they finished, Luke suggested they go out to the barn. "My dad went out to feed the horses and it's taking him longer than it should. You'd have to keep an eye on him, but without his knowing it."

"I did the same with my own dad before he passed away."

Experience with old codgers. A plus.

"Pops," Luke called from the door as they entered the barn. "I have someone I want you to meet."

Abe poked his head up from Balboa's stall. "I'm busy, can't you see?"

"Take a break. I want you to meet Mike Ryan. He might be interested in the job. That's if he can stand being around a cranky old man."

Abe practically flew out of the stall. "The only

cranky one around here is you." He held out his hand. "Nice to meet you, Mr. Ryan."

Luke held back a smile. All he had to do was make his dad think they were on opposite sides and Abe was all over it.

Just then Luke noticed that Abe's wire was sitting on top of one of the hay bales. He quickly pointed Mike to the stalls, urging him forward with a hand on his shoulder. "This is Balboa, and the Appaloosa over here is Cheyenne."

"Nice stock."

Though he was looking at the horses, Ryan's eyes never stilled, making Luke's skin itch. But anyone he didn't know would make him uncomfortable right now. It wasn't as if hiring a ranch hand was all they had to think about.

"When would I start?" the man asked. He glanced at Luke. "If you decide to hire me."

The question took Luke off guard. He hadn't thought about a start date because he was so preoccupied with just finding someone. But obviously this was not a good time to bring anyone else onto the scene. "Two weeks," Luke said. "We have some things to tie up first."

"When will I know whether you're interested or not?"

It was a valid question. But Luke hadn't made up his mind yet. And he still had references to check out.

"You can start right now," Abe said.

Luke was both surprised and encouraged that his dad suddenly seemed agreeable to having someone working on the ranch. But he wasn't going to hire anyone without checking him out first. "It would be two weeks, Pops. If you recall, we have some other things to deal with right now."

Awareness dawned in Abe's expression. His gaze shot to his wire on the hay bale. Luke led Mike toward the door. "Let's say I give you a call by the end of the week to let you know."

Luke walked back to the house and just as Ryan started for his car, Jules appeared in the doorway. Her eyes went wide when she saw the man.

"Howdy, ma'am," he said and continued on to his vehicle.

After Ryan left, Luke walked over to Jules. "What's wrong? You look like you've seen a ghost."

"That man. What was he doing here? I've seen him somewhere before."

"You're right. He was at the gas station when we stopped on the way to see Abe at the hospital. And he was here interviewing for the job."

She seemed relieved, but not totally. "I don't know. He gave me the willies."

"Well, fortunately, you won't have to be working with him. Abe will." Luke went inside.

Jules followed him into the kitchen.

"Is Abe okay with that?"

"Yeah. He seemed to be. Maybe he's resigned to it. He knows he can't fight it forever."

"He's been in the barn for a long time. How come?"

"Don't know. We had a pretty heavy discussion last night. Maybe he's hiding until I'm gone."

She shifted from one foot to another. Rubbed her hands together.

Picking up on her nervousness, Luke said, "Something bothering you? Besides the fact that I looked at your messages."

He'd have been upset, too. But given their *plan,* he considered it all part of the job.

"It's not that. Come with me. I want you to see something."

ABE STUCK THE WIRE back in his ear. He'd seen doubt in Luke's eyes when he saw it on the hay bale. A look that said Luke thought he was losing it. Anger flared inside him thinking that his son considered him an old man, too sick and addled to manage the ranch by himself.

It wasn't true. Not all of it anyway. Maybe his body wasn't working as well as before, but his brain was still as sharp as ever. If he had to have someone help with the physical work, maybe that would be okay. But no one was going to tell him he couldn't think for himself.

The mirror might say one thing but Abe didn't feel any different inside than when he was twenty. He just knew more about life and its consequences now than he did then.

He hoped that someday Luke would realize that giving up love for pride was a huge mistake. Abe knew only too well that he'd forever pay the price if he didn't.

He'd wanted to explain, tell his son the whole story, but Luke wasn't interested. Maybe someday, when all this stuff with Julianna was over.

Abe's hands clenched. He got angry just thinking that someone wanted to hurt his daughter-in-law. Ex-daughter-in-law, he reminded himself. Fact was, he was glad Luke was there. If there was one thing Luke was good at, it was protecting people. He'd done it all his adult life, sometimes to his own detriment.

That his son was making the same mistakes he had, broke Abe's heart. If only Luke realized before it was too late. His own biggest regret was that he'd taken so long to realize the mistakes he'd made. And now he had to live with the mess he'd made.

A vision of Stella's face formed in Abe's mind. She was a beautiful woman. Even now. If years ago he hadn't been such an idiot… He sighed, suddenly feeling very old.

All those wasted years.

And now it was too late.

"IT DOESN'T MAKE SENSE," Luke said.

"It does to the person who wrote it. I looked up the original haiku and he's changed some of the words in this last part. I think he's giving me notice that he's going to strike, but I won't know when. A scare tactic."

"He could be bluffing."

"He mentioned the ranch in Santa Fe. I think he knows where I am, Luke."

"But isn't that the idea? Are you having second thoughts?"

Julianna paced the room while Luke wrote something on a pad of paper.

"I have to let Rico know."

"Has he gotten anything on the e-mail trace he was doing before?"

Luke shook his head. "He said it would take a while, and even then he may not get anything."

"So, that leaves us where?"

"With the same plan as before. We all continue doing what we're doing. One of us might get lucky."

"Any news about the grid?" she asked.

"Rico is getting a faculty list from the university for the time periods surrounding each crime. Jordan has some thoughts about narrowing in on staff involved in the writing programs. That haiku stuff only appeals to a certain kind of person."

Julianna stopped pacing and dropped into the chair next to Luke. She was emotionally drained. It was so hard to hold onto a hope that seemed more elusive by the moment.

She leaned over the table, resting her head on her arms. A second later, she felt Luke's warm hand on her back. Her stomach clenched.

"Do you have any thoughts?" she mumbled.

He didn't say anything for a long time, just kept gently massaging her back and shoulders, and then finally he said, "I have lots of thoughts. And they all have to do with you. With us."

With us. Lord, she wanted nothing more than to lean into him, to feel his warmth and strength wrapped around her. She wanted him to hold her and make her feel safe again.

The dull ache of loneliness she'd fought for so long

began to overwhelm her. Could they ever…was there even a thread of hope that they could maybe find each other again? Find the love they once had.

No matter how much she'd pushed those thoughts from her mind, no matter how many years she'd refused to acknowledge it, she was still in love with Luke.

She bolted upright. "Luke…we have to focus on what we need to do."

Just then her cell phone rang. Her heart leaped to her throat. She'd forgotten to shut the phone off after calling Mark. Luke glared at her, but nodded for her to answer anyway. Picking it up, she glanced at the number. Mark. It was only Mark. Relief swamped her. She stood, answering at the same time. "Mark. I'm so glad to hear from you."

Luke got up and left the room.

"What's up?" she asked, hitching her hip on the corner of the desk.

"I need you here," he said. "This place isn't the same without you."

"I can't come back yet."

"Why not? We haven't heard anything more, so why not come home?"

Julianna couldn't tell him why she couldn't. She couldn't tell him anything. But…she had a thought. "Mark, when you were at SCU, did you know any professors interested in haiku?"

"Haiku? You mean the poetry?"

"Yes."

The line was silent for a while. "I'm not sure about

haiku, but there was one prof who was big in the English and poetry department. Received all kinds of awards."

"What was his name?"

"Man, you're testing my memory here. That was ten years ago, and he probably isn't there anymore."

"It's important."

"Uh, let me think. And I've got another call. I'll get back to you in a few. Okay?"

"Sure."

As she hung up, Julianna walked to the window. What was she going to do about Luke? What *could* she do about Luke? She hadn't a clue what he wanted to talk about. *Us,* he'd said. He wanted to quit their plan. That had to be it. He didn't trust her because she'd walked out on him.

But hadn't he done the same by drowning himself in booze? And what good did it do to think about any of that now? They were done.

Pushing the thoughts away, she sat at the desk and pulled out her briefcase. She had research to do on the next story. Anything to forget the ridiculous thoughts that seemed to crowd her brain. *Us,* he'd said. She pulled up FindLaw.com and set to work on the Darnell case.

Before she knew it, it was dusk and time for her to feed the horses. Luke hadn't come back all afternoon, and she had to find him before she could go out to the barn.

She didn't have to look far. He'd already come looking for her.

"You ready?" he said as they stood in the hallway. He seemed distant.

"Where were you? I thought I wasn't supposed to be out of your sight?"

"I knew exactly where you were." He pointed to a corner of her room, but she couldn't see anything. "You've bugged my room?"

"Clever, aren't I? You can't even see the camera it's so small."

"You…you creep." She punched him in the arm, whirled around and started for the door, clicking on her wire as she hurried outside and toward the barn. The sun was dropping rapidly behind the mountains and a quick wind whipped her hair into her face. She felt weary and tired and wondered how much longer she could do this.

It had to end soon, she decided, as she opened the barn door. Luke and his team were reinvestigating the case. Wasn't that her goal in the beginning?

The pitchfork lay to the side of one of the hay bales, not where she'd left it. Was Abe getting forgetful again? One of the horses whinnied. A thrashing fluttering sounded at her side. She jerked around, heard a shrill squawk, wings flapped violently in her face. She jumped back, her heart banging through her chest. She gasped for air. Geez. A chicken. How the hell had it gotten in here?

Her eyes darted. Nothing out of place. Just the stupid bird that was now shrieking and acting like she'd scared it instead of the other way around. She calmed herself, grabbed the pitchfork handle and went to soothe Balboa.

"It's okay, boy. It's okay." Her words were as much for herself as the horse.

As rattled as she was, she knew Luke was watching her every move. With cameras inside and out, he could see everything. Oh, Lord. He was going to razz her like crazy about this later. She stuck her tongue out at the camera. Still, knowing he was there gave her a sense of comfort and security. She'd missed that. She hadn't realized how much.

After feeding both horses, she tapped the microphone, the signal that she was coming out. "I'm leaving now," she said.

Balboa whinnied.

She turned. "What's up, big guy?" She reached to brush his face, but he jerked away, skittish. She heard rustling behind her. The hair on the back of her neck prickled. She sensed she wasn't alone.

Oh, God! A scream formed in her throat, but in that split second, a hand clamped over her mouth from behind. Then an arm came around her neck like a tourniquet, pinching her windpipe…crushing her against a man's body.

She fought to get away. The viselike grip at her neck tightened. Her blood roared in her ears. She flailed helplessly at the mike. He ripped it off. She couldn't scream to let Luke know. She couldn't even groan.

But Luke would know. He was watching. She glanced at the camera. Oh, God. They were under the camera, not in front of it. Luke thought she was coming out. He was waiting for her. He'd know when she didn't come out. But would that be too late.

"Hi sweetheart," a gravelly voice hissed in her ear. "You still think I'm a crank?"

In a split-second decision, she went limp, remembering from somewhere that it would take an assailant off guard. But as she slid downward, he yanked her up by the neck, compressing her windpipe even more.

She stomped at his foot but felt only air.

"You want to fight, sweetheart?" he growled. "I like women who fight."

True horror set in. She'd set a trap…for herself. He squeezed harder. Stars flared in her eyes. But Luke would come. He had to. Unless…someone got to him first.

"You should have listened to me. Left things alone. It's your fault that I have to kill you."

Her head spun. The world blurred. His words muffled in her ears and now he was dragging her, dragging her. Where was he taking her? Balboa flashed in her peripheral vision. The gun. She'd hidden the gun behind a barrel two feet away. But she couldn't move and light and dark strobed before her eyes. Just as blackness overtook her, the grip loosened.

He thought she was unconscious. Or maybe that he'd strangled her. Somewhere in the foggy recesses of her brain, she knew not to move. He let her fall to the floor, thudding like a sack of flour. Hay matted against her face. The scent cleared her brain. She saw a glint of metal. The gun. If he thought she was passed out or dead she might have a chance. Somehow she had to alert

Luke. If she didn't, he could get away and kill again. She wouldn't let that happen, even if it cost her her life.

Mustering her strength, she readied her legs and then giving it her all, she leaped forward like a frog, grabbed the cold handle of the .38, rolled over and pointed it in the face of the man hovering over her.

For one fraction of a second she saw fear in his hard eyes. "Move and you're dead," she growled, no question in her mind that she meant it. It was only when he grabbed for the gun that she recognized him.

"LUKE!" Abe shouted into his wire. "Julianna isn't answering."

"Did you see anyone?"

"No."

"I've got all the cameras working. Everything seems okay. She said she's coming out."

"That was sixty seconds ago. Where is she?"

"I heard her say something to Balboa. She's calming him down." Then Luke saw movement near the side of the barn. A horse rounded the corner. Stella Hancock.

"What the hell—" Abe spat out.

A gunshot rang out. Then another.

Luke saw Stella slide off her mount and run into the barn. He bolted out the door, gun in hand. "Cover me, Pops."

"Stella's inside," Abe hollered. "Don't let anything happen to her, Luke."

Luke reached the half-open door and froze. A man's voice.

"You can't shoot me, old woman. If you do, your friend here is dead."

His heart in his throat, Luke crept around the corner to the window and eased himself up. Jules was sprawled on the floor, a man standing over her with a gun, while Stella Hancock pointed her weapon at him. Jules wasn't dead or the man wouldn't be dealing with Stella. But she looked badly hurt.

Anger gnawed at Luke's insides. If anything happened to Jules… It was his fault. He never should've allowed her to do this…

It took everything in his power not to rush inside. If he did, the guy might panic and shoot. His hands shook as he readied his gun. He had to stay calm. Think. Dammit. He wasn't in any position to get off a shot, not without endangering Jules and Stella. But it was the only way.

He aimed dead on and pulled the trigger.

Almost simultaneously another shot rang out. The man crumpled. Luke raced for the door. He had to make sure the guy was down for good—and that Jules was okay.

As he tore inside, he saw Abe at the back of the barn, rifle in hand.

CHAPTER SIXTEEN

JULIANNA AWAKENED to bright lights and the dry scent of alcohol. The first thing she saw was a big vase of roses next to the bed...and then Luke's face came into focus.

"Hi," he said.

She smiled. "I'm alive? Or is this a dream?"

"You're alive."

"My head hurts."

"The doc says you'll have a sore leg and a headache for a little while."

She glanced down at her leg but the covers blocked her view. She reached for her head and felt bandages.

"It was a clean wound on the leg, the doc said. The head wound is minor, a graze. A week or two and you should be as good as new."

Luke smiled, but his eyes looked sad.

"Did we get the bad guy?"

Luke nodded. "He's behind bars as we speak. My dad had called the sheriff immediately after we heard the shots, and Yuma was there before the ambulance."

Julianna pushed up on her elbows and Luke came

closer to help her, puffing up the pillow behind her head. "I got the gun," Julianna said. "But he overpowered me. I think it went off and hit my leg. I don't remember exactly."

"You're alive, that's all that counts."

She smiled. "A lot of good that gun training did, huh?" Her leg throbbed and her head hurt, but it didn't matter. The sicko was in jail.

Luke gently sat on the edge of the bed. "You had a narrow escape."

"What happened after Stella came in? It's all a blur in my head."

"We're still not clear on it either. But what we do know is that he was taking aim when Stella made an appearance. She surprised him enough so when he shot you, the bullet only grazed your head. I heard the first shot, but when I got there, I saw Stella had her gun on him. Just as I was taking aim, our bad guy went down."

"Who—?"

"Abe." Luke smiled proudly. "The old guy is still a crack shot. He'd come in from the back."

"Where is he now?"

"Out in the hall with Stella. You up for seeing them?"

"Absolutely."

"I'll send them in."

He stood, started to go, but she caught his sleeve. "The man. He was the one who came for the interview. I recognized him. He was right there in the house." The horror of it hit her.

"We're still getting the facts together, but we're pretty sure we have—" Luke's voice cracked "—the person who took Michael from us."

Seeing the pain in Luke's eyes was almost her undoing. But hearing that they might finally have justice for Michael was simply too much for her brain to process. She pressed her face into her hands, tears suddenly streaming. Luke put his arms around her, holding her tight, and then she felt his body shake.

They shared the bittersweet tears, their sadness mingling with the knowledge that finally there was closure for Michael. Their son was at peace with the angels and now, God willing, maybe they could find peace themselves.

After what seemed like an eon, Luke pulled himself together, rubbed his eyes with his shirtsleeve and brushed the tears from her cheeks with his fingertips. He stood, ready to leave.

"There's someone else here, too. Your friend Mark. He was instrumental in identifying the guy."

"Mark?"

"He said you asked him about a professor at the university. He got the name and when he couldn't get hold of you on the phone, he e-mailed it to you. Rico picked up on it and with some other e-mail data he'd received, they got a search warrant for the professor's house. While the psycho was at the ranch, they were collecting evidence from his place."

Choking on his words, Luke shoved a hand through his hair. She'd never seen him like this before. Not even when Michael had disappeared. He'd always kept his emotions buried.

"They found a knife with animal blood on it and figured it's probably the calf." He took a big breath and then went on. "So far they've collected enough evidence to put the guy on death row. His name is Anton Orion. Hence the star clue. Weird, I know."

She put a hand up to stop him saying more. She was familiar with all the cases from her research. She didn't want any more details, she didn't even want to know if they'd found anything that belonged to Michael. It was enough that their beautiful son would finally rest in peace.

She wasn't sure Luke could handle telling her either, and her heart ached at seeing him in so much pain. Between that and the wrenching emotion of knowing they'd finally found justice for their son, words simply wouldn't come.

Their eyes met in a mix of emotions. And then Luke turned and walked out the door.

THREE DAYS LATER, Luke paced across the patio as he waited for Julianna to arrive and get her things. She'd told him her friend Mark would give her a ride from the hospital because they had a lot to talk about.

Just as well. He'd had time to do some thinking. And had managed to find someone to stay with his father. Someone Stella knew, and Abe seemed okay with that.

"Pacing won't solve any problems, son."

Luke turned and saw Abe settling himself on a chair.

"It's cold out here, Pops. Might not be a good idea for you since you've—"

"Maybe for you it's cold, but it isn't to me. I've lived here all my life and I can handle a little chill."

Luke raised his hands. "Okay. Okay."

After a moment of silence Abe said, "Waiting for Julianna?"

"Yes. She's going back to San Francisco."

"You sure she wants to do that?"

He looked at his father. "That's what she said. Why wouldn't I be sure."

"Because people don't always say what they mean, that's why."

Yeah, Abe had told him that before. Was there something he knew that Luke didn't? "She's with her…friend from San Francisco."

"So?"

"So, that's what she wants."

"Is it what you want?"

Luke felt angry and mad and hopeless and torn between what he should want and what he really wanted. His emotions felt as if they'd been pulled inside out like an old shirt and tossed in the trash. Still pacing, he raked a hand through his hair. "Hell no. But what I want for me doesn't matter. I want her to be happy, even if that means she's with someone else."

"Well, that sounds noble as all get-out."

This was ridiculous. How could his father, a man who never went anywhere, had hardly had a decent conversation with anyone in twenty years have any clue what he felt? "It's not noble. It's reality."

"So you're saying that you love Julianna, but instead of telling her, you'd rather see her with someone else?"

Talking to his dad was pointless. "That's not what I'm saying and you know it."

"Then maybe you should forget your high-falutin' pride and tell her."

"Pride?" Luke scoffed. "That's ridiculous. It's not about that."

"Okay. Whatever you say. My theory is that if we want something bad enough, we just have to bite the bullet and ask for it, even if the result might hurt like hell."

"And you live by those words?"

Abe's expression turned thoughtful. "No. I haven't for years. But I plan to. The other night made me realize I've wasted a lot of time. But I'm not going to squander what little I have left. Not if there's one iota of a chance I can do something about it."

Luke heard gravel crunch in the drive, saw a truck pull up. It was Stella's truck. He watched as the woman got out and then came around to the passenger side. She opened the door and his jaw dropped. Jules, holding a cane in one hand, turned to get out. Stella reached to help her.

Luke practically sprinted through the patio gate to the truck. "What's going on? Where's Mark?"

"If you let me come inside, I'll tell you."

Luke blanched. "Sorry. Here, let me help you."

Stella moved out of the way and just as Luke took Julianna's arm to help her out, Abe sidled up.

"Hello, Abraham," Stella said.

Once Jules was on her feet, Luke scooped her into his arms and carried her toward the house. He didn't want to hear what his father had to say to Stella. How could he feel good about a relationship between his father and the woman he'd had an affair with while Luke's mother was dying?

But as he thought it, the bitter emotion he'd carried for so long just wasn't there. It seemed unimportant now. He'd almost lost Jules, and the significance of that made everything else pale in comparison.

Was it wrong for his father to want to share the time he had left with someone he'd once loved? Still loved apparently. No, Luke realized. There was nothing wrong with that at all. And he'd give anything to do the same with Jules.

As they went inside, Julianna's cheek brushed against Luke's. He inhaled, breathing in—for possibly the last time—the scent he remembered so well. Remembered even in his sleep.

What he wouldn't give to erase all the heartache between them. He heard Stella and his father laughing in the background and, in that single moment, he realized he had to let go of the past. There was no going back. There was only the future.

Inside, he put Jules on her feet and before she had a chance to speak, he said, "Wouldn't it be better to stay a few more days to recoup?"

"Maybe."

"Abe would like it."

"And you?"

"What do you mean?"

She shrugged. "Nothing. Nothing at all." She looked down, then started for her room. "I think I'd like to rest right now, if you don't mind."

"Sure."

Watching her hobble down the hall and close her door, Luke banged his palm on the table. Dammit. Why did everything have to be so hard? Why did loving someone have to hurt so much?

He went to the cabinets and searching for a glass, he found a bottle of Jack Daniels. His adrenaline surged. He picked it up, stared at the label. He felt a sudden urgent need. One drink. It wouldn't hurt. Everything else in his life was so screwed up, it would feel good to find oblivion for a little while.

He needed a drink. Badly. He could almost feel the smooth, yet biting liquid sliding down his throat. One drink. He gripped the bottle tighter and tighter until his hand started to shake. A vision of Julianna and Michael flashed through his head. A powerful vision that was all he needed to place the bottle back on the shelf.

Pride, his father said. Was that what was keeping him from telling Jules how he felt? He didn't think so.

But how would he know unless he told her?

SHE MUST'VE DRIFTED OFF, Julianna realized when she awoke two hours later. She'd been dreaming, not the anxious, fearful dreams she'd been having for the last month, but dreams of angels and exotic places. Of

Michael and Luke and of playing on the beach together. For five years whenever she'd dreamed of them, she woke up in a sweat, anxious and tearful.

But this dream was soothing and wonderful. They'd been a family, the kind of family she'd always longed for.

If only it could be that way.

But it couldn't. Luke's job was still his main focus, and as much as she wanted things to be different, they never would. She knew it. Luke knew it. The only person who didn't know it was Abe.

Still, as she stretched out her arms and legs, she felt a sense of calm she hadn't experienced in a long time. It had been so long since she'd awakened smiling. Even before the threats, she'd been an anxious person. Or maybe driven was a more apt description.

She'd been relentless in her research, gathering information from families and other sources, writing article after article on the missing children, so relentless she didn't even have a life outside her stories. Luke was right, she was obsessed.

She could've died because of it. With the realization came the thought that she didn't want to live like that anymore. She'd been existing. Not living. But there was another reason. While keeping the stories in the public eye was important, she didn't feel the compelling need to write them that she had before. When Mark told her he wanted the series to end, that he wanted her to focus on something else for a while, other stories that were equally important, she'd felt a sense of relief.

But that feeling brought questions. Had she only

been doing it for Michael? Had she convinced herself she had all these altruistic motives, when her goal had really been selfish? Had she been living a lie?

By the time she left the hospital, the thought that she was a fake began to eat at her. And if Mark didn't want her to write about missing children, what was she going to write about?

The ringing of her cell phone on the nightstand startled her. Then she remembered the man who'd been threatening her was in jail. She pushed to a sitting position. "Hello."

"Julianna Chevalair? This is Tom Black from NBC News."

Hearing a knock at the door, she said into the phone, "Excuse me," then, "Come in." She'd had police at the hospital to intercept the media and hadn't anticipated them calling here. But of course they'd want all the information they could get.

As Luke entered the room, she handed him the phone. "It's NBC News. I have no idea how they got this number."

"This is Detective Luke Coltrane, LAPD. Can I help you?"

Julianna listened as Luke told the reporter that the police didn't want to compromise the case and they'd release more information when they could.

"Thanks," she said after Luke hung up. "I never know what to say in situations like that."

He came over to the bed. "No comment usually works."

She smiled then pointed to the bottom of the bed. "Sit down."

Instead, Luke pulled up a chair. "Don't want to bump your leg."

He looked serious, as if he had something disturbing to say. "The doc said it's fine."

A hollow silence filled the air.

"How's Abe?" Julianna finally said. "I heard him talking to Stella."

"They've gone riding. I think Abe has something important to say to her."

"She loves him, you know."

"I'm getting the drift."

"I know you don't like her, but it would be good for him to have someone. I mean someone he cares about—not a hired hand."

A petal from one of the roses in the vase fell off onto the bed. Luke picked it up, and holding it between two fingers, he studied the petal. "Nice flowers," he said.

"They are. Mark is a sweetheart. A little intense sometimes, but his heart is in the right place."

He pulled closer. "And where is that?"

She frowned. "Where is what?"

"His heart. Your heart. Are you in love with him?"

She stifled an incredulous croak. "With Mark? Whatever gave you that idea?"

When he didn't say anything and she saw the look in his eyes, she felt her throat close. She said softly, "Would it matter if I was?"

Luke stared into her eyes. "Yes. It matters because I can't imagine you with anyone but me." Still looking at her, he stood, shoved his hands in his front pockets. "It matters because I'm still in love with you, Jules."

Her heart raced. Words stuck on the back of her tongue. She wanted to say she was still in love with him, too, but— *But what?*

"I never stopped loving you, and if there's any chance for us, I'd do just about anything to make it happen."

But—what would happen if every time she looked at Luke she thought of Michael and what they'd lost? It had been like that at the end. She couldn't deal with the guilt and the shame. What would happen when he was away every night and she was alone in that house?

When she didn't answer right away, he said, "I don't have any big epiphanies about what happened between us except that I let you down. When I couldn't find Michael, even using all my expertise, I felt so inadequate. I couldn't live with that and that's when the drinking got out of hand. I—I failed you. I failed Michael and our marriage."

She placed a hand over his lips. Tears welled in her eyes. Oh, God. Her heart ached for Luke. She'd been so caught up in her own pain she hadn't recognized the extent of his. He was the stoic cop. Always in control. How could she have not seen how much he hurt? No wonder they couldn't help each other. How could they when they couldn't help themselves?

She took his hand in hers and quelled the flood of tears about to burst.

"Then we both felt inadequate, Luke. You told me before that I wasn't to blame, you told me many times.

But *I* knew I was and I couldn't live with that. Every time I looked at you I was reminded of it. Reminded of Michael. That's why I left."

His eyes searched hers. He steepled his fingers at his chin. She could almost see his mind clicking.

Finally he said, "Remember that night on the beach when you said you felt Michael in the wind, that it felt like his arms wrapping around you?"

She nodded.

"That's what I feel whenever I think about him now. I didn't at first. Like you, I railed at the injustice, I felt the sorrow so deep within me I thought I'd die from it. I wanted to forget and I found an easy way to do it. But one night when I reached for another drink, I saw Michael's face as clearly as if he were there, and something inside me came to life. I didn't take that drink and for a few days I kept remembering more and more. His smile, his laughter. And it felt good. I felt happy to have had him in my life, if even for a short time.

"I finally realized that I didn't need to forget. What I needed to do was remember Michael and to celebrate the time we had together."

Tears filled her eyes.

"Remembering our son and the love he brought to us is important. I never want to forget that, and I don't want to forget what we had either. We loved each other and just thinking about that is a lot better than having nothing. Yes, we had problems. And sometimes they seemed insurmountable. But that didn't make me love you any less. I cherish the love we had, Julianna. I always will."

Julianna reached for him. He'd revealed more in the past thirty seconds than he had in the whole time they'd been married. If she'd ever doubted his love for her, she couldn't now. Her heart broke for him and for her and all they once had. He was right. They'd had love. They'd had love and hope and a future and she'd thrown it away.

Like a bright sunrise lighting up her mind, she realized Luke was right. She didn't need to forget, she needed to remember. She needed to remember all that was wonderful between them. Including Michael. Everything else was an excuse. An excuse to run away just as she'd done when she'd left home to marry him.

God, it was all so clear now. Though she'd loved Luke with all her heart, she was the one who'd married for the wrong reasons. Not him.

Dangling her feet over the edge of the bed, she tried to stand, wobbling as she did. Luke caught her and they both landed in the chair, her on his lap.

He held her tight in his embrace, as if he might lose her again if he let go, and then he rested his forehead against her shoulder.

She pressed her lips against his head in a gentle kiss, and in doing so, she released a frail hope…

Drawing back to look at him she said, "Luke, when I left, it wasn't because of you or your drinking or anything else you did," she said, her voice hoarse with tears. "It had nothing to do with my feelings for you. I loved you then and I still do," she whispered. "With all my heart."

He pulled back. "And I you. I never stopped." His lips

met hers. Softly, sweetly, lovingly, and in that moment, all the longing and the passions, all the emotions she'd denied herself for so long welled up inside. The pain and sorrow of the past faded in the wake of hope.

It had been so long since she'd felt hopeful. So long since she'd even thought about more than one day at a time.

Her future was with Luke. Their future was together. It had always been. No, they wouldn't ever get over the loss of their son. But Michael had been the culmination of their love, and he deserved that love to continue.

And when Luke kissed her again, her heart swelled with love—and the promise of tomorrow.

EPILOGUE

One year later

"VERY FEW LIVES are what we expect them to be,"
Abraham said to his daughter-in-law sitting beside him
with her notebook and a tape recorder. "And I'm no orator.
I doubt what I have to say will be of interest to anyone."

Julianna, pregnant with his son's child—his grandchild—looked radiant, just as his wife Lizzie had looked
when she was carrying Luke. Abe had doubted he'd
ever have another grandchild after Luke and Julianna
lost Michael.

But now that a new life was growing, a life that was
part of him as well, he didn't think about his own mortality as much. He supposed he should be at seventy-one,
but knowing a part of him would continue on in this world
made it easier to face that he wouldn't be around forever.

Not that he planned on going anywhere soon. Shoot,
he'd just gotten married and had a whole second life to
live with the woman he'd been in love with for more
than sixty years. He'd been a fool to waste so much time.
When Stella broke off with him, his damned pride

wouldn't let him forgive her. Then Lizzie died and he'd been overcome with guilt and retreated into himself. Well, he'd lived with false pride and guilt long enough. He was still alive and he planned to enjoy every second he had left.

"Okay, Abe, before I start the recorder, I hope you don't leave anything out just because I'm your daughter-in-law or because you're afraid I'll be judgmental. I'm a journalist and we're not allowed to judge people. But if you don't want me to know something, I'm okay with that, too."

Abe pulled himself up in his favorite chair, the worn leather lounger now shaped to his body after so many years, the chair Lizzie had always threatened to burn years ago. "So, what's the point of keeping secrets? It wouldn't be my life."

She smiled. "I like that philosophy."

"Why are we doing this again?"

"For our family history. So your granddaughter will know her heritage."

"It used to be people didn't know what the baby was going to be until they had it. I'm not sure it's a good thing to find out all these things before they happen."

"It was necessary because of my age, Pops. The tests show if there's anything wrong and can also tell if it's a boy or a girl. Modern medicine has come a long way."

He didn't like it. He didn't like a lot of things happening in this so-called modern world. But he had to live with it. He'd buried himself on the ranch for too long. Now he and Stella were going on a honeymoon to

Hawaii. He'd never in a million years thought he'd see Hawaii again. But then he'd also thought he'd die in a Vietnam prison camp.

"So, are you going to write a story about me, or what?"

"Gee, I hadn't thought about what I'd do with it, Pops. I just wanted to record the information befo—" She frowned. "Before I have the baby and I get too busy."

He placed a hand over hers. "You want the information before I kick the bucket. That's okay. It's good. But I'm not going to do that for a while, so we do have time."

"Okay. But I'm here now. And we probably won't be back until after the baby's born."

"Fine with me, but remember we're coming to Los Angeles when the child gets here. Stella wouldn't have it any other way."

"Me neither, Pops." She smiled sweetly. "So, where do you want to start?" Julianna asked. "Can you tell me about your childhood, your parents?"

"You want me to tell you everything?"

She smiled. "Yes, I do."

He shifted in the chair. He hadn't thought about his parents in a very long time. Not since he'd left home at sixteen. He'd put them out of his mind like he did most hurtful things, things he couldn't do anything about.

No point in thinking about all the nights he'd shivered with fear in the corner. Mostly he remembered that he'd just wanted it to be over, one way or another.

"It wasn't a noteworthy childhood, just a kid growing up on a poor ranch. A mother and father who didn't have much and who died too young." His father hadn't died soon enough for him. "I left home at sixteen."

"What about school?"

School. The thought conjured the singular most important day in his life. The day he'd met Stella Nez. He was ten and it was her first day at the tiny two-room school. One room each for two grades. She was in the lower grade, and she'd just come from the reservation.

He'd thought her the most beautiful girl he'd ever seen. Her straight, shiny dark hair went all the way down her back, and her eyes weren't dark brown like most of the Navajo kids, they were a lighter color, like his pinto, Chakura, that his dad had won from some drunk during a card game.

He'd seen her standing alone on the edge of the playground when a couple of the bigger kids went over and started shoving her, calling her names like half-breed, saying she should go back to the reservation.

He'd gotten mad. He didn't like bullies, people who picked on others for no reason at all. People like his father.

That's when he strode over. He didn't say anything, but planted his feet apart and stood in front of her with his arms crossed. One of the boys spit on him, called him "Injun lover," as if that was the meanest thing they could say.

Hell, he'd heard a lot worse. The girls called him names, too, and one threw a rock as she was leaving, hitting him in the forehead. But he stood there.

He didn't know what to do or say then, so he sat on the grass and after a minute, she sat next to him but not too close. The sun was burning hot overhead and he started sweating. He remembered that because he didn't want her to see him sweat. Or smell him either.

They didn't say anything for the longest time and then finally she asked, "How'd you get that black eye?"

He shrugged. "Bumped into a door at night." He pulled his shirt tight at the neck and tugged his sleeves down to hide his other bruises. But he knew she'd seen them.

"Want an apple?" she said, reaching into her pocket, then held one out to him.

Her voice was soft and she had an accent, the kind the kids had who came from the reservation. Like she'd just learned English or something. He rubbed the apple on his sleeve and took a bite. It was the best apple he'd ever tasted.

"IT's OKAY, Abe. We can do more later," Julianna said then shut off the recorder. Abe had told her about the two-room school, and meeting Stella for the first time, and then his mind seemed to go somewhere far away. She figured they'd done enough for the day.

"I'll be outside," he said, getting up to leave. "Stella will be back soon and we're going shopping for luggage and all that, then we have to look at plans for the new house."

Julianna smiled. "That will be fun." Abe and Stella had decided to build a new house on the property between their two places. It would be a place of their own, not one that he'd shared with Elizabeth or she'd shared with her husband. Abe wanted Luke to take over the ranch, but Luke was still undecided. He loved his job. She knew that. They had both made some concessions when they got married again, Luke in not working so many hours and she embracing the time they shared even if it was less than she wanted.

Still, she couldn't think of a better place to raise a child than here on the ranch. She felt a need to get away from the city altogether. A new beginning. She could do her job from almost anywhere, but she knew Luke would never leave the LAPD. So, they'd made another compromise. They'd keep the house in Venice and the ranch. How they'd divide up their time was the question.

Luke came inside. "Look what I found in the storeroom." He held up a baby rocker. "It was mine when I was a kid."

"It's adorable."

"There's more. A crib and an old high chair."

"Are they useable?"

"I don't see why not."

"I can't believe your father saved all that stuff."

Luke's eyes softened. "I can't either. I guess no matter how much we think we know about a person, we can never know it all."

She smiled wide. "Like you saying your dad fired the shot that saved me. I heard that's not the case."

He grinned. "But he doesn't know that. As far as I'm concerned, he saved us both."

She reached up to kiss him.

"So what do you think about the baby furniture?"

"I think it's a sign."

He gave a skeptical glance. "Now you're sounding like your mother again. A sign of what."

"That this should be our home."

Luke put the chair down. The doorbell rang. "That's the sheriff."

"Sheriff Yuma? What's he coming here for?"

She saw a glint in Luke's eyes. "He's got a job for me." He eyed her narrowly. "If I want it."

"Oh, my." She couldn't think of anything else to say. She wanted this to be their home so much, but only if Luke did, too.

The doorbell rang again. Luke started toward the door, but then he stopped and took an envelope from his pocket. "Here, hold this for me."

"What is it?"

"A letter from my mother. We'll read it together."

Stability is highly overrated....

Dana Logan's world had always revolved around her children. Now they're all grown up and don't seem to need anything she's able to give them. Struggling to find her new identity, Dana realizes that it's about time for her to get "off her rocker" and begin a new life!

Off Her Rocker

by Jennifer Archer

Available August 2006
TheNextNovel.com

HN53

HARLEQUIN®
NeXt™

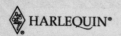

American Beauties

SORORITY SISTERS, FRIENDS FOR LIFE

Michele Dunaway

THE MARRIAGE CAMPAIGN

Campaign fund-raiser Lisa Meyer has worked
hard to be her own boss and will let nothing—
especially romance—interfere with her success.
To Mark Smith, Lisa is the perfect candidate for
him to spend his life with. But if she lets herself
fall for Mark, will she lose all she's worked for?
Or will she have a future that's more than
she's ever dreamed of?

On sale August 2006

Also watch for:

THE WEDDING SECRET
On sale December 2006

NINE MONTHS NOTICE
On sale April 2007

Available wherever Harlequin books are sold.

www.eHarlequin.com

HARMDAUG

If you enjoyed what you just read,
then we've got an offer you can't resist!

Take 2 bestselling love stories FREE!

Plus get a FREE surprise gift!

Clip this page and mail it to Harlequin Reader Service®

IN U.S.A.
3010 Walden Ave.
P.O. Box 1867
Buffalo, N.Y. 14240-1867

IN CANADA
P.O. Box 609
Fort Erie, Ontario
L2A 5X3

YES! Please send me 2 free Harlequin Superromance® novels and my free surprise gift. After receiving them, if I don't wish to receive anymore, I can return the shipping statement marked cancel. If I don't cancel, I will receive 6 brand-new novels every month, before they're available in stores. In the U.S.A., bill me at the bargain price of $4.69 plus 25¢ shipping and handling per book and applicable sales tax, if any*. In Canada, bill me at the bargain price of $5.24 plus 25¢ shipping and handling per book and applicable taxes**. That's the complete price, and a savings of at least 10% off the cover prices—what a great deal! I understand that accepting the 2 free books and gift places me under no obligation ever to buy any books. I can always return a shipment and cancel at any time. Even if I never buy another book from Harlequin, the 2 free books and gift are mine to keep forever.

135 HDN DZ7W
336 HDN DZ7X

Name	(PLEASE PRINT)	
Address	Apt.#	
City	State/Prov.	Zip/Postal Code

Not valid to current Harlequin Superromance® subscribers.

Want to try two free books from another series?
Call 1-800-873-8635 or visit www.morefreebooks.com.

* Terms and prices subject to change without notice. Sales tax applicable in N.Y.
** Canadian residents will be charged applicable provincial taxes and GST.
All orders subject to approval. Offer limited to one per household.
® are registered trademarks owned and used by the trademark owner and or its licensee.

SUP04R

©2004 Harlequin Enterprises Limited

HARLEQUIN *Romance*

A family saga begins to unravel
when the doors to the Bella Lucia
Restaurant Empire are opened...

The Brides of Bella Lucia

*A family torn apart by secrets,
reunited by marriage*

AUGUST 2006

Meet Rachel Valentine, in
HAVING THE FRENCHMAN'S BABY
by Rebecca Winters

Find out what happens when a night of passion is followed
by a shocking revelation and an unexpected pregnancy!

SEPTEMBER 2006

The Valentine family saga continues with
THE REBEL PRINCE by Raye Morgan

www.eHarlequin.com   HRBB0706BW

Join Sheri WhiteFeather in The Trueno Brides!

Don't miss the first book in the trilogy:

EXPECTING THUNDER'S BABY

Sheri WhiteFeather
(SD #1742)

Carrie Lipton had given Thunder Trueno her heart. But their marriage fell apart. Years later Thunder was back. A reckless night of passion gave them a second chance for a family, but would their past stand in the way of their future?

On sale August 2006 from Silhouette Desire!

Make sure to read the next installments in this captivating trilogy by Sheri WhiteFeather:

MARRIAGE OF REVENGE,
on sale September 2006

THE MORNING-AFTER PROPOSAL,
on sale October 2006!

*Available wherever books are sold,
including most bookstores, supermarkets,
discount stores and drugstores.*

Visit Silhouette Books at www.eHarlequin.com SDETB0806

HARLEQUIN®
Super Romance®

COMING NEXT MONTH

#1362 A TEMPORARY ARRANGEMENT • Roxanne Rustand
Blackberry Hill Memorial
All Abby wanted was to spend a quiet summer filling in at a small hospital in the beautiful Wisconsin woods before going back to teach nursing. But this temporary arrangement is far from quiet. Especially since single dad Ethan has the only vacancy in town.

#1363 THE HORSEMAN • Margaret Way
Men of the Outback
When Cecile meets Raul Montalvan—a mysterious Argentinian—she knows she has to break her engagement with a man she doesn't love. Not that she really expects anything to happen with Raul—because as attracted as they are to each other, she can't help but sense his reasons for being in the Outback are not what they seem....

#1364 BEACH BABY • Joan Kilby
A Little Secret
Nina Kennerly has a full life, but she's always regretted giving her daughter up for adoption and losing her first love, Reid. Now her grown daughter has found her—with her own baby girl in tow!—and Nina may finally have a second chance at the family she always should have had.

#1365 FAMILY AT STAKE • Molly O'Keefe
Single Father
Widower Mac Edwards's twelve-year-old daughter has spun out of control. Now he's in danger of losing custody of her. The one person who can help keep his family together is Rachel Filmore—the woman he once loved...and the woman who broke his heart.

#1366 A MAN OF HONOR • Linda Barrett
Count on a Cop
Heather's father was a bad cop, which is why she'll never depend on a cop again. Out on the streets, helping runaways, she's forced to accept Officer Dave McCoy's protection, but she'll never trust him. Not until he proves where his loyalty truly lies.

#1367 REMEMBER TEXAS • Eve Gaddy
When marine biologist Ava Vincent accepts a job in Aransas City she has no idea her estranged brothers live there, too. Ava ran away as a kid and carries a secret so shameful she believes no one can ever forgive her. Yet when she meets Jack Williams, a widower with a troubled son, she discovers she wants to have a future with him. Still, she can't believe anyone can accept her past, much less Jack.

HSRCNM0706